BURLINGAME PUBLIC LIBRARY
W9-BMO-469

Love's Alchemy

A JOHN DONNE MYSTERY

Love's Alchemy

Bryan Crockett

FIVE STAR
A part of Gale, Cengage Learning

GALE
CENGAGE Learning

Farmington Hills, Mich • San Francisco • New York • Waterville, Maine
Meriden, Conn • Mason, Ohio • Chicago

All Scripture quotations, unless otherwise noted, are taken from the Seventeenth-Century Bishops' Bible.
Five Star™ Publishing, a part of Cengage Learning, Inc.

LIBRARY OF CONGRESS CATALOGING-IN-PUBLICATION DATA

Crockett, Bryan.
Love's alchemy : A John Donne mystery / Bryan Crockett. — First Edition.
pages cm. — (A John Donne mystery ; 1)
ISBN 978-1-4328-3025-0 (hardcover) — ISBN 1-4328-3025-2 (hardcover)
ISBN 978-1-4328-3020-5 (ebook) — ISBN 1-4328-3020-1 (ebook)
1. Donne, John, 1572–1631—Fiction. 2. James I, King of England, 1566–1625—Fiction. 3. Espionage—England—History—17th century.—Fiction. 4. Conspiracies—England—History—17th century—Fiction. I. Title.
PS3603.R6353L68 2015
813'.6—dc23 2014038497

First Edition. First Printing: March 2015
Find us on Facebook– https://www.facebook.com/FiveStarCengage
Visit our website– http://www.gale.cengage.com/fivestar/
Contact Five Star™ Publishing at FiveStar@cengage.com

Printed in the United States of America
1 2 3 4 5 6 7 19 18 17 16 15

To my mother, Karleen Burch Crockett,
and to the memory of my father, Dale Rees Crockett

ACKNOWLEDGMENTS

Several good friends have read this novel with a critical eye and have offered valuable suggestions, many of which are incorporated into the story. While any faults in the result are entirely my own, the novel has been much improved by thoughtful, often challenging readings by Mark Osteen, Robert Miola, Barbara Braun, Richard Lee, Tom McCoog, John Bonn, Deni Dietz, Diane Piron-Gelman, and especially those harshest and most helpful critics of all: members of my own family. These readers include my brother Gary Crockett, my sister-in-law Marla Crockett, my brother-in-law Randy Scholfield, and the critic at once most supportive and most likely to provide that sort of challenging but spot-on advice the novel has needed: my wife, Pamela Crockett. In her many suggestions, Pamela has always been right. Well, almost always.

Chapter 1

1604

In the London air musty with smoke and ancient piss on cobblestone, Timothy Burr considered the groat in his hand. "A plague upon this for a beggarly sum."

Jack feigned his surprise. "A plague, do you say? Then it will die, Tim, and I would not have you in danger. No, give it me again, and I will see it buried in my pocket." As Jack reached for the coin, Burr pulled it back and held it against his ear.

"Wait. It speaks to me." The slack-jointed old man doled out his words without hurry, without urgency. "There is life in it yet, if only a little. Yes, its thin and dying voice, most faint, whispers that a fellow would revive it. It pines toward the grave but for want of a friend. Have you another?"

"Let it die, Tim. 'Twere mercy not to infect another of its kind."

Unfazed, Burr said, "Then a stronger. Have you gold about you?" The old knave's gray-peppered beard hung like a bedraggled willow. The folds on his face tapered to a peak in the middle of his forehead, half-shielding the eyes and giving him a perpetually funereal look. Even the man's voice drooped. "Gold is restorative; gold is stout; *gold* is incorruptible."

"Ah, Tim." Jack placed a hand on Burr's shoulder. "Though incorruptible, gold has corrupted the hearts of many men. I would not for a golden world have you among them."

"Your compassion, Master Donne, knows no bounds. Your

compassion"—here Burr cleared his throat and rolled his eyes as he held the coin close to him in one hand and extended the other—"is legendary."

Well, the performance was worth a reward. Jack fished for another groat but could not find one. Blast the old scoundrel, it would have to be a shilling.

Burr took the coin and said with evident appreciation, "*This* may prove restorative. No golden angel, this, but it will serve."

Jack removed his black velvet hat, the one Anne had told him that morning sat so handsomely on his head—she must have noticed it was getting threadbare but said nothing about that—and swept it in an exaggerated courtly bow.

One would hardly know the day was yet full, with hours to go before sunset. A darkling mist hung about the air, or some internal vapor clouded the mind. It was only the plashing of a pack-horse along the streetside puddles that brought Jack to his senses long enough to avert a wetting. He dodged nimbly to the other side of the street, only to be met a minute later by four hounds: two younger ones frisking about, sniffing here and there, and two older ones moving straight ahead. Behind the dogs came three horsemen riding abreast, one of them trotting directly at him. He darted back toward the wetter side of the street, snuffled at along the way by one of the younger hounds. Jack recognized the rider in the middle: it was the Earl of Bedford, husband of the alluring young countess he had just visited.

The three men were on their way home from a hunt: a gutted wild boar was tied behind the saddle of one of the Earl's companions. The other had a deer similarly fastened. Slung across the withers of the Earl's horse hung two rabbits, bound together by the hind legs. The Earl stared dully ahead while the two other men talked across him.

How, Jack wondered, could young Lucy Harrington have consented to be matched with such a dullard? Well, no doubt she had not been given a choice: she had been only thirteen at the time. A decade ago, it must be. Probably her father—or maybe Queen Elizabeth herself—had arranged the marriage. Even at thirteen Lucy had a reputation for her learning and wit. Captivated by her cleverness and dark-eyed beauty, wealthy young blades had courted her. Then, still young, she had been married to this oaf.

The man's short, fat legs ended in heavy boots with thick heels—no doubt, Jack thought, to elevate him when he stood beside his lithe-bodied wife, who would nevertheless rise some three inches taller than her squat husband. The man's sparse, lank hair, rheumy eyes, lumpy nose, and foolish-hanging nether lip did nothing to improve his appearance. As the horse trotted, the Earl's lip joggled and bobbed as if attempting to free itself from the dreary face.

Jack moved on. His mind played half on the verses he would write for the Countess and half on what Anne might think of such doings. How could she object to flattering lines when Lady Bedford stood as near as he had come to patronage since his fall from grace? Maybe something like this: *Some that have dipped love's quill. . . .* No, too obvious. *Some that have dipped love's well. . . .* Not that either; something about alchemy, or mining treasure: *Some that have deeper digged love's mine than I. . . .* After all, Anne knew as well as he how much the family needed money. *Say where his*—something—*happiness doth lie. . . . Centric:* that was it. *Say where his centric happiness doth lie.* Yes, Anne knew well enough they needed money. Why then had he not told her about the bracelet? With all he had confided to her over the years, why this? Lady Bedford was nothing to him. Surely he was nothing to her. Those flirtations of hers were doubtless no more than that. Doubtless. She was a countess, far above his station. And married. While Jack was a seeker after patronage, a man with a troublesome past and a wife of his own. More than a wife: his life's love, bone of his bones. Lady Lucy—yes, she had let him call her that—liked verbal sparring, and her husband the thick-booted Earl of Bedford was not her intellectual equal. Surely that was all. She liked Jack for his poems, liked the verses well enough to give him gold for them.

I have loved, and got, and told.
But should I love, get, tell, till I were old,
I should not find her hidden mystery.

Yes, that would do for a start. Anne would understand. Flattery in a poem to a patroness was mere convention, nothing more. Yet he had not told her. . . .

As he walked down Highgate Street, with its mossy, teetering alehouses and its clumps of raucous apprentices on half-holiday jostling their way to the theaters and bear-baiting pits, he recollected this latest visit with the Countess. As usual, Timothy Burr had stood playing the impassive servant, looking like a favorite hound. His face said to the world, *I am sad but trusty as a latched casket, faithful to the end. Secrets are safe with me.* But Jack was not taken in.

He recalled how Lady Bedford tilted her head to one side, saying with a pout, "But how could you lose it, Jack?" This young countess, now, was a puzzle: artless and childlike at times, shrewd and forbidding at others. Those deep brown eyes sometimes welcomed the world, sometimes sharpened enough to dissect it. The proud, narrow hook of a nose gave her a falconish look. Still without turning to her servant she added in half-coy surprise, "Do you hear, Timothy? Jack has lost my gift to him."

Burr did not respond.

"It was most ungrateful of him to lose it, were it not, Timothy?"

Still no answer; had it been Burr's cue to speak, he would have known it.

"No. He has not lost it," Lady Bedford went on. "Jack would never lose it, for when I gave it him he pledged to keep it always by him, and ennobled the giving of it with the prettiest terms of thanks that ever I heard. He has not lost it. No, I think he has given it to his wife. She must be a great beauty to command such a gift from such a man as Jack. *Is* she a great beauty?" Jack held her gaze. "Or perhaps he has given it to some minx to wear as his token. That is what he has done. Some wanton minx has it, some strumpet. Perhaps I shall tell his beautiful wife. Shall I tell his wife, Timothy?"

Nothing.

"Timothy." This time her voice was crisp.

"My lady," Burr said dryly, "Master Donne's ways are ever unfathomable. Mere mortals cannot plumb the depths of them."

With a musical lilt Lady Bedford said, "Oh, *I* can fathom them. What is the name of this minx, Jack? Is she raven-haired, like you? Or is she fair? Has she waves of hair as fine as yours?" Lady Bedford moved up close to him, very close, and lifted a hand to touch one of his locks. Almost he could hear her heart beating; almost he could feel it. If he lowered his eyes, no doubt he would see the rhythmic tremor in her breast. "Has she lashes like yours? Has she lashes long enough to make . . . one . . . weep?" A beating heart; iambics of the flesh. She moved her hand to lay it softly on his cheek, and he held her gaze as she asked again, "Is she fair, Jack?"

He spoke evenly. "My lady, I have said: your bracelet is lost."

She turned away, exasperated—or putting on a good show of it. "Well, then. You must find it. You simply must—" She whipped back to him and asked again, "But how could you lose it? You knew it was most dear to me." When Jack nodded gravely, she added, "And most dear to buy. The gold in those seven chains was pure, more pure than the twelve gold angels the piece cost."

Twelve! The goldsmith had given him only five angel-nobles for it, and four of the coins were gone already to his creditors. The other he had spared to buy meat, flour, and eggs for his family. Surely Lady Bedford did not mean him to make restitution. The bracelet had been a gift, and he was here to get another, not to be charged twelve angels for the one already sold. He spoke softly, letting the velvet of his voice drape about her: "My lady, I kept it ever near my heart, for in color it was like unto your golden locks." No; too easy, and she knew it. Besides, her hair was hardly gold; it was a fierce, dark auburn-red setting off a pale face. Squint one eye and it seemed an unpromising aspect. Yet somehow she had a striking way about her: a strangely haunted beauty.

"Color like my locks? Then my next armlet for you shall be woven not of seven fine gold chains but as many thin strands of ruddy-brown hair."

"Nay, do more: knit me up a shirt of your rich, ferruginous hair that I might better do my penance for the loss." Ugh, too grotesque, and she knew that too.

"Ferruginous! Listen to that, Timothy. He would snatch me bald. He would have me wear some rusty syphilitic French crown, and not a good angelic English one. And for what? A hair shirt for his penance. No, Master Jack-a-napes, I would have my twelve coins again, to melt them into what you have lost, and give it to one more faithful."

Well: no more underestimating her. "My lady, that were too cruel. Though I have strayed, melt not twelve angels from their first creation. Heaven appointed them at your hand to provide all things for me, and serve as my faithful guides. Shall these twelve innocents bear mine own great sins? Dread judge, shall they be both martyred and damned, punished in the furnace for offenses not their own? Burn them not in hellish flames; cast them not in seven-fold chains."

She smiled: at last he was winning her. "How your twelve golden martyrs found themselves in hell is more than I can say." He smiled too, and she paused before adding, "Burn but a candle for me then, to write some verses by. Pen me a poem. And if I like it well enough, may hap, *may* hap I will forgive you."

"I think my heart shall serve for candle wax, for you have melted it." Hm. Not so good, that, but not bad. And almost true: he could well grow fond of this woman. . . .

Enough. Beside that road lay the dragon.

A slight inclination of her head, the gesture of one used to having her subtle commands obeyed, declared the interview over. With a graceful, understated bow of his own he said, "You shall have the verses, Lady Lucy." Ah, she did not flinch at the familiar address. It was a good sign.

Back in the parlor, Burr found that Lady Bedford had set down the book he had fetched for her. She had taken out her needlework but had not started on it; instead she sat staring at the space where Jack had stood half an hour before. Burr waited. After a while she narrowed her eyes and asked, "What do you think, Tim? Can we trust him?" He waited. "Can such a man be trusted?" Outside, a carriage creaked by. Then, "Tim."

"Trusted to do what, my lady?"

"Why, to do what we ask. To aid us, in whatever way, in our dealings with that canker-hearted little crook-back in Ivy Lane."

"I know not, my lady. What might this Jack have to do with Lord Cecil?"

"Oh, come, Timothy. You know all things; your ignorance is

false as a pledge of love. This man Jack Donne is resourceful, and we are resourceful. Can we trust him?"

"My lady, I think we can trust him no farther than he can be thrust—with his pockets full of gold."

"My gold."

"Yes, my lady."

"Hm. I would like to trust him." She absently bit her lower lip, then shook her head and began to ply her needle. "It may be you are right. But did you note that he did not bend to my flattery?"

Burr shifted his weight slightly. He paused before saying, "I did note it, my lady."

"He was unmoved, was he not?"

"He was, my lady, except—"

"Except what, Tim?"

"Just this, my lady: I noted . . . some expansion of his codpiece."

Lady Bedford laughed. "Well, his heart perhaps he keeps to himself. But. . . ." She worked a few stitches. "Still, I *do* wish we could trust him, head, heart, and all."

"Madam—"

"No." She cut him off; Burr's tone was enough. She needed his observations, not his sympathy. "No, I think you are wrong. Man though you may be, you do not know men as I do. There is something about this John Donne, this Jack, as he would have it."

"Something. But my lady, search not too deeply for what it is. Before he married, he left many a maid wishing they had not been so curious. For it was they whose depths were plumbed, and not the other way."

"I see." She moved as if to stand but then settled back into her chair and returned to her needlework. "But I am no such silly wench." Burr watched cautiously as she stitched away: her movements were too quick, too nervous. "His wife," she said, "must be no fool, to get such a man as this Donne to marry her."

Burr spoke softly, carefully. "Assure yourself she is a fool indeed, Lady Lucy, for she gave up a great fortune to marry the man."

"*Did* she? Who is this wife?"

Burr waited a moment before saying, "Madam, I know not."

"Come, Timothy. Something of her you know, and something of the man. This much *I* know of him already: he thinks my flirtations make me but one more empty-headed, shallow-hearted woman, and now you behave as though you thought the same. But even if you misjudge *me* after all our years of acquaintance, you seem to have acquired some knowledge of Master Donne. How did you come by it?"

Burr spoke off-handedly. "I saw him but a little in his most profligate youth, when I was in the Earl's employ."

"Southampton. Yes, this Jack is just the sort of hanger-on Southampton would have about him."

"Just so, my lady, and no better than a hanger-on." Perhaps she was beginning to see the danger. Yes, her attention moved back to the needlework. At length he ventured to ask, "Might I attend to the cook? I fear she will have the kitchen at sixes and sevens."

Lady Bedford ignored the request. "Southampton: an Essex man. This Jack Donne was of the Essex party at the rising, then?"

"At the rising? I did not note him. But all was confusion that day. I think he fought under Essex at Cadiz, though."

"Ah. He is good with his sword, then."

Resolved not to take this bait, Burr said only, "So it is bruited about, my lady. I know not." Burr waited, but she continued with her needle as if she hadn't heard. No doubt she would make him stand there until he offered something more. He said, "If this Jack Donne was not at the rising, it was because he had read the writing on the palace wall. And if Essex thought about the man at all that day, it was only to think here was one more hanger-on that could not be trusted."

Lady Bedford put the needlework into its basket and picked up her book. After half a page she put it down again, turned to Burr, and said firmly, "But you know the man. Is there nothing to commend him?"

"Nothing." Burr's tone suggested he meant what he said, but in fact he spoke too quickly, too emphatically; it was clear Lady Bedford could see there was something more.

She pressed on: "Timothy, I would have you tell me what you know. You are in his confidence, are you not? An intimate."

"I tell you, my lady, I am *not.* I . . . I think he lets no man close to him." No sooner had the words left him than he knew they were a mistake.

Her eyes brightened. "That may be, Timothy, but a woman is not a man. I have read some of this Jack Donne's poems. He needs but a woman who comprehends the heart that stirs beneath the words. The man is tormented. He longs for understanding, for . . . release."

Burr allowed a note of pain to play in his voice: "My lady—"

"I tell you I *need none of this pity.*" With a glare she made him stand awhile before continuing. But she kept her voice calm: "What of his wife? Tell me what you know of her."

"Less, even, than I know of him."

"Come: you already said she gave up her fortune. You mean it became her husband's when she married, do you not? You mean Jack Donne is a spendthrift."

Burr exhaled forcefully enough to quiver his mustache. "*No,* my lady." She waited until he had no choice but to continue. "I think she had some prospect of a very favorable marriage, but while still little older than a girl she allowed this Jack to steal her from under her father's nose."

"*Did* she? Whose nose was this father's?"

"Some . . . great man's. My knowledge is imperfect." She waited. "Some . . . relation of the Lord Keeper's, it may be."

"Really."

"So I have heard bandied about, my lady."

"He had her with child, then, and Lord Keeper Egerton—or the girl's father—or both—were angry."

"No. Or . . . I think not. Or . . . angry, yes. With child, no."

With a too-studied air of unconcern she asked, "Children since? Legitimate ones?"

"Some two or three, it may be; I know not for certain."

"Pregnant now?"

"My lady—"

"Say on."

This would never do; the exchange had already gone too far. "Lady Bedford, I have told you all. That is the end of my knowledge, the whole of it, the sum of it from south to north, from start to finish, from alpha to zed."

"Omega."

"Omega, then, if you would Greek it. But I have told you all."

"Well." She picked up the book again. "See to the cook."

As Jack passed the Savoy, with its usual collection of hawkers, cripples, beggars, half-wits, whores, and thieves gathered outside the gates, he stopped short at the sight of an old woman he recognized at a distance, her back bent and her hand stretched in hope of alms from a foppish young blood who knocked her arm out of his way as he passed, sparing only a sneer for the benefit of one of his three attendants.

The light blow to the woman's arm was enough to tip her off

balance. Her cane waved feebly just off the ground. Jack hurried toward her but was too far away to catch her before she went down: not hard, luckily, but with a rolling fall that landed her in a skinned-over puddle of muck. Several of the onlookers laughed. Jack watched as the young man turned, saw what had happened, and joined in the laughter. But then the courtier stepped over to the frightened-looking old woman—she did not seem to comprehend what had just happened—and extended a hand to her. She took his hand, and he lifted her two or three inches, just out of the puddle, then released his grip. The old woman dropped into the muck again, splayed on her back, her legs spindled in the air.

The young man doubled over with laughter, then turned and continued walking. Jack picked up his pace, making a point of roughly shouldering the young man as they met. The man stumbled, uttered a cry of protest, and put his hand to the hilt of his sword. Jack was unarmed, but he had known men like this. He stared coldly at the sputtering courtier, turned his back, and continued toward the woman. He heard the command from behind: "Stop, miscreant!" The accent was Scots. Jack kept walking. To spurn, ridicule, and perhaps hurt such a poor old creature as this: a widow, a woman he knew to be kind, honest to the bone. Jack gently lifted her to her feet, made sure she could stand, and spoke to her in a soothing voice.

Breathless, gasping, she put a hand to her chest as she leaned unsteadily on her cane.

"Stop, slave, do you hear?" Jack ignored the Scotsman. "Whoreson bastard!" Mrs. Aylesbury—the very woman in whose house Jack had spent so much time during his days at Lincoln's Inn—teetered on the point of a swoon. Jack heard the Scotsman's rapier slide from its keep. The woman's eyes grew wide, and she uttered a little cry. Something about that sound, that inarticulate sigh of dismay, froze Jack where he stood. The blood rose in his veins, and his hands flexed murderously. He made sure Mrs. Aylesbury could stand on her own, and turned.

The Scotsman had removed his cloak, tossed it to one of his servants, and taken a few steps forward, his sword extended. Jack looked at him coldly. "Miscreant," the man repeated. *Slave.* Jack began to walk slowly toward the Scotsman, who said, "I will teach . . . I. . . ." Jack picked up his pace. The man stepped back as his speech faltered, until he stood within inches of the stone wall of the Savoy. As Jack strode to within three paces, the Scotsman's sword wavered. Now Jack moved within reach. The man lifted the blade to strike. Jack snatched the swordsman's right hand in his own left. He heard the rapier clatter to the pavement, the snap of tendons or bones, the sudden howl of pain. A fierce backhanded blow cut the sound short. The courtier's head jerked to the side and thudded against the stone. The man slumped to a heap. Jack reached to pick him up and hit him again, but two of the servants held him back. "Stop!" shouted one. "Y'have kilt him arready." The young Scotsman lay there bleeding from both sides of his head.

The other man holding Jack said sharply to the youngest of the three, a thin, freckled servant hardly older than a boy, "A constable, Rafe, find a constable. To it, now." The young servant hesitated. "Avaunt!" The young man looked at the cloak in his arms, dropped it to the ground, and turned.

"No constables," said Jack. Something in his voice stopped the youth where he stood. Jack shook himself free of the other two, glanced back at the wide-eyed Mrs. Aylesbury, reeling as she leaned on her cane, and knelt by the bleeding man. He felt for a pulse, snatched a feather from the gaudy hat that had fallen a few inches away, held it under the Scotsman's nose. Nothing. Nor any heartbeat. Onlookers, some tattered and gap-toothed, some smug and oily, some eager-eyed and nattering, had begun to gather in the shadow of the wall. A plump, red-faced ballad-monger, a smirking fishwife, and the sweepings of the London streets—wastrels, beggars, and grit-faced children—jostled for a better look. But it was Anne whose image filled Jack's mind, Anne as she would look when she heard the news. The sorrow in her eyes said he would never see their children again, said the law would make him pay the price of this murder, said she would love him nonetheless, even as he dropped from Tyburn gallows. He pulled his sleeve across his forehead to dispel the image.

Jack took the man's head in his hands and examined the wounds. They did not look deep. He thumbed open the eyes, but they were rolled too far back to show whether they held any life. Still kneeling, he grasped the prone courtier's belt and lifted until only the man's heels and the back of his head touched the pavement. An instant after Jack released his grip and the body thudded to the stones, a loud rasp of inhalation startled several onlookers into exclamations of their own. The courtier lay still for a moment, then began to sputter and cough.

Jack rose. "Take him home," he said. The three servants hastened to lift their gasping, wheezing master as if they'd been given a sudden reprieve. Jack picked up the man's cloak from the ground, wiped his bloody hands on it, and tossed it onto the courtier's sagging body as the servants hurried away with their burden.

He turned to Mrs. Aylesbury. She stood there dazed and pale, hand to wizened lips. He gently took her elbow and led her away from the crowd, which parted before them as if he had issued some silent command. She looked to be on the point of a swoon, so he held her up. At last she heaved a great breath and leaned against him huffing until she could say, "Master Donne! Lord help us, I thought that gallant was like to strike you dead, I was *that* affrighted." She fidgeted with her shawl.

"Noooo," he said soothingly. "No harm done. No harm."

"But he drew his blade! And there I stood astonied, watching." She looked at him out of her creased eyes as if he might have missed the point: "Astonied."

He let her breathe awhile, then asked, "But what brings you to the Savoy?"

"Well, there's the bread and cheese they gives out at the 'spital, but it don't always go around, does it, and with all the deal of shoving and shallying at the gates and the urchins tugging at the loaves—worse than the cutpurses, they is—well, it's a pity but a poor old woman has to beg alms betimes, Lord help the wicked." She looked at him not, as he might have expected, with shame or defiance or expectation, but with wonder.

"But Mrs. Aylesbury, what of your money? What of your house? Have you no lodger?"

"Oh, yes, same house as you've visited often enough, Master Donne, back when you studied the law, and a lodger I keep still, though I think this young man you wouldn't know: a commoner sort than Master Goodyer what lived there in your time. My, didn't that Henry Goodyer cut a figure! And didn't you all look handsome as peacocks, and as proud, when you wore your finery! But a decent man, a workaday man, my young Jeremy Jakes, and like to make a good husband when he's put by a bit more against his marrying day. And a pretty lass *she* is."

Jack nodded. "He pays his rent, then, this Jeremy Jakes?"

"Oh, yes, Master Donne. Without fail, somethin' wonderful. You know I would not have it otherwise." She chuckled.

Slow as she was to see where all this was leading, he would work her around to it. "But Mrs. Aylesbury, if you have your rent, why do you beg?"

"Lord help us, Master Donne, I cannot ask Jeremy for more than rent, not for alms-money. He needs to save, as I said, against his marrying day."

Jack seemed to ponder this deeply, then said, "You are right,

Mrs. Aylesbury, not to burden him."

She added in a whisper, "He doesn't know I come here."

Jack felt himself strangely troubled, as if some dark herald of sorrow had half-appeared, then begun to withdraw. "Is there . . . no one else?"

"No one," she said quietly. "All dead and buried, down to the last."

He shivered, and the act seemed to shake away the apparition's lingering shadow. "Yet you have just said you have your rent. Why do you not use it to buy food? Have you borrowed from someone who demands payment? Does someone steal your money?"

She tucked in her lips and nodded, then said, "Aye, more's the pity."

"Which is it?"

"Ah, the pity of it."

"And the money your husband left you. Is that gone too?"

Mrs. Aylesbury shook her head. "Gone. All, all gone. The last farthing." Then she brightened a little. "But Father Gerard is a great comfort, back again from the north country. Have you heard Mass from him? He—" Her fingers shot to her lips as she made the realization: "But I forget myself! I forget that you left the Church. . . . Oh, what have I done? What have I done to Father Ger—" She hesitated for a moment, a look of horror in her eyes. "Palmer! His name is Father Valentine Palmer, not. . . . Oh, did the Lord ever see such a fool as me? Oh, Master Donne, please don't. . . ." She clasped her burled hands together.

Jack held her lightly by the shoulders and said, "Listen to me."

"But what have I done?"

"Listen! I care not one whit who is Catholic and who is Protestant. *Not one whit,* do you hear? This Father. . . ." He knew well enough she had called him "Father Gerard." He had never met the priest but knew of him and knew of his doings: John Gerard was a man to be loved, feared, hated, worshipped almost by some. But Jack thought it best to say, "Father . . . whatever his name—I have forgotten it already—is safe. What I want to know is this: who is taking your money?"

"Why," she said as though it had been clear all along, "the pursy-wants. Twice fined, I've been. Did I not say so plain as a pikestaff before? Fined, I've been, for going to Mass instead of the heretic ch—" Her chapped fingers went to her lips again. "Oh, Master Donne! I mean no disrespect for your heresy, rest yourself sure of that." She crossed herself. "When tongues went wagging after you took the oath of disallegiance to the Holy Father, I said to them, bold as a game-cock I said, 'Master Donne is a good man and must have his reasons for turning heretic, or he wouldn't do it,' I said, bold as a game-cock I said it. And I'd say it still." She lifted her dewlapped chin in proud assurance of Jack's heretical virtue.

He felt a little stab of shame but hardly attended to it after that talk of the pursuivants. The mere mention of them made the afternoon mist hang heavier in the air and the sewage kennel along the street smell even fouler. The pursuivants were no better than the tax collectors of New Testament times. Jesus may have found a way to love such bloodsuckers, but Jack hated their latter-day incarnations. True, he was no papist. Not anymore. But the throne's fear-mongering, its painting the Catholics as some vast army of enemies to English freedom, its licensing of these leeching pursuivants to bleed the life from the honest Mrs. Aylesburys of the realm for but going to their secret Masses instead of the required services, made his hands heavy with vengeance. He looked at his palms, lined with their runic traces of the Scots courtier's blood, as if his hands bore through all the generations of men the indelible mark of Cain. Almost he could feel his fingers, crooked and hard and tight around a pursuivant's neck.

As so often before in his vexation, sometimes even in his rare moments of peace, words came to him unbidden. Visiting from some ancient realm just beyond the threshold of hearing but plain and insistent nonetheless, they took dark, prophetic soundings in his dreams, and they redounded as he lay awake. At times they penetrated to his very bones. Other times they skimmed along as innocent diversions, mere trifling puns—like gamesome children with a spinning-top. Or maybe at those times they only seemed innocent, as might befit some witty daemon in disguise. *Cain/Cane/Abel/Able.* Here he stood able-bodied but not Abel-souled. He stood the apostate, the outcast, bearing in his soul the murderous curse of Cain, and these pursuivants he would murder were his brothers in Christ—Protestants, members of his own adoptive faith—while here stood bent-backed Mrs. Aylesbury, surely an Abel whose sacrifices were pleasing to the nostrils of God. A Catholic Abel who was not able-bodied but in need of a cane, a woman who could do no murder to save her own life. He turned the conceit this way, that. A poem one day, perhaps. Or not.

Maybe, the old suspicion came to him once again, all his versing was but a cheapening of prophecy into poesy: a hopeless attempt to evade the horrors within him, to busy his mind with pretty conceits when he should attend to the word of God. Maybe he was called to be not a Jack nor even a John but a Jonah, and all his hauntings foretold the coming of the leviathan that moved all its vast, slow bulk beneath the waters, ever nearer, the sea-beast that would swallow him up and belch him forth on the coast of some forsaken Nineveh. God was calling him to a fearful, holy work—to martyr himself, perhaps, not gloriously before admiring throngs but in a darksome corner—while here he sought to mince clever phrases for one vain patron or another at a corrupt and godless court. He wished he knew.

In his childhood all had been simple. The old faith was the true one, and he was ready to follow the examples of his daring Jesuit uncles, men who would face down the Devil himself to defend the Church of Rome. Uncle Jasper had told Jack of his most glorious great-great-grand-uncle, Sir Thomas More, who had defied the hellhound, the eighth Henry, and had joked with the henchman on his way to the block. Such was the strength of More's faith, and such was the faith of Jack's uncles and his pious mother. The uncles he would not see for weeks or months, for their business was secret and dangerous. But when he saw them they told him stories of the miraculous lives and glorious deaths of the saints of long ago, of the Jesuits' own adventures in Protestant England, of the souls they had brought back to the true faith from the heretic church, of the saving Masses they had offered in secret, of the priest-holes made by the lay-brother they would not name (but he thought he heard his Uncle Jasper say "Owen" one night when Jack lay awake long after midnight), holes and ingenious secret closets where they had lain hidden for hours or even days while the pursuivants had torn asunder a Catholic nobleman's house. One day, they said—and young Jack himself prayed—he would join the ranks of the Jesuits. He would take the vows of poverty, chastity, obedience, and the Jesuits' special vow of allegiance to the Church and the Holy Father. If Father Jack saw a matter as white and the Holy Catholic Church said it was black, then it would be black. If all went well, he would save many souls, then die—perhaps die sweet Saint Sebastian's death, pierced by a hundred arrows for the love of the Blessed Virgin.

Then, in young manhood when he knew the Jesuit vows were not for him, he had dreamed of fighting with the sword for the Catholic cause. He would lead troops in desperate charges to liberate cities lost to Protestant despots. Wounded with bullets and arrows, he would be cared for by grateful Catholic maidens who would fall in love with him in the soft lamplight. They would weep silently with heads bowed, their long, dark hair rivering loose about his wounds, as the priest came in to administer the Last Rites.

Such dreams had heated the blood of his youth. But now, twenty years later, he knew the futility—no, the damnable madness—of the Jesuit cause. If it was heresy to turn against the Jesuits and the pope who sent them to speed young men like his brother Henry to their graves, then Jack Donne would prove a heretic. With a clear conscience he would stand before the Almighty on the Day of Doom. Then why did it nettle him when Mrs. Aylesbury said he had turned heretic? She meant him no offense, but her words stung.

No, he had made his decision in good conscience: catholic meant universal, not Roman, and the nearest thing to a universal faith in his native land was Protestant, the Church of England. Still, he had not made his decision lightly. Months of reading the arguments on both sides had stretched into years. He knew more theology than . . . well, than almost anybody else. Not more than Sarpi, maybe, or Andrewes. . . .

But why was he wrapped in such thoughts? Why must he always be carried away from what lay before him? Here he stood in a street, not in a lecture hall disputing theology with the Venetian friar Sarpi or the London preacher Andrewes but in a street with Mrs. Aylesbury, where she stood with her chin in the air, and she seemed to want assurance. "No, my friend," he said, "you may be sure I hate the pursuivants as rootedly as you do yourself. More, it may be."

She leaned toward him conspiratorially and half-whispered, half-spat, "I'll tell you whose doing it is. It's this bunchback serpent Robert Cecil that now goes styling himself the Lord Essendon."

The woman's eyes were red-veined, liquid with anger. Never had he seen such venom in her.

"It was Cecil as made the vile Scotsman king," she said. "The king what promised live and let live to the Catholics. He promised it. He made the promise to some four or five of the Fathers, and I've heard Mass from one as heard him say it with his own ears. Now the pursy-wants is worse than ever they was under the Queen, and that was a half-deal more than bad. I say it's all this Robert Cecil's doing. It's him what sets King James against us." She darted her watery eyes about, then lowered her voice to a bare whisper: "I know good Catholic men what say this Cecil is the Anti-Christ." She furtively crossed herself.

To reassure her, Jack crossed himself too. "Mrs. Aylesbury, I think you are right. Not perhaps about the Anti-Christ, but the human source of your woe is Lord Robert Cecil. Lord Salisbury is his next title, some say."

The old woman waved a gnarled hand in disgust. "What needs he or any man of all these titles? Cecil. Essendon. Salisbury. All his names hiss like snakes."

Jack smiled. There was poetry in the heart of even the unlettered Mrs. Aylesbury. He lifted his palms as if to say, *but what can any of us do*? She lowered her eyes, chewed her underlip, and fingered her shawl. He asked, "What does Father Ger—what does Father Palmer tell you to do?"

"Christen forgiveness," she mumbled. "Patience."

"Well, then." He reached into the flattened little leather purse in the pocket of his cloak. His fingers hesitated over the coins. He had thought to spare only the one angel-noble he had reserved for his family's food; all the rest he would give the old woman. He knew by feel exactly how much it amounted to: four shillings and a silver half-crown. But after he pressed the lesser coins into her hand, he reached back into the purse, took out the golden angel, and added it to the others. "I wish I could help you more."

"Oh, but Master Donne! You have arready done more than what—"

He cut her off with a deep bow and a graceful sweep of his black velvet hat.

She did her best to return the gesture with a curtsey. He heard the faint creak of her knees and helped her upright again—or as close to upright as Mrs. Aylesbury ever got—then hurried along his way. Anne and the children would be waiting, and the walk would take a full two hours.

Chapter 2

Something slowed him as he neared the house. Jack came to the top of the rise and caught his breath at the sight of Pyrford Place, his young friend Francis Wolley's mansion, or latest plaything, sprawled golden and russet in the glancing sun. As usual the thought of continuing to lodge at Pyrford troubled him. True, Wolley said the Donnes were to stay there always and forever. He loved Jack, he said—loved Anne, too, who was after all his cousin. But then, Wolley loved the latest blend of tobacco, his newest tapestry, the bronze Adonis that Giovanni da Bologna had cast for him in Florence. The next day Wolley's loves would be hates. King James was right that tobacco was the Devil's weed, the tapestry was moth-eaten, the Adonis mocked him. How long until Jack and Anne were no longer welcome? True, they could live for weeks almost unnoticed in their end of the house if Wolley chose to ignore them. The troubling thing was that even if Francis Wolley was a fickle, overgrown boy, Jack was a man. He should be plying his talents, making a name. With Lord Keeper Egerton he had been doing just that. And then Egerton's niece had come along. . . .

The gilt-edged colors of the house took him back to his first sight of Anne: very young then—just fourteen—with all the glories of youth and all the graces of womanhood intermingled as she sat reading on a bench of woven willow in the garden at York House. The afternoon sun, the same sun that now tinted the cold stones of Pyrford Place, had played along her copper-gold hair as it lifted and eased in the breeze. Her green dress too had softly billowed about her bare feet, billowed and relented. Head inclined slightly to one side, she had kept her gaze lowered to the book that absorbed her, oblivious to the black-clad intruder ominously named Donne.

He had stood there for several heartbeats, half-hoping she would look up, half-hoping she would not. Seldom at a loss for an apt thing to say, he had opened his mouth to speak but found his tongue dry and useless. What an odd thing: a mere child sat before him, and he stood unable to talk to her. He began to ease backward along the path he had come by and was about to disappear behind a hawthorn hedge when the Lord Keeper himself burst into the garden from the opposite side.

"Ah! Donne! There you are. I've been looking. These papers want your eye." Jack nodded and mumbled his greeting to Lord Egerton as he pretended to have been just that moment walking into the garden. Meanwhile, the girl darted an untroubled glance at Jack before rising to make a curtsey first to Egerton and then to him. "But have you met my niece Anne," the Lord Keeper continued, "come from the country to stay with us for a time?"

"No," Jack said, finding his voice clear again and turning to her, "but the meeting pleases. Pray, what do you read?"

"Ovid," said Anne, with just a touch of pertness.

"Ah," Jack said, "then you know your Latin. That is good."

She shrugged. "Some I know."

"More than some, I should think. Ovid can be difficult."

Now her smile spread. "Oh, but beautiful. One of his verses can be worth all the trouble of learning the language." She held the book to her breast as she said,

illa velut crimen taedas exosa iugales
pulchra verecundo subfuderat ora rubore.

Lord Egerton said absently, "What? Yes, girl. You know your Latin. . . ."

"That is Daphne," Anne said, "as she clasps her hands about her father the river-god's neck and asks him to grant her perpetual virginity."

Lord Egerton cleared his throat. "Yes, the *Metamorphoses.* You were better to read Caesar, my dear. Your Caesar is more wholesome, better suited to the young, than your Ovid."

"Caesar!" said Anne. "All those battles, Uncle, all those wars. How are they wholesome? And Caesar's writing is not beautiful, not like Ovid's."

"Well, I suppose one must read the *Metamorphoses* at some time," said the Lord Keeper. "But consider your youth, my dearest, and be governed by wisdom." Having closed the matter, he turned to Jack to discuss the papers.

"Oh, but these are not the *Metamorphoses,*" Anne said brightly. She held the little calfskin-bound volume in her hand.

"How is that?" said the Lord Keeper, the conversation already half-forgotten. "How . . . but you said you were reading Ovid."

"Oh, I am," she said with wide-eyed satisfaction. "The *Ars Amatoria.*"

"*What?*" thundered Egerton, thrusting the papers into Jack's grasp and snatching the book from his niece. "Where did you lay hold of *this,* child?"

Jack watched closely. She did not flinch, did not blush, did not blanch. "Why, in your library, of course, Uncle."

"But . . . who gave you the run of my library?"

"You did, Uncle. Yesterday."

"I. . . . So I did. But that was. . . . That was for. . . ." Jack looked on, amazed. Never had he seen the Lord Keeper, legendary orator and legal counselor, member of Queen Elizabeth's Privy Council, so put out. "That was *not* for the *Ars Amatoria,*" Lord Egerton proclaimed.

"But why not?" asked Anne. "The *Ars Amatoria* is the art of loving. We are placed on earth to love, are we not? Is there to be no art to it?"

"There is to be *no loving.* Not for you."

"No loving! But our Lord Jesus commands us—"

"Enough!" Egerton turned to Jack, who did his best to maintain the requisite air of decorum. "Master Donne: I have hitherto plied your brains and your hand: your brains increasingly in matters of state, some of them weighty, and your hand in scrivening. The latter service as my amanuensis I have valued largely for the fluidity and grace of your Italianate script. Henceforth, however, I shall employ some other scrivener, and you shall devote a portion of each day to undoing some measure of the harm my niece's prior tutor has done the child, apparently without her good father's knowing it."

"I should be honored," Jack said.

Anne replied, "And I should be pleased to be . . . is *diseducated* a word, Master Donne?"

Jack arched an eyebrow. "If it were, what would you think of it?"

She wrinkled her nose in thought. *"Diseducated:* I should call it *uglificatory."*

Jack smiled. Lord Egerton said, "That, my dear, I think is not a word."

"Just so, Uncle. Master Donne, it is clear, thinks neither is *diseducated* one, so I fancied a made-up description would be just the thing. But I must be wrong. Have I already displeased my new master?" She looked up at Jack through bright green eyes.

"Not at all. The first lesson augurs well."

"Good. Since I am to be diseducated, I shall now forget that I have learnt it."

Egerton looked at his niece and blew out an exasperated

sigh. "Enough, young malapert. Master Donne, this creature to be diseducated has learnt her Latin, her French, her Italian. . . . Am I correct?"

"Yes, Uncle. Some of each."

"What else?"

"A little Greek."

"Greek!" said Jack. "What think you of it?"

She pursed her lips for a moment, then said, "A rocky language, like the country. Full of echoes. Good for poetry, I think. But I know only a little."

"Well," said Egerton. "Improve her languages, Jack. If she does well, give her Hebrew for a treat. If she misbehaves, set her to arithmetic for a fortnight on end."

"Ugh," said Anne. "Arithmetic."

"And she may begin reading theology. Calvin and Beza should suffice."

"Oh, Uncle! Both are dull. Let me read Luther. Luther has *life* to him."

"Calvin and Beza, good Protestants both."

"Please, Uncle. No such suffering as Calvin and Beza. We Protestants do not believe in Purgatory." It was all Jack could do to stifle a snort.

Egerton said sternly but, Jack thought, with a gleam in his eye, "My dear, I have spoken." He lowered his bushy gray brows before adding, "You are excused from the garden."

Anne said with a sprightly air, "Cast forth from Eden, like—"

Egerton held up a hand in warning, and his niece seemed to know enough to hold her silence while he said, "No more in my library, do you hear, not until Master Donne has perused it. Scriptures only until then." She curtseyed and left.

Lord Egerton pocketed the book and took Jack's arm. The older man seemed more weary than usual, his beard more hoary, like some long-suffering patriarch of the Old Testament. "Have men-children only, Jack, men-children only." They walked a few steps before he added, "Still, I love that child like none other in the wide world." Jack could tell from the little hitch in his voice that the Lord Keeper would weep if he said more, so Jack kept his eyes ahead and walked on, silent.

Now he moved down the hill through the lengthening shadows toward Pyrford. In the few years since that first glimpse of Anne at her uncle's house—three years of improving her education and letting her improve his sense of wonder, and then three of marriage and children—he had come to shed all the Lord Keeper's loving tears, and more. He knew in his very bones what it was to love Anne More like none other in the wide world. Yet that first meeting in the garden seemed a lifetime removed.

He found her now stirring the fire into flame: poker lightly wielded like a foil in one hand, baby held to her hip with the other. He took up the infant, sat on the cushioned bench, and watched as Anne propped the poker in the chimney-corner. Pressing with both fists against the small of her back, she arched away the stiffness. Constance waddled over from her seat on the lowest of the stairs to protest her baby brother's privileged spot on her father's lap. Jack helped her up too. Anne puffed back the fugitive wisp of hair that had fallen across her forehead and eased into a smile as she watched Jack try to hold Little Jack away from both Constance, who wanted to push the baby aside, and his own face. The boy had taken a liking to Jack's beard of late and had a fine, healthy grip. He squared the baby around to face the fire, and the boy promptly forgot about the beard as the flames flicked and darted around the smoldering back-log. With his free arm Jack half-hugged, half-restrained Constance. She squirmed against his grip until he let her slide to the floor where, having made her point, she sat and watched the fire.

Anne said to Jack, "You've walked from London."

"Yes: Bedford House." Best get it out now; she would know soon enough.

"Bedford House! What took you there?"

"Verses. Patronage." He added, "It may be."

"From the Earl of Bedford? How did you come to know him? He likes your poems? But how so? A great clot-poll, is he not? A blockhead. But what did he tell you?"

Before answering, Jack looked for a moment at the fine curves of her body in the firelight. Marriage and motherhood had taken the edge off her youth, her eagerness. Yet as usual, the regrets about the loss of her fortune seemed all Jack's, not hers. And although childbearing had been hard—very hard—motherhood deepened her beauty rather than famished her spirits. Only from time to time did a vague shadow creep in about the corners of her eyes, a darkness that Jack had not learned to penetrate.

But she had been asking about the Earl of Bedford. Jack found himself saying, "Yes, he liked 'The Ecstasy.' " A stab of guilt: he had never met the Lady Bedford's husband. The nearest he had come was watching him pass by in the street. Why tell this little lie? What made him do such things?

"No wonder," she was saying. "I like that one, too."

Where, like a pillow on a bed,
A pregnant bank swelled up to rest
The violet's reclining head,
Sat we two, one another's best.

Little Jack reached toward his mother, who took him up as she asked, "But what did the Earl say? You haven't told me what he said."

"He said . . ." Jack shifted on the bench. "He—"

"He was not wholly pleased, is that it? Or he did not grasp the sense of it, more like."

Ah, a way out: "Not entirely. But Lady Bedford—"

Anne's eyes widened. "The *Countess* read your poem?"

"Yes. And liked it. Somewhat."

"Now, *that* were a patroness. Jack, this is—" Anne pulled back her head a bit as she considered the matter. "They say she is become a great friend of the new queen. And she liked your poem! Well, why would she not?" She recited more of the lines:

A single violet transplant,
The strength, the color, and the size
(All which before was poor and scant)
Redoubles still, and multiplies.

She spoke with both wistfulness and wit. Jack nodded. "The poem already earned me gold," he said. "I paid Hilliard four angels against his loan."

"Four angel-nobles! Did she give them or lend them?"

"She gave them, or . . . it."

He could see that Anne noticed the slight disturbance in his voice. A hint of a cloud crossed her face. "It?"

"Yes, she—" Why did he find this difficult to say? "The gift was a token that I sold."

"A token." He knew she had met such evasion from him before, and he knew she did not like it. Why then did he simply not admit the truth at the start? But something in him held back even as she asked, "What manner of token?"

"A bracelet," he admitted, trying to sound matter-of-fact, as if a bracelet were simply payment and not a lover's gift. "A mere bauble that I took and sold."

"A bracelet," she said. Then, as if stunned, she added, "Lady Bedford gave you a bracelet." All the color drained from her face. Jack had never loved her so much as at that moment, never been so sorry all his evasion had hurt her. He stood and took her in his arms, and she wept a little on his shoulder. He held her until Constance's tugging at her dress made her pull away. "Well," she said as she dabbed at her eyes with a sleeve, "I am not surprised she liked it. You told me it was written from the heart."

"It was. It is." He spoke firmly as he stood and looked at her. "I wrote it for you, and still it is written for you." It was the truth. Then why did it sound otherwise when he said it? Damn his . . . whatever it was that made him sound that way. It was the truth, though: he was sure of it. He had written the poem for Anne, and it was still her poem.

There was a strain in her smile. "Of course you must show your poems to others. It is merely . . . a necessity."

"For patronage. A formality. A courtesy. Nothing more."

"Nothing more." She turned away slightly. "How else is one to get him a place?"

He caught the reference.

For God's sake hold your tongue and let me love.
Take you a course, get you a place,
Observe his honor, or his grace;
And the King's real, or his stamped face,
So you will let me love.

It seemed long ago he had written those lines, but it was only three years. He said slowly and plainly, "We needs must eat, and it takes money for that."

"Yes," she said with equal firmness. "We must. And do you think our Heavenly Father does not know we need to eat, and more than bread alone?" This talk of Providence again. He winced, but she continued. "Have these little ones gone hungry, for bread or meat or love? Even if you speak but of the fruits of the earth, then Francis—"

"Francis! Yes, your cousin will suffer us to remain at Pyrford. Francis Wolley will stuff us as he stuffs his Christmas geese."

Jack began to pace, his hob-nailed boots clicking on the fine blue-gray Wilmcote flagstone that Francis had just installed, carted all the way from Warwickshire because the color of the old flooring wouldn't do. When the baby started to cry, Jack raised his voice above the noise. "While other men make their way in the world, I will prevail upon your cousin to decorate a *room* with us."

Anne bobbed the baby gently and tried with a look to get Jack to soften his tone. Neither infant nor husband, though, would be quieted. The one had a lusty set of lungs and the other ignored her silent plea. She said calmly, "He is as much your friend as my cousin. We remain here more for his love of you than—"

"I will offer witty conversation," Jack said, his voice building even louder, "when Francis fancies wit." Jack's gestures grew almost comically expansive. "And when his guests know of my disgrace—which is to say when his guests are friends with your father Sir George More, the new-minted Treasurer to the Household of the Prince of Wales—which is to say when Wolley's guests are any lords or ladies in the whole of England—as when King James himself came a progress to Pyrford and our part was to linger in the shadows of the staircase in the great hall while your father's men or trained apes or whatever they fancy themselves bowed and scraped before His Majesty—then I will remain demurely out sight and discreetly of *earshot*!" This last word rang so loud that the baby stared, shocked into momentary silence while the pewter wash-basin hummed with the reverberation. Then Little Jack started up again in earnest, louder than before, and Constance shrieked as if to outdo them all.

Jack started to storm out of the house but thought better of it. For several seconds he stood with his hand on the latch. *My disgrace*, he had just said: another unintended dart at Anne. She was the one who had been done out of grace, had been stripped of her father's favor. Willingly she had given up a fortune for love; Jack had much less to lose, and much to gain if Sir George had released her dowry. Or so the world saw the match. He knew, or he knew when the Devil wasn't whispering otherwise, that he too had married entirely for love. He had married Anne, not her money. Or did one ever marry entirely for anything? Without her fortune she would never have had the learning, the languages, the wondrous wit that had so captivated him over the years at York House. But of one thing he was certain: His wife was utterly unlike the other women he had known, learned or not. It was Anne he had married, and it was Anne he loved still, for better or worse. And at the moment he was the one making it worse.

His shoulders flagged. Turning to her with as apologetic a gesture as he could muster, he reached for her hand. For a moment she looked as if *she* would leave. She stood her ground, though, as her jaw tightened and the unaccustomed cold fire flickered in her eye. She did not take his peace-offering, but left his hand hanging in the air. Jack held only her hard glare while he felt his pulse throb in his temples.

But then, all unaccountably, she cocked her head and mugged such an antic look amid the din that he smiled in spite of himself. From somewhere inside him came a chuckle, and it was answered by one from Anne. Then he laughed, and so did she. He started to go on about Francis but could not get out the name without laughing. Before long he backed against the wall, slid to the floor, and sat convulsed until he coughed and tears ran to his collar. Anne came to sit beside him. Both children crowded onto her lap, quiet and rapt, fascinated by the spectacle of their father so convulsed.

Of course she was right. Of course God—or, in the meantime, Francis (Anne would say it was God working through Francis)—

would provide. The baby sat there in his mother's lap, hale and fat and like to live. Constance's eyes glowed in the firelight.

Jack and Anne sat without talking but holding hands for a long time: until the logs had burnt to embers, the baby had nursed himself to sleep at Anne's breast, and Constance lay with her thumb in her mouth, her head on Jack's lap. Then Anne let go of Jack's hand, stretched her free arm, and yawned. He was tired too. But the matter was unresolved, and he did not feel right going to bed like this.

"You know I pray," he said. "You know I pray for guidance, for a way to serve the Lord. The church, though, is not the path—not for me."

"But how do you know?"

"Anne, a minister must be called of God, must lead a blameless life."

She paused momentarily before asking, "And where is the blame in yours?"

"Nowhere, now." Tender as he felt toward her, the words sounded almost bitter—almost as if he wanted to wound her with his life's blamelessness. But what could he tell her? That God judged the motions of the heart and not the outward doings, that his heart was corrupt even if his actions weren't? That he desired to sin but forced himself to refrain? Was that even true, or only the foul Fiend whispering that it was true? Was it only because he was timid and not because he was good that he refrained from lifting Lady Bedford's dress and thrusting her against a wall until she screamed with pleasure? No matter; what would Anne think if he confessed to any such desire? The theology of her own church accounted for these temptations, but he doubted she had ever felt the sudden tug of adultery. He forced himself to speak softly: "We've talked of this. My present actions do not stand in the way, but my past ones do."

Her tone was firm. "Yes, we have talked of it. And do you

believe me when I say I have forgiven you your past?"

Well, her forgiveness was easily enough granted: the other women had come and gone before he met her. "Of course I believe you."

She spoke crisply. "You believe then that I can forgive you but that God cannot."

"No," he said wearily. At another time the word might have exploded from him, but now he was too spent for shouting. "No, no." Jack knew full well that God had forgiven him, but somehow the knowledge pined in his soul and made it cold. "It is . . ." he said uncertainly, "it is that I have no sign, no inner assurance, of the Lord's favor for the ministry."

"What, you think a priest of the Church of England should not be married, is that it?"

"No. Yes. I don't. . . . Yes. I will not deny it: there is something of the Catholic still in me that rankles against a married priest. A priest must give his *all* to the Church. I have seen men. . . ." The images crowded into his mind now, as they had so often troubled his dreams.

Uncle Jasper, newly back in England as head of the Jesuit order there, was taking him to the vast, three-cornered gallows at Tyburn to see the execution of the great Campion: the quick-spirited Jesuit who had visited Jack's house only a few weeks before. When Jack's mother objected that a nine-year-old boy had no business witnessing a bloody murder, Jasper told her it was no mere gruesome spectacle but a glorious celebration, and besides, having the boy with him would aid in Jasper's own disguise.

Uncle Jasper had read to Jack several times the copied-out letter Father Campion had written to the Queen's own Privy Council, challenging all the most learned Protestants of the land to debate. The boy had part of the words by heart, and they gave him a thrill every time he said them aloud or merely ran them over in his mind: *Touching our Society, be it known to you that we have made a league—all the Jesuits in the world, whose succession and multitude must overreach all the practice of England—cheerfully to carry the cross you shall lay upon us, and never to despair your recovery, while we have a man left to enjoy your Tyburn, or to be racked with your torments, or consumed with your prisons. The expense is reckoned, the enterprise is begun; it is of God; it cannot be withstood.*

And then, racked out of his natural form, consumed by prison, and battered from the drag behind the innocent, strong-necked horse, Campion had stood weakly on the platform at Tyburn. In front of the very fire that would burn his inmost parts, he prayed for the forgiveness of his tormenters as the crowd cursed and jeered. Jack stood close enough to the gallows to hear some of the priest's words. No longer a bold challenge to the powerful, those words—*Look tenderly upon them as you look even now upon your blessed Son*—had filled Jack with love for the man and his cause, sick-hearted hatred for the mob and the torturers. Then Campion's eyes had rested on Jack, with a look that said he would happily die another death if it would relieve the boy's heated tears.

It was then, when perhaps the martyr needed him most, that Jack had turned away. He heard but did not see the gurgling struggle for breath at the noose's end, heard despite the clamor of the crowd the rip of live abdominal flesh as the dull blade parted it, heard the sizzle of the priest's guts tossed onto the fire, heard the hacking at the limbs.

Now, as Anne sat beside him asking about the ministry, the sister-image to Campion's martyrdom troubled Jack's mind. Some dozen years later after the hanging, drawing, and quartering that still pulsed through his dreams, Jack's dying brother Henry, blackened out of his youth with plague-sores, lay gasping out pathetic prayers in his prison cell. It was the priests and all their mindless allegiance to Rome that had cost his brother his life. It was their marriage to martyrdom and death. It was their damnable, suicidal faith, and Jack's tears had burned against them as Henry refused, for fear of spreading the pestilence, to let Jack hold him as he died.

Now he said none of this to Anne. She had not seen these deaths, and he was glad of it. "The church is not for me," he said, "unless God gives me some sign of it."

"Well," she answered, shifting both sleeping children into Jack's lap while she rose from the floor, "that's as may be. God will provide." The usual Protestant platitude. Then she added, "But the signs of the Lord lie hid in the book of the world. Turn every leaf." She knelt, carefully picked up Constance, who remained asleep with her thumb in her mouth, and took her upstairs to bed.

Little Jack erupted with what seemed a quart or two of the milk he had just drunk, then went on sleeping peacefully. Jack propped his head against the wall and looked at the ceiling, the smell of half-digested milk rising about him. He held the baby with one hand, pushed himself stiffly upright with the other, and, when he could not find a rag near the wash-basin, went in search of one by the light of a rush-candle he touched off from the fire's embers. After a minute's search he found a cloth draped over a chair in the next room. He poured water from the ewer into the basin, dampened the cloth, and did his best to clean the baby and himself.

When he carried Little Jack up to bed, Anne was busy at her hymns and prayers over Constance, so he laid the baby in the padded crib next to the little girl's bed where the prayers would do for both, and went back downstairs to do what he could to walk away the day's lingering troubles. Once again he began to pace, this time more slowly than before. He had just brought home the hope of patronage: the bracelet had not fetched its worth, it was true, but enough for some little celebration. Yet the gift had somehow set him at odds with Anne. The flagstone clicked beneath his boots. When he had come even with the door for the third or fourth time, a sharp knock startled him into reaching for his absent sword.

Chapter 3

Reaching for his sword-hilt: a habit from the wars, or from all those years of practicing with Henry. But he had not worn his sword to Lady Bedford's house; the leather belt was cracked and shabby, and the scabbard wanted polishing. There was no need for a sword now anyway. He was in his home—well, Wolley's home—and it was only a knock at the door. A sharp knock, though, certainly not like the musical tapping of Wolley, who might not deign to knock in the first place. And the hour was late. Instinctively Jack glanced aside. Yes, his sword was in its wonted place, on a high shelf in the corner: near enough, if he needed it. Despite his irritation at the hard rapping on the door, Jack paused before lifting the latch as he remembered the encounter that had spurred his years of sword-practice with Henry.

He had been only ten or eleven, Henry a year younger, when they rounded a corner to find three older boys huddled around a dead cat on a narrow street. Jack recognized the leader of the three: Tom Purvis, a short, stocky youth with a limp hank of hair that hung in a greasy strand before his face. The boy had served a year or two as Jack's father's ironworking apprentice before the good man's death, and the spark-burns on Purvis's hands and face proclaimed him an ironworker still. "Look here," Purvis had said, "it's Jackie Donne, what should be an apprentice like us, but now as his father is dead and his new father too fine for the trade, little Jackie puts on airs."

"No," Jack had said, "I think laboring for an ironmonger a noble trade."

"He thinks it a noble trade! Listen how he puts on airs." Purvis tried to match his tones to Jack's—"I think working for an ironmonger a noble trade"—then scoffed. "His new father the doctor sends him to school to learn how to put on airs, instead of work." One of the bigger boys flanking Purvis snorted, and the other stared ahead stonily, jaw clenched and hands flexing.

"I put on no airs," said Jack, "and I mean no hurt to any of you."

"He means us no hurt! Did you hear that, Dickon? He means us no hurt."

Dickon, the one who had just snorted, now guffawed. "Oh, 'e means us no 'urt. Well, then, now we can breave easy, then, if 'e means us no 'urt."

Purvis gave Jack a shove. "Now do you mean us any hurt? Your filthy Jesuit uncle will not help you hurt us, for he has fled London, has he not? Do you mean to hurt us, Jackie Donne?"

Henry pulled at his brother's sleeve. "Jack, we should go."

Without taking his eyes off Jack, Purvis said, "You'll go when we tell you to go." The big, grim-faced boy took a step forward and stood louring over the frail-boned Henry.

"Stand away from him, you," Jack said.

The boy said nothing, but with an upward blow, lifted Henry off his feet and sent him sprawling to the pavement.

Jack launched himself at the big boy, hooked his foot behind the boy's, and made him stumble and fall onto his back. Jack swung his fist but hit nothing as he felt himself jerked back, and a knee in the stomach made him double over and left him gasping for breath. From the corner of his eye he saw that Henry's head was bleeding. Still bent at the waist, Jack watched as Dickon advanced on him, an idiotic grin on his face. Jack lunged forward, butting the boy in the midsection with the top of his head. Dickon staggered back and tripped over the grim-faced boy, who had just started to get to his feet. For the moment the two lay in a tangled heap. Jack turned to Purvis, who stood with a cruel smile on his face. In his hand he held a knife. "Say you put on airs since you went to school instead of work. Say it."

Jack coughed out the word: "No."

He jumped back as Purvis swung the blade. The bigger boys were untangled and starting to rise. Purvis tried a jab with the knife. Jack dodged to the side, then elbowed Purvis in the ribs. The knife clanked to the cobblestones. Jack reached for it, but Purvis kicked it out of the way. Now Henry was standing, weaving a little, and Jack felt someone grip his arm. Henry turned and ran. Hardly believing what he saw, Jack watched his little brother disappear around a corner. It was Dickon holding his right arm, and now the other big boy gripped his left. Jack sagged at Henry's betrayal, hardly caring when he saw Purvis creep into view, a menacing smirk on his face. Purvis pulled back his fist, and Jack felt it slam against the side of his head. When he looked up, the same fist was on the way again. This time it hit him just above the eye, and it seemed no time passed before he felt the warm trickle of blood. Purvis's next blow came in low, and once more Jack had to gasp for air. Purvis said, "Shall we teach Jackie Donne to put on airs, now his father is dead and his filthy Jesuit uncle is gone? Shall we carve it into him?" Dickon made an incomprehensible sound of approval as Purvis turned, then walked to the curb where his knife lay in a puddle of rainwater. He picked it up and moved slowly toward Jack. "What shall I write on him? I know my letters too, Jackie. I need none of your schooling to know my letters. What shall I carve upon him?"

Another half-witted sound came from Dickon. Purvis held the edge of the blade to Jack's forehead, slowly increasing the pressure until Jack felt his skin give way. Now blood trickled around his other eye.

Then a sharp cry made Purvis pause. "Here, Uncle Jasper! Here! Hurry! Jack needs you!" It was Henry's voice. He sped around the corner, looking back into the street he had come from, frantically beckoning to someone still out of sight. "Hurry!" Henry spun around and shouted to his brother. "It's Uncle Jasper, Jack! He's come back, on his horse. He has his sword, and—" Henry turned back to the street. "Quickly, Uncle Jasper!"

Now Jack could hear the steady clop of a horse. Purvis hesitated, then turned and bolted away. The grim-faced boy released his grip, gave Jack a smack in the back of the head, and ran. Apparently unable to comprehend what was happening, Dickon still held tight to Jack's right arm. Jack turned and with his left fist hit him in the nose as hard as he could. Immediately Dickon released his grip, held both hands to his face, then looked at the blood on them. Jack smiled. "Your friends are gone, and my uncle is come. He and I will break your pate together." Dickon looked up, and the horror slowly dawned in his eyes. He looked around for his friends, turned, and ran.

At that instant a hostler leading an old mare rounded the corner and stopped when he saw Jack, whose grin stood out amid the streams of blood on his face. "Henry!" Jack shouted. "That were a device worthy of Ulysses." He laughed. "I thought you had deserted me."

"Never," said Henry. "I heard the horse, and it was all I could think to do."

The hostler, hardly able to piece out what had happened, stood scratching the back of his neck.

Jack put his arm over Henry's shoulder, and the two strode home to tease their horrified mother. After that the two brothers practiced daily with blunt-tipped swords.

Now, as he stood before the door glancing at his sword on

the high shelf, the whole encounter with the three boys having flashed though his mind in a few images, another series of knocks—even louder this time—disturbed the quiet of the night. "Anon, anon," he said impatiently. He fetched the candle from where he had set it on the washstand, undid the latch, and opened the door. There stood a plumed, silk-stockinged, taffeta-jacketed, officious-looking stranger with a cudgel in one hand—no doubt the instrument he had used to strike the door—and a piece of folded parchment in the other. The man had a clean-shaven face, squinting eyes, and an upturned nose.

"Master John Donne?" he asked in a needling voice.

"I am," said Jack. "What is it that would have you batter the boards as to wake all the sleepers in the house and half the sleepers in the churchyard?"

The visitor gave Jack a supercilious glare. "Only this," he said, "a message from no lesser personage than the illustrious Lord Robert Cecil, Baron of Essendon, Secretary of State and Chief Privy Counsellor to His Majesty King James, Master of the Court of Wards, *et cetera, et cetera*. . . . Would you like me to continue with my master's titles, or would you prefer me to depart with his missive to you? Or"—he pulled back the letter and held it daintily in the air—"would you have me deliver it?"

Cecil! Good God, Cecil. . . . What could Robert Cecil want with Jack Donne? Whatever it was, it could scarcely bode well. Could this be Anne's uncle's work, Egerton's backdoor way of trying to help? But the Lord Keeper was hardly one to work through Cecil, hardly one to trust his niece to such a serpent, even if the twisted little man did run James's kingdom for him. Cecil! All of it surged upon Jack at once: all of it, somehow compressed into this moment, while the overdressed messenger stood before him with the parchment in his hand. This instant contained all messages, from God or the Devil or both: messages about patronage, power, providence, fate, freedom, family

. . . all of it. His eternal life, his soul—maybe the lives and souls of innumerable others—teetered and reeled on the point of this precarious now. But perhaps it was always so. He breathed. "I will take the paper." The messenger smirked, his little victory won, and swaggered away with his cudgel tucked under his arm.

When Jack latched the door and turned, Anne stood on the stairs in the faint glow of the rush candle. "They slept through the noise," she said, for once failing utterly to read his thoughts. "What sort of creature makes such a sound? Was it a dragon too courteous to burn the house without asking?"

"Yes," he said abstractedly. "Ah . . . no. Not so courteous. A messenger from Cecil."

"Cecil." Her playfulness vanished. "Robert Cecil, you mean. The King's. . . ." Her voice faded.

"Agent." He supplied the neutral word but mentally added a few others: *Plotter. Henchman. Spymaster. Devil.*

"What does he want?"

Jack looked at her for a moment, then at the parchment. "I don't know." He broke the wax and opened the letter. He and Anne took it in at once:

> *Lord Robert Cecil the Viscount Cranborne requires your attendance at his house in Ivy Lane at an hour and a quarter past dawn tomorrow. Which appointment you are to fail not on peril of the King his displeasure.*

Cecil's *house in Ivy Lane:* he made it sound like a cottage, but Jack knew it to be a sprawling mansion covering blocks of London, a fortress flanked to the south by Bridewell—once a hospital, now a cruel workhouse, almost a slave market—and to the east by the broad, open sewer of Fleet Ditch. Bridewell and Fleet Ditch: apt reminders of the poverty, sorrow, and stench that clung to the outskirts of power.

"Viscount Cranborne?" Anne asked.

"One of his new titles. Earl of Salisbury is next, they say. But no matter. They are all stuffed into his little personage."

"What could this summons mean?" she asked.

He shook his head slowly. "I know not. Friendly employment of some sort?" he suggested hopefully.

"If it is, it doesn't strike the ear so; *peril of the King his displeasure* has an unwholesome ring."

"It is but . . . a custom, a formula. Cecil dictated, said *et cetera,* and his secretary filled in the rest."

Anne knew when she was being coddled. "Come, you have been secretary to a Privy Counsellor. If you were penning a letter from the Lord Keeper, a friendly letter offering friendly employment, would you write such a phrase?"

"No. But your uncle is not Robert Cecil."

"Just so."

They stood silently until the candle guttered and all was dark.

"What will you do?" she asked.

There was real fear in her voice: a rare thing. What could Anne know about Cecil that frightened her so? Had her uncle been talking? That would hardly be like him. Lord Keeper Egerton, ever the Christian gentleman, would not gossip even to his male friends, much less to women or girls. On the Privy Council he had kept his distance from Cecil—Jack had watched the politic dances by day balanced against the literal ones in the courts by night. As Egerton's secretary Jack had been like a playgoer at the stagings of statecraft: the farces, revenge tragedies, masques, and interludes. Two or three dozen times he, Jack Donne, had stood near enough the little hunchbacked form of Robert Cecil to wring his neck. He could do it with one hand. Yet no doubt when he saw Cecil tomorrow the man would not recognize Jack's face at all; Cecil spared none of his attention for anyone or anything not useful to him.

Jack answered her: "What can I do but go to see him? He is the most powerful man in England, after King James. Or including him. But what makes you worry? What do you know of this Cecil?"

"Nothing else than what I have seen with my eyes, heard by my ears, or noted by rumor—which is to say I know nothing at all. For rumor is ever untrusty, and at my uncle's house in the Queen's reign I exchanged but a few words with Sir Robert as one of our dinner guests, some three or four times. Once or twice with my father at Loseley. There was nothing untoward in anything he said." She paused. "Only, a chill crept along the edges of his words."

Jack nodded in the dark.

"Oh," Anne continued, "and once when I was alone in my father's library, Cecil stumbled in and spoke awkwardly, as if he had entered the wrong room. He stayed a few minutes, spat out some pleasantries, and left." She added in a quieter tone, "My uncle does not like him—despises him, perhaps, if my uncle can despise any man. He would never say it, but I know it is true."

"Well, so it may be. But come what may, this Cecil is but a man. Make him not into a devil, whether or no he be called in the streets *Robertus Diabolus.* As you say, rumor is untrusty. Cecil is a man. As am I: a man, and no fool. So fear not. I too can be nimble with a word, and were it to come to a contest of the wits—"

"Jack!" She startled him with the force of the interruption. "*This* is what I fear, as much as I fear Robert Cecil: I fear Jack Donne fetching the notion it is his business to cross words, which is more fell than crossing swords—with Robert Cecil. Well, he will not kill you with his sword, but he may kill you with a word. It will happen some behind-door way, and the man will lament your death as much as the maiden in your poem lamented the passing of that flea she purpled her nail withal."

Jack held up both palms in the dark. "I am schooled."

"You have *children.*"

"All abject submission, I, upon the morrow. I shall hear what he desires, and come to tell you as early as I may."

They stood holding each other in the dark until Anne said, "To our prayers?"

"Hm. Prayers."

Early the next morning Jack said he had slept some, but even by the flickering light of the lantern Anne could see it was otherwise. His eyes, always dark, had lost their wonted spark. Shadows tinged the skin beneath them.

"You look very fine," she said. "The clothes sit well upon you."

"I look . . . black. As ever."

"Just the color for this meeting. Nothing for show, but well-fitted. You look fine."

"I must go."

"Yes."

It was yet above an hour until dawn; he had checked the stars and the progress of the moon. He would borrow a good horse from Wolley's stables: a man must arrive at Lord Cecil's house in some sort of style. Ah! Wolley's fine Andalusian stallion would be just the animal, and so the ride into London would barely take an hour—much less if he let the stallion run. And the fine, proud animal would like nothing so much. The horse was the fastest Jack had ever seen—and Francis, for all his foppish delicacy, one of the finest riders. There was no denying it: the man looked good on a horse.

By no means did Jack want to be late, but he had no need to tire the Andalusian. There was plenty of time.

Anne kissed him goodbye and watched him walk along the path to the stables until he disappeared around the corner of the hedge. He walked as if conscious that she was watching him: confidently, loosely, as if merrily setting off to the wars. She closed the door softly and went back to sit at the table, wrapping a woolen blanket around herself against the morning chill. The children slept upstairs. Instinctively she started to say a prayer for Jack but stopped before she had well begun. In the parable Jesus urged the seeker to keep knocking, keep pestering the master, and Paul said to pray without ceasing. But she had prayed enough for now.

The lantern's flame hissed faintly as it writhed in its fitful dance. Shadows jerked and flickered on the walls. As she sat with her head tilted and her hair hanging loose, she looked into the smoky globe that shielded the lantern's little fire. Her reflected face, pulled and warped all out of its proper form, stared back at her.

And Lady Bedford: in the morning Jack sees the enchanting Lady Bedford. She likes his verses well enough to ask for more of them. No, likes *him:* likes him well enough to give him a bracelet of gold. Then in the evening Robert Cecil sends for him. Lucy, Countess of Bedford, and Robert Cecil. If the two were in league, Anne had never heard it, but amid the complicated ravellings of court alliances it seemed likely enough.

Anne's distance from court affairs left her knowing little about how to help her husband. Most days the allure of life at court did not enter her mind at all. Other times she was grateful to be free of the machinations of courtiers. But sometimes, as now, she chafed against the role she had chosen. It might have been otherwise. She could easily have married a nobleman: even before she turned fifteen, several had made their desires plain. But the stirrings of her heart—moved by Providence and love together—had led her to choose Jack. She did not regret her choice. Or not often.

Maybe if she mustered what little she did know, she could piece together some manner of help for him. . . . Where to start? Prayer: always start with prayer. But once again she found she could not pray, not now. Her heart was not in it, and somehow she knew that mouthing the words would not be pleasing to God, that for this task he wanted her not to pray from the heart but to use her head. The Lord had, after all, given her a good one. Well, what did she know? Just this: whatever Cecil—or Cecil and Lady Bedford—wanted from Jack, it would have to do with politics and it would have to do with religion. For everything having to do with Cecil had to do with both. She picked up the torn loaf that lay before her, turned it, put it down again, drummed her fingers on the table. But to know only that was to know almost nothing. So much was true of anyone at King James's court, true almost of anyone in England. What else then did she know? Start at the first: James, an odd man from an odd land. The Scots Protestant king with the Catholic mother the Queen of Scots and the Catholic wife, Anna of Denmark. James was the Protestant who had come to power by dangling the hope of tolerance before the Catholic faction on one hand and the Puritan on the other. Then when all was secure, the new king had used Cecil to clench both hands into fists.

And Lady Bedford. The Protestant Lady Bedford had grown fast friends with James's Catholic queen, Anna of Denmark. Jack said the new queen had become the only person in England allowed to hear Catholic Masses without fear of torture and death. Was Lady Bedford, then, trying to convert the Queen to the new faith? Or was the Countess secretly . . . ? Anne had seen Lady Bedford only once, at a great gathering at Loseley, years ago. Anne had been a child of eleven or twelve, Lucy the Countess of Bedford already married at only thirteen or fourteen—yet seeming years and years older. Proud-looking she had been, with a quick eye. Beautiful, yes. Perhaps. At least the young men seemed to think so; her doltish, droop-lipped new husband the Earl of Bedford had kept a watchful eye on her. At the time Anne had seen no use for the haughty, learned young countess who bantered with the bachelors home from university—had run off instead to play with her cousins.

Now Anne fingered the smooth edge of the wooden trencher in which lay the sodden remnants of the broth-soaked bread Jack had pretended to eat before he left. What was left of the loaf rested before her on the table. She absently tore off a little piece and chewed it slowly.

. . . And there was Jack, summoned: the handsome scholar-soldier, the troubled poet and statesman-in-the-making spurned by his Catholic family and then his wife's Protestant one, unrewarded hero of the wars, ignored by Raleigh and Essex, finding a place at last with her uncle, and—she couldn't help a wan little smile in the lamplight—falling desperately in love with a wealthy, fair-haired young maiden against all the rules. Like a tale of passion in Boccaccio. Or one of Shakespeare's love stories for the stage. Her smile faded. A tragedy, it might be. Who could say before the last act? One thing was sure: comedy or tragedy, Cecil would make a fine villain. The third Richard, perhaps, or Iago.

Anne drew the blanket closer about her. The pre-dawn chill made her breath hang in a faint cloud before it fell away into the shadows. But it was the thought of Iago more than the cold that made her shiver. She and Jack had seen the play at the Globe not a fortnight since. One of Wolley's maidservants had stayed with the children. True, Jack was no Othello, and she no Desdemona. There should be nothing to fear then from this Cecil, Iago or no. Yet for days the play had not left her mind. When they had come home afterward, she had gathered the sleepy children into the big bed, held them to her, and wept. Jack had not understood, or not quite. He too had been moved by the play but in a different way. Swept along by the words, the spell of the verse, he had wanted to find Will Shakespeare afterward and talk with him—had not understood that they must get home to the children and hold them, hold them.

Warmed by Wolley's fine horse, Jack rode along the Bankside under the cold, fitful stars. Just visible across the river in the first blush of dawn rose the great, blunt-topped summit of St. Paul's, its steeple still not rebuilt after the lightning strike over forty years before, the flat-roofed remains nonetheless rising hundreds of feet above the London streets. Nearer at hand to his right stood the humbler-looking structures that in a few hours would house all manner of entertainment and depravity: the bear-baiting pits, the brothels, and the theaters, first the Swan, then the Hope, then the Globe. Before him spanned the architectural wonder that always took his breath away: London Bridge, with its twenty massive stone pillars that carried a highway across a quarter-mile of water. Teetering out over the river all along both sides of the bridge, supported by struts angling down to the piers, hung the shops. Some were made of stone and rose two or three stories. They tempted travellers with London's finest goods: velvet caps, colorful silks from the Orient, gleaming jewels set in laceworks of silver and gold. But now all the shops stood shuttered against the night.

Jack had time to spare—too much of it. He eased the Andalusian to a stop and watched the sun rise over London Bridge. As the stars faded, the eastern sky flushed with promise. But he could also make out the heads of traitors—or men executed as traitors—impaled on pikes fixed to the bridge's gatehouse, rotting and gaping in their grotesque parodies of human woe. There they stayed as a warning to walkers and riders over the bridge until the quarreling birds had pecked them clean and carried away even the hair to line their nests. When only skulls remained, new traitors seemed ever at the ready to supply their heads. Absurd, insane these contraries seemed: the glorious hues blushing across the sky and the blackened death-masks on the bridge. With a grim eye Jack turned away, pulling the rein a bit too brusquely. The good horse moved obediently but snorted at the indignity. Jack reached down to give the stallion a pat on the side of his neck and a gentle word to let him know he meant no hurt.

Yes, any man summoned by Cecil—or a piece of any man—might end on London Bridge. But it would not be John Donne. Not unless he knew—*knew*—that God willed him to die a martyr's death. Nor would he succumb to the Jesuitical fantasies of his youth. No, he would stop his ears against the bewitching bridal song that lured him into those soft, scented folds of oblivion. Never again would he fall in love with death, pursue her: never dream of hunting her down, ravishing her, and becoming one flesh with her. He must remember the heads on the bridge. In marrying death he would become one flesh with her, but one dead flesh. He would not succumb. He would not. Anne was his wife, and no one on earth was more alive than she. He shared a single flesh with a living woman, with life herself. To choose martyrdom now, unless God did the choosing—*all* of it, and made His Inscrutable Will as Scrutable as he made it to Jonah—would be to choose not just death but everlasting adultery.

As Jack approached the bridge's gatehouse, grinning with the teeth of its raised portcullis, one of the heads impaled on a pike seemed to fix its desperate gaze on him, as if to warn not the others making their way across the bridge but Jack himself that death awaited him on the other side. He looked away and tried to let the easy, rhythmic clop of hooves on cobblestones calm him. When he came to the crest of the bridge, he could make out on the far shore the Tower of London. Perhaps Raleigh was already awake and pacing within the Tower leads, like a caged panther—as beautiful, as proud, and, in the wild, as quick to pounce. Jack had seen him in his glory. Raleigh had looked like Mars himself as he and the shimmering Essex commanded the English forces at Cadiz. But now, first Essex and then Raleigh had fallen prey to this Robert Cecil. Well, maybe Essex had fallen prey to himself, but Cecil's hand was in that, too. Raleigh, though, had been Cecil's friend, and the twisted little hunchback had betrayed him. Even at Jack's distance from the doings at court, he could see just how it had all fallen out. And now that he had made his move, Cecil would have to see that Raleigh spent the rest of his life in the Tower. If he ever gained his freedom, Raleigh would look for revenge.

Jack had been inside the Tower's walls just once, some twenty years before. In those days he had all but worshipped his uncle Jasper. As head of the Jesuit mission in England, Jasper Heywood had embodied all Jack's aspirations for his own life. The man sparkled like the gem that bore his name. A brilliant, spirited seeker of adventure, a soldier and courtier who commanded his sword and his wit with equal dexterity, a scholar of both deep learning and good humor, a handsome priest who garnered respect and inspired devotion wherever he went, Uncle Jasper told stirring tales to Jack and Henry, tales of the fearless saints of old, tales of the English Jesuits and their outwitting of pursuivants and spies, their hairbreadth escapes, their clever disguises—Jasper's favorite being open, ostentatious travel as a diplomat.

Young Jack had wept, then moped about the house for days when he learned Uncle Jasper had been recalled to Rome. Two weeks later, when news reached London of the storm at sea that blew the ship back to the English coast, where Uncle Jasper was captured and sent to the Tower, Jack felt a secret, guilty thrill to think he might see his uncle again. For three months he talked of little else to his mother, until at last she agreed to take him with her to visit her brother in the Tower. She absolutely refused, though, to allow Jack's younger brother to accompany them. So it was Henry's turn to sulk.

When the day came young Jack steeled himself against the terrors he would soon witness. Uncle Jasper would lie bound in chains, confined in a narrow, dim-lit keep. Rats would scuttle about his feet as the rack-weakened priest stared at his visitors through haunted, bloodshot eyes. The sight of his faithful nephew would help revive the man, help restore him to his rightful, fearless self. Then, with Jack's help, he could escape. Although young Jack had never walked inside the massive fortress called the Tower, he knew well enough the moans and plangent cries of the inmates at the Clink and the Marshalsea, the fetid stench, the gritty faces pressed between iron bars, the meager, ragged arms outstretched for alms or crusts of bread.

Unsurprisingly, the guard who admitted Jack and his mother through the Tower's outermost portal bore a furtive look. He seemed to recognize Elizabeth but looked none too pleased with the business of leading the two to Uncle Jasper's cell. The man did not so much as glance through the contents of the large baskets Jack and his mother carried. He simply led them at a brisk pace through roofless, moist, moss-walled walkways. Even in the open air, the rankness of the place made Jack's gorge rise. But he kept beside his mother and did not vomit. At one point the guard motioned the visitors into a deep shadow while another, keys jangling, crossed a passageway before them. Then the guard led them around a corner and under a torch-lit archway. Jack looked up at the ribbed vault of the entryway's ceiling. At the base of each of the four ribs a different grotesque, stone-carved image flickered in the torchlight: a snarling monster, a demonic skull, a horrified human face. But the visage that most frightened Jack simply leered eagerly, as if it were welcoming yet more human souls to pass beneath its gaze and never emerge after. Jack had to force himself to look away and move on.

At last they came to Uncle Jasper's cell. The guard turned the key, pulled open the thick-ribbed door on its heavy, creaking hinges, and let in the two visitors. Jack's mother motioned for the guard to follow them inside. The man hesitated, then looked about him and stepped into the room. She said, "We will call again at noon one week from today. There will be four of us: the two you see before you and two who look like an old husband and wife. The woman will be hooded and bent over a cane. Supporting her will be a gray-bearded man with a broad-brimmed hat."

The guard looked at Elizabeth suspiciously. "This couple: will they be old indeed, or only made to look old? And will the one with the cane in fact be a woman?"

"These things you needn't know," Elizabeth said.

"If admitting them would imperil my life, I must needs know," the guard replied.

"But let us into this cell, let us out again two hours later, and your office is done. Here are thanks for your pains." She handed him some coins.

"But if these men be Catholic priests, my life were forfeit."

"Fear us not, but trust in the Lord."

The man looked dismayed by that admonition. "If they be Jesuits, Topcliffe will embowel me alive."

When she said nothing, he extended his hand to return the money. "I cannot do it."

Elizabeth gently closed his hand around the coins and said, "How fares your dear wife? Has her sickness passed?"

"No," the guard said quietly, "she fares worse."

"And the three little ones. Have you someone to care for them while you are here?"

"My wife does what she can, but she grows tired and faint."

"Is she fevered?"

"Aye."

Elizabeth hesitated only a moment before saying, "My husband is a doctor. Tomorrow he will visit her. With him will come one who will serve as nursemaid for your wife and caretaker for your children. There will be no expense to you."

The guard slowly withdrew his hand and pocketed the coins. "I thank you."

"One week from today," Elizabeth said. "Noon. Meet us at the gate. Two hours."

The guard nodded his thanks, stepped into the passageway, shouldered the door shut, and locked it from the outside.

The room was darksome—Jack had been right about that—and his eyes were only now beginning to adjust; he could tell more by sound than sight that the chamber was large. The air felt cool but not dank or cold. Two thick candles glowed on a table, and behind them Uncle Jasper, dressed in gentleman's finery, sat in a comfortable-looking chair. His finger traced the page of a book open before him. The priest did not so much as look up—as if receiving visitors from outside the walls were the most ordinary thing in the world. Then, his finger pausing on the page, he said, "There: a good place to stop." He raised his head, and his face brightened. "Ah, my dear Elizabeth: a *most* welcome sight. And young Jack!" He rose and embraced his sister, then his nephew. Jack held on tighter and longer than might have been quite seemly, but he didn't care. Nor did Uncle Jasper or Elizabeth protest. At last the priest ruffled the boy's hair and said, "So. You must have campaigned long and hard to talk your mother into this visit." Jack nodded, only then releasing his grip on his uncle. Jasper put his hands on Jack's shoulders, held him at arm's length, and looked into his eyes. "It is well," he said. "You are old enough to aid us in our cause, and with more than prayers alone."

As if to shift the ground before the idea had time to take root in her son's mind, Elizabeth said, "I have brought food and drink for us all. Jack, you will take some wine with us. But not too much; I trust not the water hereabouts to qualify the wine, so you must drink sparingly and keep your wits."

Jasper smiled. "A fine young man. Taller by three inches, I think, since last we met. If they let me keep my swords for exercise within these walls, I would try blades with you."

"Henry and I practice at home."

Elizabeth said, "And too lustily you practice. I doubt not but one of you will soon hurt the other past all cure."

They ate a leisurely meal: roast fowl, beef-and-cabbage pies, crisp apples, honeyed bread, and good Spanish wine. Jasper told them the story of the storm in the Channel, the near-shipwreck, and the party of pursuivants that met them on the Sussex shore—pursuivants or ordinary thieves, more like, looking for plunder if the ship should split. But as it was they had to content themselves with searching for crucifixes and rosaries, which they found in plenty. It was not long before one of the passengers, pressured by a pursuivant who salivated at sight of the poor man's daughter, identified Jasper as a Jesuit.

"It is by God's own blessing you were spared the gallows," Elizabeth said.

"Yes," Jasper replied as the customary gleam faded from his eyes, "I suppose it's a blessing to be spared the gallows. To say nothing of the drawing and quartering. Or it would be a blessing if I could say my fellow-priests at the trial shared in it. I had prepared my soul for a goodly death, but the Queen would not have it so."

Jack's mother had not told him about the Queen's intervention, had not even told him of the trial. He said to his uncle, "Queen Elizabeth herself spared you?"

"She did. She knew I counseled my Jesuit brethren not to seek out maryrdom, but to abide by the law if they could. She knew I told them to administer the Sacraments and to renounce rebellion. Besides, I think she remembered my days as her schoolmate, or she remembered your grand-uncle's music and jesting in her father's court." Jasper paused before adding, "But there were six of us at the trial, and I alone was spared." He said it as if being spared were a burden.

"They died well," Elizabeth said quietly. "They sang a *Te Deum* on the way to the scaffold."

Jasper nodded. Brightening a little, he said, "We sang one at the trial, just after our sentence of death. At that time I had no thought of a reprieve. Well, I suppose I might have known: I did, after all, carry the tooth in my pocket."

Jack's mother turned to him. "Your kinsman Thomas More's tooth," she said. Jack knew the story well enough, but he let her tell it. "When your uncles determined to enter the Society of Jesus, both secretly wished to claim the relic, but each said the other should take it. On the eve of their departure, the tooth miraculously split into two, each a complete tooth; through the good Sir Thomas's intercession, the Lord saw fit to bless them both with a wonder-working relic." She added warmly, as if the point might be missed, "It was a miracle."

Although feeling flushed with the wine, Jack refrained from suggesting it was no miracle but a rotten tooth, cracked and ready to fall apart. His mother might insist that each relic was complete, but Jack had seen the one Jasper carried. If that was a whole tooth, it was a sorry one.

Jasper was saying wistfully, "Singing that *Te Deum* with my friends while the justice pounded his gavel in fury. . . . Never have I felt so happy."

Jack could see his mother was torn: moved, perhaps, by the thought of condemned priests singing songs of thanksgiving for the gift of martyrdom, by her brother's reprieve while the others went to their horrific deaths, by the bittersweet fear that her son would follow in her brothers' risky path, by her reading in the boy's expression the beginnings of doubt. Jack could hardly bear the look on her face; he felt he had to say something. He looked away from his mother and asked his uncle, "Is it long of the Queen that you live so well?"

Before Jasper could answer, Elizabeth said, "What do you mean, he lives well? Your uncle lies in prison."

No, his uncle Jasper did not lie in prison; he sat, and in a cushioned chair. He watched the priest, wondering how the man would respond, and said, "But this chamber is large and clean. You have books and light to read them by. Did the Queen give order for them?"

Jasper smiled. "No, good friends gave order for them. Friends like your mother, and many other of the faithful. I thank God for such friends. No, Jack, it is money that buys comfort in prison."

"They moved you here from the Clink. Did you live so well there?"

"What a thing to say!" Elizabeth snapped. "No more wine for you, boy."

Jasper looked at his nephew carefully. "No, perhaps not so well as this, but I thank God I fared well enough—again, thanks to faithful friends."

"I have seen them at the Clink," Jack said. "The prisoners there are hungry and dirty and sick."

"Many of them are, yes," Jasper said.

"Were it not well for you to give some of your money to them, that they might have food?"

"Jack!" Elizabeth rose from her chair. He knew she was glaring at him, but he kept his eyes on the priest.

Jasper calmly held up two or three fingers, a slight gesture to stay his sister. "My friends give me money that I might fare well. That is their wish. I feed the poor here as I fed them at the Clink: with word and with sacrament. Comfort of the soul."

"But you could buy them comfort of the body as well. Money, you said, buys comfort."

Elizabeth raised her hands. "I know not where the boy learnt such impudence."

"Oh," said Jasper calmly, "I think he did not learn it, but it runs in his blood. Our father had it in his, I have it in mine, and"—here his eyes gleamed—"it may hap even my sister did not escape it entirely."

"Well, I am sure he did not learn it of me."

Jasper said, "But the question is well asked. When our Lord visited the house of Mary and Martha—this was long after he had raised their brother Lazarus from the dead—Mary anointed the Lord's feet with costly spikenard. Tell me, Jack: who was it who said she had done ill for not selling the nard to feed the poor?"

"Judas Iscariot."

"It was. Our Lord said Mary had done a good and holy thing; Judas was wrong to rebuke her. So too has your mother done a good and holy thing, as have others who have eased my lot. It would be wrong of me to deny them their wish."

The argument came straight out of the Gospel, and it came from Jack's beloved uncle. Yet somehow the boy remained unconvinced. It was in fact what his mother feared, what he himself feared but felt powerless to stem: the young growth of doubt, the quickly flourishing questions about his elders, the Jesuits, the Roman Catholic Church. He could see that Uncle Jasper had cast him as Judas in the analogy, just as the priest had cast himself as Christ. That hardly seemed fair-minded, especially in light of all the places in the Gospels where Jesus insisted on feeding the poor. Jack pressed his luck: "Yes, but when the rich man came asking what he must do to find everlasting life, our Lord said, 'Go, sell the things that thou hast, and give to the poor, and thou shalt have treasure in heaven.' "

Elizabeth was pacing now, arms folded, but she said nothing. With a wry little smile Jasper asked, "How old are you now, Jack?"

"Twelve."

"Twelve years old. Just the age of our Lord when his parents missed him on their journey home after the Passover feast, and they returned to find him in the temple disputing Scripture with the rabbis and wise men of Jerusalem. The men were astonished that a mere boy spoke with great authority."

Elizabeth stopped pacing and glared at her brother as if he had insulted her son. "Jasper," she said, "you must not put such ideas—"

"I but say that Jack is of the same age," the priest replied. "I make no further comparison." Jack was glad to hear that. He had bristled at being compared to Judas Iscariot, but this would be worse. To be likened to the young Jesus of Nazareth would put an intolerable burden on him, one he knew he would never be worthy to bear. Surely Jesus never had such thoughts as Jack harbored, never longed to pull the clothes off a girl like Katherine Fletcher, whose soft body moved so fluidly beneath her dress as she helped her father at the butcher's shop.

Elizabeth sat again, and the three ate and drank in silence for a few minutes. Then Jasper said, "Still, it is true Jack will prove a credit to the Jesuit order."

"That's for our Lord to decide," Elizabeth said. "And not for some while yet, I pray."

To live as a Jesuit: to serve the Blessed Virgin without a trace of fear, to outwit the pursuivants in a holy cause, to inspire the devotion of admiring maidens, to navigate grateful souls along the secret currents of a forbidden faith. A year, a month, even a week ago young Jack would not have hesitated to swear he would one day join the priesthood despite his longing for the likes of Katherine Fletcher. Now, though, now that he had finally been allowed to visit his uncle in prison, now that he had seen how Jasper prospered even within the Tower's walls—a sight that Jack knew should make him grateful—somehow all this, more than his youthful lusts, made him doubt his calling.

And in all the twenty years since, the dark doubts remained.

Chapter 4

Jack let the reins lie slack, whether unconsciously steering with his knees or otherwise somehow allowing the stallion to sense his reluctant desire to move toward Cecil's house. But by some means horse and rider conspired to make their way steadily toward Ludgate until they crossed the little bridge over the thickly gurgling muck of Fleet Ditch, with its noisome welter of human and animal excrement, its offal discarded upstream by Smithfield sausage makers, tripe dressers, and cat-gut spinners, its dead dogs, its occasional body of some poor suicide, unworthy of burial in sanctified ground—and, when God was merciful, its rainwater. Jack's eyes burned with the disgrace, the shame, the stench of it—the criminal indifference of his beloved city toward the awful fact of death. He took up the reins, sat tall, and steeled himself for the interview with Cecil. The horse eased off the bridge and, looking proud and stepping high, made his way around to the front of the house. Jack announced his appointment to the stout, crop-haired soldier at the gate, who examined a paper and let him pass. Once inside the grounds Jack dismounted and left the horse to the care of a well-dressed groom who seemed to know the worth of such a fine Andalusian. The man led the stallion off to Cecil's stables, promising to take good care of him. A kind-eyed old doorman nodded gracefully as he showed Jack inside and walked off to inform Lord Cecil of the visitor's arrival.

The spacious anteroom gave off a pleasing smell. Often

enough when Jack had found himself inside a stuffy, musty, greasy, or smoky room he had stepped outside to breathe more freely. This was the opposite. Fresh-cut boughs of evergreen trees, seeming somehow to purify rather than merely scent the air, stood here and there, artfully arranged among the tapestries. A few crushed leaves of aromatic herbs in ornamental bowls added an invigorating flavor to the air. This room alone told Jack something about Cecil's tastes—not that what he saw came as any surprise. Everything here was finely appointed: well-crafted furniture, artfully woven tapestries with scenes from the *Aeneid,* books in a handsome case, an ample fireplace with a good supply of quartered, seasoned oak and ash, and a well-tended fire. All this was to be expected for a man of Cecil's position: he must entertain ambassadors and kings, and they must be treated well. Yet while lavish spending had become commonplace among the wealthy, nothing here spoke of extravagance. Here all was reasoned, ordered, sane: life as it should be.

With a touch of unease Jack saw that this was exactly how he himself would appoint such a room, had he the means to do it. A reasoned, ordered, sane life was the one he too would live—or so he had often thought. But even with the money and power of Cecil, could he live such a life? Would the seething moil in his mind ever settle into steady reason? He doubted it. No, Robert Cecil, not Jack Donne, was the reasonable one. And what had *Robertus Diabolus* done with God's great gift of reason? Raleigh, no saint but innocent of treason, paced within the Tower walls. Heads of other innocent men, congealed in their frozen howls, haunted London Bridge. The poor, weak, and sick who in another time might have gone to Bridewell Hospital now sweated and toiled their life sentences in Bridewell Workhouse. The desperate men so poor and forgotten and lonely they took their own lives floated or sank or hung on snags in Fleet Ditch not fifty yards from this room.

The kind-eyed doorman appeared, said that Lord Cecil was ready, and led Jack through a series of rooms—one for music, one with a large oaken table for meetings, one with an armor collection, one for games, the great hall for banquets, dances, and masques—entertainments that could hardly come naturally to the little hunchbacked Cecil—and at last to Cecil's study, which might have doubled as his library. It was a room to take Jack's breath from him: large, with a high timbered ceiling, but made comfortable by fireplaces at both ends, well-lighted by high clerestory windows along two walls. But especially this: below the windows, books—hundreds upon hundreds of them. Perhaps Cecil would allow him to explore the collection later, but he could hardly peruse the books now. He removed his velvet hat as he bowed, only slightly—he did not want to appear obsequious—and said, "Your lordship."

Cecil had aged a decade in the three years since Jack had seen him. The little man ebbed even thinner than before, paler, his long, contorted face more cadaverous, his back more hunched. A deep crease ran vertically along his left temple, making his high forehead seem to bulge outward, as though the brain within had expanded beyond normal bounds. Yet his eyes maintained their enigmatic calm. "I see you admire my books," Cecil said.

"Very much."

"These few I keep about me." Cecil motioned for Jack to take a chair—an intricately carved one with a padded seat—and continued. "There are more—many more, and other copies of some of these same—in my library. In the last three or four years I have—wherefore I know not—taken to improving my store of books: buying smaller libraries, sending agents here and there to find those volumes I lack." With half a smile, half a grimace he added, "A whim."

"I fear," Cecil continued, "I must entertain the Count of Villa Mediana when you depart." He held up both palms and shrugged as if to say in a single gesture, *What can one do? The Spaniards insist on sending these doltish ambassadors along with the real negotiators, and the dullards must be entertained along with the rest.* "Otherwise," he continued, "you could spend the morning here and the afternoon in the library. But perhaps your passing the whole day in the library will suffice?"

Cecil had already found Jack's weak spot. "I should be honored," he said.

The little man nodded. "Master Cobham tells me you arrived on a fine Andalusian war horse. Your own?"

The library, now the horse. . . . Jack looked Cecil steadily in the eye. "No, my lord. My circumstances are straitened of late. The stallion is borrowed."

"Still," said Cecil calmly, "you chose an Iberian breed. Most thoughtful of you." He bowed his head briefly in a good imitation of Jack's earlier gesture. "Most thoughtful. You might have chosen an English breed or a French, or a Netherlandish. But you chose a Spanish, knowing that you were coming to see me, and knowing that most English hate all that has to do with Spain."

"I did choose the horse with some care."

"You know then of my efforts to forge a treaty with Spain."

"I do."

"What think you of the idea? You fought the Spanish at Cadiz and the Islands, did you not? Under my Lord Essex and Sir Walter."

Essex and Raleigh: the two mighty men Cecil had deposed. As if to say, *Who, then, is this Jack Donne to oppose my will?* Jack replied with a little shrug, "We were at war with Spain. Lords Essex and Raleigh commanded the ships. I fought for England under their command."

"And all of England thanks you." Another little nod. "But what think you of a treaty with Spain?"

Jack spoke briskly: "We should have one, but we should sacrifice little for it—certainly not our independence. No alliance, merely peace. For Spain needs an end to the wars as much as do we."

Cecil pursed his lips and sat back in his chair. He eyed Jack for a moment before saying, "His Majesty favors an alliance with France."

"So I have heard."

"Yet your counsel runs counter to the will of your king."

"You asked where my counsel lay, my lord, not my allegiance."

"Well replied. The Lord Keeper asked your counsel many a time, and I can tell you he misses it now. But. . . ." Cecil let a little sigh escape. "His Majesty has his crotchets, and he favors Sir George More's bluntness over the Lord Keeper's equanimity."

So Cecil knew all: the King favored Anne's father, and so Jack was to receive no employment at court.

"The King," Cecil went on, "is a great lover of bluntness." He tipped his head to one side and asked, "But why Spain? Why not France? His Majesty's grandmother Mary of Guise was French, and his mother the Queen of Scots might as well have been. He says an alliance with France would isolate Spain, already poor with her wars, and the Anglo-French would rule the world together."

Jack would not take this bait. "His Majesty, begging your lordship's pardon, is wrong. An alliance with France gains nothing. With it, our wars with Spain in the Low Countries continue, and the Spanish block our sea trade to the Mediterranean, to the East Indies, and to the West. The coffers of England are soon depleted, then those of Spain. The French are left to violate the alliance, as they have twice broken alliances with us before, and rule alone. A Spanish truce—but no alliance—ends the wars, opens the sea routes, and brings a market for good English cloth the world around. Our coffers wax full, and we remain independent of foreign powers."

Cecil raised one eyebrow, apparently in admiration. Without thinking, Jack leaned forward and pressed on: "And with our wealth we may in Christian charity aid all who suffer, like those who toil and slave in Bridewell a hundred yards to the south. Now, very now, we could do something for them." Even had Cecil not twitched in his chair, the wave of dismay would have washed over Jack for going too fast and too far, and he would not have been able to hold back the heated flush that rose to his cheeks.

"Well," said Cecil crisply, "we may hope to help them, when the funds allow it. In Christian charity." Abruptly he changed the subject. "My friend Sir Walter hates the Spanish with a passion you must know only too well, if you served under his command."

"He does, my lord. *Hates* is not too strong a word."

"Sir Walter favors, then, His Majesty's policy for France and against the Spanish. And if Sir Walter were free to influence the King in this matter. . . ."

Cecil paused and looked expectantly at Jack, who dutifully filled in the rest of the sentence: "It would spell the ruin of England."

"Yes. The ruin." Both were quiet for a while, and a look of what appeared to be genuine sadness overtook Cecil. Even a tear gathered in the corner of an eye. "I hope to see Sir Walter walk free once the truce is signed."

Jack remained silent. He must use his head independent of his heart for a while—ever a hard thing for him—and he could not see what response Cecil wanted here. Perhaps none. Jack knew Cecil must have no intention of freeing as powerful an adversary as Raleigh. Perhaps Cecil wanted Jack to think that even *Robertus Diabolus* had a heart. Or perhaps he merely wanted to show that he had the power to imprison and free even the greatest men in the land. In any case there seemed no advantage in either supporting or opposing Raleigh's freedom. Jack waited until Cecil moved on.

"So the blunt Sir George was incensed when you married the pretty, nimble-witted Anne More."

Pretty, nimble-witted. So Cecil remembered Anne. Or he had taken the trouble to inquire about her. Jack said, "He was, my lord, in something of a rage when I revealed the union to him, although he liked me well enough before. It is true she could have made a better match, but she loved me, the choice was hers as much as mine, and as a member of Parliament and secretary to the Lord Keeper, my prospects for prosperity at court were excellent."

Cecil nodded, as if to say all this was true—as far it went. But it did not go far. "Sir George sued for an annulment, did he not?"

"He did, and I won the suit. The marriage was held legal, but Sir George. . . ." Jack paused.

After a moment Cecil said, "Yes. Your circumstances are straitened. I understand; you need not continue." The little man shifted uneasily in his chair, and his voice both quieted and somehow sharpened. "But do you know why Sir George waxed so angry? Do you know why he sought the annulment?"

Of course Jack wanted to know; had the question not played over his mind a thousand times? Had it not plagued him for three years? But what was Cecil's device here? "I do not know the reason. Always I have wondered. Some poems I wrote, it may be, about other women, before I met her. Or her youth: she was seventeen. Yet she had the comprehension of a woman much older. Or . . . I know not what."

Cecil waved a hand to dismiss such ideas. "Many young men write poems, and Sir George knew she was full able to choose for herself." He closed his eyes for a moment, bit his lower lip, and then said, "What I am about to break to you I have told no man, excepting Sir George, and so I rely upon your confidence."

"You have it."

"I ask you to repeat this thing to no man. Your wife you may tell, but only if you judge her able to hold all in like confidence."

What could this mean? What manner of thing could be meet for only Jack and Anne? "I pray your lordship proceed."

Cecil took a deep breath, then said, "My own dear wife Elizabeth died in the year of the raid on Cadiz."

"I remember, my Lord." He would have added, *All of England mourned,* but it was not true. To the common Englishman the death of the wife of *Robertus Diabolus* caused little grief. But such a plain, quiet, devoted wife as Elizabeth Cecil deserved better. Jack said only, "She was a good woman."

"She was. None better. And I mourned her. And for a few years I tried in vain to fill the void she left, fill it with affairs of state. Each night I slept but two hours or three, and the rest of the time I worked, busying myself with the security of England. And then after a time it happened that I attended a banquet at Loseley, where Sir George's daughter—your Anne—had come home from the Lord Keeper's for a visit. Before, when I had seen her she had been but a girl. But now . . . I was. . . ." Here Cecil's voice broke. "Charmed. Stricken." He swallowed, regained his composure, and continued. "Upon hearing her speak, upon observing her motions. . . . When it came time to converse with her, my words stopped in my throat. I, who have talked with ease to the powers of the earth."

His confusion moving toward horror, Jack looked on as Cecil continued. "I loved her, Master Donne. None of this did I say, or even fully know that night, for I was taken by surprise. Never had I felt such things: never. Such a violent assault upon the heart!" He smiled crookedly. "For once I understood why young men—and I was no longer young—write their poems and sing their songs of love. I, the bunchbacked maker of kings, mover of armies, and master of spies, in love with a young maiden. You see why I beg your confidence."

"I do," Jack said weakly. He felt himself drifting, lost at sea without even some passing piece of a spar to grasp and keep him afloat. Why was Cecil saying these things? Why unburden himself to Jack, of all people? Why now? What did he want?

Cecil let his gaze drift, as though he no longer saw anything in the room. "For some days after that banquet at Loseley—days that seemed without end—I tried to master these new sensations, to calm them at least, or to transform them into something useful. But they would not be conquered or changed; their torment would not relent. And so I ventured back to Loseley, where Anne remained, and I broke with Sir George. I received his assurance that she was not yet affianced to any man, I adumbrated my intent to marry his daughter, and I extracted from him—with great difficulty, let me tell you, for his deep desire was to proceed with a wedding at once—his oath to do nothing and say nothing to her unless I gave him leave: unless, that is, I could be certain of her affection. For that to me was all in all: I would not brook this marriage if her heart spoke against it. I arranged to speak with her."

Jack tried to still the waters that swirled about him and within him. He *must* keep his wits. Had Anne ever spoken of such an interview with Cecil? Yes! Just hours before, she had told him Cecil had once exchanged some awkward words with her at Loseley. How had she put it? He seemed to have stumbled into the wrong room.

Cecil went on: "She sat on a bench by the window in her

father's little library, her feet crossed and a book bound in calf-skin open on her lap. As before, my words limped forth half-formed, broken, palsied. From the pieces, she gathered that I inquired what she read. 'The *Arcadia,*' she said. 'Ah, S-S-Sidney,' I stammered. She told me that no, this was not Sidney's *Arcadia*—would that it were, she said, for Sir Philip's was like honey on the tongue (my knees went slack when she said those words)—but Lope de Vega's, and she had found it a tiresome pastoral, unworthy of the great Lope's talents. 'You read Spanish,' said I, stupidly stating the obvious. There followed a broken exchange about her languages, her likes (of all earthly things, she said, books alone did she covet), and her learning. When I inquired after the source of her education, she had much to say of you." Here Cecil looked at Jack again, this time with a steady, moist, unreadable eye. "And although she did not say as much, it was clear by her countenance that she loved you."

Jack steeled himself against the assault; until he knew why he had been summoned here, what was there to do but maintain an unyielding gaze?

Cecil let his own gaze drift again, and continued. "From this alone I did not lose heart, or not entirely. For young ladies *will* fall in love, and I knew that Anne More of Loseley—as she herself could not fail to be aware, even had she not been quick-witted—must be matched (begging your pardon, Master Donne) with someone of higher station than the son of an ironmonger."

Jack held his peace. He could protest that his mother's family was ancient and noble, but if Cecil had searched so deeply as to find that his father, dead these twenty-five years and more, had been an ironmonger, then Jack knew better than to invoke his mother's nobility. No, Cecil would not bait him into admitting that his mother and all her family—all but Jack himself—lived illegally, traitorously, as Catholics.

Cecil continued: "And so between my halting speech and unpromising aspect, I presented, I am afraid, no very appealing personage to a young lady of Anne More's sensibility. Neither did I receive at her hand any eagerness of welcome, nor yet any rebuff nor shadow of disdain. From these signs I deemed it best not to pursue my quarry further on that day, but neither to abandon the chase. My strategy you will find, I think, familiar: I retired for some days and plied my pen. I wrote her a sonnet."

"A sonnet!" The exclamation escaped before Jack could check it. Cecil seemed the least likely of all men to write love poetry. "You . . . wrote a sonnet for Anne."

"I did. And labored over it for many hours—days, even. I wrote, blotted lines, and recast them. For of all things I feared she would read it and laugh."

"Did she ever receive it?"

"No. Nor will she ever receive it, nor will any man or woman, for I have burnt the paper."

"Why? Were you not pleased with the verses? Good poetry is, as you must have discovered, most difficult to write."

"It is difficult indeed. But in the end I was satisfied. The lines, I thought, would have moved one of Anne's tender compassion to pity, mayhap to love."

This was maddening. What game was Cecil playing? If he desired Anne, if he wanted Jack dead, why had the man with all the power not done away with his lowly, disgraced rival two or three years before? It would have been easy enough. Was it a point of honor? Or did Cecil see Anne as spoiled now that she had lost her virginity? Or. . . . "When," Jack asked, "did you write this sonnet?"

Cecil said softly, "I think you have guessed the answer."

Jack's mind numbed with the realization, yet he found himself saying clearly, "At some time, I would hazard, just after Christmastide following the Queen's last Parliament."

Cecil placed his long fingers together, held them to his lips, and nodded. "You have it," he said. Then his head lolled to one side, and with a little moan he exclaimed, "O, that I had proceeded with more haste! That poem, or the labor I poured into it, spelled the destruction of my only hope for earthly happiness. Imagine, if you will, Sir George's confusion—then his fury—when letters arrived from you and from me on the same day. From you, an epistle delivered by no other than the Wizard Earl!—of him I would speak with you anon—but a letter boldly announcing the glad tidings of your marriage to his daughter, as though you were within your rights to claim a girl of her standing, still in her minority, without her father's leave; and a letter from me begging Sir George to speak on my behalf, and offering her the sonnet I had enclosed." He turned his watery gaze to Jack, as if expecting some manner of explanation or word of comfort or cry of protest or . . . Jack hardly knew what.

"Why do you tell me these things?" he asked. "Why now?"

With a little flutter of his hand Cecil waved the questions away. "For all his righteous wrath, Sir George did one thing well that day: he saw that he must not shout to the world that Sir Robert Cecil desired the hand of a girl who had eloped with the son of an ironmonger. No. He must not make me look the fool. Sir George, I am told, roared his displeasure to the very rafters upon receiving your news, but he spoke of mine to no one. That very day he rode to London to disclose to me my sorry fate. He returned the letter and the sonnet. The paper on which the poem was writ I have committed to the flames, but the words are deeper burned, here." He touched his forehead. "Here." He touched his heart. "Will you listen to them?"

"I will." Perhaps this was all Cecil wanted? A chance, for what reason God only knew, to recite a love poem to the husband of the poet's beloved? Maybe Cecil somehow thought using Jack was the only way to exorcise a demon that had haunted him these last three years. Jack hardly knew what to make of such a prospect. Certainly much worse could befall a man summoned before Cecil than to be made to hear a bad poem. But after so many disappointed hopes, to be so summoned, to steel oneself for the encounter, and then to be so used. . . .

"You are a poet," Cecil said, "so you can tell me where it is wanting. And you are Anne More's . . . lover."

"I am Anne Donne's husband."

"And so, I trust, her lover still. You can tell me, then, whether the words would have moved her to pity, and to love."

"Say on, my lord."

Cecil eyed him for a few seconds before beginning. Then in a steady voice, with nuanced tones as if he had read poetry aloud all his life, he recited the lines:

If but thy lightsome footfall might but pause,
While, halting, limping, I made up the pace
To take thy side; if thou wouldst turn thy face
To mine and not recoil despite just cause,
And were thy touch a balm to mend my flaws,
Or would thy beauty's gentle force new-trace
Some faintest shadow of thy soul's sweet grace
Upon this visage bent from nature's laws,
Then, then, dear Anne, my upright noble form
Which never in this life was blessed before
Could smile on tempests and could laugh at storms.
Thy whispered prayer, enriching one most poor
In spirit, breathing godly strength, ensures
Though trembling still, I dare to ask for More.

When Jack spoke he found his throat had contracted, clouding and half-obscuring his words. "My wife would have taken the verses to heart. It pleases me she did not receive them." It was true. All might have been different had Cecil written the poem a few days earlier. No. He must not think such a thing. Never had he questioned Anne's faithfulness to him, and already this twisted little creature was making him do it. But that poem. . . . It did not seem the work of one scheming to make his rival jealous. It was a cry from the heart of a man used to denying the heart's urgings, of one who had by hard experience learned to rely on his head in its place. Counterpoised against Cecil's agonized desire to be healed by Anne's love, agony forced into the confines of a sonnet, the lines from one of Jack's cynical old poems alighted in his mind:

Though she were true when you met her,
And last till you write your letter,
Yet she
Will be
False, ere I come, to two, or three.

How empty those words seemed, how shallow the mind that had spawned them, now that he had known and loved Anne, now that he sat before such a wretched man as this who had loved her without her knowledge, loved her in silence these three years. "You . . . summoned me to hear this poem, my lord."

"I did, yes." Cecil closed his eyes and breathed deeply before saying, "In part."

"In part."

"I would have you know, Master Donne, I am no heartless creature. What is said of me in the streets—and even in the halls of the Court—I know well enough. Though the knowing of it pains me, I will confess to using this false repute for the good of the realm. When courtiers, ambassadors, and counts have learned by rumor to fear me, much may be accomplished." He shrugged. "But I am not without a soul. What I do, I do for the good of all England: for you, for Anne, for your little ones, for all true subjects of the King."

This, now: this sounded like the Cecil Jack had expected. When a man made such protestations that what he did was for the greater good, then what he did was like to be foul. And somehow the mention of Anne and the children seemed a threat. Jack asked plainly, "What is it you would have me do?"

"I would have you serve your king."

"And this service you would have me do: it is, I take it, dangerous."

"It is." Cecil shifted in his chair. "But this thought, Master Donne, must have entered your mind already: If I, a widower, desired to make Anne Donne a widow, I could have made her one ere now, and easily might it have been . . . done."

Jack looked at him steadily, refusing to speak. At length Cecil continued. "Nor do I mean so to dispatch you now. The task is dangerous, yes, but no more so than similar work I have assigned to others, not one of whom I would lightly give over to an early death. No, these are men all England needs alive. As are you. I would not commit the sin of David, when. . . ." Cecil opened a hand in invitation for Jack to fill in the rest.

Jack obliged: ". . . lusting after Bathsheba, he appointed her husband Uriah to the front of the battle, where he was certain to be killed. Second Samuel, eleventh chapter."

"You are precise, Master Donne. Perhaps when this business is finished, a vocation in the clergy awaits."

Jack said darkly, "I doubt it, my lord."

"Well. Time enough for that. But for now I would have you know I would not commit the sin of David."

Jack could not resist a little taunt. "But why not? God forgave him. Even in King David's sins God smiled on him."

Cecil snapped, "But God has not smiled on me!" The force

of the eruption took Jack by surprise. Quickly reining in his tone, Cecil added, "Or God has kept his smiling countenance hid."

Jack watched as Cecil ruffled through a pile of papers on his writing-table, pretending to look for some piece of business, then straightened the stack. When the man appeared to have regained his sense of composure, Jack said, "So the Almighty withdraws himself from you, as well."

With a wry grimace Cecil said, "To some he seems to speak often, and at length." Then without a trace of irony he added, "But me he would have cry out, and cry again."

Jack nodded. Here was a kindred spirit. That did not change the fact, he must keep aware, that the man was powerful, treacherous, and still very much in love with Anne. But beneath it all, a kindred soul.

"This service I would appoint you," said Cecil, "is voluntary. I would not force your hand."

Well, yes and no. Some things were truly voluntary, some in name only. "Say on, my lord."

"You come from a family of . . . I will say it: notorious Catholics."

"I do. But my family might change the word *notorious* to *faithful.*"

"Catholics," Cecil continued, "descended from no less a rebel than Sir Thomas More."

"Yes, my great-great grand-uncle. But again my family would change a word: he was not a rebel but a martyr."

"Of course." Cecil brushed the air with his fingers as if such distinctions were trifles. "Tell me: your family descends from Thomas More. Does not Anne's as well? Sir George More shares the rebel's—excuse me, the *martyr's*—name."

"There is no relation."

"Truly? Curious, that she should share the name of this rebel."

What was the hunchback thinking: an annulment based on kinship? "Anne is my wife, not my kinsman."

"Well, in any case, Sir George her father remains a stout Protestant, as do all his children. And your own conversion to the true faith is well known. But so are your doubts. So are your troubles. So is your . . . want of employment worthy of your talents." Cecil paused and looked at Jack expectantly.

"Say on," Jack said.

"Need I? Do you not guess how I ask you to serve?"

"I think I smell it, and I think I do not like the way it smells. You ask me to feign reconversion to the Catholic faith, to spy upon my brethren."

"Not upon your brethren, Master Donne. Upon those who would overthrow the King by violent means. Such men are no brothers of yours, nor of mine, nor of any true Englishman's."

"And of those who are peaceably Catholic?"

"They are traitors under the law, as you know, but I do not ask you to reveal anything of the truly peaceable. Only the violent: only those who preach martyrdom to our young men, filling their brains with visions of heavenly glory, if only they will blast God's anointed rulers with the hellish fire of their pistolets and their petards. Only the Jesuits and those who would follow them in their foul plots against the King and all his godly realm. I ask you to enter into their company, and help me thwart their plans. For the good of all. Think of your little ones."

The heat rose in Jack's face. His color must have changed, but he did not care. "My little ones, Lord Cecil, were better served if I stayed near them and worked by some honest means to feed them. I will tell you or any man I care not a jot whether England is Protestant or Catholic, so long as men may live at peace."

Cecil shook his head slowly. "But Master Donne." He dealt out the words one by one: "Men. Will. Not. Live. At. Peace." Holding up both hands, as if speaking to a child, he said, "That is why we must stop them when they go awry."

Jack's anger rose. "If you but tolerated the Catholics, if you but let them hold their Masses without molesting them, do you think they would hatch these plots? James of Scotland promised toleration before you made him King." Cecil raised his eyebrows. Jack thundered, "Well, let him be tolerant!"

A voice from the other side of the door said, "Lord Cecil?"

Turning to the door, Cecil replied crisply, "Leave us, Master Cobham. It was nothing."

Cecil turned back to Jack and said, "Shouting for tolerance. You see? Men simply will not live and let live. Even those who wish to do so soon begin to shout. Then they begin to shoot. And finally the nation is torn by civil war. If only it were so simple as tolerating Popish Masses. But I see that in your passion you are merely rehearsing the part of the indignant Catholic."

Jack bit his lower lip for a moment, then said, "I cannot do this thing."

"You cannot." The two men stared at each other. "Very well. I said the choice was yours."

"And what consequence follows my refusal?"

"Consequence? If there were one, would it not have been more prudent to ask before the refusing?"

"More prudent, yes. If prudence were my aim."

Cecil leaned forward. "Ah, I see. You have some loftier purpose. I applaud you. Still, should prudence not govern the wrath of a man with a wife and children?"

Jack asked sharply, "What mean you by that?"

"Nothing," said Cecil. "Nothing at all. Do you take my meaning otherwise?" He moved his chair back and stood. "I thank you for your time. Master Cobham will show you to the library."

Jack picked up his hat as he stood. "I ask again, my lord: the consequence."

"And I have said: none at all. All is as it was before." He paused, then said, "Well, mayhap a constable will call on you about Lord Hay's nephew, whose head you broke yesterday at the Savoy. But apart from that. . . ." He gestured toward the door as he bowed his head very slightly. "Again, I thank you."

So Cecil had not only heard about the incident but knew who had been involved. His spies must be everywhere. Jack said, "Hay's nephew, is he? Somewhat wanting of his uncle's prowess, I should say, as well as his courtesy. Well, I care not. The man drew his blade upon me, with my back to him and all unarmed. I but defended myself."

"Yes, yes, so it is reported," said Cecil impatiently. "Doubtless you have naught to fear, if the young man lives."

"Well, I will brook that chance," Jack said. "Is there aught else?"

Cecil sat again and stared coldly at him. Jack waited a few heartbeats, turned, and took a step or two toward the door before he heard, "Only this: I am a patient man." Jack turned slowly back as Cecil continued: "I think you must agree I have been patient with you today." Jack waited with his hat in his hand until Cecil added, "For three long years I have remained patient. But I am flesh and blood. Good day." It was as though ice had filled the air, and Cecil's words had cracked their way through it to Jack's ears.

He stood still. "What means this?" he asked.

"What means what?"

"Your words: you have been patient, but you are flesh and blood. Come: be plain with me."

"Are the words not plain? I have been patient, but patience

wears thin. I am flesh and blood, as are we all. What is plainer than that?"

Jack tried once again: "You will say no more?"

Cecil rose, put his hands on the table, and leaned toward Jack. With menace in his voice he said, "I have spoken. Construe my words how you will."

There was no need to go on. Anne had seen it, or part of it, even the night before: *He will not kill you with his sword, but he may kill you with a word. It will happen some behind-door way, and the man will lament your death as much as the maiden in your poem lamented the passing of that flea she purpled her nail withal.* What Anne had not foreseen was that after Jack's death she would not long remain a widow. The thought of her with Cecil. . . . And the little ones: in later years they would not remember Jack at all, would always think of this scheming, hunchbacked man as their father. There was no choice to make. If this creature was to be outdone, it would have to happen later. Jack said, "Let us discuss this appointment."

Stiffly Cecil motioned for Jack to sit, then said, "First: as for the Wizard Earl. . . ."

Chapter 5

Anne looked up from the dough she was kneading while Constance stood by the corner of the table, waiting for a piece. The single knock had hardly faded when the door swung open to reveal an elegantly dressed man striking a dramatic pose, one hand on a hip, his fine-featured face turned in profile. He wore a close-fitting doublet of pale green, mustard-colored hose, and gleaming new riding boots. Behind him stood a broad-hipped young maidservant with downcast eyes. "Where is my Andalusian?" the man demanded without turning his head.

Anne smiled at the performance but kept kneading the dough. It was already resilient, ready to rise on its own for an hour or two. The cool flesh of the lump, though, yielding to the impression of her fingers and then slowly reassuming its shape, somehow left her unready to release it. She turned half her attention to her cousin. "Your. . . ." What was it he wanted? "Francis, do come in."

"My Andalusian!" said Wolley without turning his head.

Ah. Of course: he meant the big white stallion. "Oh," she said, "it must be the one Jack borrowed. It was early, and he did not want to wake you."

"My Andalusian!" Francis whipped his head around and said in theatrical tones, "I am in consternation. I am aggrieved. I take umbrage!"

"Oh, come in, Francis."

"Well," he said, and bowed elaborately, "I will condescend."

He strode into the room, looked around, and said in his normal voice, "But truly, Anne, these walls *must* be painted afresh. Or tapestries. Would you like some tapestries? I could find some that would set off the blue of this flagstone to advantage." He turned to the servant, who had remained outside, uncertain whether to enter, and said, "Come, come, come." As she entered, still with lowered eyes, Wolley mouthed to Anne, "She is *new.*" Then aloud he said, "Abigail, this is Mrs. Donne. You are to whisk her children away for the afternoon, and set her free. She will come and fetch them home later."

"But Francis," said Anne. "They haven't eaten."

Francis squeezed off a little piece of dough and gave it to Constance, then took a bigger one for himself. While still chewing it he said to Abigail, "And see that the cook gives them some. . . . What is it little children eat? What do you eat, Constance?"

"Dough!" Constance said.

"See that the cook gives them some dough. Here, child, take another dollop with you." Wolley started to pull off a big piece, but Anne stayed his hand.

"Not too much, Francis!" she said. "It hasn't risen."

"Well." Wolley took a yet bigger piece, gave Constance a small part of it, and kept the rest for himself. The child looked at him enviously. "I am big," Francis said. "You are small. The big get much; the small get little. That is the way of the world." Constance stuck out her lower lip. He did the same.

Abigail came over, smiled shyly at Constance, and offered a hand. The child backed away a step and reached for her mother's skirt. But Anne said, "It's all right. Go with her." Constance grudgingly reached to take Abigail's hand. Anne said, "The baby is asleep. I will bring him when he wakes." Abigail curtseyed awkwardly and led the child outside.

"Thank you, Francis," Anne said. "I could use the time to

read. Or to think." She sat in the chair at the end of the table.

"Oh. Reading. Thinking. I do as little of either as I can." As Wolley spoke he rolled the piece of dough he held into a ball. "But if you must punish yourself with reading and thinking, then why do you not let my servants tend your children every day? Must I come and foist servants upon you? *Foist:* a good word, that. I had rather feast than foist." He took a bite of the ball of dough as if it were an apple, then said, "I shall have Jack work the conceit into a poem. But Anne," he went on as he gestured with the lump, "take some servants as your own."

The offer sounded wonderful. What a blessing it would be to have servants again. . . . "Thank you," she said. "But I prefer things as they are."

Wolley watched her skeptically for a few seconds before saying softly, "Take just a housemaid and a cook, then." She turned her eyes away as he continued: "Why knead your own bread? We have loaves enough six rooms away."

"You are kind, Francis, most kind." She looked him directly in the eye. "But do you not see it is difficult for us—for Jack—to live by your generosity?"

"Oh, Jack and his pride. Pride! The deadliest sin of the seven." Wolley swung a foot over the bench, sat astride it facing her, and said as if he were scolding a child, "It was Lucifer's sin, you know."

Now she acted the patient mother. "Yes, Francis."

Almost immediately he was back up again, storming toward the door. "And as for that devil of a husband, where in hell has he taken my Andalusian?"

"Oh, Francis. That is much on my mind. He was summoned before Lord Cecil."

Just before he reached the door, Wolley stopped. He stood stock-still for a moment, as though the name had frozen him.

He turned slowly to look at her. "Cecil! Why did I not hear of this?"

"The summons came late last night. We did not want to disturb you. But Francis, what could it mean?"

"Cecil. Anything. It could mean anything. The man's mind is a labyrinth. I . . . I hardly know what it might mean."

"All day I have thought of little else."

"I well imagine." He walked over to her, sat on the bench, and put his hand on hers. "Summoned at night, and made to appear next morning?"

"Yes."

"Anne." He looked into her eyes. "Has Jack *done* anything?"

"What do you mean? No! He. . . . No. He owes a little money, but hardly—"

"Owes money? Anne, *tell* me these things. I will give Jack money. How much?"

"I don't know. A few pounds, I think. But he does not want. . . . Francis, do you not understand?"

Wolley slowly shook his head. "Pride."

Anne could see by her cousin's strained smile that he was trying to put a good face on the matter. With his free hand he tossed the ball of dough a few inches into the air, caught it at its peak, then took another bite. "Tell him to keep to gluttony," he said with his mouth full. "Much better for the soul."

Anne would not be distracted. "He may return soon, or tonight, or tomorrow, or . . . I know not."

Wolley furrowed his brow. "Cecil did not summon him over a few pounds. It is something else. You say he has done nothing."

"No. Nothing but look for patronage. Yesterday he visited the Earl of Bedford."

"Bedford?" Wolley looked as if the very name insulted him. "He can no more comprehend one of Jack's poems than I can write one in the Arabian tongue." Wolley looked puzzled. "The

Earl of Bedford. Hunting with the King, I thought he was. In Hertfordshire."

"Oh," Anne said faintly. Well, it was best to let it out; Francis might be able to help her piece things together. "And . . . Jack saw Lady Bedford, I think."

"Ah! That were a different matter. Your *Lady* Bedford has a wit to match. . . ."

Anne tried to keep the accusatory tone out of her voice. "To match whose?" Jack's, did he mean? Was Francis going to say Lady Bedford was a better match for Jack than Anne herself could ever be?

Wolley fingered his beard, apparently oblivious to her fear. "To match Cecil's, I was going to say. I wonder. . . ."

"Yes?"

"She and Cecil? I know of no relations there, but she and the new *queen*. . . . Perhaps all is well. Perhaps Lady Bedford has arranged some appointment for Jack at court. Or . . . I know not."

"Or what, Francis?" What was he hiding from her? If Francis suspected some ugly truth, did he not think she could bear it?

"Nothing."

She pressed him. "What is it?"

"It is nothing, I say."

Maybe it was best to be plain: "Do you suspect some . . . some ill-doing between her and Jack?"

Wolley looked momentarily confused, then said, "Oh! No. No, you need have no fear on that score. Jack thinks the very moon and stars hold in their spheres but by your sweet influence."

It was clear Francis did not share her fear—or even comprehend it. She said, "Moon and stars. Perhaps you had better leave the poetry to Jack."

"Gladly. Loathsome stuff, poetry."

Anne smiled.

Francis continued, "I was only thinking. . . . You were best to know: it was only that. . . . How to say it? I do not *like* the Lady Bedford. She frightens me."

Anne let a little laugh escape, then put her hand to her lips.

"Well, she *does*," Wolley said. "She makes me think of a harpy. But if I need to confront her or any other beautiful, dragonish creature to help you in this business, you have only to say the word."

"Thank you. I know you would do that."

"If only Elizabeth were still on the throne! Then it were an easy matter. The old queen *adored* me. At least before she soured toward all of us at the end. But in the old days I would simply ask, and problems would be solved. This new Scots king, though: his taste in men is *most* peculiar."

"He likes my father."

"Oh. Yes. . . . Your father. A stout man, your father, and true."

Folding her arms, she pulled back. "Go ahead, Francis. Say what you mean."

"A stubborn man, then. *That* is Jack's problem, don't you see? Your father blocks his advancement. The King blocks Jack's advancement, because of your stout father."

"So I fear."

Wolley looked at her as he would look at a woman he loved, if he fancied women at all. "Ah, Anne," he said, "how did such a father beget such a child as you?"

Again she smiled. "Still, I love him."

"Aha! *That* is the deadly sin of . . . something or other. I'm sure it's in the list somewhere." He looked around as if he hoped to find a list of sins posted on a wall. "Well," he said. "To your reading, or thinking, or whatever such perverse activity you please. Or. . . ." He spoke tenderly: "Would you have me stay?"

She knew Wolley's offer was genuine, but she also knew he could hardly sit still for long. "No, Francis. This waiting is difficult, but so it will be regardless. I thank you, though."

He stood, rubbed his hands together, and said, "I must take another of my horses for exercise since your miscreant husband has stolen my Andalusian. When he returns I shall have to give the man a thrashing." He took another lump of dough.

"Oho!" said Anne. "I should like to see this thrashing."

"No, no, it were too bloody for your tender eyes. Perhaps for your sake I shall spare him."

Anne inclined her head toward him. "Nobly done."

With his chin in the air, Wolley strode out the door. He spun around, bowed deeply, and said, "For thee, my lady, no price too dear."

When Anne moved to close the door, she hesitated a moment in the hope of seeing Jack approach, as if he were likelier to do so just as Wolley left than at some other time. But as her cousin rounded the corner to the stables, only a wren's fitful flight from one branch of an elm to another disturbed the stillness of the air. She eased the door closed and returned to the dough—or what was left of it. Absently she continued her kneading. This waiting. . . . Maybe she should have asked Francis to stay. Well, soon Little Jack would awaken. She would nurse him, then take him to Abigail, then read until Jack arrived with news, bad or good. She worked the dough into a lump and covered it with a damp cloth to let it rise. After washing her hands in the basin, she turned toward the next room, with its shelves of books, but hesitated before going to retrieve one.

Instead she sat in the carved oak chair by the window and allowed the silence of the day to settle around her. Not a leaf stirred in the great poplar outside. She took a deep breath, blew it out, and closed her eyes. Such respite should be welcome after the early waking to see Jack off, then the clamor of the children, then Francis. But her heart and her mind were restless; she could not give herself over to the quiet.

Waiting. . . . Why was it always the woman's lot to wait? The men could stride about the world, imposing their wills upon it, while the women stayed behind and waited. Why the women? Only the high-born among them—the late queen or a countess like Lady Bedford—could enter the affairs of men, even direct them. If a lesser-born woman raised her voice in protest of any male scheme, she was put down—and by other women as much as by the men—as a harridan and a shrew. No, a woman's lot was to linger by the fireside, look to the children, busy herself with all the little tasks of a goodly household. Not that Anne begrudged such things when her heart was untroubled; the doing of them was as good a way to serve God as any. But today she chafed against this waiting as if her true calling lay otherwhere.

Maybe this was how Jack felt: well-fitted for public office by both training and inclination, he had been shut out from the affairs of men, denied entry into the life that all his learning and all his native talents had proclaimed was his by right. Well, had Anne Donne not similar gifts to Jack's, and was her learning not like his? Was she not better born? Was she not more fit than all but a few of the men to direct the affairs of others? The thought made her even more restless.

The Countess of Bedford would never sit and wait if her husband were forced into trouble. She would do something: go to Cecil and confront him, or otherwise use her influence at court to get what she lacked. Anne's eyes narrowed. Never had she liked Lucy Harrington, but now she felt a smoldering spite. This woman who would do what Anne could not had given Jack a bracelet, like as not a love token. If the Countess merely admired Jack's poems, why had she not come forth with ready money, as a patroness ought? Perhaps she had none about her at the time. But that was doubtful. No, the Countess of Bedford had designs on Jack, and Anne More would not stand for it.

But what could she do? The bitter spite welled within her. She pushed herself up from the chair, stood at the window, and pressed her fingers to her forehead. Such thoughts were unworthy of her. She knew her Christian duty: to think well of others, and forgive them if they wronged her. But she knew also that such knowledge would little avail her now. There was something delicious about this unfamiliar spitefulness, something she was unwilling to put aside. Yet she did not like the agitation.

Augustine said our hearts were always restless till they rested in God. But where was she to find God and heart's rest: at home while her husband cast about the world until he fell victim to some scheme of Lucy Bedford's or Robert Cecil's, or both of them in league, or . . . ? She hardly knew.

This moment: focus on this moment. What was God telling her now, with this agitation, this taste of spite? To forgive Lady Bedford? She was not even sure the Countess had wronged her, so what was there to forgive? And Jack: had Jack no part in enticing the alluring young countess to give him her golden love token? No: Anne knew the thought itself was poisonous; she must not think it. Did Francis, though, suspect as much? It did not appear so, but perhaps she misjudged him. Perhaps Francis knew it to be true but would not betray Jack's trust.

Well, what of Jack and his own heart's ease? Suppose some honest cause lay behind the summons. Suppose Jack were to be appointed to the post he deserved. Would *his* mind then rest at last? Would *he* then cease to chafe and fret? She doubted it. Jack would be happy for a while, but not for long. Even in his time at York House, when Lord Egerton had trusted him and given him some scope to use his mind in affairs of state, Anne had sensed something of the troubled waters that churned within him. She had been drawn to those dark waters as one is drawn to watch a gathering storm.

Out of the corner of her eye she caught some movement outside the window. She looked toward the stables, where Jack would first appear. But it was only a brindled cat padding across the yard. The sight gave her a shiver, as if it were an omen of ill. She knew better than to believe in portents: the vicar said such things were vain, Catholic superstitions, spawned by the Father of Lies and sustained by the Devil's spokesman on the papal seat in Rome. Yet compared to what she felt, the vicar's imprecations seemed thin and insubstantial, mere whispers against the wind.

She glanced toward the stairs, wondering whether to go and waken Little Jack. The baby would perhaps take her mind off her cares. No, the child needed his sleep. She went into the next room, the small one where Jack kept his books. More than once of late he had mentioned selling them: an act she thought would break his heart, and very nearly hers. What did she want to read? Something from another land. Something that had nothing to do with the troubles of this time. She laid a finger atop a volume of Virgil's *Eclogues,* and the act of reaching for the book stirred in her a sense of mystery, a feeling that she had lived this moment before, that now, as before, someone was standing behind her watching. She turned, her finger still on the volume. No one. But the feeling lingered.

Then it came to her: a scene from a few years before. Having just returned to York House after staying at Loseley for three weeks, she had gone to her uncle's library, pulled out his copy of this very book, sensed someone behind her, and turned to find the Lord Keeper's thin-boned Irish servant Marjorie standing in the doorway. "Begging your pardon, Mistress More," Marjorie said, "but you were after being told, be it any hour whatever, when your uncle and Master Donne should arrive from Windsor."

"Yes," Anne had said, trying not to sound too eager. "I have something to ask my uncle." Marjorie gave her a little half-smile, as if she knew it was Jack that Anne wanted to see and not the Lord Keeper. Anne's attempt not to return the smile ended in her blushing. She avoided Marjorie's eyes as she moved to the door. It would not do to let her growing attraction to Jack become the talk of the servants. But the three weeks away from York House had seemed interminable. During those weeks she had turned sixteen: old enough, surely, to be thought a woman and not a mere girl.

Upon entering the parlor she saw to her dismay that the Lord Keeper had brought several men home for supper. It would be a long while before she and Jack could get a few minutes to themselves. Or perhaps she was not in his thoughts at all. The guests were distinguished, but she cared nothing for that. She suffered through the introductions: in addition to her uncle and Jack there was the dull-eyed, palsied Lord Buckhurst, appointed Lord Treasurer upon old Burghley's death; the dour politician with a gray spade-shaped beard, Lord Monteagle, a man for whatever party was like to be in power; Monteagle's brother-in-law Francis Tresham, a thin-whiskered, frightened-looking man who kept watching others to see how he should behave; Jean Richardot of Artois, a shrewd-looking diplomat just arrived in London; Henry Percy, the arch-browed Wizard Earl of Northumberland; and the Earl's cousin Sir Thomas Percy, a furtive-looking man with sweat on his face.

Anne had met the Wizard Earl two or three years before, and he seemed to remember her. A man whose disordered thoughts always seemed to race ahead of his speech, he nodded to Anne and said, "Your father. Well, I trust. At Loseley. Splendid, the house. Magnificent gardens, green place to grow. As a child. Magnificent, the gardens. But now a lady, lovely." He nodded again.

"Yes, your Lordship, I thank you, and am happy to say my

father is well. I was with him at Loseley not two days since, and when I see him again I shall give him your regards."

"Yes, regards. Very best, Sir George. Lovely gardens."

Somehow she knew Jack must be smiling at the exchange, but she avoided glancing his way. For one thing, Jack liked the Wizard Earl, and so did she. It would not do to let the Earl see them smiling at his expense. For another, she must show her uncle no sign that she thought of Jack as anything but her tutor. And it would harm nothing to put on a show of indifference to Jack himself. *She* had certainly had to wait long enough, with no word from him whatsoever through the three long weeks. Why should *he* not have to wait awhile?

At dinner she was made to sit between the sweaty Sir Thomas Percy and the doltish Lord Buckhurst, who hardly spoke at all through the meal. Percy bit off his words as if it pained him to speak them, as if some fierce anger lay beneath all that he said. A dangerous man, he seemed. All the while she conversed with him, supplying a dozen words for his every two or three, her mind was on Jack, sitting near the end of the table with the Wizard Earl. She wondered whether Jack was watching her.

But no, during the lapses in her painful conversation with Percy, she could hear that Jack and the Earl were chatting merrily away: now about hawking, now about astronomy and Galileo's treatise on Archimedes, now about the new "necessary" that the man Owen had built for the Earl: a closet of water mounted on the wall of a jakes, so that when the water was released, it carried one's merds away with a great rushing noise. "Sir John made one for the Queen," the Earl was saying. "Harrington. Elizabeth's godson, he is. And this Nicholas Owen—you must meet this man Owen, Jack—heard about Sir John's necessary for the Queen. Never saw it. Heard about it merely. And built one for me, what? You must come and use it, Jack. Only three in England: the Queen's, Harrington's own, and this. Owen: he is your only man for invention, this Owen. 'Sblood, the very Daedalus of England, Owen is. Must see that you meet him."

At that moment Lord Buckhurst coughed to get Anne's attention. He extended a trembling hand toward the muttonchops, which she dutifully served him.

When at last the meal was over and the after-supper pleasantries had been exchanged, Anne went directly back to her uncle's library in the hope that Jack would know to find her there. She took down the *Eclogues* and sat in the chair facing the casement, where she could read by the evening light.

Softly sounding aloud the supple cadences of Virgil's Latin, she had finished the first of the eclogues and had spoken a few lines of the second when she caught the bold, confident sound of Jack's step in the hall outside. Then he stood before her. She rose from the chair as if directed by an unseen hand, and she fought the urge to run into his arms. His look said he would welcome the embrace. But he was her schoolmaster. With both hands she clutched the book to her breast.

"I missed . . . our lessons," she said. "This waiting has been difficult." He looked at her with something like wonder in his eyes. Hardly knowing what she was saying, she added, "While we were apart I busied myself with trifles. Gathering bits of grammar from the ground."

He looked puzzled. "Gathering. . . ."

Her thoughts swirled in some confused response to the urgings of her heart, but words came to her unbidden. "Each day, being away from you and your influence, a morsel of Latin or Greek would fall right out of my head. I would pick up the pieces and put them in a basket."

He leaned against the doorpost. "You did well to save the parts. And the arithmetic? That, I trust, remained in your head, where it belongs."

"Oh, no! It all fell out on the first day. I left it to the birds, thinking it would help them multiply. But eating of it, they only tore themselves asunder by division, most horrible to behold. This mathematics is a dangerous thing, and to be avoided at all cost, I think." She hazarded a step toward him. He straightened, standing squarely in the doorway now. Almost breathless, she took another step toward him, then another. She was near enough to take in his scent: he smelled at once of earth and air. At Loseley she had missed that smell as much as much as anything else about him.

He opened his mouth to speak but hesitated a moment before saying softly, "I too missed . . . our lessons. It is very . . . very good to see that I have such an eager pupil. Very good."

Without any decision to do so, she moved still closer until she stood within inches of him, near enough to kiss him if he would but incline his head. "Ah," she said as she looked up at him and searched his face. There was no certainty in those dark eyes with their little flecks of green, and no hint of seduction; what she saw looked more like sorrow tinged with regret. She had a fleeting thought that his eyes reflected at least a few bits of the pure sapphire-green of her own. "But I fear I am such a slow learner," she continued, "that you must be my . . . schoolmaster for all our lives. Do you think we could spend all our lives together?"

He exhaled heavily, stepped around her, and moved to the window, where he stood with his back to her as he looked into the waning light. "What would your father say to that?"

She bit her lower lip. "I do not know."

He turned to face her. "Why? Does he say aught about it? Does he not like me? Does he not think me a good prospect for a . . . for a lifelong schoolmaster?"

She lowered her eyes. "He speaks only of others. He talks not of my love . . . of learning . . . but of my marrying: marrying this nobleman or that, all of them landed and wealthy, none of whom I would have—if I had my will. But he is my father."

He closed his eyes for a moment, then said, "Well. On the morrow we have Latin and Greek to insert back into your head, and the arithmetic that has unaccountably subtracted itself. Bring your basket of pieces."

On another day Jack would have liked nothing better than to spend the afternoon in a library like Cecil's. The rows upon rows of shelves held nearly every book he might want to read: leather-bound volumes in Latin, Greek, Hebrew, French, Italian, Spanish, English; collections of maps on parchment; chronicles, scriptures, myths; philosophy, natural history, theology; mathematics, architecture, music, theorics of art; poems and tales of adventure and love. But today Jack could hardly hope to keep his mind on any of them. It was only of late, Cecil had said, that he had turned his mind to book-collecting. Had he done so with Anne in his thoughts, knowing her love of reading? How long had the hunchback schemed to bring her to this house, to this very room? But if that were his aim, why invite Jack to go home and tell her so? Why confess his love for her? Surely she would hate Cecil now that he had used her to force Jack's hand, whereas before she had hardly thought about the twisted little man at all. Could it be that her indifference hurt him more than her hate? Or did Cecil think he could somehow turn her hatred into love, once Jack had died as a spy in some dirty business? And was there no truth to such an idea? The stage-poet Will Shakespeare's Richard III, a hunchback even more grotesque than Cecil, had seduced the Lady Anne Warwick just after killing her husband. Women had ever been drawn to strength, and Cecil had already proved himself the stronger. Maybe, then, Jack should say nothing to Anne, should merely tell her that his work was secret.

No. Cecil wished him to think such thoughts, to entertain such doubts. Anne Donne was no shallow, power-hungry harlot. Nor if Jack died would she prove the grief-stricken, confused Anne Warwick of Shakespeare's imagination. Yet the scene on the stage had rung eerily true. After Jack's death, would his wife, though faithful, not grieve in confusion? Cecil's sonnet had moved Jack despite all his suspicions; how much more would it move the woman for whom it was composed? Or if poetry did not seduce her, what of force? Would not Robert Cecil, who had just forced Jack Donne to do his bidding, though Jack was faithful and in his right mind, easily do the same with a grief-stricken young widow? And even if he couldn't force her hand, would not her father demand the marriage?

Or could Cecil have been telling the truth—that he wanted Jack alive rather than dead, and the confession of love was a way of exorcising the ghost of a woman who had been denied him? Jack knew Cecil to be above all a practical man. Maybe he had simply found the readiest way to achieve two ends at once: add a spy to his ranks of intelligencers and rid his mind of the image of an impossible love. Maybe.

As Jack sat agitated in his enemy's library, surrounded by leather-bound volumes that distilled all the fruits of learning from time immemorial, all at once his mind cleared. There was no book in the vast room that could show him his course. Only one path lay before him: he must tell Anne all, trusting her to know best what to do when the time came, and he must take on the task of spying in some way that satisfied Robert Cecil and at the same time outwitted him.

Chapter 6

Old Timothy Burr's chair sat as near the fire as Lady Bedford's. What was the woman thinking? Some half an hour ago she had addressed him almost as her equal, inviting him to join her at the fireside. They had chatted about the biting February wind that swirled outside, rattling shutters and scattering bits of debris along the streets; about the men and women gaining or losing favor at the royal court; about the new treaty with Spain; about her husband's brief letter just arrived that morning from his latest hunting trip with the King—not a letter, really, as much as a catalogue of animals killed in the hunt. Now Lady Bedford brought the talk around to Jack Donne and his latest visit. Burr listened and watched carefully. He registered a faint note of stiffness in her tone, and she crossed her hands on her lap at the mention of the man's name. So this was the reason she had asked him to sit and talk with her by the fire: all this had to do with Jack Donne.

"It was on one of Donne's first visits here—you remember, Tim, we talked about the bracelet I gave him—on that very day I sent word to Lord Cecil that this man Donne was just the sort to do good service to the King. There has been some delay, but by this time Lord Cecil will have given orders for him to go abroad upon a mission." She paused and watched the flames. They quivered like aspen leaves as they curled along the big oak backlog. She said, "You have doubtless guessed his mission's purpose."

So she thought as little of the man Donne as that. He had sold the bracelet or given it away or melted it for its gold, and she had turned him over to Robert Cecil. Burr said only, "Yes, my lady. I think I have guessed it."

"And, Timothy—not lightly have I done this, I assure you—I have offered your services."

Burr arched an eyebrow. "My services. In what capacity, might I ask?"

"You are to travel with Master Donne as his manservant. Prepare to spend some weeks or months abroad. Perhaps a year or two. You will of course write to me frequently. I expect to hear everything worthy of note."

Burr felt the blood drain from his face. A year or two! And abroad: that would likely mean the strange, dangerous worlds of the Spanish Netherlands, France, Italy, Spain herself. . . . Had the Countess considered his age? For an old man he felt hale enough, but to go gadding up and down the Continent with one so much younger. . . . Had she thought of the perils of the mere Channel crossing, the stormy passage that had pulled so many to their cold, shifting graves? Before he could think how to reply, Lady Bedford looked at him and softened her tone: "My dear Timothy, I am but lending you; when this business is finished you may return here and retire at ease for your last long years."

Yes, if he lived to see them. But what was there to do? Burr gathered his breath, nodded, and said, "My lady."

Quill in hand, Jack sat motionless at the little writing-table beneath the window of the narrow room that served as his library—the only library at Pyrford Place, in fact; Wolley had no great love of books. Outside, the chill wind shook against the stone, feeling for secret cracks along the walls or beneath the thatching of the roof. The house had been well fortified by the masons and joiners, but somehow the cold found ways of creeping in. Jack laid the quill aside, cupped his hands, and breathed into them. Between the moans of the windstorm he could hear Anne weeping in the next room, just as she had during the days after he had told her all: Cecil's love for her, the sonnet, the little hunchback's plan to force him into spying.

Through those days they had waited on edge, every hour expecting word from Cecil. None came. The days became weeks, then months, and while the ghost of foreboding never left off haunting the house, it faded with the passing of time.

Then, just when Cecil's plans for Jack had begun to seem more threat than substance, the dreaded message arrived. Jack was to leave within the next few days. Further word would soon be delivered.

Now Jack picked up the quill, dipped it, paused a moment above the leaf of Wolley's fine parchment, and wrote:

Sweetest love, I do not go
For weariness of thee,
Nor in hope the world can show
A fitter love for me.

No, that would not do; the mere mention of another love would awaken Anne's suspicion, groundless or no. He tried again:

When thou sigh'st, thou sigh'st not wind,
But sigh'st my soul away;
And when thou weep'st, unkindly kind,
My life's blood doth decay.

Hm. Not good enough, not for Anne. Why should he seem to blame her, even in the conceits of poetry? Already she laid blame enough upon herself: had she not somehow allowed Robert

Cecil to think she might love him? Last night in her desperation she had offered to cut her hair, disguise herself as Jack's page, and go with him on his travels. When he had asked whether she could really leave the little ones in another's care, she had broken into coughed-out sobs intermixed with keenings of dismay.

Now the wind relented for a moment, and he could hear nothing from the next room. Maybe she had finally come to see there was no solution short of his plan—a desperate one, she thought—of trying to outwit *Robertus Diabolus.* Jack pressed his cold fingertips to the bridge of his nose, took up a blank leaf of parchment, and started again:

Our two souls, Anne, which still are one
Though I must go, endure not yet
A breach, but an expansion,
Like gold to airy thinness beat.

He whispered the word *expansion,* drawing it out to four syllables instead of the usual three. He smiled. Yes, that was the sort of music Anne would savor. Around such an image he could build a poem worthy of her.

Still there was no sound from the next room. He rose, rolled his head to ease the stiffness in his neck, stretched, walked to the doorway, and stopped when he saw Anne. Bundled into a blanket, she sat staring into the fireplace, having let the fire burn low. With a stick from the woodpile, Jack jostled the embers into flame, then tossed on several more pieces. Anne turned her red-rimmed eyes to him.

He said, "The children are . . . ?"

"With Abigail." Her tone, like her posture, said she was drained; there were no more tears in her. "I'll get them in a few minutes," she added. "It's almost time to feed Little Jack."

"I will miss them," he said.

She nodded. The fire began to hiss and pop. "They won't remember you." She said it matter-of-factly; there was neither spite nor sorrow in her voice. "If you don't come back."

He rubbed the back of his neck. "Well. A blessing that may be. For them."

She gave him a rueful little smile and said, "A blessing."

He added, "But I will come back." Anne looked back into the fire but did not otherwise respond.

A sharp knock, followed by two more. Jack glanced at the door before turning back to Anne. She did not move but sat as if nothing could startle her. Jack strode over and opened the door. The same officious messenger who had come from Cecil months before, the same yellow-plumed popinjay with the same cudgel, stood with another sealed letter in his hand. The man cleared his throat and opened his mouth to speak. Without a word Jack snatched the letter and closed the door.

He tore through the waxen seal. The letter was signed only with a *C.* Jack read:

D,

You are this day licensed to travel wheresoever you will, in England and all foreign lands, in the company of one Sir Walter Chute. This Chute will be furnished with £400 of his own monies for expenses pertaining to your travels. Know ye I have it by certain report that this Chute desires most sincerely to be converted to the papist faith. This his earnest desire, which he has been given to think you share, shall lend a greater color to your enterprise. By no means are you to allow our designs to be known to this Chute. He has been informed that although his rank and station exceed your own, all choice regarding your movements wheresoever, and all control of the aforesaid £400, lies with you alone.

The manservant to attend you both shall be one Timothy Burr, whose worth is known to the Crown. This Burr has been informed of all. He and Chute will call upon you in three days' time.

The task I have set you is to seek out, wheresoever you may find them, any and all Catholic men or women who would proffer any degree of bodily harm whatsoever to our most Godly Sovereign, or any of his lawful ministers. Seek ye out all such, but in especial one Englishman whom the papist hellhounds call only Guido; we know him not otherwise, nor whether this Guido be his true Christian name. Mayhap he sojourns in England, mayhap in the Low Countries, where he has fought betimes under the command of the traitorous Sir William Stanley, mayhap otherwhere.

We further require you to burn this missive in the sight of the bearer. Vouchsafe him not to read it, but only to see it burned.

C

Anne was now standing beside him; she too had read the letter. She looked at Jack, then opened the door. The messenger still stood there in the swirling wind, this time with his arms folded, the cudgel cocked at an angle. With a smug look he asked, "Does the Lord Cecil Viscount Cranborne desire thee to perform any act in the presence of my person—to wit, to perform an act without my suffering the door to be shut before my very face, as thou, a notorious rudesby, I warrant, hast shut it?"

Jack reached beneath the man's red velvet cloak, grasped him by the shoulder of his pale blue doublet, and began to pull him into the house. The man brandished his cudgel, which Jack snatched with his free hand. With a bit more force than he intended, Jack pulled again, hard enough to send the messenger sprawling onto the floor. Having tossed the cudgel clattering onto the flagstone beside the man, Jack strode to the fireplace and offhandedly flicked the letter into the flames.

Furious, the messenger hissed, "Cecil will hear of this!"

Jack knelt, his face a few inches from the man's, and said evenly, "You have seen what you came to see; the missive is committed to the flames. Go and report to Cecil that I will do his bidding, but the next time he sends you I shall toss you into the fire after the letter."

The man sputtered a few incomprehensible syllables, picked himself up along with his cudgel, and hobbled out the door, slamming it after him.

Her eyes wide, Anne slowly shook her head. "Oh, Jack," she said, "that were not wise."

Jack shrugged. "Cecil is no fool; he must know his man is a dandiprat."

Anne eyed him closely and said, "Even so, we knew such a letter would arrive. Lord Cecil told you as much. What need you use his underling so roughly?"

Jack hardly knew what to say. "I . . . I looked at him standing before me, grinning his pleasure with the letter in his hand from that devil incarnate who has caused you to weep. I. . . . You are right; I should cuff the master, not his man."

Anne latched the door, then turned to face him. "You should cuff *no* man. *This* is what I fear, do you not see? It boots you nothing to give Robert Cecil further cause to hate you. Has he not cause enough already?"

Again Jack shrugged. "If he hates me, I had rather have him fear me too." When Anne started to object, Jack changed the subject. "But Timothy Burr. I know the man. He is Lady Bedford's old manservant. Now he is to be mine. I wonder at it."

Anne turned away from him and spoke very quietly: "So Lucy Harrington has her hand in this."

"So it appears. But whether Burr is a spy she and Cecil have set to watch me, or her gift to me, I hardly know."

Anne spun to face him, angry tears in her eyes. "A *gift*? She gave you one love token already. Has she cause to give you yet another gift, and a far greater one?"

"No! Burr is a spy, more like. You have nothing to. . . ." He looked at her reddened eyes and said, "This is how Cecil would have it, don't you see? He sets Burr to spy on me, and he sets me to spy on Chute, and like as not he sets Chute to spy on Burr. And now he sets you, my life's love, at odds with me. It is all as Cecil would have it."

Still angry, Anne said, "But this new servant of yours is not Cecil's to give. He is the beautiful Lady Bedford's."

Jack held up his empty hands. "I tell you none of this business is my doing!"

Anne exhaled forcefully, looked around as if she had lost something in the room, then said, "You are right. We must not let Cecil divide us." Her brow furrowed, she asked, "What, then, of this Walter Chute? I have heard the name but know not the man. Do you?"

"No better than you," Jack said. "Never has he spoken a word to me, nor I to him." He added bitterly, "But he is one of the great throng of men the King has knighted, as he has knighted your brother and the husbands of your sisters while your father whispered him lies about me."

"My father does not lie!" Anne said with surprising force. Then she added more softly, "He only thought you a lesser match for me than the King's own Secretary of State. And can you fault him for the thought? No, my father is guilty only of thinking I could ever live as wife to a wretch like Robert Cecil, a knave as misshapen in body as he is cankered in mind."

Jack tenderly brushed an errant strand of hair from her face and said, "I know. I know. . . . But what am I to do?"

She corrected him: "What are *we* to do? For I will not have you piece out this business alone, though I cannot travel with you."

This would not do. "We must not put both ourselves in harm's way. The children—"

"Fear me not," she said, and added wryly, "Doubt not but I shall prove more circumspect than you have shown yourself today."

He put his hands on her shoulders. "But—"

"Enough." She spoke as if the matter had been settled. "Though the serpent part us in body, I will not have him sunder us in soul."

How could he disagree? The very poem he had just left off writing said the same.

All business, she said, "Now: know you any *Guido*?"

He thought for a moment, then said, "None. An Englishman, the letter said. But the name is Spanish, or Italian. I think it must be feigned."

She nodded. "Where will you seek first?" After a moment she added, "And what will you tell Cecil if you find this Guido?"

"As for where to seek, I hardly know. In England to begin, I think: among the London Catholics—I had best see the Wizard Earl before Chute and Burr join me—and then among the great Catholic houses in the North. Or maybe Warwickshire. And after that. . . ." He hesitated to mention the Continent; Anne had wept enough already. "As for what to tell Cecil, I pray God I may know that when the time sorts."

The sadness or profound weariness he had seen in her before the messenger arrived settled into her eyes again. "I have a gift for you," she said blankly as she turned to a little cabinet under the stairs. She pulled something out, but he could not see what. "Lady Bedford gave you a bracelet woven of seven chains of gold. I give you a plainer one. You will see it comes from my head, but know that even more, it comes from my heart." She held out the gift: a strap of plaited leather jesses interwoven with. . . . He held it to the light of the fire.

"Your hair," he said. "This is a bracelet of leather and your own hair."

"Tie it about your wrist, that you may have something of me with you wherever you go."

"With all my heart." She helped him wrap the bracelet around his left wrist and tie the ends together. By the light of a rush-candle they went out to the little building that housed Wolley's forge. There Jack found a sharp knife and two pairs of long-handled tongs with tight-fitting jaws. He dipped his left hand and wrist in a water-basin to soak the leather, then pulled it out and took a set of tongs in his free hand, using the jaws to grasp one free end of a knotted jess. He told Anne to take the other tongs and pull on the other end. In this way they tightened all the knots. The bracelet fit snug on his wrist, too tight to slide off over his hand. Jack picked up the knife and cut all the loose ends close to the knots. "Now:" he said. "If ever I were to remove this token, by cutting or untying it, I would not be able to tie it on again. It is here to stay."

For the first time in days, he thought he saw her lips ease into a little smile.

The next morning Jack walked the half-mile from Pyrford Place to the River Wey and waited only a few minutes until a boatman came around the bend. The river wound lazily here, and only a dozen yards or so across. Jack gave the mossy-toothed oarsman a shilling and told him to let him off at Syon House. "House!" said the boatman. "Pellis, more like." He eyed Jack with evident envy. "Ah, the Wizard 'imself, then, is it? 'Slid, these Percys lives loik kings, doon't they? Always 'ave, time out of mind. What's 'e, Northumberland's eighth earl in the chain? Nointh?"

"Ninth," Jack said as he sat back for the ride downstream. The receding tide made the man's rowing easy. The oarsmen going upstream had to ply it harder.

"And you know such a man as that! 'Sblood, 'e could 'ave a feast wif a tun of ale ever' noight and never want for money, never feel the pinch."

Jack smiled. "So he could."

"Would I could put on such a frolic *one* noight!" The oarsman wheezed out a chuckle. "That would set the tongues weggin' proper." After a few more strokes he asked, "But do you not fear his wizardry? These cunning-folk 'ave power somethin' fearsome." He eyed Jack as if his black garments might betoken some dark allegiance.

"The Earl is a good man," Jack said, "and gives of his plenty to the poor. A good, pious man. His wizardry is but a love of the new learning—as well as the old."

The oarsman slowly shook his head. "Somethin' fearsome. Well, there's small harm in rowing to the water-gate at Syon House, I ween."

In an hour or so the Wey joined the Thames, and not long after, the battlements of Syon House loured into view. A few minutes more and they pulled up to the water-gate. A leathery guard with a few tufts of gray hair escaping his cap recognized Jack from prior visits and swung open the iron gate to let the boat pass. Before the gate was fully open, Jack asked if the Earl were home; he might be at one of his houses in the country. The guard nodded, grunted "Aye," and pulled the boat up to the landing. Jack stepped out, walked up a half-dozen stairs, and let himself into the anteroom. Meanwhile, the guard sent a sour-faced, barefoot boy sulking up to tell the porter of the guest's arrival.

In a few minutes the Wizard Earl himself appeared, smiling broadly. The man had tousled hair, a broad, boyish face, and clear blue eyes. He eagerly beckoned Jack in, saying, "Come, come. . . . Jack, it's. . . . You must see it, this optic glass of Harriot's. He . . . just yesterday, he. . . . Goodyer is here, too. You know Henry Goodyer. Of course you do. From your. . . ."

"From our time at Lincoln's Inn."

"Yes, yes, studying the law: I remember. But this invention of Harriot's. And such a simple device! Has to leave soon, Goodyer, but you'll catch him. He's up in the. . . . All the heavens! Left it with me to study, Harriot did. Or amuse. . . . Well, he has another at his house. But truly, Jack, how are you?"

"Well enough," Jack said. Even this little lie chafed. He was here to deceive this good man, a man with much to lose, a man who had always been kind to him. True, some four years ago when he had delivered Jack's ill-fated letter to Sir George More, the Earl had shown himself helpless to prevent Sir George's rage about the elopement, or to quell the old man's wrath once it had been aroused. But he had tried. Jack would never forget that.

And Goodyer was here at Syon House, too: Henry Goodyer, Jack's old friend from their time studying law together. Of all men on earth, it was Goodyer who really knew Jack Donne, really understood the workings of his mind and the stirrings of his heart. At any other time Jack would have welcomed such a meeting of friends; what could be better than to talk with the Wizard Earl and Henry Goodyer about some new device of Thomas Harriot's? But already the shadow of Robert Cecil had fallen across the gathering.

Cecil had said months before that he wanted to hear something of the Earl's doings, and Jack had stalled as long as he could. He would do all in his power to protect the Earl, but the report had to sound credible. Jack would very much like to tell the Wizard everything; the good man bore little love for Cecil, especially now that Raleigh had been sent to the Tower. But the Earl could hardly keep a secret. He was always blurting out things others of his rank would know better than to say.

No doubt Cecil hoped Jack could provide evidence that the

Earl was part of some Catholic plot, or at least was aware of one. Everyone knew the Wizard was Catholic, but everyone also knew he was not very eager to promote the cause. That much Jack could confirm in a report to Cecil without harm to the Earl. And as a well-born Protestant loyal to the crown, Goodyer would be of no interest to Cecil.

The two men walked briskly past palatial, well-ordered chambers that the Earl seemed not to notice. Up two flights of stairs at the end of a narrow, dank hallway a battered door stood ajar. Ah, yes, this was the place the Earl called the schoolroom. Only once before had Jack been here, four or five years since. Then as now, the pungent musk of tobacco had hung in the air. Harriot had been in the room then, and Raleigh had left only a few minutes before. The talk that night had moved freely from the Twelfth Night revels, to the old queen's likely successor, to the strange prophecies in the books of Daniel and Revelation, to the Algonquin language of the Indians Harriot had befriended in Virginia.

Now the Earl pushed open the door, which creaked faintly on its hinges. The room was both large and cluttered. Books lay in careless heaps, some open, some not, some with scraps of paper crammed with notes holding places in the texts. Maps, charts, and drawings of all sizes hung hastily tacked to the walls, in some spots partly obscuring the ones that had been put up days or months or years before. Astrological charts vied with geometric proofs, sketches of strange plants and animals, alchemical ciphers, and architectural plans. The floor and tables stood heaped not only with books and papers but stoppered or open flasks and vials of colored liquids, bowls of herbs, boxes overflowing with partially dismantled machinery of every sort. Still intact were a theodolite and several astrolabes of varying complexity: armillas both equinoctial and solstitial, and a large planisphere with intricate brass rings and movable sights. Four or five chairs and end tables stood at various angles around the big fireplace. A generous pile of split firewood had been heaped into a corner. Someone—Jack guessed it was some thoughtful manservant forbidden to tidy the room too thoroughly—had at least cleared the floor of books and papers in a rough semicircle around the fireplace, which had been fitted with a well-made screen.

Henry Goodyer rose from one of these chairs to greet Jack. Goodyer's clear, brown eyes shone with the eagerness of a child-like intelligence. Cradled in his hands lay a metal tube with a smaller tube protruding from one end. Goodyer said, "Jack, this device—"

The Earl said, "Wait, we'll show him." He rooted through the firewood until he found a small wedge-shaped piece. He took the tube from Goodyer, tucked the wedge under his arm, and with his free hand hastily stacked some books on a long, narrow table beneath a window that looked out onto the river. He put the wedge on top of the stack and held the device to the wood so that the tube angled down toward the river. Then he put his eye to the smaller end and slowly swiveled the instrument. After a few seconds he said "Aha!" and held the tube firmly in place as he stepped aside and said, "Now you look."

When Jack put his eye to the tube, at first he could see nothing. Then he closed his other eye and shifted slightly to the left. Suddenly the tube was filled with light, and. . . . "Jesu!" He jerked back and tripped over a box, spilling parts from dismantled clocks and watches. From the floor he pointed to the tube and said, "What is *that*?"

The Earl was laughing so hard there was no hope of getting an answer from him, so Jack looked to Goodyer, who was making some effort to stifle his own laughter as he reached a hand toward Jack to help him to his feet. Jack ignored the offer, quickly picking himself up and peering out the window. All looked as ever it did: the river lay glimmering in the midday sun, boats and barges lazily made their way upstream or down, trees on the far shore rose above their wavering reflections in the water. Laughing and coughing, the Earl collapsed into a chair. Jack put his eye to the small tube again, then pulled away and looked carefully out the window in the direction the device pointed. Yes, there stood a rough-faced boatman on a barge moored to poles driven into the riverbed. It was the man's toothless face that Jack had seen through the tube. But the image had been much larger—as though the man hung in the air a few feet outside the window. Again Jack looked through the instrument. The monstrously enlarged visage of the man on the barge squinted in the sunlight, scowled, and spat. Jack turned to the Earl, who still sat convulsed in the chair, now coughing uncontrollably.

"Percy," said Jack, "Harriot made this?"

The Earl nodded and coughed.

"This is. . . ." Jack took a moment to sort his crowded thoughts. The device could be put to a thousand good uses. "A ship's watchman," he said, "could descry a pirate's vessel at a great distance. A general could tell the enemy's numbers and direct his own troops to advantage." The Earl nodded again as he began to gain control of his coughing. Wide-eyed, Jack said, "A spy could. . . ." Then it hit him. As if stunned, he said faintly, "A man could turn it on the heavens."

The Earl drew his sleeve across his face to wipe his watering eyes, coughed once more, took a deep breath, and blew it out. His face sobered. "He could. We have."

"And?"

Goodyer answered: "Blemishes, Jack. The sun has blemishes. And the moon: every child knows her face, botched and mottled in color, like a painted harlot. But it is not just pied; it is also rough, with hills and vales." He paused to let Jack absorb all this, then said, "And there is this: Jupiter has little moons that fly about him. Four of them."

"You mean . . . they circle him?"

"They do."

"Then his crystalline sphere. . . ."

"There is no sphere. There cannot be. Jupiter is not lodged in any sphere, or the moons would shatter it in passing through."

It was all a wonder. Copernicus, then, must be right: the earth was not at the center of all, surrounded by crystalline spheres. He asked, "Then by what power does all hang in the quintessence?"

The Earl shrugged. "I took it to show Raleigh in the Tower yesternight. He says it means there is no God."

Jack considered the idea. The new way of thinking about the stars and the planets unsettled the mind somewhat, but Jack knew his own theology ran far deeper than Raleigh's. "No, it means no such."

Goodyer said, "That's just what I was telling Percy when he went down to meet you. You see, Percy, Jack agrees: it does not mean there is no God. It only means the Church of Rome needs better mathematicians, and better watchers of the skies."

The Earl said, "Well, I know not. But will you smoke another bowl?"

Goodyer put up a hand and said, "No, I have had enough. You know I have unhappy brains for tobacco, and in any case I have stayed too long; I am promised home before sunset. Jack, next time we will talk longer. Come and stay with us. Stay a week or two."

"Would that I could."

"Well, write then." Jack promised he would. To the Earl, Goodyer said, "No need to see me down. I know the way."

When Goodyer had left, the Earl said, "So you think Copernicus was right."

"I suppose so, yes. Well, we all suspected it. And Goodyer is right too: the problem is not with Copernicus but the Mother Church."

"Yes, there are many problems with the Mother Church. Many problems. But . . . one does not get to choose his mother."

Seeing his opening, Jack said, "I have felt of late the pain of separation from my mother." That much, at least, was true.

"Then you. . . . Wait: are we talking about your mother Elizabeth Heywood Donne, or your . . . ecclesiastical mother?"

"Both."

"Then go back to her, Jack; she will welcome you. Whichever mother we're talking about."

"I intend to do precisely that."

"Precisely which?"

"Precisely both: rejoin the Church of Rome and rejoin my mother Elizabeth, whom I have not seen these several years."

The Earl beamed as he rose from his chair. "Jack Donne, a Catholic again! Well, I knew. I *knew* one day you'd. . . . Did I not say this very thing to you? I knew one day, one day you would come home."

Jack returned the Earl's embrace, doing his best to disguise his queasy sense of betrayal. "Thank you," he said.

"Ah: brave tidings, these. Careful, though. I will. . . . Must be careful. Protect you if I can. But. . . . Spies everywhere."

"You're right. Spies are everywhere. Whether my action be wise, perhaps only God can say." He thought it best to change the subject back to the optic tube. "But this device: there is no telling where its uses might end."

"Yes. No telling. Harriot says he has written to the Tuscan Galileo in Florence. Sent him drawings of the instrument. And more stars. Harriot says he has seen stars in the black void, stars invisible to the eye. Think of it, Jack: new stars—new worlds, maybe—hang in the firmament."

"New worlds. . . ." Jack fingered his beard and took a few slow steps along a path through the room's clutter. He said, "Who knows of this?"

"None but the three of us. Harriot, you, and me. Oh, and Raleigh."

"And Galileo. You said Harriot had written to Galileo."

"Ah, yes. Galileo. I forgot."

"And Goodyer."

"Of course. Goodyer."

Jack said firmly, "Percy, that makes six already. Can you not see that this thing poses a threat to us all? Catholics especially. Already Cecil wants us dead. Already King James has betrayed us. We do not want to give them cause to move against us. Do you not see the danger?"

The Earl looked unconvinced but said, "I suppose. . . ."

"You must say nothing of this thing: tell no one else. And warn Raleigh and Harriot not to speak of it. I will write to Goodyer. I wonder I did not smell it from the start. Already men murmur you hold a School of Night within these walls. Some whisper that you—and Raleigh—are atheists."

The Earl lifted his palms as if his innocence were self-evident. "I am no such."

"I know. But that matters nothing. Do you not see? Cecil, or some other enemy, will say this instrument offers proof that you are."

The Earl scowled. "Cecil. But for Cecil, Raleigh would walk free." The Wizard looked sadly at the device and after a moment slumped back into his chair and said, "You are right, I suppose."

Jack turned a chair to face his friend's and sat. "Tell Harriot to write again and warn Galileo."

The Earl pursed his lips, then nodded. "You are right. As usual." He leaned forward, and his face regained some of its eagerness. "But Jack: how can a man hide *this*? We draw the very heavens near to us!"

"We will not hide it. We cannot—not for long. Only, we must take care how and when to reveal such a thing. Cecil is ever watchful, ever crafty." Jack paused a moment and said, "I myself might be a spy, employed by Cecil to *claim* I would rejoin the Church of Rome."

The Earl dismissed the idea with a snort. Jack continued, "And the King! You must know this king has whimsies in him: superstitions and fretsome irks. Where a man is called the Wizard Earl—a *Catholic* man—the Scots king will suspect dark magic."

The Earl shrugged as if to say *I know, but what can I do?* From the table beside him he picked up a rounded, flat-bottomed flask of greenish glass. A narrow pipe angled off near the top. Next to the pipe the Earl had fixed a small basin, hardly bigger than Jack's thumb. The Earl had lined the bottom of the little basin with fine wire mesh. Another slender pipe descended from a hole beneath the mesh into the murky water that half-filled the flask. The Earl put the first pipe to his lips and inhaled, sending bubbles through the water from the bottom of the second pipe. "You see?" As the Earl grinned, his livelier eyebrow darted even higher than usual. "One takes in the air but not the water. The water cools the smoke. Doesn't burn the throat, the lungs."

"What smoke?" Jack asked.

"Ah!" From a box on the floor beside his chair the Earl pulled a broad, brown leaf, tore off a piece, and stuffed it into the little basin. Then he picked up a long pair of tongs that had been propped against the fireplace. He moved the screen, stirred through the ashes until he found a small ember, pulled it out with the tongs, and dropped it in with the tobacco. As the leaf smoldered, the Earl inhaled some of the smoke and passed the flask to Jack, who took in a deep lungful. The scent of the smoke pleased, but Jack's nose, throat, and lungs rebelled. He stifled the urge to cough. His eyes watered, and he felt light-headed. As he passed the basin back to the Earl, Jack sneezed.

"Raleigh . . . the Indians, the old ones," the Earl said. "Great restorative, tobacco. In Virginia. Raleigh has seen it. Cures everything. The Indians, the wisest of them. Only the old, wise ones are allowed to smoke it. Some of them, Raleigh told me this: never get sick. He has seen it. The wise ones. With his own eyes. Some are so wrinkled he says they must be two hundred years old."

The Earl scraped the flask's ashes into the fireplace, loaded the little bowl with tobacco again and said, "Let us smoke to your salvation. Bosom of the Mother Church. Home. They do this in the Indies. Virginia too. Glad occasions like this, and solemn ones. The Indians."

They passed the flask twice more before Jack said, "Not three days since, I spoke of my resolve with a priest of the old faith. A great help and a comfort he proved. He asked me, then, if I knew the whereabouts of one Guido. He seemed to think it was a matter of some import."

The Earl's arching eyebrow fell as he considered the matter. "Ah, Guido. . . . His Christian name, is it, this Guido?"

"I know not. The priest did not say. Or would not."

The Earl leaned forward in his chair as he asked, "Which priest? Most of them I know."

Jack's left hand began to tremble slightly, unaccustomed as he was to this lying to a friend. Or maybe the trembling was an effect of the smoke. He was a little queasy, lightheaded, unsure he could think quickly. So he named the first priest who came to mind: "John Gerard."

"Ah. The Jesuit that escaped. In London again, is he? Tall man? Rides a horse like he was born to it? With the Dowager, last I knew. Falcon. Beautiful. Back again, is he?"

"When he heard my confession, yes. Dowager, did you say?"

"What? Oh, Eliza Vaux, I thought. Dowager of Harrowden."

"Ah. Of course." So Father Gerard was, or had been, in Northamptonshire with Eliza Vaux. Jack had to tread carefully here. He put his right hand on top of his left to still the faint tremor.

The Earl showed no sign of suspicion. "But again. Welcome home, Jack. Bosom. Bosom of the Mother Church."

"Thank you."

The Earl sat back in his chair. "The Netherlands, I thought he was."

Puzzled, Jack asked, "Father Gerard is in the Netherlands?"

"No, no," said the Earl. "Guido. Guido. . . . What's his family called? By God's bodykins, I have forgot it. I know of only one Guido. Voss, or Foss, or. . . . Well, I know of one such. Fights in the Netherlands. Englishman, but fighting for the Spanish, not the English. Where I heard that, I cannot. . . . I think Stanley mentioned him in a letter. Or. . . ." He ended with a shrug.

So some English Guido served in Sir William Stanley's army, as Cecil had said he might. Surely this was the man Cecil wanted found, fighting his own countrymen after Stanley's defection to Spain and the Spanish Netherlands.

They smoked another flask of tobacco. "I have something to ask," Jack said. The Earl waited for him to continue. "An old widow I know, one who showed me great kindness in my youth, a good Catholic: the pursuivants have bled her dry, and now she spends her days begging at the Savoy."

The Earl looked pained. "Why do they . . . ? They do themselves more harm than good. Much more of this . . . they'll rebel. The people will rebel."

"Sometimes I think Cecil wants a rebellion so he can have a few thousand heads to crack."

The Earl nodded. "And crack them he would. Blood in the streets."

The men talked on until a well-dressed servant entered with the news that the evening's guests had arrived. "Guests?" asked the Earl. "I'm not expecting any. . . . Who?"

The servant spoke without surprise, as if used to the Earl's lapses in memory. "The Count of Villa Mediana and his lady, my lord."

The Earl winced. "Oh. Yes. Evening with. . . . A trudge. Like a trudge through the mud. Jack, tell Lawrence here."

"Tell him about an evening with the Count? I don't—"

"No, your widow, of course. Tell him how to find your widow at the Savoy. She will be provided for."

"Oh. I thank you."

The Earl waved away Jack's thanks and put on the exaggerated accent of a stiff Spanish courtier: "I am the Count of Villa Mediana, and when I ope my lips, let no dog bark."

Jack laughed, and the servant looked as if he wanted to.

In his own voice the Earl said, "And his wife! The evening will drag itself sore. Hours. Cannot subject you to it, Jack. But come below to meet them. Then you can escape."

Chapter 7

Dressed in soggy finery and seated on a magnificent Friesian war horse, Sir Walter Chute led the way through the rain along the muddy road to Harrowden Hall. A mile or two back, one of Chute's little jennets had begun to show signs of going lame, so Jack now plodded along beside the pony. Burr's mare was so small and sway-backed the lanky old servant's feet hung within a few inches of the ground. "Master Jack," said Burr, "once more I ask: allow me to change places with you. It is unbecoming for a servant to ride while his master walks." Having already settled the matter, Jack gave a slight shake of his head and trudged on in silence until Burr added, "Or at least allow me to dismount this . . . this noble steed and walk beside you."

In no mood for negotiation, Jack said only, "The mud is thick, and you are old."

Burr considered the matter. "The former is evident by the sucking sound of your boots, and the latter I cannot deny. I must be almost as old as this venerable flop-eared beast I ride."

Chute turned his chubby, boyish face to them and said cheerily, "You both may ride. Jack, your little nag but feigns. I think she is not truly lame."

Jack said, "I think she is."

"Ah, well," Chute said airily.

The journey had only begun, and it was most like to last month upon month. Already the absence from Anne and the children seemed somehow to have taken a life of its own. It was a blind, unthinking, unhurried beast, gnawing its way into all but a few of Jack's thoughts; respite was rare. Already he longed to go home.

What would Anne be doing now? Her duties to the children would have pulled her from her torpor soon after he left, her tears spent and her spirits tractable. Her unborn child would move within her, perhaps stirring her into remembrance that Jack's temporary absence spelled the best hope for the growing family's lasting support. Constance and Little Jack, even in their petulant demands, would prove a blessing in distracting their mother from her sorrow.

The three men and their three beasts plodded on. After an hour they rounded a bend, and Harrowden Hall rose before them, its grounds looking unkempt but its honey-colored stone glistening in the rain. Finding no footman at the main door, they followed a path to the back of the house, where the large stables offered shelter. They saw no one, but from somewhere in the shadows came the sound of a hammer. When Chute's big horse snorted and pawed the ground, the hammering stopped. From the shadows emerged a short, bandy-legged man with a ring of coarse silver hair around a bald spot so cleanly circular it made him look tonsured. He calmly watched the strangers through steel-gray eyes, taking their measure. If he was suspicious he was placidly so, as though the truth would be revealed to him if he but waited for it. Perhaps only fifteen or twenty years older than Jack, the man was already lined with the creases of old age. The face made Jack think of a high tor carved by the wind for age upon age, the sculpted folds etched by neither great joy nor great pain: no more than the harrowed bark of an oak grew from joy or pain within the tree. The sinews in the man's arms looked as if they wielded strength all out of proportion to his size.

As he dismounted, Chute said, "Oats for my horse, my good

sirrah, and hay for the others." The gray-eyed man did not move. "Oats, I say," Chute continued irritably. "Here, take the reins." The man made no move to take the reins. His voice faltering, Chute added, "My good. . . ."

"Your good sirrah. Is that what I am, then?" The tone was serene, with a touch of Welsh in the accent.

"Forgive my friend," Jack said. "We are all of us, man and beast, wet from the ride."

The man nodded. "That I can see."

"Our business here is with the Dowager," Jack continued. "We would thank you for any help you might provide our animals." The bandy-legged Welshman reached out a hand for the little nag's reins, and Jack led the pony two or three steps forward.

His brow creased in concern, the Welshman knelt and put his hand to the pony's left foreleg. "Warm," he said. "She'll want a poultice of comfrey and vinegar on this fetlock. You won't be riding her for a few days."

His face flushed, Chute said, "My good man, she is my horse, as are these others. I shall be the judge—" Jack held up a hand, and Chute fell silent. Burr could not suppress a little smile.

"We would be grateful," Jack said to the man. "My name is John—or Jack, if you like—Donne. This is Sir Walter Chute and this, Timothy Burr."

The leathery little man eyed all three before saying, "Donne. A Welsh name, is it not?" When Jack nodded, the man said, "There are Donnes 'round Swansea still. An old family, and a good."

"Distant cousins," Jack said. "My branch lived in Rhyl before King William's time."

The bandy-legged man smiled a little, the lines on his face gathering around his eyes. He said simply, "Rhyl," as if he missed a place long ago left behind.

"We Chutes have always been English," Sir Walter said as he removed his gloves, "and we always will be. None of your Irish, Scots, nor Welsh in these veins."

"Well," said the little man, "your English mother must think you the very pink English apple of her pink English eye."

Chute looked at the bandy-legged man warily, but the Welshman's expression betrayed nothing. Burr, on the other hand, let out a snort that he tried to disguise with a cough. "Well," said Chute, "I note that we have told you our names, but you have not told us yours."

"So you have," said the bandy-legged man, "so you have." As he began to unsaddle Jack's pony, he said, "My name. . . . Business with the Dowager, do you say? Business of what sort?"

Before Chute could begin his reply, Jack cut him off with a glare, then pulled a letter from his pocket. "We bring greetings," Jack said, "from the Wizard Earl."

The Welshman's features softened. "Ah. That, I think, will sort with Lady Vaux. How fares the Earl?"

"Well, when I left him," Jack said.

The man extended a hand to Jack and said, "Owen. Nicholas Owen." The name sounded somehow familiar, but Jack couldn't think where he had heard it. Owen's handshake was strong, his fingers callused. He shook Burr's hand, too, then turned to Chute and hesitated. "Something too rough for so fine-veined a gentleman, I fear."

Chute blushed a little as he tried to think of a reply. After a few seconds he said, "Well, I care not. I can be as hale a fellow as the next, I warrant." He reached toward Owen, who took his hand and clasped it briefly, then went on unsaddling the horses. Jack and Burr helped while Chute strolled about, humming a tune.

When the horses were stabled and feeding, Owen led the three through the drizzling rain to the mansion's back door.

Once inside, he said, "The kitchen here is warmest, and I'll warrant the best place to dry yourselves." With well-feigned concern he nodded in Chute's direction and said, "If, that is, Sir Walter here does not think it stooping."

Chute glanced around the kitchen as if sizing it up for inspection and said brusquely, "No, no, this will serve."

Owen added, "Our ways here in the country, as you can see, are homelike. Get yourselves comfortable, then—beer in the firkin there—and I'll tell Lady Vaux you're here." Jack gave Owen the Earl's letter to take to the Dowager, and the three settled into the warm, strong, yeasty beer.

In a few minutes the Dowager appeared: a large woman with a broad jaw, iron-gray hair, and one eye perpetually squinted. She gave the three men a shrewd, sharp appraisal. So formidable did the woman appear that Jack imagined she could easily command men. The look explained what people as far away as London had heard: Eliza Vaux was the one being on earth who could cow her late husband, legendary for his fits of rage. Anyone else who suffered George Vaux's wrath would come away hurting. But when Eliza told him what to do, he had obeyed, often without protest.

It was even said that when she visited London, Eliza Vaux always made a point of carrying a rosary in full view of anyone who cared to look. Jack could not remember ever seeing her in London, but so went the rumor. And it was said that never once had anyone—pursuivant, constable, agent of the Crown—called her to task for her open Catholicism, nor had she ever been arrested. Now that he saw the Dowager Lady Vaux in person, Jack could well believe it. The fines on her once-wealthy household, though, had been heavy.

She paused in the doorway and motioned the three men to sit again. "Welcome to you all," she said, her voice surprisingly warm. "You'll have noticed the house and gardens are fallen off somewhat—more of that anon—but I trust you may consider yourselves at home nonetheless." Jack thanked her for the respite from the weather and introduced his companions. Lady Vaux looked at old Burr for a moment as if she knew and did not much like him, but if that was true she said nothing about it.

As the group sat around the kitchen fire, steam rose from the three travellers' garments. The talk was of horses, hawking, and the news from London. After the third or fourth piggin of beer—Lady Vaux drank as heartily as the men—she said, "Master Donne, might you join me in the hall on some business the Lord Northumberland bespeaks in the letter you brought from Syon House? We shan't trouble your friends with the like, as it concerns only yourself." The red-cheeked Chute sat with a vacant smile on his face, but Jack noticed that Burr stiffened a bit and narrowed his eyes.

"Of course," Jack said.

Burr watched them leave. He hadn't missed Lady Vaux's sharp look at him, and he wondered what lay behind it. Well, maybe she remembered him but couldn't think where or when it had been. Maybe what he had seen as a look of disapproval was merely her wonted expression when she tried, but failed, to call up a memory.

He remembered, though. She had been in London the only time he had ever seen her, perhaps a dozen years ago. She and her sister-in-law Eleanor Vaux had visited Burr's master at the time, the Earl of Southampton, to ask some favor. Apparently Southampton had refused the request, and the two had told him what they thought of the refusal. For after they left, Southampton looked as if he had found himself on the wrong side of the Lord on Judgment Day. The man did not sleep until the third day after.

Burr took a sip of ale. Chute reached with his empty piggin and said, "Another, Tim. Damnable muddy country, this north country. Damnable muddy country. Good English beer, though. But what makes this north country so damnably muddy?"

"Rain, I should think, sir." Burr filled the vessel and handed it back to Chute.

"Rain, is it?" said Chute. "Damn this damnable rain."

When the Dowager had closed the door behind her she said, "Well, Master Donne, my friend the Earl writes of you warmly. But the burden of his letter seems to concern some change impending in your life. Am I near the mark in guessing he dares not commit the matter plainly to paper?"

"You are not near the mark," Jack said. "You have hit it."

Looking squarely into his eyes, the Dowager said, "And the Earl thinks I may be of some aid."

"He does." It was true enough, and Jack was confident no hint of dissembling crossed his face as he continued: "When my brother Henry died for sheltering a Catholic priest, my grief was such that I left the Mother Church. I meant to have no more to do with her."

"I see." Still she watched him closely.

Jack found himself looking away as he said, "It was a mistake." Well, there was some truth in it. In certain dark moods he still thought it a mistake. At such times faint voices from the past whispered his faithlessness, and accusations of treachery troubled his dreams. Yet Henry and the priest he sheltered had died, both of them horribly. And for what? For their allegiance to an enthroned, triple-crowned Italian bishop. No, God had not shed his beam of light on Rome alone, nor on Wittenberg nor Canterbury. All beams shone from the same sun. Yet the dark, whispering voices persisted. . . . "I would repent my sin," he said, "and join the Church again."

The Dowager waited for perhaps a full minute—it seemed to Jack an hour—before saying, "You *would* rejoin the Church.

Well, you would do so if . . . what?"

Jack found he could look her in the eye again. "There are no *ifs,*" he said. "Lady Vaux, it is true I harbor doubts. They torment my heart, and I would find a priest to settle my soul. I confess to you doubts in plenty, doubts in especial about the Jesuits and their doings. But know this: my resolve is clear. I set no conditions. And what is more, I swear before you and Almighty God, on peril of my salvation, that I mean no harm to you nor any priest—nor to any other Catholic woman, man, or child."

The Dowager let another silence pass, during which Jack thought he heard a faint footfall in a room overhead. Lady Vaux held his gaze and said, "There are many who mean no harm; that is nothing. The question is this: do they *do* harm?"

Spoken like a true Catholic. And, false Catholic though he was, in this instance he agreed: much depended on his doing no harm. He said quietly but firmly, "I have told you my intent. If you cannot or will not help me, my friends and I will thank you for your hospitality and be on our way. But I think you can help me."

This time she eyed him for only a few heartbeats. Then she said, "Well, something in me misgives, but I think so too. For the Wizard Earl's sake, at least, I will trust you. I remind you, though: good men's lives hang in the balance."

"I am well aware of it."

"And what of your two companions? Can we trust *them*?"

"That, my lady, is a very good question. I know neither man well. Circumstances have brought us together for a time. But Chute—"

"He's the one that looks like a cherub?"

Jack smiled. "Yes. Chute I *think* you can trust, in so far as his religion tends. His wish to join the Church appears genuine. Yet I counsel you to hold. I would fain know the man better before

I hazarded much on his faith. On his ability to keep counsel I would rely even less. Of the other—old Burr—I am also unsure. In any case, my aim is to go with them to the Spanish Netherlands and there let priests whose lives are less in peril try their faith."

She nodded. "It is well considered." After rising from her chair she said, "I will occupy your friends while you make your confession. Afterward, come down and join us for supper." He thanked her.

The Dowager led him up the stairs and into a narrow, windowless room. A faint yellow light glowed from an oil lamp hanging from a chain affixed to an overhead beam. The only other objects in the room were two unadorned chairs, one of them near the lamp. Lady Vaux motioned for Jack to sit in the other, a few feet away. She left the room.

A few minutes later a tall, broad-shouldered man entered and sat opposite Jack. He was dressed as a country gentleman at his leisure, in a leather jerkin and faded blue breeches. In the dim light Jack could not see the man's face clearly. When the stranger sat, the glow from the lamp behind him formed a faint nimbus of light around his head. The big man watched Jack for a while before saying, "So you would rejoin the Mother Church."

"I would. Are you a priest?" If he was, he certainly didn't look the part. The man sat forward in his chair, which was of normal size but seemed too small for him. His feet were planted wide apart.

"There might be one hard by, but I would fain speak to you first."

Jack leaned toward him, extended his hand, and said, "I am Jack Donne."

"Catesby," the man said as he shook Jack's hand with a firm grip. "Robin Catesby."

Jack tried to remember where he had heard the name. Then

he had it: "Ah! You rose with Essex in '01."

Catesby nodded.

"I fought under him at Cadiz," Jack said.

"Aye. Would that I had too. But the bitch-queen had me mewed up in the Tower on a false charge in '96." Catesby reached above him to unhook the lantern from its chain. He held it to his left, turned his head to the right, and pulled back his hair. The top of Catesby's ear was missing, as though someone had taken a pair of shears to it. "A bullet took it off in the rising." He set the lantern on the floor before him and relaxed into his chair. "I had no more finished saying a rosary than the ball came that close. It was the Virgin looking out for me, seeing to it the shot didn't carry more of me away." Catesby put his hands on his knees and sat back in the chair. "Essex would have made a fine king of England, would he not? No Catholic, he, but he would have made friends with us all. At the least, he promised toleration."

Jack shrugged. "So did the Scotsman."

Catesby turned his head and spat. "That's for the punk-livered Scots turncoat. Had he kept to his word, we had served him well. But as it is . . ." Catesby didn't need to finish the sentence; there was murder in his voice. "England needs true sons: true to the one God and to God's one Church." Jack slowly nodded his agreement. Catesby asked, "Are you such a man?"

"If God gives me strength."

Catesby stood, picked up the lantern, and said gruffly, "Aye. You were best pray that he does." He stepped forward, leaned until his face nearly touched Jack's, and added, "It will go well for true sons of the true Church, but for intelligencers and spies, it will go very, very hard."

Jack could see the pores in Catesby's nose, and he could feel as well as smell the garlic-laden breath. His own heart-blood was pounding in his ears, but he held steady, showing no outward sign. He crossed himself, forcing Catesby to move his head back an inch or two, then glared silently at him before saying, "That's as it should be."

Catesby hovered for a few heartbeats, searching Jack's eyes. Then, apparently satisfied, he set the lantern on the floor, straightened, and strode out of the room.

Jack took a few deep breaths to calm himself. He closed his eyes and thought of Anne, picturing her on the settle by the fire, her head inclined a little to one side, Little Jack asleep in her arms while Constance sat nearby and stared wide-eyed into the flames. He heard a faint rustling in the room, and when he opened his eyes, there sat an affable-looking gentleman, shoeless but otherwise dressed impeccably. Jack introduced himself and explained that Lady Vaux, then Robin Catesby, had led him to think he'd be meeting with a priest.

"Oh, but I am one," the man said. "Palmer. Father Valentine Palmer."

"Ah." Of course. A Catholic priest must stay disguised somehow, and this Palmer wore his clothes so easily he seemed a born nobleman. Where had he heard the name? In a moment he had it: old Mrs. Aylesbury, trying to cover her blunder. Jack's eyes went to the man's wrists. A sleeve covered one, but the other . . . yes, there it was. "You're John Gerard."

The man raised his eyebrows. "But who told you so?"

"The scar on your wrist. You've hung from the manacles."

Gerard's easy smile faded. "I have. Hung from the manacles and stretched on the rack." He pulled back his sleeves and held up both wrists. "Topcliffe's work."

A tingling stuttered along Jack's spine. "A madman, Topcliffe. Cecil picked a right reprobate for his rackmaster general."

With a rueful little smile the priest said, "I can assure you Topcliffe takes great pleasure in his vocation."

Jack hardly knew what to think. Here before him sat either a hero or a fool: a Jesuit who revealed no information under torture and now was back for another trip to the rack. "But you escaped from the Tower."

"I did, with help from friends."

"You made it to Rome."

"Yes, and I am here for only a few hours longer. I'll be on my way back to Rome before you leave this house."

Jack wondered if it was true. Certainly if the priest had any notion Jack was a spy, it would be a sensible thing to say. "I heard you could hardly hold the rope strung across the moat."

Gerard said, "I could not grasp the rope at all, but only drape my arms about it. I used my legs to move along the line. It was by God's grace alone I 'scaped a drowning. Much time passed before I could so much as hold a pen and write." The priest added quietly, "But the pain in the wrists and the hands—terrible as that pain raged, so much so that I like not to remember it—was not the worst. After you hang from Topcliffe's manacles for two or three hours, your belly bursts inside you. I could scarce say a prayer, for all the spitting out of blood. . . ." Both men were silent for a while. Then the priest's smile returned. "But here I am, by God's grace."

His thoughts a mixture of wonder and disgust, Jack pressed the point. "You *escaped.* You landed safely in Rome. And your superior sent you—*you,* a man whose face was known to Topcliffe and all his henchmen—your superior sent you *back* here?"

Gerard shrugged. "He did, for this short mission. But not before I asked him."

Jack leaned forward. "Father, is this not madness masking as devotion? Do you not know that if you are caught, the King will fear you Jesuits all the more? He will make it his business to tighten his grip on *all* Catholics."

The priest sat looking at Jack for a moment before saying

calmly, "Master Donne, God will hold me to account not for the King's sins but for mine own. I am called to minister to the flock of the Lord. Shall I not answer the call? The Lord's sheep famish for want of the Blessed Sacrament. Which is more godly: to save these aching bones of mine by suffering the sheep to starve, or to feed the sheep by suffering upon the rack? Which road leads to Paradise?"

Jack had answers in plenty. He quickly turned over possibilities. One: priests in the Protestant Church of England, no less than priests in the Catholic Church of Rome, fed the faithful with the Body and Blood of Christ. Two: the Jesuits risked not just their own lives but the lives of all who housed and fed them. The Act Against Jesuits made that clear. Three: while they claimed to do no more than minister to the faithful, the Jesuits worked like Machiavels toward a Spanish takeover of England—or at the least, turned a blind eye to those who worked for it. Four: once in power, the Catholics would prove as bloody as the Protestants. Five: the Jesuits had fallen, as Jack himself had fallen in his youth, half in love with death.

Jack had spoken only the first of his objections, though, before Gerard interrupted him: "Come. Are you here to argue theology or confess your sins?"

"I have been confessing them, Father. My sins are my doubts."

"Not all doubts are sins."

"Tell me if this is one of them: I doubt that you and others of your order do more good than harm with your presence in England. Do you not make civil war more likely rather than less?"

Gerard pressed the tips of his fingers together, then let his hands rest on his lap. He said, "You are right that we must weigh probable results along with godly motives and charitable deeds. But you may be sure that among those deeds is the dissuasion of our hot-blooded young men from acts of rebellion. If we priests were not here to turn them from violence, who could do the same? They know they are bound by their faith to obey us." He paused, then said, "Have you other doubts?"

As if that settled the matter of the Jesuits and their endangering England. "Yes. Doubts about my decision to rejoin the Church of Rome." Gerard waited for him to continue. Jack asked, "Are there not many paths to the truth?" After a few seconds he added, "Do *you* have them, these doubts?" He was surprised by the earnestness in his voice.

This time the silence lasted a long time. Jack sat waiting uneasily. Finally, Gerard said, "Do I have doubts? Taking holy orders does not silence the voice of the fiend. But we are here for you, not for me. Do you succumb to your doubts, or do you resolve to stand firm against them?"

"But Father, I would know: do you suffer these plaguing doubts?"

The priest closed his eyes and let out a heavy breath. "Regarding the authority of our Lord and his Holy Catholic Church? No," he said quietly. "Or not often, and not for long. Those few foul whisperings I now hear are now most faint, and easy to answer. But this certitude of soul has not come to me cheaply. I paid dearly to get it, and still I pay for it daily. I can assure you that the gift of certitude is as real as you or I, and that it is offered to you as well as me. If a man daily, hourly puts his trust in the Lord and His Holy Church, over time the fiend's whisperings lose their strength."

"I would I could believe you," Jack said. He meant it. Or part of him did. What would he not trade for a settled sureness like Father Gerard's? But those Protestants he most admired—Morton, Andrewes, his own wife Anne—were similarly sure, and their beliefs differed from Gerard's. Protestant and Catholic could not both be right in their certitude that theirs was the one true church. He said, "I believe—or I desire to believe—

that the faithful of the Church of England as well as the faithful of the Church of Rome will be saved."

"In that case why would you risk life and limb to engraft yourself anew into the Holy Catholic Church? You seem to think the hasty-cobbled church of the eighth Henry will serve you well enough."

Jack shifted in his chair. "I hardly know how to answer." He thought for a moment, then said, "In these late years I have been like a child lost. My earthly mother renounced me when I joined the new faith. Now she is fled to Antwerp. I would see her again; I would be reconciled with her before she dies." Again it was the truth.

"Are you certain she renounced you, or perhaps did she renounce only your apostasy? Perhaps the source of the curse you felt was your own conscience and not your mother's heart."

"Perhaps."

"Go on."

"And as I would return to the arms of my earthly mother, I would return to the bosom of the Mother Church. In especial, I would return to the warm embrace of the Holy Mother, the Blessed Virgin Mary."

Gerard nodded slowly, then said, "These are reasons you would return. Tell me why you left."

"The decision came only after much prayer and study, I can tell you that. For years I agonized." He paused to gather his thoughts, trying to recall whether his motives through all those years had been pure.

"And did the agony," Gerard asked, "redeem the act?"

"No, I suppose not. Or I would not be here."

"There you have it. Suffering never redeems a wrong. The question is whether, in the end, you allow the suffering to lead you to decide aright."

"Then are we damned for a wrong choice, even when the

way is not clear because it is thick with rights and wrongs on both sides?"

"Come. You know better than that. Wrong choices can be redeemed, but by Christ alone, not by mere suffering. If our agonies bring us to Christ, they have done their office. But go on: tell me how you came to leave the Holy Church."

"First, I watched my brother Henry, cast into Newgate Prison only a few days before, die of the Black Death infesting that hellish place. His crime was but giving shelter to a Catholic priest."

"Which?"

"Father William Harrington."

"Ah, yes, young Harrington. I knew him. He died well, a glorious martyr's death."

"Glorious!" Jack raised his voice despite his resolve to stay calm. "That is the kind of talk that cost my brother his life, and you your own, almost. From the cradle on, our uncles, Henry's and mine—Jasper in his tales, Ellis in his letters, Jesuits both, these uncles—filled our hearts with longing for this heaven-hellish gift of martyrdom."

"Gift of martyrdom? The gift is steadfast perseverance in the faith," the priest said quietly. "I do not long for martyrdom. If it comes I am ready. But I knew your uncles. In your youth, it may hap, you misconstrued their tales and their letters. In any case I know your uncles did not cause your brother's death. Or Father Harrington's. It was the English apostates—the Protestants and atheists—who did so."

"Harrington: you say you knew him, but were you with him at the end?"

The priest said, "No, more's the pity. My superior forbade me to witness the holy martyrdom, lest I be recognized and captured."

"Well, I watched him die. When Topcliffe cut him down,

before that madman showed the priest his own guts and burned them in his very sight, Harrington wrestled with him."

"Yes. I have heard as much. A noble struggle, were it not?"

Jack's gestures grew expansive. "Father, the man was terrified. He wanted to *live,* not die a martyr's death. You could see it in the way he fought. And what of you? *You* wanted to live when you escaped from Topcliffe and the Tower."

"Of course I did. As long as God wishes me to minister to his flock, I wish to live. When God calls mc home, I wish to die. And it is true a martyr's death is best. Your uncles did well to teach that much to you from your cradle, though you seem to have forgotten the lesson. Thanks be to God I have not forgotten it." The priest had begun speaking sharply, almost like a schoolmaster chiding a pupil. He closed his eyes and took a deep breath—as if to ward off infection from whatever agitations this strangely argumentative pilgrim, this half-penitent apostate, had brought into the room with him. The priest's voice was calm when he continued. "Yet martyrdom is not mine to seek out. When Harrington wrestled with the hangman—when I escaped from the Tower—we were but discerning God's will for us. He willed Harrington to die then, me to live now. I know not why. Our part is but to discern God's will and do it."

Now Father Gerard sat patiently, an easy smile on his face, looking like some mildly pleased nobleman watching his beloved child at play. He waited, so Jack pressed him: "Do you not see it, Father? You Jesuits, with your fourth vow: you invite the Pope to rob you of your birthright. You vow to let a Roman bishop steal from you the gift of reason. Is that not madness? What if the Pope is wrong? Many have been; any man of reason can see it. A child can see it."

Gerard said, "The Pope is like a holy alchemist who distills the wisdom of the ages into one substance, simple and pure. Why do you trust your powers of reason, or why should I trust mine, above the rarefied wisdom of fifteen hundred years and more?"

Jack would not give up this easily. "Ignatius—the founder of your own Jesuitical order—says if you see a thing as white, and the hierarchic Church sees it as black, then it is black. How can you live with such a saying?"

Gerard furrowed his brow. "Are you here to confess your sins, or to talk me into renouncing my faith? If the latter, you had as well persuade the wind cease to blow."

Jack looked at the priest, tried to calm himself, and bowed his head. "I have come to confess my sins and receive absolution."

Burr watched the steam rise off his boots, tipped back his chair, closed his eyes, and let his head rest against the wall. Months lay before him—years it might be, Lady Bedford had said—satisfying the whims of this Walter Chute. Lady Bedford had proven a demanding enough mistress, but at least she commanded a fine wit. Burr let a little moan escape. Chute seemed not to notice; he was sawing the air with his mug as he tunelessly mumbled a catch about Kate Greengown and her bawd. Well, at least there was Donne for company, worthy of trust or no.

When the song had ended, Chute drained off the rest of his drink, wiped his sleeve across his lips, and shoved the empty piggin into Burr's ribs. The old servant squinted an eye. Chute leaned forward and said, "What ho, Burr! Another dose of ale, shall we?" Chute could have done it well enough himself from where he sat, but Burr dutifully rose and dipped the beer from the firkin. He wondered what business might concern Eliza Vaux, Jack Donne, and the Wizard Earl.

Guessing the kitchen must be the only warm spot in the house, Burr glanced about the room. Once before, back when he served the Earl of Southampton, Burr had visited this house to deliver a sealed message from Southampton: a dozen years ago, it must be. Back then Harrowden Hall had been magnificent. A dozen fires blazed at once in various rooms. Sir George Vaux held court like one of the nobles of old.

At the time he brought the message, this Lady Eliza, now the Dowager of Harrowden, had been in Warwickshire visiting her sister. And now, just as the Dowager's gardens grew rank with weeds, even the kitchen showed signs of neglect. Cobwebs hung between some of the beams, and the floor could use a good sweeping. The Dowager was right: the place certainly had fallen off. Well, the cause was not hard to guess: the Scotsman king had laid crippling taxes on these Catholic houses since coming to the throne. Probably the Dowager paid the fines too for keeping recusant from the Church of England services. No doubt she had harbored priests here. Some of these Catholic strongholds of the North were riddled with priest-holes, cunningly crafted hiding places the pursuivants could not find when they came to ransack the place. Probably Harrowden was such a house. Conceivably a priest lay hidden somewhere near even now.

As if picking up on Burr's thoughts, Chute looked around the room, spread his arms, and said expansively, "Is this not well? Is it not well that we three Catholics travel together, as on a holy pilgrimage?"

Burr glared at his master and said in a harsh whisper, "Speak within-door, my lord. Even here."

His eyes wide, Chute said, "Oho!" and put a finger to his lips. "Shhh. . . ."

Just then Eliza Vaux appeared in the doorway. If she had overheard the exchange, she didn't show it. The Dowager took a chair and said, "So. Your friend Donne tells me you are bound for the Netherlands."

"He does?" Chute said, looking confused. Then he caught himself and said, "Ah, yes, the Netherlands first. I remember me: Jack wants to visit the Low Countries on our way to Rome. It's Italy, for my blood. My Italian is excellent. I excelled in Italian at Oxford. Do you speak Italian, Tim?"

"Little enough, sir."

Chute yawned. "No matter. You may rely upon my Italian," he murmured, his eyes half closed, "when we visit Italy."

Burr said to Lady Vaux, "Sir Walter and I, as must be evident to Your Ladyship, have made free with your beer. Do you not find that some contain it better than others?"

The Dowager smiled. "Of a surety, I have found it so." She turned to Chute. "Sir, would you have somewhat to eat with your beer?" But Chute's head, heavy with drunken sleep, had already fallen to his chest.

CHAPTER 8

It was odd, this request to meet at Windsor Castle. What could the woman want? Lady Bedford considered the possibilities. Most likely this Anne Donne had come with a plea for patronage on her husband's behalf. Or maybe jealousy drove her to ask just the opposite: the end of relations between Jack Donne and Lady Lucy Harrington Russell. Or Anne suspected Lady Bedford's hand in Jack's work for Robert Cecil. Or she knew England's Queen Anna was staying at the castle, and she wanted to use Lady Bedford to pass along some plea to the Queen. Or she simply missed courtly life since her disgraceful elopement. Well, it should be easy enough to find the answer; the girl was no doubt a simple, impetuous creature.

But the young woman the porter admitted was clear-eyed and clever-looking, a woman perhaps not beautiful but very pretty, one who seemed to bear a wry sense of her own limits as well as those of others. With a noncommittal half-smile Anne took Lady Bedford's delicately extended hand. She kept her curtsey shallow and unhurried.

Lady Bedford said, "How good to see you. How fares life at Loseley? Does your father still lord it in high style?"

"Too high for my liking," Anne said. "But I have not visited in these three or four years. Relations with my father have been strained for some time."

"Ah, there you must be careful. I just last night, at this very palace, heard a new play by the man Shakespeare. It is all about ungrateful daughters, and I have to tell you: it does not end well for them."

"Oh, *King Lear*!" Anne exclaimed. "Jack and I heard it at the Globe not a fortnight since. It is . . . devastating. I wept for hours afterward."

"And your husband? Did he weep?"

"A little, I think." Anne added a bit ruefully, "But he saw me home and then went to the Mermaid to drink with the author. It was almost dawn when he came home, drunk and full of the raucous life of the alehouse. He wanted to bandy words with me, as he had done with the Shakespeare, Jonson, and the others."

Lady Bedford chuckled. "Yes. That sounds like Jack."

"But does it? He has a family, and almost always he does right by us."

"Ah, but all of London knows that in his youth he bandied more than words. Your husband's witty poems bodying forth his exploits have been copied out from hand to hand to hand, so that everyone in London who can read has collected two or three of them."

"Oh," Anne said, "I don't think it's as bad as that."

"Bad! Why should you think it bad? You have married the most notorious seducer of women in all of London. *Married* him. So that he behaves as he should." Lady Bedford laid a finger on her cheek as if she were deep in thought. "Yet I wonder. Does he not chafe against the constraints of the marriage bed?"

"I pray he does not."

"Then all is well. You have tamed the wildest man in the city."

Anne shifted in her chair. "Tamed? No, I would not call Jack tamed. But he is faithful."

"And so you trust him to go to the public playhouses."

"And when the fare suits, I go with him."

"But you must come to hear plays at Court! The King's Men—Burbage, Armin, Shakespeare, the whole lot—play for us often."

Anne said, "We have not been. . . . But that sounds well. I have not heard a play at Court since my marriage."

"Then that must be remedied. Ah! I shall have the man Jonson pen a masque, and he shall include a part for you." Lady Bedford took both Anne's hands in hers. "But you are blushing! Don't tell me a girl so sprightly is shy of playing in a masque."

Anne hesitated a moment, then said, "A rumor bruited about has it that you played a part in a masque bare-breasted."

"Yes?"

"It is not true, is it?"

"Oh, quite true. Why should it not be? I played the part of Venus. Is the Goddess of Love to go about in a bodice and farthingale?"

"But you are married. And a Christian of the reformed Church of England."

Lady Bedford laughed. "But of course I am. What has that to do with my breasts? God made them, and they are shapely. I bared them to his glory."

Anne asked, "For my part in the masque, would I be . . . ?"

"Wrapped in muslin head to foot, if you like. Perhaps Jonson could write you the part of an Egyptian mummy."

Anne smiled. "Or maybe something between the mummy and Venus."

"Done."

Now that Lady Bedford had drawn the first measure of this Anne Donne, it was time to put her to the test. As she led her to a small parlor, Lady Bedford said, "Your husband has told me all about you."

A glint of eagerness flashed in Anne's eyes. "*Has* he?"

"Well," Lady Bedford replied as she motioned for Anne to sit, "perhaps not so much as you might hope, but it seemed the right thing to tell you."

"Oh. I see. I suppose there is not much for him to say."

"Not much to *say*? How do you mean? An heir to Loseley Park, cherished daughter of no less a personage than Sir George More and favorite niece of the Lord Keeper himself, a girl with every prospect of a match with a wealthy country squire—perhaps even a baron or a viscount, if things were managed properly—a child who chooses to cast away all to marry a scrivening apostate Catholic for *love*? Oh, I should think there would be a very great deal to say."

"Yes," said Anne, meeting Lady Bedford's dark eyes, "I married for love. After all, the realm holds many a woman who marries for wealth, many a woman who would go so far as to marry a fool, had he a title and gold enough. One need not look far at all to find such women. They are . . . common."

So Jack Donne's wife had some fight in her. "You are right," said Lady Bedford. Some have been born to such stations as to find themselves obliged by the *Crown* to marry fools." She looked at Anne carefully for a few moments before adding, "If you numbered me among these women I would perhaps not gainsay your claim. Indeed some of us, but that we were good Christian women, would look beyond our marriages for worthy lovers."

Anne said quietly, "Then thanks be to heaven for good Christian women."

"Yes. Thanks be." Lady Bedford smoothed her skirt. "But I see you are great with child. How many will this make?"

Anne brightened a little. "Three."

"Three! And for one so young! I fear you put yourself at risk in going about London on visits such as this when you are so very near your groaning."

"Not so near," said Anne. "Some two months off, I think. Maybe more."

"Well, you swell so fulsome already that no doubt the child will be hearty and stout."

"If God wills it."

"If God wills it." Lady Bedford glanced at the door as she found herself saying, "So far, God has not willed it for me."

"No? But you too are yet young, only a year or two, I think, older than I. In good time, I trust, children will grace your home."

The girl seemed earnest. Lady Bedford said, "True, I am but twenty-three. But I have been married these ten years."

"And no . . . ?"

"Oh, I have been pregnant."

"How many . . . ?"

"Three, the same as you." The tears began to gather in Lady Bedford's eyes. This would not do. This would not do at all. Despite her effort to maintain control, she found herself saying, "One of them was quickened in the womb as long as yours there." Her clear, authoritative voice became very quiet. "It—*he*—was alive. I could feel him move within me. Then. . . ."

Anne reached out a consoling hand, but Lady Bedford turned away and dabbed at the corners of her eyes with a lace kerchief as she said, "It may be just as well. I have grown accustomed to a life of influence at Court. Children would perhaps prove as much burden as blessing."

Anne started to protest but checked herself, saying only, "Perhaps."

Suddenly the very picture of composure, Lady Bedford looked squarely at Anne and said, "So: what news from your fine husband? I have not seen him this long while, and he owes me a poem."

"It is about him that I have come."

Lady Bedford arched an eyebrow. "No doubt."

"Do you not know what employment has befallen him?"

"Why, no. I thought perhaps you had come to solicit my aid in procuring him some office, perhaps that you were come to try my influence at Court. If not that, tell me what is on your mind."

Anne looked anything but one well-born lady calling on another: some cold, pregnant child, rather, as she hunched forward a little and clutched her arms with her hands. A large clock stood against the wall behind Lady Bedford, ticking away. Anne said, "Jack has been sent away by Robert Cecil."

Lady Bedford did not allow her expression to change. "Sent away, you say."

"Yes. I dare not tell you more."

"I think there is no need to say another word. Doubtless I can guess near enough. Robert Cecil, like all men—*nearly* all men, anyway—is a simple creature. He desires only power. All his doings serve merely to augment the power of the Crown, which is to say, to augment power for himself as he directs the Crown. Such a man is strong but hardly in a way I find appealing. Such a man is incapable of . . . complexity; incapable of love, for instance."

Anne looked briefly at the floor in front of her. Lady Bedford noted the glance as well as the faint flush rising along Anne's throat. After considering what these signs might mean, she said, "So, you wish me to intercede with Lord Cecil."

"No!" said Anne with surprising force. "I wish. . . . I think there would be nothing to gain in mentioning my name to him."

A brief spark of compassion or curiosity flickered across Lady Bedford's eyes. Then she shrugged. "I suppose it is just as well. Lord Cecil and I are presently not on the best of terms." There was no need to tell the girl more.

"I see. But the Queen remains here at Windsor, does she not?"

Lady Bedford narrowed her eyes. "She does."

"And you share her confidence, do you not?"

"I do."

"And the King loves her, does he not? I mean to say, he thinks well of her, listens to her counsel."

"He does. For a man so fond of boys, King James thinks highly of his wife. Unlike the eighth Henry, James of Scotland sees his queen as something more than a brood-mare for men-children."

Anne smiled. "I thought so."

A maidservant arrived with a tray of cakes and two crystal goblets of wine. She placed the tray on the table. After dismissing the servant with a nod, Lady Bedford handed Anne a glass and said, "And you would have me intercede with the Queen on your husband's behalf. You wish me to direct her to keep Robert Cecil at arm's length."

"No. Yes. I mean, any help you can offer would be most welcome. But Lord Cecil must not suspect my hand in the matter."

"Of course. You may rely upon my discretion."

"But what I really wish to ask is whether you might introduce me to the Queen."

For just a heartbeat or two Lady Bedford looked taken aback. Then she smiled wryly, placed her hand on Anne's, and said, "I like you. I can see full well why your good husband calls you *lectissima.*"

Anne's eyes widened with delight. "Oh! He said that?"

"How very like him, is it not? He means it in its full, double sense."

"Yes," said Anne, "*most choice* and *most learned.* Wonderful. He said that of me?"

"Well, indirectly, yes. If you must know, he said it of me, but I am sure he was thinking of you."

Anne withdrew her hand. She looked as if she had been stabbed. After closing her eyes for a time, she said quietly, "There is a third sense."

"A third?"

"Yes. The word can also mean *most readable.* If Jack said it of you, he means he knows how to read you."

Lady Bedford laughed, a little uneasily. "No man, I think, knows how to read me. Not even your dark-eyed husband."

"Well. I suppose that is a good thing."

Lady Bedford asked pointedly, "Good for me, or good for you?"

Anne let out an exasperated breath. "I know not. But I came here hoping our benefit might be mutual. If you are . . . fond of my husband, surely helping him stay alive is of some interest to you. To me it means everything. Is it in your power to grant me audience with the Queen?"

"Well. As I say, I like you. I can put your plight to her in its fairest light. But I know not how to say this other than to say it plainly: I am quite sure *she* would not like you. Her tastes are most . . . selective. Your seeing her is out of the question."

"You don't seem to understand. I fear for my husband's life. I would do something to help him."

"But you *are* doing something. You are talking with me, and I will talk with the Queen."

"No, *I* would do something."

Lady Bedford rose and extended a hand. "I shall give the matter further thought. As for now, I am expected for dinner at the King's table. I must bid you good day."

Anne took Lady Bedford's extended hand, curtseyed half-heartedly, and turned to leave. Lady Bedford sharply clapped her hands twice and called, "Sirrah!" Before Anne had reached the door a portly footman entered. "Bring Mrs. Donne a coach. Take her wherever she will."

The footman, who must have known the maidservant had just brought refreshments, glanced at the untouched cakes and wine and registered only momentary puzzlement before bowing and saying, "My lady."

The thick-wristed helmsman peered nervously into the darkening north, but the captain remained unperturbed. He assured the queasy-looking Chute that the spire of Antwerp's Cathedral of Our Lady would pull into view within the hour. "The wind holds fair from the west," the captain added. "I think we'll make port well ahead of any squall." Chute looked unconvinced, then alarmed. He put a hand over his mouth and lurched to the aft rail. The captain turned to Burr and laughed. "What cheer, good Timothy? You look near as greenish as Sir Walter."

Burr said, "I have no love of this pitching about in a great wooden casket on the vasty deep, were it the fairest day in June. But to commit ourselves to the waves in the February wind! As you are unaware of the season, I must think you have all been struck to very midsummer madness."

"Why, Tim," said Jack, "this is the fairest February day I have seen in half a year of Februaries. The sea lies calm."

"Lies calm! I know who lies, and it is not the sea. The waves I think rise half again as high as the mast. By God's eyelid, I would we had reached dry land. I could kiss your good dry land, be it netherland or no."

But for Chute's occasional retchings, the men fell silent for a time. Shivering patches of gray light glanced off the undulating waters that stretched away on every side. The ship rose, creaked, and plashed with a steady rhythm: a slow cadence to calm the mind. As Burr's look faded to a sullen pout, Jack's thoughts drifted to the otherworldly calm that had stayed Essex's fleet for days upon days back in '97. Jack had written about it, and he remembered the lines:

Our storm is past, and that storm's tyrannous rage,
A stupid calm, but nothing it doth 'suage.
Storms chafe, and soon wear out themselves, or us;
In calms, heaven laughs to see us languish thus.
No use of lanterns; and in one place lay
Feathers and dust, yesterday and today.

In '97 one poor soul, crazed in that calm by a fevered calenture, mistook the green waters for a field near his house in Cornwall and leaped overboard. A boat was lowered to fetch him, but by then the seaman had already gone under. It was just as well; the fever would have taken him within hours anyway.

It had been yet more days before a breeze arose and the fleet straggled home treasureless, without even having attacked the Armada. A year after the daring raid of Cadiz, this bootless voyage to the Azores had proved the beginning of the end for Essex. Nor did it one whit advance Jack Donne.

Now, though, the ship carrying Jack, Burr, and Chute made fair for Antwerp, plowing before a rising wind. Our Lady's cathedral rose steadily ahead. Lesser buildings took shape around its bulk. The stone lacework of the spire told of a graceful Catholic world long gone, a world of honest artisans united in their striving heavenward.

Or so Jack allowed himself to imagine, part of him knowing all the while it wasn't so. Simony and strife, corruption, would-be reformers brutally put down: all of it had been there all along. The city's wealth had funded that magnificent edifice on broken backs, the mortar pinked with the blood of the poor. Still, the cathedral took one's breath away.

Before long, as the sky darkened into storm behind them and the mate barked orders to the crew, the helmsman steered the ship into the broad, brackish waters of the Westerschelde. Chute knelt half-swooned against the rail, his forehead pressed onto his fist. Burr glanced furtively about, as if to glimpse some subtle enemy lurking along the shore. Jack was quickened by the sight of so many ships, so much bustling trade, as the crews hurried to finish their work ahead of the storm.

Anne tried to contain her fury as she rode from Windsor Castle in a carriage drawn by a team of strong-necked, wide-flanked horses. To be toyed with as Lady Bedford had just done! The churning within her felt unfamiliar, extravagant and alluring in its demand that she submit to it with her whole being. Men—many of them—had underestimated her. In their unthinking way they assumed her to be one more ignorant girl. But never had a woman treated her so. The jealousy that had for months smoldered within her now fanned into the burning purity of hatred. Oh, it was delicious, this hatred, hot and dangerous and delicious. All at once she knew what had always mystified her: how people could do violence to one another. She imagined herself slipping a crippling poison into Lady Bedford's wine, or throwing a vial of some caustic vitriol into her haughty, hawk-like face.

By the time the travellers' coach pulled into the narrow street where Jack's mother lived, bursts of wind and rain shook against the carriage walls. Chute had insisted on hiring the coach instead of walking in the rain, but now he complained that the swaying carriage was no better than the ship. Some of the houses were ramshackle affairs, looking as though the storm might blow them to the ground. Jack wondered whether his mother had fallen on hard times. She had told him she had funds enough to live comfortably. Had she been lying, knowing that her son was too poor to send her much money? But soon the condition of the dwellings improved. A minute or two later the carriage came to a stop before Jack's mother's house: sturdy-looking stone with a half-timbered upper story, not spacious but more than adequate.

Elizabeth came to the door herself. The few years since he'd seen his mother had taken their toll: the silvered streaks in her hair had blended to a uniform gray, and she had thinned. Even so, she carried herself straight and retained some of her youthful vigor. She stepped into the rain to embrace her son before saying briskly, "Come, come, come, in from the rain. I've a big fire in the parlor where you can dry yourselves. And I'll get you something warm to drink."

Jack introduced his traveling companions to her. Burr said, "Somewhat to drink would warm the heart, as does the sound of a good English voice."

Chute said, "True enough. I am ignorance itself in this Dutchman's tongue. When the hostler spoke to us it seemed the gibbering of an ape. Your son knows enough to get us by, but I cannot tell a single word from the rest. Nor your French nor Spanish. Italian, though: I can speak your good Italian, like a native son."

"Are you bound for Italy?" Elizabeth asked.

"We are," said Chute, "and a merrier trio ne'er set foot upon good Roman soil."

"Well," Jack said, "we know not whither we will travel. To Italy it may hap. Or no."

Chute gave him a pained look and said, "We hope to go. We are bound to go. I think we will."

The men sat near the fire while Elizabeth and her maidservant, a fair-haired, plain-faced woman named Kaatje, busied themselves in the small, dimly lit kitchen. Once the women were gone, Chute groaned and said his queasy stomach wouldn't allow him to eat or drink anything. But when the mugs of steaming spiced wine appeared he took one and drank as readily as the others. Next came a course of mutton, eggs, and bread, which everyone, including Kaatje, ate not at the table but from trenchers on their laps as they sat about the fire.

Chute and Burr went to their beds in an upstairs room shortly after supper. Jack remained behind and talked with his mother while Kaatje cleaned the trenchers, bowls, and utensils in the kitchen. As far as Jack's mother knew, he was still an apostate, a Protestant. Yet she had welcomed him with an easy grace. Perhaps the years had slackened the fervor of her religion.

Elizabeth said, "Your letter told me little about your business in the Low Countries. This business: is it secret, or may I know of it?"

"You may." He spread his hands on his knees. "I have of late reconsidered my allegiance to the Church of England." It was true enough. How many times had he asked himself whether he had made the right choice? But he had resolved to remain a Protestant, and it pained him to mislead his mother.

She brightened. "So you're coming back!"

"So it would seem."

She rose with surprising quickness and embraced him. Damn this half-lying.

She backed away, holding his shoulders at arm's length as she said, "And the others?"

"The same. Both would be Catholics." That much, as far as he knew, was true of Chute, maybe even Burr. Like as not, though, Cecil had sent Burr along to keep watch on Jack. It would be easy enough for Burr to find ways of posting reports to Cecil.

Jack talked with his mother for over an hour. She wanted to know all about Anne and the children. "My one great regret," she said, "is never seeing my grandchildren. But I am a marked woman in England. My part in the good father's escape from the Tower is now known. I dare not risk returning."

Jack said, "Your part. . . . *You* helped Father Gerard escape?"

"I did. I supplied the bark that bore the father away, and I furnished the rope that let him reach the boat. He had persuaded a guard, a secret Catholic, to throw across the moat from the top of the Salt Tower a weighted string to where four of us—three trusted men and I—stood upon the shore. These hands tied the string to the free end of the rope, which the guard pulled up the wall to where he stood. He knotted the rope fast to a cannon atop the tower. Father Gerard climbed along the sagging line—with great pain and difficulty, I can tell you, for the manacles had stretched and snapped the sinews of his wrists—until he reached us on the shore. The good John Arden escaped in the same way. My doings on that night are now known, for the oarsman I hired was caught. The man betrayed us when Topcliffe fixed him to the rack. So I dare not go home. Nor could I write to tell you of it, for fear of harming you."

Jack hardly knew where to begin. "But . . . ," he stammered, "why did you not tell me about this plan of escape? I could have taken your place that night."

With a knowing little smile she slowly shook her head. "Jack," she said softly, "that was in '97. You had left the Church by then. You spoke of the Jesuits with nothing but contempt. Were these Catholic men who aided me to trust you to help a Jesuit escape?"

"You mean . . . were *you* to trust me."

Her eyes took on the look he remembered from his childhood, a look that said she knew of his wrongs but loved him still. "Yes, if you would know. I was not sure I could trust you. Why should I have thought otherwise?"

He chided her for not knowing he could be counted on, told her he liked to see no man, Jesuit or not, tortured and confined to the Tower. "But these Jesuits," he added, "do you not see the path they lay out for our young men leads to the scaffold? Do you not know the Jesuits play into the hands of Cecil, Topcliffe, and the rest, giving such tormentors good excuse to ply the manacles and the rack?"

She gave a little shrug and said, "Thus is it ever among the faithful. Are they to cease being holy because others are cruel?"

"No. But they might cease urging men to the torture chambers."

She tilted back her head in thought: a little shift in posture Jack had seen a thousand times but hadn't thought about in years. Somehow it made him at once love her and miss her company even as she sat before him, made him feel the weight of all those years apart.

"I think," she said, "many who are caught have done no wrong. Others have committed crimes for the benefit of the Church without the good fathers' blessing. Such men have acted on their own. Those who find a scheming Jesuit behind every hedge look upon the world through eyes of fear. And for this the faithful suffer, the Jesuits most of all."

They sat quietly while the embers glowed in the fireplace. The rain slanted against the shutters. After a time Jack asked, "Did you know Father Gerard returned to England for a time?"

"No," she said. "I thought he stayed in Rome after his escape."

Jack shook his head. "I spoke with him not a fortnight since."

She smiled. "Back for more, is he? I might have known."

"I told him it was madness."

She asked how he had come to meet Father Gerard, and he told her what he could. Then Jack said, "He heard my confession. He absolved my sins."

"Praise be."

Jack closed his eyes and said quietly, "Mother, I have such doubts as I quake to look upon."

"Not all doubts are sins."

"Hm. Father Gerard's words exactly."

She reached over and patted his hand. "Well. I will pray that God settle your doubts."

"Thank you," he said.

"Will you pray the same for yourself?"

Jack promised he would. After a while he asked whether she knew any Englishman calling himself Guido.

"None, I think," she said.

"I heard the man was in Sir William Stanley's employ."

"Oh. Well, you might ask Sir William."

"You know him?" She spoke as Stanley's familiar, as if he might be sitting in the next room.

"Oh, certainly. He has dined here often enough."

"So he is near."

"Yes, near enough. He commands a Catholic regiment camped hereabouts. If you like, I will send word to him. Maybe he can join us here."

Jack thanked her and asked her to write him. They talked awhile longer, mostly about King James and his court. Jack assured her he had little enough news; since his marriage he had enjoyed hardly any commerce with courtiers. He thought of Lord Hay's nephew, the Scotsman whose pate he had bloodied at the Savoy. Apart from Jack's encounters with Robert Cecil, about whom he said nothing to his mother, the young Scotsman was about as close as he had come to the court.

They watched the embers fade, and when the air grew chill they went to their beds. Jack had insisted that old Burr take the truckle-bed in Chute's room. Jack's pallet amounted to a straw mattress on the floor of the little room that doubled as his mother's library and sewing closet. Thanks to Kaatje, the mattress had been covered with linen and two thick blankets. But the flagstone floor beneath the mattress was hard and cold, his sleep fitful.

★ ★ ★ ★ ★

Francis Wolley sat with his brow pursed, the creases in his young forehead an unaccustomed thing. He idly opened and closed the latchet of an ornamental mulberry-wood box on the small table beside his chair. Anne watched him, remaining silent.

"Well," he said to her at last, "I'm not surprised the raven-eyed, the dragon-livered Lady Bedford would not hear of it. But you must know that neither can I simply hide you under my cloak and deposit you in Queen Anna's chambers. She would have my head. Now, if it were the *old* queen. . . ."

"I'm not asking you to do that, Francis. If you can do nothing more, at least keep your eyes open, and your ears. Some pathway will present itself."

"Hmph. You and your faith. Well, Providence may seem to show you a path, but Prudence tells you to leave well enough alone. . . . Oh, don't give me that look. I know that look. You could use it to curdle cheese."

Chapter 9

Anne kept the Wizard Earl's brisk pace along one of the labyrinthine corridors of Syon House. A plump, matronly servant followed, limping and wheezing. As the Earl chatted away—something about clocks, pendulums, pinions, and gears—Anne turned two or three times to offer the poor woman a sympathetic look. But the servant kept her head down, arms pumping as she plodded along. Finally the woman gave up the chase, stopping and puffing, her hand on her chest. She called, "Milord! Whither run ye?"

The Earl was saying, "And Anne, just as you arrived—clock room!—and just as you arrived, a remedy. That very moment, a remedy. Timely, no?"

"Timely. After all, the remedy is for a clock, is it not?"

"A new kind of—for a clock, yes. Oh, timely! For a clock, I see. Yes, very good, Anne. You have some of Jack's. . . . A new kind of pivot, this would be, with a weighted—one end weighted, the other notched. A notched sort of latchet, you see, that links with a pinion. That way, when—but here we are!" He turned into a room overlooking the courtyard, a noisy chamber cluttered with timepieces of every sort, on every surface: tables, walls, floors, even depending from the ceiling. It was a room busy with machines vying to outdo one another with their clatter. The Earl glanced around, bemused, as if he had lost his way. "Where did I . . . ? Haven't fashioned it yet, only drawn it. But the very moment you. . . . Where did . . . ? The paper: I laid the paper. . . . Well, no matter. Ah! That's it: I wasn't here. Schoolroom, must have been, where Jack and I. . . . With Harriot's glass. But no matter. I wanted you to see my clocks." He made a sweeping gesture as if Anne might not have noticed them.

There were table clocks, bracket clocks, and hooded clocks run with wound springs that turned gears, clicking with the linking and unlinking of metal parts. On the floor stood long-cased clocks powered by weights and governed by pendulums with pear-shaped bobs. Even the lamps were clocks, with markings on the glass to tell the hours as the oil burned. Most of one wall was taken up by a huge chamber-clock, ancient-looking with its cast-iron mechanism. "Two centuries old," said the Earl as he saw Anne looking at it. "From a castle in Lombardy. See? The hand that marks the hour is fixed; the dial turns behind." Anne told him she liked the craftsmanship of the brass dial with its engraved figures of the sun, moon, planets, and stars. She could hear the piece's works clattering but couldn't help noticing the clock was several hours off, reading just after nine in the morning when it must be nearly mid-afternoon. She glanced around the room: no two clocks, in fact, seemed to agree on the time.

The maidservant appeared in the doorway. His back to the door, the Earl somehow knew she was there: perhaps he heard her above the din as she tried to catch her breath. "Two centuries," he said. "More, it may be. Betsy, you missed three this morning that still want winding: the tall one by the door, the bronze drum on the low table, and—what was the third?—well, no matter. Ah! The little one in the maplewood case." The servant gave him a put-upon look and moved to adjust the weights in the tall case by the door. The Earl led Anne to a table beneath a window. "But this: this is more ancient still. Or the type is. Water. Far more ancient. Made it myself, but the type is old. You see? It drips, here. Steady drip. A *clepsydra,* the Greeks called it."

"*Clepsydra.* Oh, I see: a *water-thief.*"

"One drop at a time, yes. The water's height in the bowl here marks the hour on this board. But I added this: a dial, moved by the weight of the bowl, as it gets heavier through the day."

"Were it outdoors," Anne said, "you could use a stream to supply the water and never have to fill the cistern at the top."

Betsy said, "I would thank you for that, milord."

The Earl smiled in his eager, childlike way and said, "Yes, just so."

Next to the water clock a large, cone-shaped armature of steel rods with a brass chute spiraling down the outside rose above a tray containing wheels, gears, and two clock-hands of differing lengths. "What's this?" Anne asked. "It reminds me of the Tower of Babel."

The Earl laughed. "Yes. Mayhap the talk of Semiramis of Babylon put you in mind of it. But it is a clock. Runs for just two or three hours. My favorite nonetheless. This one's flaws I know, I think; I am perfecting the design. Twenty-four hours, at least, the next one. But look." He reached under the base of the cone, and she could hear him turning a crank or key. "Now," he said. "The weights inside are at the top. They supply the force." He touched a lever at the base, and a chain began to turn, conveying to the top of the cone little hinged cups, each containing a steel ball. When a cup reached the top it struck a platform and tilted, releasing the ball. One by one the balls aligned themselves at a gate, which opened to let a single ball pass. It rolled down the chute, slowly winding its way around the cone, until it triggered a mechanism as it dropped through a hole at the bottom. At that moment the gate opened at the top, and another ball began to descend. The first ball rolled to the chain, where the next empty cup scooped it up. "The eighth part of a minute from top to bottom," the Earl said. "Each ball. This spindle moves, turning these two gears, and they turn the hands. This one marks the hour; this, the very minute!"

"Astounding," said Anne, at once captivated by the machinery and eager to get on with what had brought her to see the Earl in the first place.

"And this," the Earl said as he moved to a table near the fireplace. He returned cradling a small clock in his hands.

Anne watched one more ball descend before turning to the Earl. "Oh!" she said, drawing back a step. "It's. . . ."

"Yes. A skull. Keep it in sight, good for the soul. *Memento mori.*"

Anne leaned a bit closer. She could hear the thing ticking. "It's. . . . How do you . . . ?"

"Ah, the best part: turn death on its head!" He rotated the skull bottom-up and lifted the jaw, revealing a dial. "Control time," he said, "and you control death. No? You look . . . how? Unconvinced."

"It's just that . . . death is already controlled. And so is time."

"Yes, yes, Providence. Be sure: I but cooperate with the Providence. Perfectly pious, this activity." He watched her as she turned her head slightly away. "Anne. What, doubtful still?"

"Yes, somehow." She looked at him. He had the eyes of an innocent, overanxious boy. "Lord Henry, a thing can be pious but not prudent."

"How is this imprudent? Any of it."

"Yours is the church, remember, that put Giordano Bruno to death."

"Yes. Dark day. Friend. But stubborn, Giordano. Heresy, they said. And a spy for Walsingham. But I don't believe that."

"Nor do I. But Bruno was condemned by his own countrymen to burn at the stake."

"Published things he shouldn't."

"And in *this* country you don't have to publish anything. You are already a heretic for merely remaining a Catholic." Anne noticed that Betsy was beginning to take an interest in the conversation, so she lowered her voice. "You must be prudent: this talk of controlling time—"

"Yes, though it is but the first step." The Wizard Earl seemed unaware of the maidservant's eavesdropping, but he lowered his voice to match Anne's. "The first step is understanding time: marking it, measuring it. Clocks: prudent, perfectly."

"But you think marking it will lead to the control of it."

"The first step, yes. Control it." He lowered his voice still more. "*Reverse* it, perhaps." Before Anne could protest, he hurried on: "The whole course of it will take learning, craftsmanship, alchemy, philosophy, prayer. . . . Plenty of prayer, be sure."

She folded her arms. "Theurgy?"

"Mayhap, yes." He added in a whisper, "But not . . . what's the word?"

"Goety."

"Even so. Yes, goety."

Anne said in a low whisper, "But whether white or black, you talk of *magic*. Some of the learned say all of it proceeds from the Devil."

"And some say wrongly."

She let out a little puff of exasperation. "You miss the point. Even if God allows theurgy, King James does not. You put yourself—and your friends—in danger."

"Years, Anne. It will take years. Lifetimes, maybe. Others will complete it. But I have well begun. Measurement is only the first step."

"Measurement. Then tell me this, Lord Henry: What is the time of day?"

The Earl seemed momentarily confused, then resolved to answer. He looked from one clock to another, lifted a hand in a gesture of explanation, scratched the back of his neck, and at last turned to his servant. "Betsy, what is the time of day?"

She moved to the window and glanced at the sun. "Ha' past two, milord."

Jack sat upright on his makeshift bed, his brow moist despite the cold. Troubled by a deep sense of dread, he recalled parts of the dream. A groaning and splintering of wood, a spray of sea, the massive prow of a ship looming out of the fog, the strange, forsaken cry of sea-bird or woman. . . . The images began to fall into place: through some queasy ill-doing of his own—he could not recall just what—sea-waves raged around him as he stood alone on a stone promontory jutting from a craggy peninsula. The waves crashed at his feet, covering him with their spume, but somehow he did not get wet. Then above the roar of the sea rose a great noise of the wrenching and shivering of wood. A moment later he saw through the mist and spray the cause: a ship had run aground, breaking apart before his eyes. In the bow stood his mother, who cast on him a mournful gaze, then extended both arms—too far to reach—as the splintered ship retreated. Then somehow it was not his mother but Anne, with the same look of woe, clutching to her breast a bundle of rags containing perhaps a child. With her free arm she reached toward him. He leaned as far as he could, and the ship surged ahead. His hand brushed against Anne's, then caught a corner of the infant's swaddling as he fell from the crag, wresting the bundle from her grasp. He tried to call out to his wife, give her some parting assurance of his love. No sound emerged. He stretched to reach the child spinning above him, but the infant tumbled just beyond his grasp. He spun and plummeted through the mist, then jerked awake.

Now he held his head in his hands, rubbed his eyes with the heels of them, let out a great breath as if he had held it in a long time. A dream. Only a dream, perhaps, signifying but an uneasy sleep, no more. Or was it the bearer of some message, some truth, some course marked out by which he might spare harm to mother, wife, and child? Or did it presage a bitter, unavoidable end?

He heard someone stirring overhead, then slow, unshod footfalls on the stairs. It was Burr. The old man carried his boots in one hand while the other worked along the rail. "Ah, Master Jack, I did not want to wake you."

"I am full awake, Tim."

"You look something taken aback, if I may say."

"You may. I am. It was a dream."

"Ah."

"Do you think they mean anything, Tim, our dreams?"

Burr sat on a stool Jack's mother apparently used to reach books on the highest shelves. It was his mother, not the father he could hardly remember, nor his stepfather Dr. Syminges, good man though he was, who had first taught Jack to read, had fostered his love of books.

Old Burr began to pull on his boots. "Oh, yes, I should think so. But we may come as near construing our dreams as we may parse verbs in . . . are there languages you do not speak, Master Donne?"

Jack smiled. "Yes, Tim." He thought a moment. "The Jesuits in the Far East write of sacred scriptures of the Brahmins of India penned in a tongue called Sanskritan. I know nothing of this Sanskritan."

"As we may parse verbs in the Sanskritan tongue, then."

"And there are many other tongues whereof I comprehend not a word. As you well know." He paused. "So you think we may not read our dreams."

"Oh," said Burr, "I think they are legible. But we have lost the wit to read the book of the world, of which our dreams compose a chapter. Or it may hap a few still remember, darkly."

"You have some learning, Tim. Where did you get it?"

"Westminster. Before the time of the Queen's Scholars. Some six or eight of us with one schoolmaster. Our fathers paid him. Or mine paid his part, at least, until I reached some eleven or twelve years."

"What happened then?"

Burr considered the matter. "Master Jack, you and I like a cup or two of wine. My father liked many cups of wine."

"Ah. I see. And so your schooling ended."

"And so my schooling ended. As did much else."

While Betsy gathered a few books and papers from a pile by the door, where the Wizard Earl had apparently left them, Anne leaned close to his ear and whispered, "Could we talk privily?"

The Earl gave her a puzzled look and whispered back, "But we *are* talking privily."

"I mean without Betsy in the room. I have a thing to ask that is for no ear but yours."

"Oh, of course," he said. "She is here but for your . . . what do you call it?"

"My assurance of your honorable intent."

"Just so."

"I do not question your intent, and she may remain in the passage without the door, so that no one will question it."

The Earl told Betsy to close the door, pull up a chair, and wait outside. The servant glared at him, then seemed to consider that sitting for a while might not be a bad thing. She bustled out and shut the door—a bit louder, Anne thought, than needful.

It was just two or three days before he left that Jack had visited Syon House, but at the time Anne's thoughts had been all on his longer journey. She wished she had pressed him for more details about how much he had confided to the Earl. "You know," she said, "Jack is gone to the Low Countries?"

The Earl thought a moment, then said, "I knew he was about to set out for. . . . The Low Countries, is it? Maybe he told me so. Ah! His mother: his mother lives in Antwerp, does she not?"

"Yes. I think he is there now, but not only to see his mother. He has—" and here she let her voice carry the weight of the implication—"other business."

The Earl's face turned thoughtful, then grave. "It won't work," he said.

Anne felt her breath give way. She squeezed out barely audible words: "Are you certain?"

"Oh, quite."

"But how do you know? Is he in danger?"

The Earl looked puzzled. "Who?"

"Who? Jack, of course. It won't work, you said. Is he in danger?"

"Why should he be in danger? Oh: you're worried about his conversion." The Earl's face betrayed his sudden awareness he had said more than he should. "I mean to say, you know about that, do you not? Or no. Forget what I just said. Or didn't say."

Anne felt a little dizzy, the way she did as a child when she spun herself in circles, then abruptly stopped. She gripped the arms of her chair and said, "His conversion? Yes, I know about that." So Jack had told the Earl the story of his rejoining the Church of Rome but not the story behind it: that the conversion was feigned. Why then did the Earl say Jack's other business would fail?

"Oh, good," the Earl said. "I revealed too much, I thought. Perhaps. But why are you worried? Jack travels in Catholic lands. He'll be safe enough."

"Then why then did you say it won't work? What won't work?"

"Why, the weighted pivot, of course, with the notched end. It won't work because the rod that fits into the notch would interfere with—"

Anne's burst of laughter startled the Earl into silence. It was the first time she could remember laughing since Jack's departure—for some time, even, before that. She allowed the laughter full reign, and the Earl's bemused look only spurred it on, as did his sudden realization, some moments later, what she thought so funny. The Earl began to chuckle too, and by the time it was over, Anne was wiping the tears from her face.

Finally the Earl asked, "But what of this other business of Jack's? You said he had other business."

Anne tried to keep her tone light. "Yes, an Englishman called Guido. Do you know him? A Catholic."

"Guido. Someone else was asking. . . . Who was it? Someone. . . . Well, I know not. But I have heard of the man. It is important that you find him?"

"Yes, very."

"Let me. . . . One or two of the Jesuits, I think, are in London. Let me find them and make some inquiries. If they know his whereabouts, I will send word to you."

The travellers had stayed in Antwerp almost a week when word came back from Lord Stanley: he would be most pleased to dine with Jack's mother and three converts to the Old Faith. He had business in the city in four days' time and would be honored to visit on Saturday night.

On Friday Chute went out on his own to buy Jack's mother a gift. After three or four hours he hadn't returned. Burr said, "Lost, no doubt. Wandering these labyrinthine streets in search of this house, a stranger to the Dutch tongue, the Spanish, and the French."

"But his Italian—" said Jack.

Burr rolled his eyes. "Is excellent. Must we go and look for him, Master Jack?"

"I suppose so. But it's just as well; my mother could do with some respite." Elizabeth started to protest, but Jack could see he was right.

The two men walked for perhaps half an hour, encompassing several blocks. They saw no sign of Chute—only cloth-merchants, carters, fishmongers, a trio of chattering, jostling apprentices just out after their day's work, a cluster of boys bolting from a schoolhouse, a street-quean who traced her fingers along her neck as she looked longingly at Jack. When Burr lingered a moment outside a tavern, Jack said, "How about somewhat to drink?"

"The way you read my thoughts, Master Donne, is more than canny."

Once inside, Jack and Burr waited near the door to let their eyes adjust to the dimness within. It was a large room. At a table in the back a group of men, already drunk before the winter sun had set, sang a bawdy catch in Dutch. The simple refrain was easy enough to decipher, easy to set in an English rhyme:

Lift up a flagon to Greasy-Lipped Gret;
She loves every drinking man she's ever met.

As Jack started to move toward an unoccupied bench to their left, Burr reached to stay him. The old man pointed toward a small table to their right. There sat Chute with his back to them, leaning over the table in earnest conversation with a dark-browed, olive-skinned man. Jack edged nearer. Chute was speaking quietly, so Jack had to stand within just a few feet to hear. As the song across the room ended and Chute's voice became clear, Jack felt his pulse quicken. *Dutch.* Chute was speaking Dutch—and fluently.

Jack looked at Burr, whose habitually impassive face for once registered surprise: the old man's brows arched over his red-rimmed hound's eyes. Jack listened, mentally translating Chute's words. *No,* he was saying, *he thinks me a true papist.* When Jack turned back to the table, the dark-browed man opposite Chute glanced up to meet his eye. Jack turned away as untellingly as he could and eased Burr along the wall and out the door.

Once outside, Burr said, "My old ears are untrusty, filled as they remain with a continual chorus of locusts and crickets, with God knows what other creeping things to swell the din. Am I nonetheless correct in identifying Sir Walter's jabber as the very tongue we hear spoken in these streets?"

"You are."

"No Italian, that. What does it mean?"

Jack hesitated. What had Chute just said? "*He* thinks me a true papist," not "*They* think. . . ." The *he* could be Cecil, or Jack himself. But if *he* meant Jack, what then of Burr? Had Chute simply left the servant out of account, or did it mean Burr was in league with him? Jack looked into Burr's sagging eyes, but they betrayed no sign. Well, even if the old man couldn't be trusted, there was no point in letting him know Jack suspected him. He said, "It means Chute is a spy."

Burr considered it. "Well. That puts the two of us in something of a bind, does it not?"

The next night Sir William Stanley sat at the head of the table, the sucked-clean bones of a capon arranged in neat rows on the trencher before him. He made a point of keeping his face composed, his wind-chapped lips turned up slightly as if in mild contentment, as Elizabeth told a tale of Jack's misbehavior in childhood. What to make of this gathering? Most likely all of it was true, just as Elizabeth had said: two converts to the Church of Rome and their old servant, also a would-be Catholic, on a trek to Catholic lands. It was clear Elizabeth thought it true—and faithful Catholic that she remained, welcomed the event. But what woman could not be easily misled?

Englishmen in the flush of youth turning Catholic, setting out for adventure on the Continent: that much was hardly unusual. Stanley had seen plenty of them, and this Walter Chute looked the part. But Jack Donne could no longer be considered young—he must be around thirty—and he spoke with a canny command of his wits. The man bore watching. The old servant must have grown up during the time when England was Catholic. Perhaps he simply wanted to return to his childhood faith. Or maybe he travelled in league with Donne or Chute or both, having joined the ranks of Cecil's spies.

As Kaatje cleared the table, Stanley took from his pocket a flat wooden box containing a deck of Primero cards. Elizabeth set a neat's-leather coin-purse on the table before her. Chute pulled out money of his own and said, "I must extend fair warning: I seldom lose at Primero."

"Time will tell," Stanley said. "If you can win our Elizabeth's money, you must needs play with more skill than many a man I know."

"Do not fear it," Chute replied. "Only I must grant due warning to our charming hostess: when I play, I play to win. The fair sex must expect no gentle treatment at my hand. But then, upon game's end, I shall graciously restore all I have won from her." Having said this, he rose and bowed deeply.

Elizabeth glanced at Burr, flashed him a little wink, then nodded solemnly to Chute. "In that event," she said, "I shall decline the recompense. But the event has yet to come to pass."

Stanley allowed himself to grin, then dealt the cards. He paused as he came to Burr. Jack said, "Join us, Tim."

Burr replied, "I fear—"

"No fear," Jack said. "I will stake you. I think, in fact, it is the only way my money is like to multiply. You know the game?"

"Oh, yes, although your faith in my prowess may be misplaced. Nonetheless at the least you shall learn a valuable lesson about investing your money unwisely."

"Well worth the stake."

Stanley dealt the rest of the cards, and the bidding began. Chute wagged his head a little and smiled smugly as he won the first round. He raked in the coins and said, "I warned you, did I not?"

After that, though, his luck changed. When he produced a primero, Elizabeth held a maximus. When Chute triumphantly displayed a maximus, Elizabeth trumped him with a fluxus. At one point she even drew a chorus: when she laid out all four knaves, Chute slammed his cards to the table in disgust. In the next hand Elizabeth bluffed with a mere numerus, taking the coins after everyone else passed. Jack won only three or four hands all evening, Stanley just one or two. Burr took in far more than his share. At the game's end, sizable stacks of coins stood before Elizabeth, while Burr's winnings lay carelessly heaped in a pile.

Elizabeth nodded to Chute and said, "We must play again sometime. I am sure your luck will return when we do."

Stanley watched the color rise along Chute's face, pinking his cheeks and purpling his ears as he replied, "Tonight it proved luck. Then you will see skill."

Burr slid his pile of coins toward Jack, who shoved them back. Burr objected: "I am but your servant, playing upon your stake—albeit a good and faithful servant, not like the one in the Bible who hides his talent under a bushel, or howsoever the story goes. Or say I am your alchemic stabler, making two pieces of barren metal breed." In the end the two agreed that Burr would repay only the few shillings it took to make up Jack's original stake, so that the old man pocketed a tidy sum.

Stanley continued to watch the men closely. Especially this Jack Donne proved a puzzle. There was no clear reason to doubt he was sincere about his conversion, but there was something about him. . . .

Elizabeth stayed with the men after the game, puffing the bowl in her turn as Stanley passed around his tobacco-pipe. At length Jack said to him, "Father Gerard told me I would do well to seek out an Englishman called Guido, but the good father knew not where the man kept himself. Have you heard of this Guido?"

Stanley took care that his eyes betrayed nothing of his suspicion as he said, "Gerard told you this, did he? Yes, a worthy pioner, this Guido, as crafty with a petard as any I know. He fought under my command, and fought ably, not two months since. He is gone now, gone to Rome. He stays there, I think, at the English Jesuits' college."

"Aha!" said Chute. "Rome! I knew in my very bones we were bound for Italy. When do we depart?"

"Soon, I think," Jack said. "I fear we have overtaxed my mother already."

"You have not," she protested, and she sounded as if she meant it.

Stanley turned to Jack and said, "Your mother's graciousness is without limit—as is her beauty."

Elizabeth's look said she had heard such things from him before and did not much like hearing them, but at least she nodded in acknowledgment.

Without so much as a glance at Chute, Burr added, "And as of tonight, so is her wealth."

Chute paused a moment, then said, "Well, tonight I care not what you say, sirrah Tim. We are bound for Rome!"

"One other thing," Jack said to Stanley. "Has he any other name, this Guido?"

Stanley looked Jack in the eye just long enough to say, "None that he cares to use. His work, my work, and yours, Master Donne—fighting for the Mother Church against the apostates now controlling the English throne—requires some circumspection. The Jesuits in Rome will know him by the single name. It will be all you need." He put on a smile and turned to Chute as he added, "But I trust you shall find that Rome answers all your hopes. And the Jesuits there are most hospitable."

Chapter 10

The Wizard Earl's note lay open on the table: he had not been able to learn from the English Jesuits any news about an English Guido. When Anne first read the message, her heart misgave. Then she found herself half angry at the Earl for failing to choose his words with enough care to avoid trouble had the letter been intercepted. She closed her eyes in prayer, asking God to give her patience and to show her a way to help Jack. And not two hours later, her prayers were answered.

Anne embraced her cousin, who stood pouting before her. Then she held him at arm's length and said, "Thank you, Francis! This is the sort of intelligence I can use. Somerset House, you say? Tomorrow?"

Francis turned from her and replied, "Yes, tomorrow, if you must know. This new Scots porter trains today with the old, then tomorrow keeps the post on his own. But I like it not. This whole business of paying her servants for such information: it can lead to no good. If I can pay them to talk, then so can someone else, and they will prove no more loyal than a Frenchman. For my own name's sake I say I like not this business." He turned back and faced her. "But even more for your sake. What you propose, in so far as I understand it, puts you in danger. Do you not think Queen Anna will arrest you the moment she sees you?"

"I will be alone. Do I look like a threat to any woman or

man? I will trust my tongue to work nimbly enough to forestall any arrest."

"Think of your children."

"I *am* thinking of them. The children need their father home again, and I work to that end."

"Well," he said petulantly, "I like it not."

"I understand. But I thank you, Francis. Now no word of this to anyone."

"Oh, fear me not on that account. I would fain forget my part in it."

The next morning the splendid coach Anne had hired with her cousin's money pulled up at the gatehouse of Somerset, where Queen Anna of Denmark kept court while King James remained at Westminster. Anne handed the new porter, a dull-eyed young man with red hair and a carbuncular face, a card on which Francis had written, in a disguised version of his beautifully florid hand, *The Lady Bedford.* The porter took the card and held it next to a short list of names. He looked from card to list and back again for what seemed minutes. He scratched his head. At last Anne tried to turn her nervousness to irritation as she said, "Come, sirrah: what, are you a porter and cannot read? Where is the usual man at this post? I am the Lady Lucy Harrington Russell, Countess of Bedford. I know my name is there on the list. Give me the paper, and I will show you."

"No, no, not necessary," the porter said. "I know my letters, and can see the name here on the list, plain enough. You may proceed." Anne snatched the card from the porter's hand as he nodded to the coachman.

Inside the marble-columned anteroom, Anne gave the tall, dour-faced doorman another card, this one reading, *Condesa de Mediana.* He took the card and said, "My lady Countess, I am afraid I do not understand. I was not informed of your visit today."

"Not . . . eenformed? Monsieur Cecil, ze Secretary: Cecil, 'ee give me assure. . . . I am sorry very much: my Angleesh, no ees good. *¿Habla Español? Parlez Français?*"

"No, my lady, English only, and Danish. But Secretary Cecil sent you, do you say?"

"Yes! 'Ee say call on ze Queen today. At zis houer."

"Very well, then. Pray have a seat, and I will return momentarily."

"Pray?" She placed her hands together in a reverent posture and gave him a quizzical look.

"No. Sit. Here." He gestured toward a chair. "Sit, please, and I will return soon."

"*Si!* Soon."

Anne sat as he disappeared into an adjoining room. She smoothed her dress, the same one Francis had bought for her visit to Lady Bedford. The stiff bodice exposed more flesh than Anne would have liked, but Francis had said such was the fashion among the Spanish. He said the dress looked lovely on her. Exquisite, even.

A moment later the doorman appeared again. He knelt and motioned to the open doorway as he said, "Her Royal Majesty, Anna of Denmark and Norway, Queen of Scotland, England, and Ireland."

The Queen entered, attired no more elegantly than Anne. Two ladies-in-waiting followed. Anna of Denmark was a plump woman with pale skin, a large straight nose, wiry blonde hair, and kindly eyes. Anne dipped into a deep curtsey as she took the Queen's extended hand. The doorman said, "The Countess of Villa Mediana." The Queen gestured her to rise, then moved to embrace her.

Anne used the moment to take the greatest chance of that risky day, trusting everything to the rumor that the Queen held secret Catholic Masses to which her husband turned a blind eye. Just after kissing the Queen's cheek, Anne whispered, "Father Gerard sent me."

The Queen took a step back, a look of alarm momentarily crossing her face. Almost immediately, though, her expression changed to curiosity. For several heartbeats she peered closely into Anne's eyes. The Queen then whisked a hand toward her ladies-in-waiting and said, "Leave us alone for a time. We will occupy the blue room." She spoke carefully, as if making an effort to suppress her words' remaining Northern inflections, both Danish and Scots, as if conscious of conforming each utterance to the London courtly dialect. The effect was to make her sound distant and unapproachable, but her gestures flowed with welcoming ease. The attendants stepped aside as the Queen led Anne down a hallway and into a small, sparsely appointed room. "This chamber," she said as she sat, motioning for Anne to do the same, "will be changed, even in a few days. Most of the—how do you say?—*furnishings* have already been removed. Do you know the man Inigo Jones?"

"I have heard the name, and I think my husband knows him. An architect, is he not?"

"Yes. That is the word: *architect.*" The Queen was so careful to pronounce every part of the word she gave it five syllables. "Mr. Jones has designed all the changes. Even now, he is with his. . . . How do you say . . . his *pictures*?"

"His drawings. His plans for the renovation."

"Yes, *drawings.* What is this *renovation*?

"It means *a thing made new again.*

Queen Anna nodded and said, "I see." She folded her hands in her lap, then said, "So your husband knows him."

"I think so, yes."

"And when you speak of your husband, I do not think you mean Count Juan de Tassis of Villa Mediana, do you?"

Anne lowered her eyes. "No, Your Majesty."

"I met Señor de Tassis at the peace conference here last summer. He said his wife the Countess was old and ailing." With only a hint of a smile the Queen added, "Either you are not the Countess or your recovery has been remarkable."

Anne took a deep breath. "I needed to see you."

"And here you are. But *who* you are, I have not yet learned."

"My name is Anne Donne. Before I married I was Anne More, Sir George More's daughter and the Lord Keeper's niece."

"Ah. And your husband?"

"John Donne, who was the Lord Keeper's secretary before we wed."

"Oh, yes. I have heard something of this marriage. Sir George has not been—how do you say?—*sparing* of his displeasure."

"Quite so."

"You said Father Gerard sent you. Might I ask whether that also was untrue?"

Looking directly at the Queen, Anne said, "It was quite true." She thought she carried off the deception—an entirely unaccustomed thing for her—fairly well. In fact she was surprised at how easy it seemed.

The Queen's face remained unreadable, a blank mask, as she replied, "You are subject to arrest: not only for falsely imposing upon our person but for commerce with a Catholic priest, and what is more, a Jesuit priest."

"I am aware of my guilt and of the risk to myself, Your Majesty, and I beseech your pardon. Know, though, I have information that concerns the safety of the realm, and of the Royal Household in especial."

The Queen relaxed in her chair, as if learning about threats to her family were the most ordinary thing in the world. "Speak on."

"I devoutly believe Father Gerard when he says that he and

the other Jesuits desire no harm to any rightfully appointed sovereign: not to your family nor any other lawful princes. The Jesuits are here only to administer the sacraments to their flock."

With a languid wave of the hand, the Queen replied, "They say these things, yes."

"I believe them. And a token of their troth is that they have sent me to warn you about a hot-headed Catholic who means violence to your family."

The Queen fingered the string of pearls about her neck. "And who might this—how have you said it?—*hot-head*—be?"

"He is an Englishman called *Guido,* known by no other name to the good father. This Guido must be found and stopped before he sets his plan in motion." Anne knew nothing of any plan against the throne, whether hatched by Guido or anyone else, but why else would Cecil have set Jack on the trail of the man? Perhaps the lie's plausibility was what made it easy for her to deliver it with conviction.

"But what is this plan?"

"I do not know, nor does Father Gerard. But he has learned from some conscience-stricken soul that evil plans are laid, and that Guido lies at the heart of them."

"I see. But why do you come to me with these news? Why not to his Majesty—or rather, to his chief minister, Lord Cecil? He is the one who busies himself with such matters, not I."

Anne hesitated. She had anticipated this question but somehow found the words difficult to form. Her stomach knotted, and tears pooled in her eyes. She gathered a deep breath before saying, "As a secret Catholic, I am afraid to go to him. He would want to know where Father Gerard stayed when I talked to him, and Lord Cecil might not believe me when I told him what I now swear to you: I know not the whereabouts of Father Gerard or any other Jesuit. Father Gerard was about to travel when I spoke with him, and he did not tell me where he is bound. Nor would he have told me if I had asked."

"So you fear Lord Cecil for yourself, and for the Jesuits."

"Yes. Lord Cecil would perhaps blame me and almost certainly blame them for this business. But they are not at fault. I thought that with your Catholic friends, you might make inquiries enough to learn this Guido's whereabouts. You could then reveal these news to me, and my husband would do the rest."

The Queen rose from her chair, took a few paces, and stood looking out the window at the courtyard below before asking, "What makes you think I have Catholic friends?"

"I do not know that you do, your Majesty. But Father Gerard thought it would be good for me to talk with you, if I could find a way."

The Queen turned and eyed Anne for a long time before saying, "I see. You ask me to take in hand a weighty affair of state, and to trust you with the same. Are not such things matters for men—for his Majesty, Lord Cecil, and the others in the Privy Council?"

Hardly knowing how to reply, Anne said haltingly, "But we women. . . ."

With a wry little smile the Queen said, "I have always found the—how do you say it?—the *function*—of ladies in affairs of state rather too—what is the word?—ah, *circum*—"

"Circumscribed?"

"Yes, I think that is the word. *Circumscribed,* or—how do you say?—*limited.* Do you not find the same?"

"Oh, yes!" Anne said.

"I will find out what I can. Expect to hear from me soon."

Jack sat at his mother's writing-table. He dipped his pen but held it above the paper. He wanted to write a poem for Anne, but first it was time—long past time, in fact—to send a report to Cecil. Jack had not written since sending a short, uninformative note upon landing at Antwerp. What to write, though? He could report making contact with Sir William Stanley, and should Cecil use another of his spies to verify the account, the details of time and place would agree. Nor would the report put Stanley in any further danger than the man himself had already chosen; Stanley had long since declared himself the enemy of Protestant England. He was protected in the Spanish Netherlands, and in any case nothing Jack said in his report would prove damning. As for this Guido. . . . Jack held the pen, hesitating. Stanley had said Guido was in Rome with the English Jesuits. Almost certainly Guido's life would be forfeit once Cecil learned his whereabouts, maybe even in the Catholic stronghold of the English College in Rome. Jack would have made up a little lie—would say perhaps that Guido had gone to the Jesuit seminary in Rheims—but like as not, Chute was also reporting to Cecil. Maybe even Burr could not be trusted. Cecil's scheme for this whole venture seemed to rely on Jack's finding Guido by using his wits. Chute's commission, or even Burr's, would be to kill Guido. What then had Cecil ordered the other two to do with Jack himself? Once the three companions found Guido, Jack would have to watch his own back. In the end he saw no choice but to tell Cecil the truth, trusting that when the time came he could protect himself. Maybe the Jesuits in Rome could help.

Jesuits. Jack could hardly think the word without rankling. The very sound of it turned him queasy with the memory of his brother Henry's last hours of agony. Yet now he found himself wondering whether his response accorded with the threat the Jesuit priests really posed. Were they in fact stirring England's young Catholics to bloody rebellion? Or, as they claimed, did they risk their lives but to bring the sacraments to the faithful, whose souls pined and famished for their lack? Certainly Robert Cecil wanted him to think of Jesuits exactly as the twisted little man already thought of them: as fanatics who, in their blind allegiance to the Pope, threatened to bring England to its knees. But did the real Jesuits he had known match Cecil's portrait? Father Gerard hardly seemed the wild-eyed firebrand. As for Jack's Jesuit uncles, in childhood he had known his Uncle Ellis only through the priest's letters to England and the stories Jack's mother told. The letters were at once inspirational and witty, and Elizabeth's tales were filled with nothing but her brother's heroic resolve. But Uncle Jasper: Jack still wavered between remembering him as a thoroughly faithful Christian, willing to risk all for his Lord and Church, and a showy leader careless of the lives of the young men he stirred to supposed martyrdom.

In the failing light, Jack gave up trying to write to Cecil. He turned to his mother as she sat at the hearth. Sir William Stanley had left soon after the game of Primero, and Burr and Chute had gone to bed. The fire smoldered in a few smokeless, blue-gray embers. The only light came from a lamp that had begun to sputter, its oil all but spent. "I want to ask you to do something for me," Elizabeth said.

"Of course. Anything."

"There is a treasure of untold value I have kept hidden hereabouts for some dozen years. Much trouble went into getting it to me here, getting it out of England. Still, our hope is that one day, in happier times, it will return to its home. For now, though, I would ask you to take it to the English Jesuits in Rome. Give it to Father Parsons there; he will know what to do with it."

"Of course."

"Wait here." She disappeared into her bedroom and closed the door behind her. Jack sat for what seemed a long time. He knew by the glow beneath his mother's bedroom door that she had lit a lamp. A few minutes later he heard her turn the key to another door, or perhaps to some piece of locking furniture. She returned to the fireside with a plain but well-made wooden box, a cube that just fit in her slender lap. She inserted a brass key into a lock in the box's side. She lifted the lid, gently folded back some cloths inside, and carefully handed the treasure to Jack.

The first thing he noticed was the smell, at once musty and bespiced. Tilting the lamp a little to see by the faltering light, he peered into the box. It took him a heartbeat or two to make out the contents. The instant he did, he nearly dropped the box. Staring up at him through vacant eyes—or holes where eyes used to be—lay a human skull. Three small patches of skin and hair still clung to the crown and the sides of the head; the aromatic scent must come from some mummifying preservative in the cloth.

"What—who—is this?" he asked. He stared at his mother, whose expression was peaceful, even beatific.

"It is a relic of wondrous power," she said. "Through it—through *him*—many prayers have been answered, my own prayers and those of others. He has already blessed me beyond all reckoning. After my prayers yesternight I received assurance that it is time to turn him over to the holy fathers. My plan was to return him to England, had King James kept his word. But hopes for that are past. One day I think he will once again see English soil, but for now take him to Father Parsons in Rome; your sojourn to that holy city is providential."

"Perhaps," he said drily. "But whose head is it?"

"Have you not guessed? This is our kinsman, Sir Thomas More." The lamplight was nearly spent, but still his mother's face seemed to glow.

Thomas More. Jack's great-great-grand-uncle, or a piece of him—the man whose smooth forehead had sheltered perhaps the most brilliant mind in England, whose eloquent lips had amused the learned with their wit and moved the mighty with their counsel—now gaped stupidly at his latter-day kinsman, a few ragged teeth hanging here and there along the jaws. One of the missing teeth had split between Jack's two Jesuit uncles, both gone now to their graves. And More himself was reduced to this. *Well, all flesh is grass,* Jack reminded himself, *even Thomas More's. And bone is only tougher grass.* Still, the more Jack peered into the casket in his hands, the more the bones seemed to take on a tremulous light, the faintest whisper of a greenish gleam, along cheekbone and jaw. A mere trick of the sputtering lamp, perhaps. Or was it something more, something Elizabeth's luminous eyes devoutly beheld? What manner of man did these empty sockets and thin-boned jaws bespeak? Faithful martyr or mere fool?

Thomas More. Maybe a riddling poem lay in the name. Thomas. *Thom:* Hebrew for fathomless depth, or *Toma:* Aramaic for twin, for mere redundancy. A twinned, split tooth, nothing more. More. *Mehr:* Teutonic for something beyond what lies in hand, or*Moros:* Greek for fool, as the good Sir Thomas well knew. A fool for Christ—a saint someday, perhaps—or a mere fool for the Pope: a worldly pontiff if the world had ever seen one. Pope Paul III, the one who fathered three bastard children, the one who dispatched the nettlesome Ignatius of Loyola by making him head of a new religious order: the Jesuits, with all their missionary zeal.

For the thousandth time dark doubts troubled Jack's mind. There had been a time when he would have gladly gone the way of More: would have tossed away his own life for the sake of the Holy Catholic Church as frankly and as cheerfully as had his kinsman. In those days the Holy Virgin often graced Jack with her love, assuring him more than once with the same divine message that had brought comfort to Julian of Norwich two centuries before: *All shall be well, and all shall be well, and all manner of thing shall be well.* He had believed the promise with his whole heart. Yes, there had been such a time. Then he had left that church for another, convinced that the leaving of it was God's will despite the hurt it cost his mother. After all, had not Our Lord said that he who would not spurn father and mother for the sake of the Kingdom of God was unworthy to be a disciple? Yet at any point would Jack Donne have given up his life, smilingly or otherwise, for the sake of the Church of England? He doubted it. Had he merely taken the easy path in abandoning the forbidden church for the officially sanctioned one, all the while fooling himself into thinking he was doing God's will? Had he in truth played the traitor to God, to the Catholic Church, to the Jesuit order, to his own family, perhaps to his innermost self? Were the very bones of his kinsman Thomas More mocking him with their mindlessly maniacal grin? Did they taunt him while they revealed to his mother the viridescent promise of a glorified, resurrected body? Here she sat without a trace of accusation, with nothing but love in her eyes. In that moment Jack felt utterly unworthy of that love, felt himself nothing but a traitor to her and to so much else: a hired henchman of Robert Cecil, the twisted little lord who leered after Anne More. Maybe the gibbous-backed schemer was seducing her even now.

From aught that Jack could read or hear of him, Thomas More never felt such doubts. Even at the end, when More's prison-weary legs could hardly bear him up the steps to the scaffold, he remained the faithful jokester. To the lieutenant he said, "Pray, sir, see me safe up; and as to my coming down, let me shift for myself." Then he told the crowd—some jeering, some weeping—that he died the King's good servant but God's first. Next, after reciting the *Miserere mei* psalm and heartily forgiving the huge, hooded executioner, he looked up and reminded the man, "My neck is very short; take heed therefore thou strike not awry." Last, he stayed the axe-man just before the fatal blow and draped his beard over the front of the block. "For it has committed no treason," he said. The hooded man did his work. Mercifully, one blow was all it took.

Then, through all the vagaries of chance or all the persistence of faith, the blessed head had tumbled into the box in Jack's hands. Before that, he knew, More's skull had served its month at the end of a pikestaff on London Bridge. How then could scalp or hair remain, even in these leathery patches? A miracle, Jack's mother would say. Or perhaps nesting season was simply over, and the gulls on the Thames no longer had need of it. Or maybe this good woman before him, her face somehow still aglow, had been duped. Maybe the bones in the box belonged to someone else: not the jesting, other-worldly martyr More but some thick-witted, plodding plowman whose shock at leaving the earth remained imprinted on the bones. Well. There was no good in suggesting such things to her. She believed, and that was enough. "Of course I will take this relic to Father Parsons," he said.

Elizabeth placed her hand on his, saying, "I am now certain: one day these bones will return home to England. Maybe sooner than we think."

Jack doubted it. Almost to a man, these Jesuits—Robert Parsons not the least of them—proved as shrewd in the affairs of earth as eager to hasten their trip to heaven. Once the Jesuits at the English College in Rome possessed as lucrative a relic as the head of Thomas More, emblem throughout Europe of Catholic learning and faith in an age of tyranny, they would not part with it lightly—not even to send the bones home.

"And one thing I ask of you," Jack said. "You are known in England and abroad as a faithful Catholic and a great friend to the Jesuits. And to my shame, I—your only living son—am known all too broadly as an apostate to the Church of Rome and a disgrace to an illustrious Catholic family." She started to protest, but he silenced her with a look that she seemed to register even in the faint, flickering light. "Do but this: write me a letter I may show to whatever Catholic I find. A letter of assurance that I have repented and have heartily sought the forgiveness of the Father, the Son, the Holy Ghost, and the Blessed Virgin." He crossed himself.

She gripped his hand and said, "Of course."

Feeling as if he had just betrayed her, Jack lifted her hand and kissed it, Judas-like, then folded the scented cloths back over the skull. He closed the casket and set it aside. His mother's eyes retained their glow. She said, "A marvel, is it not?"

"Yes," he replied, even as his thoughts turned to the practical difficulties of transporting the skull. He had hoped to use Chute's money to see something of the Continent: to take his time riding through France, over the Swiss Alps, and into Italy. But it would hardly do to jog along a-horseback with Thomas More's skull in a box. Even if highwaymen ignored what would surely look like a treasure chest, however Jack tried to disguise it, More's bones would be jostled to bits by the time he got to Rome. Nor would the skull fare much better without the casket. The overland journey would have to wait. Neither Chute nor Burr would welcome the news that the three travellers would have to sail, but there was no help for it. "Yes," he repeated, trying to muster some semblance of sincerity, "it is a marvel."

The lamplight was completely gone now. Jack sat in the dark, absently tracing his fingers along the plaits of the hair-and-leather band on his wrist. For a moment he thought he caught a glint of light off a strand of Anne's hair. Maybe the bracelet could furnish the conceit for the poem he wanted to write for her. Or—he felt the bracelet—maybe a poem for Lady Bedford. Or both, in two versions centered on the same conceit. Anne wouldn't like the idea, but need she know of it? He felt the stirrings of discomfort at the thought of upsetting her or hiding anything from her, but did he not need to consider his livelihood when the whole business with Cecil was finished? Was not Lady Bedford's patronage his most promising means of supporting his wife and children?

The more he thought about it, the angrier he grew. Who was Anne More to tell him what he could and could not write? Had he not remained faithful to her these three years and more? If jealousy about his relations with Lady Bedford distressed her, what was that to him? After all, he had never given his wife cause to doubt him—had never so much as reached out a hand to touch Lady Lucy—had only written some verses for her, some poems with clever intimations of seduction. The Countess liked such poetry; it pleased her—stirred her to passion, perhaps, without paying passion's price. All she paid was money. Money was the object for Jack, and what was money to Lady Bedford? It was all part of the courtly game of patronage. Clearly, she liked the part she played. She liked to think of herself as the distillation of all that men desired. Did Anne not understand that? True, at times Lady Bedford seemed willing to take the game into her bedroom, would likely do so if Jack responded to her advances. But he had piously refused to take that bait.

Bait. He had used that very image in one of his poems for Lady Bedford:

Let coarse bold hands, from slimy nest
The bedded fish in banks out-wrest,
Or curious traitors, sleavesilk flies
Bewitch poor fishes' wand'ring eyes.

For thee, thou needst no such deceit,
For thou thyself art thine own bait;

That fish, that is not catched thereby,
Alas, is wiser far than I.

It was a poem, nothing more, and the Countess ought to know as much. Yet did she not continue to lure him, not just as poet but lover? And what had he done in response? Out of faithfulness to his ever-pregnant wife he had denied himself a delight any courtier would have seized. He let his head fall back, rubbed his eyes with finger and thumb. He forced himself to think of his children, of how much he missed holding them. Somehow he knew his anger at Anne was misplaced, was really anger at himself for betraying his mother. Or maybe it was lust for Lady Bedford disguised as anger.

He shifted in his chair. Suppose he did not refuse the Countess the next time they met. Were there not far worse sins than bedding a woman like Lady Lucy? Surely her desire wanted quenching. And would she not remain discreet about a tryst with a man other than her husband, a man far beneath her in social rank? Even if the doltish Earl of Bedford discovered his wife with Jack, would the fool not easily enough be cowed into silence? Maybe Jack could even father hearty children for Lady Lucy in place of the misbegotten, abortive lumps the Earl had sired.

After all, why should Jack Donne have to bear such a heavy burden for so little reward? Here he sat, chaste in his marriage as any Puritan, spurned by the Court, dispatched by a misbegotten Machiavel on a dangerous mission that forced him to live a lie for the good of his wife and children, and now charged with bearing a dead man's pate into the very midst of the Romish thicket. Upon his return to London, did he not deserve a bit of dalliance with the likes of the dark-eyed Lucy Harrington, Countess of Bedford? He sat fuming.

Even if Jack's mother mistook the source of his unease, she sensed his disquiet: "Fear not the journey," she said. "Sir

Thomas will bless you on your way."

"Yes," he muttered ruefully. "Sir Thomas." Sir Thomas More. . . . Sir George More. . . . Anne More. . . . Why was it his lot always to be plagued by More? More and More and More.

"Well," his mother said. Her chair creaked as she rose. "For now, to bed. But doubt it not: Sir Thomas will protect you."

As he wished her good night he tried to keep the rancor out of his voice. But there was no keeping it out of his mind, which seethed with greater turmoil the longer he sat before the last of the ash-coated embers in the fireplace. After a few minutes of halfhearted prayer—mere mouthing of words to a God that seemed too distant to hear them or care about them if he did—Jack rose and began to pace.

Friends: he wanted his friends. Months had passed since he had seen any of his male companions from the old, heady days of study and revelry at Oxford and then at Lincoln's Inn, and months more would likely pass before he could be reunited with any of them. They alone seemed to understand him when he sank into these fits of fretful melancholy. He missed Anne too, but even she would prove powerless to quell this beating in his brain. Burr was good enough company but much older, and of a different cast of mind from Jack's. Nor could the old knave be fully trusted. No, he needed Tobie Mathew or Henry Goodyer or Christopher Brooke. Mathew would understand his doubts about the Church of England, Brooke his lascivious desire for Lady Bedford. But no one had a soul as comprehensive as Goodyer's, a mind as nimble, a heart as open, a spirit as rare. No one else on earth, not even Anne, knew Jack Donne the way Henry Goodyer knew him. No one's counsel was wiser. If anyone could tell him what would quiet these unruly thoughts, it was Goodyer. Not since Jack's brief encounter with Goodyer at the Wizard Earl's house had he sensed the wholeness of soul his friend seemed to bring simply by his presence, sometimes even in his letters.

Jack felt no inclination to write, but penning a letter to his friend could hardly be worse than this tormented pacing in the dark. He set about blowing an encrusted ember into heat enough to light a small piece of kindling, added a larger piece, then a larger, and soon had the fire roaring again. He found oil for the lamp, lit the wick, and sat at his mother's little writing-table with paper, ink, knife, and quill.

Without putting Goodyer's name on the page, Jack began with indirect references to his troubles, lest the letter be intercepted by some spy and used against him or his friend. But before he had written half a page, he found himself spelling out some of the particulars of his misery. By the time he had started on the next page, he was pouring onto the paper all the molten leadenness of his sinking soul. He told Goodyer of the twisted wretch Cecil's forcing him into betraying Catholics, told him of such doubts about the Protestant faith that he, the most miserable Jack in Christendom, teetered on the point of rejoining the Church of Rome. In fact, he said, unless God instructed him otherwise he intended to go through with the reconversion. In Rome he would confess all to the Jesuits, in penance offering his services as a double spy, an intelligencer ideally placed to wreak subtle, malicious vengeance on *Robertus Diabolus.* He told Goodyer of his lust for Lady Bedford, a fire that grew hotter in his loins with every word he wrote. He told his friend of the surging, savage violence within him, of his intent to leave Lady Lucy screaming with rapturous spasms of pleasure ripped from pain.

Of what these things would do to Anne he wrote nothing at all.

As if to ratify a vow, whether heavenly or hellish, he signed his name with a flourish, then pricked his finger with the penknife and squeezed a drop of blood that he let fall onto the page.

His brow moist and his breath labored, Jack sat feeling chastened and weak, as in the hour after the breaking of a long fever. The wood in the fireplace hissed and popped. Tongues of fire shifted and dazzled like moonlight on a rippled lake. He sat watching the flames until it was time to throw another log onto the embers or go to bed. Wearily, he picked up the letter with its words and its drop of heart's-blood. He leaned forward and flipped the pages onto the coals. Flames leapt up to embrace the words as if sensing some passionate, self-consuming kinship with them.

He forced himself to other thoughts. Family: he needed to think of his little family, not the siren Lady Bedford, the one woman on Earth whose seductive song he might follow to perdition. Of all women she alone could act the succubus, devouring his willing soul.

He closed his eyes tightly. Family. Think of family. Anne and the children would be long after their first sleep now. Constance would be dreaming away with her thumb in her mouth, and Little Jack would be on his back, impervious to the cold, his blanket long since kicked away to the side.

Well. Time to go to bed. Still, Jack did not stir from the chair. He sat exhausted, perhaps dozing, perhaps not, until dawn began to break.

His mother's letter in his hand, he got up and went to the little sewing closet where his mattress lay. But he doubted he could sleep. By the growing light of dawn he found black thread and a needle. With his dagger he slit through the stitching at the top of his right boot. He inserted his mother's letter between the leather plies, then took from his satchel the Wizard Earl's letter and slid it in next to his mother's. He held the boot up to the window and re-stitched the leather plies, using the same needle-holes the boots' cobbler had made. Before he had finished, he heard Chute and Burr talking softly upstairs. Or maybe it was only Chute muttering to himself, as he did from time to time. He heard someone on the steps. The needle and thread were still dangling from the top of his boot, which he hastily pulled onto his foot. From where he sat he could not see the staircase. A shadow fell across the doorway. Burr.

"Ah," the old man said. "Awake already. Is there aught that you lack?"

"No, Tim, thank you."

"Has Kaatje arrived?"

"No, I don't think so."

"Then I will lay a fire in the kitchen."

"Good."

A few minutes later he heard Chute coming down the stairs. The red-cheeked man yawned and stretched away his stiffness. As he descended he asked, "Sleep well?"

"Well enough," Jack said.

"I know no other bed to match the one upstairs for warmth and comfort, not even my softest goose-down four-poster at home." Jack had heard him say the same at least twice before, so he did not reply. Chute began to stroll about the room, humming.

There was no sleep in the offing, so Jack stoked the fire and sat to write another letter. Soon his mother came in and stood warming herself with her hands behind her and her back to the fire. She chatted briefly with him, then listened patiently to Chute's aimless natter. Burr came in and sat in the corner chair to read one of Elizabeth's books: North's Englishing of Plutarch's *Lives of the Most Heroick Greeks and Romans.* During the stay Burr had shown no interest in any of Elizabeth's decidedly Catholic volumes: polemics, catechisms, lives of the saints. The old servant seemed to prefer reading about the ancient world.

When Jack's mother remarked on the preference, Burr said simply, "I myself am ancient."

Jack traced a finger along the bracelet on his wrist. Firelight glanced off his wife's copper-gold hair interwoven with the leather bands. Beginning to feel troubled once again by the force of his desire for Lady Bedford, he wrote some lines for Anne. For her they would be a delight. For him they would serve as a sort of penance for his lust. He titled the poem *The Relic:*

When my grave is broke up again
Some second guest to entertain
(For graves are only sacred till
The churchyard grounds have had their fill)
And he that digs it spies
A bracelet of bright hair about the bone,
Will he not let us alone,
And think that there a loving couple lies,
Who thought that this device might be some way
To make their souls, at the last busy day
Meet at this grave and make a little stay?

If this fall in a time or land
Where misdevotion doth command,
Then he that digs us up will bring
Us to the Bishop and the King
To make us Relics; then
Thou shalt be a Mary Magdalene, and I
A something else thereby;
All women shall adore us, and some men,
And, since at such time miracles are sought,
I would have that age by this paper taught
What miracles we faithful lovers wrought.

The love between us, More and Donne,
In binding double flesh in one,
With fine-spun golden filaments,
Rarer than the elements
That trace the falling stars
And blazing, live no sooner than they ebb,
More fine than Vulcan's web
That snared the winsome Queen of Love, and Mars,
Shall outlive monuments of bronze and brass.
All measure and all language I should pass,
Should I tell what a miracle she was.

The firewood had burned to embers. Despite the chill in the air, Jack was perspiring—he hardly knew why—by the time he got to the last verse. The paper bore the blotted-out and superimposed words and phrases usual in Jack's first drafts, so he wrote out the poem again in fair copy. On a separate page he wrote an ordinary letter describing Antwerp's crowded streets and the fishy, boggy smell of the air—not too different from London's—then, as gently and with as many assurances as he could, told Anne the three travellers would be venturing yet farther away, even as far as Rome. He powdered and blew the ink dry, folded the pages, sealed them for mailing, and laid the letter aside for Burr to post that afternoon on his way to the docks to inquire about passage to Rome.

The poem's first draft with its blottings, hatch-markings, and revisions still lay before him. Some days had passed since he had posted any of his verses to Lady Bedford. How difficult could it be to change a few words and make a second copy for her? By the time he reminded himself he had written the poem to Anne in penance for his lust, he was already turning over alterations. He could make the verse at once lighter and more lascivious, the way Lady Lucy seemed to like her poetry. He could change *faithful lovers* to *harmless lovers,* then wholly recast the last stanza, the one mentioning Anne by name. He tried some lines, and after half an hour had cast the stanza for Lady Bedford in place of his wife:

If thou and I at last might couple,
Bodies willing, lithe and supple,
Saint Lucy's glist'ning radiance
Would slide all darksome shadows thence.
Thy husband and my wife
Might soon forgive a love like thine and mine,
Their jealousies consign
To dull Oblivion's unrememb'ring life.
If I could kindle thy bright spark to fire,
And lightened, prick the strings of thy quaint lyre,
We'd sing the world a miracle entire.

On a fresh piece of paper he wrote in fair copy the whole of Lady Bedford's version. He sealed this poem too, addressed the outside, and laid it with the other. He had no more finished with the letters than a knock at the door interrupted him.

It was, oddly enough, a courier bearing a letter: a man who said he also carried some mailings for London to place on a ship that would sail across the Channel the next morning. Jack paid the courier, took the letter from him, and told the man to wait. The message was addressed in Anne's hand. Jack tore open the seal.

My dearest J,

A courier waits at the door, so I must be brief. I trust and pray that you and your mother are well, and that this missive finds you safe at her house.

I have it on the highest authority that G, the man you seek, lies in England, and as I think, in Warwickshire: for how long, I know not. But seek not for him in any other land.

Your children fare well but for missing their father. As for me, longing for your return, I remain as ever,

Your faithful, beloved

A

Jack broke the waxen seal from his letter to Anne, dipped his pen, marked through the passage about traveling to Rome, and scrawled across the bottom of the page *Missive regarding G received. Sailing soon for Warwickshire and home.* He held the paper to the fire to dry the ink quickly, resealed it along with Anne's version of the poem, and gave both letters to the courier. Turning to Burr, he said, "Our plans have changed."

CHAPTER 11

"God's wounds! Where is Chute, that scurf-ridden, rabbit-sucking, arse-kissing son of a mongrel bitch? The ship sets sail within these five minutes, and the rat-pizzled miscreant does not show himself." Jack took a few angry paces along the dock and glared down the road Chute would likely travel, but there was no sign of him. "You told him where and when to meet us, did you not?"

Burr's face hung in its usual droop, his dour countenance reflecting no sign of urgency. "Indeed, I informed him. My instructions to him were most thorough, for the man falls something short of a nimble wit. I suppose there is nothing for it but to get aboard without him." With a wry imitation of sorrow he added, "Ah, the pity of it."

"Has he left us because we go back to England instead of on to Rome?"

"I know not." Burr stood there impassively for a time before adding, "But now I bethink me, I might have neglected to tell him we sail for England, directing him to a Rome-bound ship instead."

"Ha! By God's bodikins, I would fain board without him, but the man carries our purse."

"Oh, you need not trouble yourself on that account." Burr produced a leather pouch. "Knowing it was appointed you to distribute his monies as you saw fit, I thought it best to collect the unused portion of our four hundred pounds. Something more than three hundred sixty, I believe." He extended the purse to Jack.

"Tim! Does Chute know you have done this?"

Burr considered the matter. "I thought it best not to burden him with the information."

"Well. I could kiss you, Tim."

"That will not prove necessary."

Jack smiled. "We are well rid of the spying knave." Taking care to keep his tone light, he added, "Yet for aught I know, you might be a spy as well."

Jack watched closely, but Burr betrayed no sign of surprise at the remark. Instead, the old man replied, "And for aught I know, you might be one, too."

"Even so. But if I am, I am a spy that is glad you nicked the money. Yet why did you not tell me of this sooner?"

Burr shrugged slightly. "You might have gone to find him, Master Jack. You were ever plagued with an over-precise conscience."

Jack put his arm across Burr's shoulder as they began to walk toward the ship. "Well," he said, "for this once I am glad you are free of one. Still, I almost feel sorry for the man. Where will he find money?"

"Sir Walter carries funds of his own: hidden, as he supposes, from the world. He shall fare well enough."

The seas remained calm on the Channel passage. Bound for Edinburgh, the ship put in briefly at Great Yarmouth, where Jack and Burr disembarked and bought two good horses—a big bay mare for Jack and a chestnut gelding for Burr—to ride on their travels to Warwickshire and beyond. With saddles and gear the sum came to almost seventy pounds, but their wanderings were like to be extensive, and hiring horses for each leg of the journey would not be cheap. Later, if need be, they could always sell the animals. And for now, at least, Jack wanted a smooth-gaited horse: the less jostling of the head of Thomas More, the better. Jack had carefully wrapped the skull in a blanket, discarding the box.

On their way to Warwickshire they passed from Norwich to Peterborough, making dozens of fruitless inquiries about Guido along the way. Nor was their luck any better in Rugby, Coventry, or Kenilworth. Not only did no one in the Midlands seem to know where Guido was staying, no one claimed to know any man by that name—or so they heard from everyone they asked. Jack was beginning to think Anne must be wrong, and he worried that someone must have lied to her. The information about Guido came "on the highest authority," her letter had said. Conceivably she meant King James himself. But how could she have met the King, and why would he have lied to a good Protestant about an enemy of the state? Surely Anne was not taking the huge risk of posing as a Catholic, especially in an encounter with King James. For the same reason—and, God knew, for others—she could hardly have sought out Cecil. More likely he had sought her out, had directed her to write to her husband with the supposed news of Guido's whereabouts. Maybe Guido was nowhere near Warwickshire, and Cecil wanted Jack back in England to lure him into some trap. Sir William Stanley, after all, had seemed sure Guido had gone to Rome. But Jack did not much trust Stanley, did not like the look of those pale blue eyes. Or maybe the "highest authority" was not the King but the King's wife. Queen Anna was Catholic and might find news of Guido easily enough, but as far as Jack knew, the Queen did not ply herself in affairs of state. And how could Anne have arranged to see her? The whole business was strange.

As the two men saddled their horses to leave Kenilworth, Burr seemed unusually pensive. "What cheer, Tim? I thought you were glad to breathe the English air, wheresoever we went."

Burr came out of his reverie long enough to mutter, "English air. Yes."

"What is it, Tim? Tell me what is on your mind."

"Nothing. Probably nothing. A dream." The old man tugged the cinch-strap tight, and his gelding tossed his head.

"What manner of dream?"

Burr laid a hand on the horse's neck. "We were at Warwick, I think. At least, there was a castle, and not like the one here. At an inn a man without a hair on his body, neither pate nor beard nor brow, said he knew where Guido lay. But when he opened his mouth to tell me, I saw that we stood in water. He sank before he could speak. Then I woke."

"Water. What do you think it could mean?"

Burr shrugged. "Mayhap it means but that I dreamed."

"Yet the dream lingers."

"It lingers. And the water stank. I feel as if I stood in it still."

"Well." Jack swung himself onto his horse. "You look dry to me, and you stink no more than usual."

Now Burr seemed himself again, his eyes grown canny beneath bristling, gray brows. "Master Jack, you were ever ready with a blandishment. I thank you most sincerely. And I might add that a bath, a bit of soap-lye, and a coarse brush would do nothing to diminish your resplendence."

Jack smiled. "They have baths as well as a castle in Warwick, do they not? And that's as good a place to ride to as any."

When they arrived in Warwick in the late afternoon after a short rain, the sun invisible behind the general gloom, Burr insisted on riding around the castle. They circled at a distance of half a mile or so, the vast bulk of the castle sometimes visible between buildings, sometimes not. Burr kept turning to look at the fortress and frowning slightly after each glance. As they rode, it seemed to Jack that the massive structure loomed heavier and heavier, its ancient battlements foreboding some unfathomable loss. At last Burr said, "There. That's how it looked in my dream."

"I hope that means the inn from your dream is hard by. I could do with a stoup of good Warwick ale."

Burr looked up and down the street. "I don't remember how the inn looked. But there's a sign for the White Lion, and it seems fair enough."

"Fair enough for me."

The White Lion was anything but fair. It was so dark inside the two men thought at first it was closed. The thick, distorted panes in the high windows were smudged with layers of age-old grime. Despite the failing afternoon light, no lamps had yet been lit for night trade. The ale, though, was rich and bracing. Jack and Burr sat on a bench beneath the windows where they could stretch their legs, sit back against the wall, and watch the few half-shadowed customers hunched over their drinks. Gradually Jack perceived, partly by the hollow sound of voices deep within the dark, that the room was large, stretching far back from the narrow frontage along the road.

After half an hour or so, from the depths of the room a form emerged like a huge, swaying apparition. Somehow the footsteps made no sound. It was not as if the big man moved into the dim light, but as if the pools of thick darkness slowly poured from his body. He was enormous, a full head at least taller than even Jack and perhaps twice his weight. He had to stoop beneath each ceiling-beam as he advanced directly toward the two travellers. From neck to ankle he wore light-colored clothing: whether white or something near white was impossible to tell. His feet were bare. There was purpose in his progress if he had been waiting for the two men's arrival. He carried a large tankard that looked like a small cup in his massive hand. Jack drew up his legs so he could rise quickly if need be, and he slowly laid his hand on the hilt of his sheathed dagger. If the man saw the gesture, he did not show it. Slowly he turned and lowered himself onto the bench where the two sat. Jack could feel the thick board warp and lift him slightly as the man settled beside him.

"Good day," Jack said, turning to look at him. "Or good e'en, whichever it be."

The huge man nodded slowly, then raised the tankard to his lips. As far as Jack could tell, there was not a hair on him: neither on the pallid skin of his head nor his hands. No eyebrows, not even eyelashes. When the stranger raised his head to drink he added two or three folds to the back of his neck.

Burr was sitting forward on the bench. "What would you say to us?" he asked.

Slowly the man turned to look at Burr. "Why do you think I have aught to say?" The voice was deep and sonorous, befitting the form. He dealt the words out one by one, as if carefully laying them on a table.

Burr took his time before replying. "I do not think it. I know it."

Again the pale man slowly nodded. Then he said, "You seek someone."

Burr glanced at Jack, who gave a little nod of consent. "Guido," Burr said. "He is called Guido."

Jack thought the stranger's eyes looked in the gloom neither brown nor blue, neither green nor gray, but a pale red, like blood leached into water. The man had not blinked since he sat. He took in a deep, slow draft of ale, spanning the time it would take most men to draw several breaths. His girth expanded, then retracted as he exhaled, and there was no more movement—as if, like some leviathan risen from the deep, he needed to breathe only once every few minutes. At length he said, "Ah." The syllable was so rich, so resonant, that Jack felt the waves of it running through the vessel of ale in his left hand. His right still lay on the dagger. "Guido," the big man said as he nodded. "Baddesley Clinton."

Burr asked, "Who is Baddesley Clinton?"

A slight smile curled the corners of the stranger's broad mouth. Jack answered the question for him. "Not who; what. Baddesley Clinton is a manor house. Not, I think, far away." How he remembered as much, Jack couldn't say. Some scrap of information from childhood, perhaps, lodged in the back of his mind. But that was all he knew about Baddesley Clinton. "Who owns it?"

For the first time the big man turned a little to look from Burr to Jack. "The sisters Vaux." Jack felt a thrill of recognition, whether because he had heard before and then forgotten who owned the house or because once again Eliza Vaux, who trusted him, might be able to help. She, or more likely her sister-in-law Eleanor, could be sheltering this Guido. So Eliza and Eleanor Vaux owned not only Harrowden Hall in the North but Baddesley Clinton in the Midlands. Like as not, he and Burr would find Guido tomorrow.

Burr asked, "Can you tell us the way?"

The stranger turned away and slowly, steadily drained the rest of his ale. He rose from the bench with what appeared to be little effort. "You know enough," the man said, and he strode smoothly from them, ducking his head rhythmically under the beams as he made his way back into the shadows.

Jack found himself exhaling forcefully, as if he had been unconsciously holding his breath. Then he said in a low voice, as if the huge man might hear him amid the dim chatter in the room, "Your dream. He was the hairless man from your dream, was he not?"

Burr pursed his already wrinkled brow. "He was, and he was not. The man in my dream was nothing so large as this. I cannot remember what he wore. Not, I think, all white."

"Still, how did this creature know we were seeking someone?"

Burr considered the matter. "We were two strangers, watching the customers. Maybe he guessed."

"Yet when he asked why we thought he had something to tell us, you said you did not think it, but you knew it. How did you know it?"

Burr rubbed the back of his neck. "I don't think I did; but it seemed the thing to say."

"No. You dream of a hairless man, and that very day we find a hairless man who seems to know our business. Tim, you are a prophet."

Burr sipped his drink, then said, "If I am, I want no part of it."

"That is the way with prophets."

The two decided to put up for the night at another inn, the doings at the White Lion having left them uneasy about staying there. They found a comfortable enough room a mile or so away after taking a circuitous route and checking frequently along the path to be sure no one followed them.

The next morning the innkeeper gave them good directions to Baddesley Clinton, telling them the house was less than three hours' ride away. They rode north from Warwick as the clouds began to break, and as the mid-May sun rose in the sky, they began to feel warm and dry for the first time in days.

The two travellers found the road to Baddesley Clinton, having been told at the inn that it led after a mile or so to the manor house and that no other dwelling stood along that road. The Vaux sisters owned all the land around, and the few husbandmen who tended the small portion of cleared land had their houses in a corner of the estate fronted along another way. The road to the manor house had been cut through what Jack guessed was a remnant of the original Forest of Arden: the woods on either side stood thick with ancient oaks that looked as if no woodsman's axe had molested them, time out of mind.

The two men rode into a large clearing and stopped to look at the manor house at the center. Of itself the stone dwelling seemed warm and welcoming. But the moat that ringed it gave the house the look of a fortress. The two had to circle to the far side to find the bridge. Jack admired the design: anyone approaching the house could be seen from various vantage points within. Catholics holding a Mass would have time enough to hide crosses, rosaries, and the like. And priests: there would be time to hide priests.

The bridge was wide enough for a wagon but led to a lowered portcullis with stout-looking oak doors behind. A thin, freckled boy of eleven or twelve sat on the bank of the moat beside the near end of the bridge. He held a fishing line that he pulled from the water when he saw the two horsemen approach. Jack thought he saw the boy also pull another string, twice, this one barely submerged beneath the water's surface. Probably some sort of bell or other warning device would sound. The boy stood and squinted into the sun as he looked up at them.

Jack said, "This, I take it, is Baddesley Clinton, the Vaux sisters' house, is it not?"

The boy said, "Indeed it is not, sir."

Jack raised his eyebrows. "Not?"

"Not, sir. For you said you take it. If you take it, it is yours, not theirs."

Jack glanced at Burr, who looked back at him as if the boy spoke nothing but the purest truth. "Well," Jack said. "Then I return it, with my compliments. And so I ask again: this is the Vaux sisters' house, is it not?"

"Yes."

"Good. Then may we enter?"

"That were impossible, sir."

Jack thumbed his hat back on his head a little. "Impossible, you say."

"Impossible."

"Your reason?"

"You said 'This is the Vaux sisters' house, is it not?' And I said yes, for it *is* not."

"So this is not the Vaux sisters' house."

"That is true, sir, as I have just told you."

"Does Lady Eliza Vaux own it, or any part of it?"

"She does."

"And does Mistress Eleanor own it, or any part of it?"

"She does."

"Are the sisters within?"

"They are not, sir."

Jack slowly shook his head, took a deep breath, and said, "Your reason."

"Which reason? For there are two."

"Both reasons, sirrah, if you please."

"The first is this: the sisters Vaux are not Vaux, and yet they are. For one was Vaux and now is not, and one was not and now is. Lady Eliza was never Vaux until she married Sir George Vaux and took his name. And Mistress Eleanor was born Vaux but married, though her husband is now long dead. So: the sisters are not sisters but sisters-in-law. If they were not they would be sisters out of law, and I were loath to think so ill of them."

"I see," Jack said. "Your respect for the law does you great credit. And, if it please you, tell us your second reason, for I should like to finish this catechism before tomorrow breakfast."

The freckled boy smiled. "The second is easy: the sisters are not within the house because one of them is away at Harrowden."

"Which?"

"*Witch,* say you? Oh, no, sir, she is no witch but a good Christian lady."

Jack turned to his companion. "Did you sire this child?"

"I would be loath to think so," Burr said dryly.

"Well, God shield us from another Timothy Burr." Turning back to the boy, Jack said, "Would the sister"—he corrected himself—"sister-in-*law* be the Dowager, Lady Eliza Vaux?"

The boy put on a puzzled look. "*Would* she be? Do you not mean to say *is* she?"

Jack looked at Burr. "Tim, I am sure this riddling bairn is of your tribe. Perhaps you can catechize him."

"With pleasure, Master Jack." Burr turned to the boy. "Mistress Eleanor is within the house. If I speak true, tell me so."

"So."

Burr turned back to Jack. "What clearer answer could you seek?"

The boy said to Burr, "You see, sir, this catechism is not as hard as your friend would make it."

"Well," Burr said, "we must be kind to the addle-pated. But as for you, boy, who is your mother?"

"Why, she that bore me."

"I think she did not," Burr replied.

The boy shielded his eyes with one hand to block the sun and get a better look at Burr. "Not?"

"Not, sirrah, for no woman could bear you and your impertinence, nor no man neither. And so they have cast you out of the house and closed the gate."

"That much were true enough," said the boy. "I am glad one of you speaks truth."

Burr turned to Jack and slowly lifted his palms as if to say, *There: I have been telling you so these many months, and now a third party has confirmed it.* Turning back to the boy, Burr said,

"I think I speak truth when I say that if you went and asked Mistress Eleanor to admit us, she would do so."

"Again you speak truth, sir, as befits your years. You must teach the younger gentleman here to tell truth and shame the Devil."

"It were a lifelong venture," Burr said. "Now, sirrah, what is your name?"

"Ned Tidwell, an't please you."

"An't did not please me, would you be Ned Tidwell still?"

"I would, sir." The boy looked from Burr to Jack. "See? How clear this man reasons! We must look to the elderly for wisdom and truth."

Jack shook his head in half-serious exasperation and gestured to Burr. "Master Tim, I defer to your wisdom."

Burr nodded solemnly, leaned toward the boy, and said, "Ned Tidwell, would you go and ask Mistress Eleanor to admit us?"

"I would, sir, if—"

Burr stayed him with the lift of a finger. "If you do so within the next half a minute, Master Donne will give you two shillings sixpence."

The boy dropped his fishing line and bolted along the bridge toward the house. Jack glared at Burr, who looked him in the eye and said, "You deferred to my wisdom."

Ned Tidwell turned sideways, slipped between the bars, and pulled twice on a cord that hung between the portcullis and the heavy doors. After half a minute or so a small panel in one of the doors slid open, and the boy said, "It's me. We have guests: two friends, as they say, of Lady Eliza." The panel slid shut again, and the riders heard the sound of sliding bolts. The door with the panel creaked open enough for the boy to enter, then closed again. The bolts slid back into place.

Jack and Burr waited for several minutes before they heard the sound of the bolts again. Then the door opened and with the clanking of a chain around the belly of a wooden winch, the portcullis slowly creaked upward. When the bottom of it was chest-high, a woman's voice said, "Welcome, Master Donne, Master Burr." So the boy had remembered their names, which they had mentioned only in passing. Jack wondered how much of Ned Tidwell's evasiveness had been the whim of a quick-witted boy and how much a deliberate device to give the inhabitants of Baddesley Clinton time: maybe delaying visitors was something the boy had been trained to do.

Only with the invitation to enter did the men dismount and tether their horses to a post at the near end of the bridge. Jack unfastened the rolled blanket containing the skull and carried it with him. By the time he and Burr reached the portcullis it was high enough to enter without stooping. Then it dropped behind them with clamorous speed, slowing only within a few inches of the threshold before the spiked bottom settled into holes and the base-plate thudded into place.

Mistress Eleanor Vaux was a small woman, slightly stooped but vigorous, with dark hair just beginning to gray and piercing blue eyes set in a plain face. Jack could well believe she was no sister but a sister-in-law to the large, square-jawed Dowager of Harrowden. Eleanor's gait was quick despite what must have been painful joints. She resembled nothing so much as a light-boned bird of prey. The likeness between the sisters-in-law, Jack guessed, lay in their leather-tough souls.

Eleanor turned first to Burr and spoke crisply. "I am afraid Ned's mother, who cooks for us, has taken ill today. But Ned knows his way about the larder and kitchen. Would you be so kind as to help him prepare us some dinner?"

Before Burr could reply, the boy said, "We could have fresh fish, an' if you would let me finish catching some."

"After dinner," she said, "you may fish for our supper. But for now"—she pointed toward the kitchen—"show Mr. Burr our provisions, look to our guests' horses, and then return to help him prepare the meal."

As Ned started to slink toward the kitchen, Burr nodded slightly to Eleanor Vaux and said, "I make no promises, but perhaps the result will be edible." He followed the boy.

As Mistress Vaux led Jack away in the other direction, she said over her shoulder, "Ned tells me you know the late Sir George Vaux's wife."

"I do," Jack said. "She showed us great kindness at Harrowden."

"If she mentioned your visit, it has escaped my poor mind. Nor would it be the first thing to escape."

"She introduced me to. . . . May I speak openly, Mistress Vaux?"

"Of course. All in my poor household are friends."

"To Father Gerard. He heard my confession."

"Ah. A good man, Father Gerard. Or so it is bruited about."

So Mistress Vaux still had her guard up. Jack had little doubt she knew John Gerard well. Probably she knew every other Jesuit in the land, too.

They entered a simply appointed room. She sat, motioning him to do the same, and asked, "Did you meet anyone else at Harrowden?"

"Owen. One Nicholas Owen."

"Ah. I have heard the name, I think."

She no doubt knew Owen too, master-craftsman of priest-holes. Probably some of Owen's hiding places lay concealed in this very house. Jack would have to convince Mistress Eleanor to trust him. "Perhaps you know my mother," he said, "or have heard of her. Two of her husbands have died, and the Channel separates her from the third. She is now Elizabeth Rainsford, before that Elizabeth Syminges, before that Elizabeth Donne."

"And before she married your father?"

"Elizabeth Heywood."

"Ah! Daughter of John Heywood?"

"The same."

"Well. A good old Catholic family."

"With your permission," Jack said, then lightly drew his dagger from its sheath. With it he sliced through the stitching at the top of his right boot and used the blade to slide out the two folded papers lodged between the leather plies. "I thought it best not to carry these openly. One is from my mother, the other the Wizard Earl."

She moved to the window and held the letters at arm's length to read them. "How fares the Earl?"

"Well, when I left him."

When she had read the letters she laid them on a little table beneath the window, then shook her head, as if she hardly knew what to make of the Earl. "Some of us had hopes he—and not this Scotsman—would be king after Elizabeth. But. . . ."

Jack shrugged. "I think the Earl is the only noble in England who does not want the crown."

"The Lord knows he did no work to gain it."

"True enough," said Jack. "Too easily he let the Scotsman convince him there would be toleration for the Catholics, and that was enough for the Earl. He went back to his experiments, his inventions, and now he watches while the Catholics are harried and whipped and cast into prison. Or he does not watch. I don't think the Wizard knows how bad it is for . . . us." He had almost said, "for you."

Mistress Vaux looked at him closely. "Your mother says here that you and your manservant now count yourself among us."

"We do."

She looked unconvinced. "You asked whether you could speak openly. I ask you the same: may I speak openly and plainly?"

"Of course. I have nothing to hide."

"I wonder. Does a man who has nothing to hide say he has nothing to hide? You were a Catholic. Then you turned apostate, a Protestant. Now you are again a Catholic. How do we know which way you will face when your giddy head stops spinning?"

From a woman like Eleanor Vaux, a woman who had risked her fortune to abet Catholics—risked her very life, for women as well as men had been tortured to death for their cause—he would bear this affront. "The question is well asked," he said. "The answer is that you cannot know. You have my word, little as my word might mean to you, and if that will not suffice, you have Earl's letter and my mother's assuring you that I include myself among the faithful. I swear before God: I wish nothing but earthly peace and everlasting happiness for every Catholic in the land."

She asked, "Do you wish the same for every Protestant?"

A fiery intelligence burned in her eyes; it was best to tell her the truth. "I do."

She held his gaze. "Well, I do not. Simple, misguided believers, yes. The Scotsman, Cecil, Topcliffe, and all their spies and pursuivants, no. May they roast in hell, and the sooner the better."

"I cannot blame you for wishing it."

"Oh, you *are* a tolerant soul, are you not? Tolerant. Wishing people well but tolerant of those who do not. Tolerant. Soft of heart, soft of head, soft of soul, I fear. May the Lord help you when it comes to the manacles and the rack."

He kept his voice even. "May the Lord help me then, and help us all."

She watched him for an uncomfortably long time, then said, "There were Jesuits among the Heywoods, were there not?"

"There were. Two of my uncles, Ellis and Jasper."

"Both gone now."

"Both gone."

"But neither of them murdered."

"No," Jack said. "Jasper was in the Tower, but Queen Elizabeth allowed him, for the sake I think of his father, to leave the country and live."

She waved a gnarled hand vaguely. "So the Tudor bitch did one good thing in her life." Jack waited for her to continue. She crossed her arms and narrowed her eyes. "Have you ever seen a priest murdered by these Protestants?"

"I have."

"Who was it?"

"Campion, and then young Harrington."

She nodded. "I was there when they martyred Campion. You must have been but a child."

"Nine years old, I think."

"You were a Catholic in those days."

"I was."

"And after witnessing the manner of his death, you could leave the Church. And William Harrington's martyrdom, when you were grown."

Jack felt the heat rising along his neck and into his face, but he forced himself to keep his anger at bay. His voice was grim as he said, "I was twenty-two, I think, and my brother Henry twenty-one. Harrington did not die as Campion did. Harrington was not ready; there was terror in his eyes. Terror. My brother had been hiding him, and after Topcliffe's hellish torture—days of it—poor Henry told him where the priest lay. Then my brother died of the plague, in prison. Died horribly. Punished and unforgiven, as he thought, for his sin. Neither my tortured brother nor the tortured priest died well. Both lives were laid waste because these Jesuits stir our young men to their supposed martyrdom. I said then and I say still: it was not God's will that my brother—or Harrington—died. I will say the same in the very teeth of any Jesuit: a man can be a good Catholic and want no part of this Jesuitical martyr-making."

She darted her head toward him and said, "Tell me this: how will young men and women know to be good Catholics if no priest dares to say the Mass and bring the sacraments to the people? How are they to know, if no Jesuit dares enter the land to risk the scaffold and the rack?"

Jack did not take his eyes from hers. "If bringing the Mass and the sacraments were all the Jesuits did, then all were well. But not only do these English priests serve the Italian pope; they are the very playthings of the Spanish king. The Jesuits would make England a colony of Spain."

"And where is the harm in that, if the Old Faith is restored?"

Jack considered his answer, then said, "Mistress Vaux, we disagree. Yet I have no desire to change your mind on that score."

She did not speak for a while, and Jack allowed the silence to settle around them. Eleanor sat remarkably still. A kettle clanked faintly in the kitchen, its sound dulled by the intervening rooms. A wood-thrush somewhere in the distance trilled its easy, liquid song. A creak from upstairs. At length Eleanor said, "Well. For this time I am satisfied. For your mother's sake and the Earl's I welcome you, and I will pray for you." Jack nodded his thanks. She continued, "But you must have come seeking something. What can I do to help you?"

"The Wizard Earl," Jack lied, "asked me to find out one called Guido about some business between the two of them."

"The Earl says nothing of it in his letter."

"He would have, but I advised him not to, fearing he did not understand the risk to himself, were I caught and the letter discovered."

She nodded. "That sounds like the Earl. Sometimes I think he seems a great, overgrown boy."

"I insisted he be circumspect."

"It was well done. But of your task: I am afraid you have missed Guido by less than a day. He stayed with us for more than a month, and departed the house just yesternight."

So Anne was right: Guido was not only in England, he was in Warwickshire. Or had been until last night. "Do you know where he has gone?"

With a tone shading between resignation and bitterness, she said, "He never reveals where he will go next. Or he would never tell a woman, even one who sheltered and fed him through this month and more."

Jack paused to acknowledge the rightness of her claim, then said, "The Earl's business is a matter of no small urgency. Is there anyone in the house who would know where Guido went?"

Mistress Vaux looked out the window and absently grazed an arthritic finger along her lip.

After a while Jack said, "A priest, perhaps? I would have one hear my confession."

Still looking out the window, she took a deep breath and exhaled slowly. Then she said, "Guido is ever secretive about his comings and goings."

She had already said so, but there was nothing to be gained by reminding her of the fact. Jack let her silence work for a long time. The thrush was gone, but a mockingbird somewhere in the woods had begun a series of songs. Finally Jack said, "There is one more thing." He glanced toward the rolled blanket he had set on the floor next to his chair. "I hardly know where my travels will take me, and there will be much jostling along the way. Could you keep something here for me? It may hap I will call for it again one day."

"And what is that?"

"The head of Thomas More."

Chapter 12

Eleanor had hurried away to fetch a goose-down pillow. When she reappeared she laid the pillow on the table beneath the window, then carefully unrolled each of the blanket's layers. In a minute or two she held the bones in her hands. Reverently she laid the skull on the pillow, then set the jawbone under it where it would have fit. One tooth—a molar—remained in the blanket, as did the three little patches of skin and hair that had somehow remained delicately adhered to the skull when it was in Jack's mother's care. Eleanor placed the tooth and the patches of skin beside the skull on the pillow. Jack considered the arrangement. All in all, the damage had been light. Something short of a miracle, perhaps, but not bad.

Eleanor's face burned with what Jack first thought was fright, but then he saw it for what it was: not the craven fear of the dead, but the holy fear of awe. With evident pain in her joints, she knelt before the skull. After a moment's hesitation Jack did the same. She muttered an *Ave Maria,* a *Paternoster,* and a *Te Deum,* then crossed herself three times and tried to rise. Jack crossed himself once and helped her back into her chair.

She looked almost a different woman from the one who had shrewdly questioned him only minutes before. It was as though Sir Thomas had spoken to her words of everlasting comfort, had assured her that all would be well: that in fact all was well already.

Jack looked again at the skull. He still saw nothing but grinning bones. They stared stupidly at him. Or maybe they taunted him.

How was it that Sir Thomas spoke so clearly, and with such powerful reassurance, to these pious women? Eleanor, his own mother . . . but to Jack he had nothing to say.

Eleanor looked at Jack placidly, her usual crisp movements somehow forestalled by Sir Thomas More. "Whether you come again for him or not, Sir Thomas will find his way back into your family. There is no doubt of it."

As there was no sense and no charity in doing otherwise, Jack nodded his acceptance of the inevitability.

Mistress Vaux said, "I tell you there is *no doubt* of it, despite all your disbelief."

Jack held up his palms as if to say, *I do not disagree.* He added aloud, trying to keep his tone entirely free of ridicule, "Do you think Sir Thomas might allow you to keep the tooth and the hair in your family? Its falling into your hands was perhaps providential."

Eleanor seemed uncertain what to make of the idea. She turned and looked to Sir Thomas where he lay on his pillow. For a long while she stared at him. Then she turned back to Jack and said, "He will allow it. In fact he desires it. You may be sure these four relics will be well looked after, and honorably venerated."

"I believe it with my whole heart."

"I thank you for this most sacred gift. The Dowager Vaux at Harrowden shall have one relic, each of my two blood sisters shall have another, and one shall remain here. Sir Thomas desires it so."

"So please you, thank Sir Thomas for me. It is he who knows best, and not I."

"Yes. I have thanked him already. But the gift came through your doing, your acceptance of his desire."

Without knowing he was about to do it, Jack crossed himself again. Mistress Vaux did the same, then pushed herself up from her chair. "Wait here," she said.

After a few minutes a plump, thin-legged country squire, or so the man's clothing proclaimed, entered the room. Eleanor stood in the doorway and said, "I'm going to look in on Ned's mother." As the men sat, Jack could hear Mistress Vaux climbing the stairs. He knew the creaking must be coming from the steps, but he imagined it was Eleanor Vaux's crepitating joints.

The squire's sparse hair was the color of dried flax, his eyes pale, cold, and canny. "You are, I take it, a priest," Jack said. The man nodded. "Jesuit?"

"Perhaps."

Most of the English Jesuits were no older than Jack, but this man looked about fifty. Jack guessed he sat before the head of the Jesuit mission to England: "Garnet? Henry Garnet?"

The priest's expression did not change. "What is the difference?" he asked. The voice had the clear, cool tones of a tenor. No doubt the man could sing a rousing *Te Deum,* as Jesuits everywhere sang every time one of their own was put to death—as if the murdering were a glorious thing. "Mistress Vaux has told me of your mother's letter, and the Earl's. She said you wanted to confess. I am a priest, and I am here to administer the sacrament. What are your sins?"

Jack knelt, surprised at how willingly his body submitted where his mind misgave. He told the priest of his confession to John Gerard, told him of his doubts about rejoining the Catholic Church, of his decision to proceed nonetheless. Whether this last was entirely a lie, not even he was sure anymore. When the priest asked whether there was anything else, Jack took a risk. He said, "Just this: it is not, I think, a sin of my own, but I would speak of it. I fear that the man Guido, who was here yesterday, in league with a few other hot-headed Catholics, plans some great violence against the authorities of this land." Jack watched Garnet—if Garnet it was—as the man's cheeks flushed. The priest knew something.

"What manner of violence?" Garnet asked.

"I know not."

"From whom did you hear this thing?"

Jack dangled a bit of bait: "I . . . I had as lief betray no man's confidence."

The priest nodded. "You know I must respect the seal of the confessional; I will reveal what you tell me to no man. Not even, unless the matter be truly grave, to the Pope himself. But this is like to be of such importance, and so I impose on you an additional act of penance for your sins. Tell me but this, and you know I must bear your secret to the grave unless many lives hang in the balance: from whom did you hear this thing?"

Remembering the big man at Harrowden, the one with the bullet-shorn ear, Jack crossed himself, said a silent prayer asking for forgiveness, and lied: "I overheard it. At Harrowden I was in the next room when Robin Catesby confessed his sins to Father Gerard."

Father Garnet closed his eyes and let his head fall back. "Catesby," he whispered, half to himself. "I might have guessed it. And you say you know none of the plan's particulars?"

"None. If I did, I could work to prevent it. Catesby spoke of Guido, but he would reveal no other particulars to Father Gerard: only that his plan would usher in a Catholic king, or at the least force the Scotsman to honor his promise of toleration."

Garnet sat for a long time staring into the middle distance. Doing his best to ignore the ache in his knees, Jack kept kneeling. Garnet's silence gave Jack time to make a calculation: if the priest knew nothing of the conspiracy Jack had hit upon, the man would not have reacted as he did. If he knew of it and supported it, he would reveal nothing to Jack. If he knew of it and feared or doubted its success, or if he knew some mischief was afoot but did not know the details, maybe he would offer some hint of what he knew. Jack said, "You know this desperate device of these men is doomed to fail. When it does, things will be much worse for us Catholics. The King will take bloody vengeance, and few among even the Catholic nobles will dare resist him."

Finally Garnet said quietly, "That is true; I fear it. The Scotsman's response would be terrible." He was silent again for a while, then stirred in his chair, leaned forward, and said, "The seal of the confessional prevents me from telling you more, but I will say this much: plans have been laid for foul doings. I know not of a surety when the thing will come to pass—a few weeks, maybe, or a few months—at, I think, Coombe Abbey."

"Sir John Harrington's house."

"The same, not twenty miles distant."

"I know Harrington's daughter Lucy, the Countess of Bedford."

Garnet's face brightened. "*Do* you? If you could use her influence to gain entry into the house. . . ."

"I think I can."

"Good. I will tell you only this: the young princess Elizabeth Stuart stays at Coombe Abbey. If arrangements were made for the child to be spirited secretly to some safer place in the event of any hint of an attack on Coombe Abbey, that would not be amiss."

"Is the girl's life in danger?"

"Not her life, I think, but. . . ."

"These hot-heads plan to seize her, then. Hold her hostage in exchange for concessions from King James. Or carry her away to Spain or Italy to be raised Catholic."

"I have said enough. Too much, it may be, and may the Lord

have mercy on me if I have. Well, you have made your confession. The rest of your penance is to pray every morning for forty days that your motives may be purified."

The priest gave Jack absolution and said, "Rise. Make your way, before much more time has passed, to Coombe Abbey."

Burr had mixed some cured mutton, onions, greens, and a large dollop of goose grease in a kettle of water that now rested on the kitchen coals. When the stew reached a boil he would drop in a dozen or so eggs. Young Ned Tidwell had told him where to find food and implements but had proved useless when it came to cooking. The boy sat peevishly watching. Burr stirred the mixture with a long wooden spoon as he said, "This might not match your mother's cooking, but I trust it will serve."

Tidwell said, "Oh, it will never serve."

Burr continued stirring as he asked, "And your reason, young Master Malapert?"

"A stew can never serve. It is people who must serve it."

"Ah. Then today you, a person of sorts, will be the one to serve it. How does it feel to be subservient to a mess of pottage?"

"I had rather serve a pot of message."

"Your exquisite reason?"

"The message in the pot," Tidwell said, "might be a good one. And I fear your stew is not."

Before Burr could respond, Ned was on his feet. He stared at the kitchen wall as if looking through it into the next room, where the thick door stood against the portcullis. "Someone on the bridge," the boy said. Burr strained to listen, but he could hear no sound outside the house. He first thought the boy was lying, but Ned seemed urgent and sincere as he said, "Pursuivants, maybe. Tell the others, and I'll hold them out of door as long as I can." He bolted from the kitchen into the next room.

As Burr went to tell Jack and Mistress Vaux what the boy had said, a loud knocking rang through the house, as if someone were pounding on the door with the butt of a shaft. A stern, half-muffled cry from outside: "King's business!"

"Anon!" shouted Ned.

Burr and Eleanor Vaux arrived at the same time outside the door to the room where the priest had heard Jack's confession. There was no need for Burr to speak. Eleanor threw open the door and said, "Ware you: that's a pursuivant knocking, or else the devil that spawned him." She gathered the blanket from the floor and began, somehow reverently and hastily at once, to wrap up Thomas More's skull.

Garnet asked, "The hide in the attic?"

"I think they suspect that one," Eleanor said. "They were near to finding it last time. It will have to be the garderobe." Garnet looked momentarily dismayed, then bitterly resolved. Eleanor glanced at Jack, then at the blanket. "I have a safe place for your kinsman Sir Thomas here."

Burr hardly had time to wonder what she meant by that. He noticed a change in the light, a passing shadow, and turned to see Nicholas Owen: the bandy-legged craftsman they had met at Harrowden. Owen motioned for the priest to pass ahead of him in the hallway. "Follow us close," he said to Burr and Jack. He headed up the stairwell as Eleanor hurried toward the kitchen.

The small room with a privy—a lidded wooden box against one wall—could hold only three of the men. Burr stood outside the door, craning his neck to see. Owen knelt. From a crack low in the wall he pulled a small nail, inserted its point into a tiny hole in one of the four pegs in a broad floorboard to which the base of the box was nailed, and pulled out the peg. He did the same with three others. Then he slid the privy, still nailed to its floorboard, toward the opposite wall. The end of the board slid under the wall, into what room Burr could not say. A few seconds later the old man recoiled at the stench rising from the sewer beneath the now-open shaft: the garderobe Eleanor had mentioned, he supposed, dropping underground and issuing into the moat.

Owen set the pegs back into their holes. No longer aligned with their holes in the subfloor, they protruded an inch or so above the board. Owen looked at the priest and spoke quickly: "I'll go first, Father, then you. Give me your doublet." Garnet shuffled out of his coat and handed it to Owen, who tied the sleeves around his own waist and said, "You'll need this jacket against the chill tonight. I'll stay on the rope and help you down from below." Owen turned to Jack. "You help him from above. Then your man comes down, then you. You'll have to pull the privy back against the wall from the underside." Jack looked at the pegs. Owen said, "They'll drop into place when you've slid the box all the way. All will look as it did." As he lowered himself into the garderobe, he said, "Once you have the privy near the wall, it will be dark. It's a twenty-foot stone shaft, like a chimney, wider inside after the first few feet. At the bottom you'll be in water to your knees. There's a hidden door in the stone. We'll come out and climb onto a ledge just above the moat."

As Owen disappeared into the shaft, Burr entered the room and, with the other two, bent over the hole in the floor to see the man descend, hand over hand. At first Burr couldn't tell what Owen held onto, but after a few heartbeats he made out a thick, black, knotted rope. No doubt the rope had been blackened to make it hard to see if pursuivants raised the hinged lid on the privy to look inside.

Burr looked from the garderobe to the round-bellied priest. He doubted the man could fit into the narrow, stone-walled shaft. The priest appeared to have the same doubt. Without being able to make out the words, from downstairs Burr heard

Eleanor's voice, or maybe Ned Tidwell's, shouting something. Then there was more pounding against the door. This time it sounded not like the sharp knocks of a cudgel or staff but heavy, hollow, and loud, like the battering of a ram. More shouts as the ramming continued. Then Burr heard the sound of splintering wood.

The top of Owen's head had passed out of sight, but his hands still gleamed faintly in the room's dim light when his voice came, quiet but urgent, from the hole in the floor: "Father, there's a knot in the rope here, just above my hand. I'll guide your foot." Burr and Jack held Garnet under the armpits as he lowered himself into the garderobe. With his broad buttocks halfway into the shaft, halfway bulging over the rim at the floor's surface, he appeared to stick. Burr heard Owen's muffled voice from below: "Father, I'm going to pull." Garnet's eyes widened as his hindquarters scraped slowly down the stone-walled shaft. Now his belly spread out onto the floor around the rim, making the hole completely invisible. He looked like a man sawn in half, amazed to find himself still alive.

If Owen was saying anything now, Burr could not hear his voice; all the sound came from the priest's labored breathing and the ram's thuds below as the thick door continued to splinter. Garnet grimaced as he appeared to shrink an inch or so, his belly bulging even wider at the base—as if he were melting. Then he seemed to regain the inch of height he had lost. Two or three heartbeats later he shrank again. Owen must be pulling hard from below, then relenting. In a slow rhythm the priest bobbed this way twice more. Burr said, "Breathe out: *now.*" The priest exhaled, shrank an inch, and gasped for air as he rose again.

"It's no good," Jack said. "This shirt needs to come off." With both hands he grabbed the opening at Garnet's throat and pulled, tearing the fabric from top to bottom, stopping at the floor. Burr took one side of the unseamed garment and Jack the other. They tore the shirt sideways around the priest at floor level until the cloth came completely free. Garnet's soft, white flesh now flowed onto the floor around the top of the shaft.

In the same way as before, he slowly bobbed three or four times more. "Father," Jack said, "we're going to have to push." He put his palms on one of Garnet's shoulders; Burr did the same on the other. When the priest began to shrink as Owen pulled from below, Jack and Burr pressed from above. Garnet winced, his mouth clamped shut against letting some cry escape. As the two men eased their hands off the priest's shoulders, he rose again.

Jack said to Burr, "Grease. We need grease. Did you see any in the kitchen?"

"I did."

"The blood-suckers are near to breaching the door. Be quiet and quick."

Burr hurried downstairs. As he made his way to the kitchen he could hear that the shouts were Eleanor's: "There's sickness in this house, I tell you! You do not want to come in!" The ram thudded, and the door shivered. "Bartholomew Ridgely, I know your voice! Would not your dear mother, if she lived, die for shame to see you now?" Another crash against the door. "Bartholomew, she weeps from her grave even now!"

Burr entered the room long enough to whisper, "We need more time."

Eleanor turned to him and whispered back, "I'll do what I can, but they'll soon be in. Already they've raised the portcullis somehow."

From an urn in the kitchen Burr scooped a double handful of goose grease and made his way back upstairs. He and Jack smeared Garnet's torso. They lifted his flesh where it rested on the floor and tried to work some of the grease into the edges of the shaft. All the while Owen kept pulling, then releasing. "All right," Jack said to the priest. "We're going to push again." Garnet nodded grimly.

As Owen's next pull started, Jack and Burr leaned heavily on the priest's shoulders. This time he seemed not to rise again after dropping a little. With the next pull he moved a full two inches. They could hear his flesh scraping through the shaft. Garnet was clearly in great pain, but he let no sound escape. After three or four more straining efforts he had descended nearly to the armpits. Jack picked up the torn shirt and wiped the grease from his hands, then passed the cloth to Burr. "Raise your arms, Father," Jack said. Burr held one wrist, Jack the other. With Owen's next pull the priest dropped again, wedged at the shoulder-sockets. For two more pulls he held there. Burr tried to imagine how the scene must appear from below. Like some darkling underworld midwife, some Plutonic graybeard, Owen hung in the air as he delivered a breached and bloody man-child, a hieratic infant, into the void.

The thudding against the door below continued. Garnet had blanched almost white, and the sweat on his head ran into his eyes. "You're holding your breath," Jack said. "Blow out all your wind. All of it." The priest nodded and with the exhalation uttered a half-stifled sound like the cry of a small beast at the moment the trap snaps shut.

With a dull cracking sound that made Burr shudder and Garnet's eyes roll back, at last Owen pulled the priest free, and Burr felt the man's sudden weight. With Jack he slowly lowered Garnet into the hole until the priest whispered hoarsely, "I see the rope." Jack nodded to Burr, who released his hold on the priest's wrist. When Garnet had the rope with his free hand, Jack released the other. Burr watched the trembling, halting descent into the darkness as Jack stepped into the hall. He stood listening.

Then he was back in the room. "The door splits," he said, "but they're not yet in. Down the shaft, Tim. Do you need help?"

"No." Surprised at his own nimbleness after watching the much-younger Garnet's struggles, Burr quickly lowered himself into the garderobe, found a knot on the rope with his feet, and began his descent. On the stone wall inches before his eyes he could just make out the mix of Garnet's blood with the smeared remains of untold years of excrement.

After a near-deafening crash of the ram against the buckling door, one that left a jagged, foot-long splinter pointing an accusatory finger upstairs, Ned Tidwell shouted, "We're trying, but the bolt is jammed!"

"You lie!" came the cry from one of the men outside.

"One more," Eleanor whispered to Ned, "and we do it. Then back away spry." Near her feet lay an iron skillet; near Ned's, a heavy set of fire-tongs.

The next crash let in a shaft of daylight between the two thick doors. Ned laid his hands on the bolt, Eleanor hers on the other door's stop. She waited one second, two, three, and said, "Now!" Ned slid the bolt as Eleanor pulled the stop. The two jumped back from the doors just in time. With an explosion of sound and light, four men and a ten-foot oak log crashed into the room. By the time the men had sprawled into a heap against the wall opposite the doors, Eleanor held the skillet in her hands. She had room to swing freely, and the man nearest her did not see the blow coming. Ned heard not only the ring of the iron but the crack of the skull. An instant later the end of his tongs glanced off the head of a burly, bald, red-bearded man, half-tearing off his ear.

"Hold them!" someone shouted. Eleanor did not get in another blow. The man she had just hit tripped her as she drew back the skillet. He pinned her to the floor where she fell. The thick-necked, red-bearded man with the bloody ear scrambled to his feet with surprising speed. Ned swung the tongs again, but the man blocked them with a forearm. He hit Ned full in the face with a heavy fist that lifted the boy from where he stood and propelled him over the threshold. He lay stunned, sprawled half in the house and half on the bridge.

Eleanor struggled against the vacant-faced man who held her to the floor. He looked unaware that his skull had been fractured and that he was bleeding steadily from the back of his head. Eleanor turned her head and said to a young, gaunt man with greening teeth, "Bartholomew Ridgely, did I not tell you that boy's poor mother lies upstairs with a fever? It's the *plague*, most like. Why did you think I would not open the doors? I'll not wish the plague on you, if only for your poor mother's sake."

Ridgely said, "You leave my mother be." He turned to the red-bearded man and said, "I want no part of the plague, Sam. We must needs go."

The big man had been holding the side of his head and was now looking incredulously at his reddened hand. He murderously eyed the half-conscious boy he had hit, then turned to Ridgely to growl, "She lies, do you not see that?"

The fourth of the pursuivants, a grim, flint-faced man in a constable's buff-yellow leather, had not yet moved; the oak ram lay across his thighs. With difficulty he shoved the log aside and rose stiffly. Then he said, "Don't hit him again, Sam. I want him awake to hear the tale he tells. For now I'll have a look at this plague-ridden mother of that whelp there that near knocked off your ear, and I'll take Ridgely with me so he can see how these papists outdo the Devil himself with their lies." Without looking at Eleanor he said, "Woman, show us where the boy's mother takes her sick-bed."

The man with the cracked skull seemed only too glad to release her.

Jack had started to lower himself into the shaft when he heard footsteps on the stairs and Eleanor saying loudly, no doubt to warn anyone who remained in the closet with the privy, "I tell you she's fevered, and I've the plague on me, too, most like. You've been warned, so now you'll get what's coming to you."

Bartholomew Ridgely whimpered, and the constable snarled, "Hush."

Jack silently lifted himself out of the shaft; if he dragged the jakes into place from below with the pursuivants nearby, the sound would alert them. And he could not join Burr and the others while leaving the garderobe exposed. He drew his dagger and pressed himself against a wall, listening as Eleanor and the two men entered an adjacent room. Jack had not realized young Tidwell's mother lay so near; she had not made a sound.

He could hear the conversation in the next room. The constable said, "She burns hot, but I see no sign of the plague."

"Then you do not know the plague," Eleanor replied. "It begins like this."

A woman, apparently Ned Tidwell's mother, said in a frail voice, "Is that you, Charles, back from the dead? And little Tobias. How you have grown since I put you in the ground! Have you come to take me with you? Come and hold me!" She began to cough.

Bartholomew Ridgely sounded terrified as he said, "I am no Tobias, back from any dead. Swetnam, we must needs leave this house!"

The constable snapped, "Quiet, I told you, boy, or I'll cuff you about the ears."

Mrs. Tidwell said, "My dear husband and child. Take me with you."

The constable's voice was now urgent: "Back in the bed, woman. Back in the bed! Never come near me; I am no husband of yours."

"Charles."

"In the bed, I say!"

In spite of the danger, Jack smiled at the sick woman's performance. He heard a shuffling of feet and a confusion of several voices, then the loud closing and latching of the sickroom door. The constable said, "Sam Parvin can search that room, if he wants it searched. I'll have no more of that woman."

"I'll have no more of this house," Ridgely said.

Jack heard the sound of an open hand striking flesh as the constable said, "You'll have what you're given and do what you're told."

At the sound of boots descending the stairs, Jack exhaled. He hadn't realized he'd been holding his breath. With the remnants of Garnet's shirt Jack wiped as much of the grease from the floor as he could. He dropped the rags down the garderobe. Again he began to lower himself. His feet dangled until he found the rope. As his head dropped just below the level of the floor, he reached up and grasped one of the boards bracing the back of the jakes and began with some difficulty to pull the heavy box, heavier still for the broad floorboard attached to it, back over the hole in the floor. Even as he bent his effort on getting the jakes into place quickly and as quietly as possible so he could join the others below, the feeling he had forgotten something tugged at some part of his mind.

He froze. The letters! Just before his confession Eleanor had left the letters from his mother and the Earl downstairs on the little table beneath the window. Then she must have laid the goose-down pillow for Sir Thomas's head on top of the papers. Unless Eleanor had remembered them amid all the commotion and hidden or destroyed them, probably they lay still under the pillow on the table. He closed his eyes—hardly necessary in the dim light of the shaft—and made a quick calculation. Eleanor would have been too busy with the attack on the house to give the letters any thought. She had hurried away with the skull, and all her effort would have been bent on preserving Sir Thomas. The pursuivants would find the letters, and when they had found them, would hardly believe Eleanor's claims that no one was hiding in the house. The letters could also be used as evidence against not only his mother, should she ever decide to come back to England, but also the Wizard Earl. Jack would have to risk going downstairs to get them. Stifling a curse, he pushed the jakes back the few inches he had moved it and hoisted himself out of the hole. Since his chances of being caught were high, he could not leave the garderobe exposed; he slid the jakes back over the hole. Just as Owen had said, when the box reached the wall the four pegs dropped into place, looking as if they had never been moved. Jack wondered what the men in the shaft beneath the house must think. If any of them hung on the rope or stood at the bottom of the garderobe and looked up at the rectangle of light, he would have seen both of Jack's abortive attempts to descend, then the eclipsing of the light as the box slid against the wall.

Jack removed his boots and eased into the hallway. He thought about stashing them somewhere until he came back but decided there was little to gain by doing that. Holding the boots in one hand and taking care to make no noise, he descended the stairs as quickly as he could. From the sound of the voices he could tell that Eleanor and the two men had gone to rejoin the pursuivants in the entryway. That was good; he could retrieve the letters without being seen.

The papers still lay under the pillow where Eleanor had left them. He picked up the letters, folded them hastily, and slid them back between the leather plies of his boot. Then he crept toward the stairs. At that moment he heard someone coming. He flattened himself against the wall next to the doorway to the hall, standing still while two men passed within view: one thick-boned, bald, bloody, and red-bearded, the other slack-faced and greasy. Had either of them turned his head to the right, he would have seen Jack there, barefoot with boots in hand. But neither of the men turned. They headed up the stairs.

Now Jack had scant hope of escape. Even if he made his way back to the room with the jakes without being seen, he could not risk the noise it would take to move the jakes with the men so near. Nor could he risk dropping from the sitting-room window and into the moat: there would no doubt be more pursuivants posted outside to watch the grounds. He would have to destroy the letters. They had proved useful, but if found they would whet the pursuivants' appetite for hidden Catholics. Eleanor and maybe even the Earl would be in danger. Jack's mother was free from such trouble while she remained in Antwerp, but only if the Catholics held the city. And there would be danger, possibly arrest and torture, for Jack himself. He drew the letters from his pocket and prepared to eat them.

Then he thought of an easier way. The kitchen was as safe a room as this, and there would still be live coals in the fireplace. He passed quietly into the kitchen and worked the letters into the embers under the kettle of stew Burr had been cooking. The paper burst into flame.

Footsteps were now converging, from opposite directions, on the kitchen. Jack hastily pulled on both boots, moved to the fire, and stood stirring the kettle as the constable and Ridgely froze in the doorway. Jack said, as calmly as he could, "Would one of you tell me why you have drawn me from my studies with noises that would wake the sleepers in their graves? I ask out of mere curiosity."

The constable had drawn a sword. "Name yourself," he said.

Jack looked steadily at the man. "Why should I name myself? My mother named me long ago."

"I'll have none of that, whatsoe'er your mother called you. Now reach me that blade."

Jack unsheathed his dagger, took it by the point, and extended it, handle-first, to the constable. "I'll have that back from you when this business—whatever business you've come on—is over. Mind you take good care of it, or you'll answer for it."

The constable scoffed. "And who is it will make me answer?"

"Lord Robert Cecil."

The constable's eyes narrowed. "Lord Cecil, you say."

"The same. I am here on his business. As, I take it, are you, though you probably take your orders from some underling. You needn't have battered the house into flinders; I have already found out all there is to find."

Chapter 13

Jack turned his back to the constable and stirred the stew in the kettle.

"And what is it you have found?" the constable asked.

Jack dipped up some of the stew in the long spoon, tasted it, and seemed to approve before saying, "Someone was here: maybe a priest, maybe some other Catholic, maybe some lawful visitor. But whoever it was has been gone two days."

"And when did you arrive to find this out?"

"Yesterday."

"How did you get here?"

Jack turned and looked at the stone-faced constable. "On horseback. Would you like some stew?"

The constable ignored the invitation. "What manner of horse?"

"A big bay mare."

"And who rode with you?"

Jack saw where the question led. The pursuivants no doubt knew Eleanor Vaux's horses and had already looked into the stables to find the two new animals Ned Tidwell had unsaddled and fed. "The boy who lives here," Jack said, "young Ned, who should be tending this pot. Where is the little mitcher?"

Without taking his eyes off Jack, the constable said to Ridgely, "Go fetch him."

"Who?"

"The lad Sam laid out, you mooncalf." Ridgely went to collect the boy. The constable said to Jack, "If the cub lives here, why was he away riding a horse with an agent, as you claim to be, of the Lord Cecil?"

Jack shrugged. "I heard Mistress Vaux wanted a horse, so I gained entry to the house by sending her word I had a gelding to sell. She sent the boy to find me in Warwick and have a look at the animal. Then we rode here together."

During the exchange the constable had gradually slackened his right arm until the tip of his sword rested on the floor. Jack was sure he could disarm the man and easily dispense with the frightened-looking youth who had just left the room. But then there would be more pursuivants to contend with—at least two others in the house and probably more on the grounds—and even if he overpowered them all, where would that leave Eleanor Vaux? Jack himself could escape, but more agents of the Crown would arrive, mounting a massive search of the house. He could not betray the priest, Owen, and Burr.

The constable took a step back, leveled his sword at Jack, and shouted, "Sam! The kitchen!"

A few seconds later Jack heard two men descending the stairs. When they arrived at the kitchen, the red-bearded man said, "Ah, so you've found one."

"He says he's here on orders from Lord Cecil."

"Does he, now."

"He claims that boy you hit—but here he is. Bart, bring him in."

Ridgely prodded young Ned into the already crowded room. Eleanor moved in behind them. She stared at Ridgely, who said, "I found her with him." He avoided meeting Eleanor's eyes as she gave him the look of a mother deeply disappointed in her child.

"Take her back out, and keep her well clear of this room," the constable said. "Later we'll see if the tale she tells is the same as we hear from the lad."

One side of the boy's face was badly bruised, his left eye swollen almost shut. The constable waited until Ridgely had led Eleanor some distance away before turning to Ned and saying, "That gelding in the stable. Who rode him here?"

Ned turned his good eye to Jack, who subtly lifted a finger and pointed back at him. To his relief the boy said, "I rode him myself. And why shouldn't I?"

"And why were you riding him?"

Jack broke in: "Can't you see it pains the boy to speak? He's confirmed it; he rode here with me yesterday."

After Jack's first few words the constable shouted for him to stop. Jack did not obey. The man put the point of the sword in his right hand to Jack's chest and with his left held the dagger to his prisoner's throat. The constable said menacingly, "Another word, and I'll have your tongue out with your own blade. I'll ask the questions, and you clamp your chops. He turned back to Ned. "And why were you riding here with this man on a horse not your own?"

Jack could see the boy was thinking quickly. This time he could only hope Tidwell's lie fadged with his own. "Mistress Vaux bought the horse. Or I think she did. That was between her and Master Donne here."

Turning to Jack, the constable said, "Ah: Donne, is it?" Tidwell looked pained he had revealed the information. "Well," the constable went on, "now we have a name for you, whether it be your true name or no. We'll soon see if the Mistress tells the same tale as the two of you." He turned back to the boy. "And have the horses been stabled since yesterday?"

"Aye," Tidwell said. "Stabled and fed."

"Ah. Then answer me this: if you and Master Donne rode the horses yesterday, why were they still wet from the ride when we saw them today? And the saddles wet too."

"I know not," Ned replied. "Things stay wet in that stable."

"You lie," the constable said. "You see, here's the hard thing: the stirrups on both saddles were set for men half an ell longer than you."

"I don't use stirrups," Ned said. "I don't like them. Nor do I even like saddles, but it was to be bought with the horse, so I rode on it."

"Well, I see ye've a lie to fit every question. But that last were one lie too many. Bart, bind this man Donne's hands behind him, and do it snug. We'll see what other filthy papists lie hid in the house—a whole nest of 'em, I'll warrant, and this one wouldn't fit with 'em in the priest-hide. If there's a true tale in him, we'll have it out."

The red-bearded man looked at Jack with a broken-toothed smile.

With Owen and the priest, Burr stood waiting under the house. Their narrow ledge rose just above the water's surface. A little light sifted in through a few cracks in the foundation wall. To pass the time, Burr tried to imagine the process of the mansion's construction. It was not as though the house had been built, then a trench dug in a ring around it for the moat; the water extended under the whole. The builders must have chosen a boggy declivity watered by a stream or spring in the surrounding hills. They temporarily diverted the stream and when the ground was dry further excavated the site into a sort of pit. The walls of the foundation were laid, their solidity now betrayed only by the few cracks in the mortar, and the house was built on these foundations. The workers erected a bridge from the house to the lip of the pit, then redirected the stream into the declivity. The Vaux family—or whoever had built Baddesley Clinton—had turned a bog into a fortress.

The three men had dropped down the garderobe from the

second story. Now they stood with the floor of the main level directly above their heads. Burr alone had to stoop to stand in the space. The ledge was not long enough for even one of the men to lie on it, let alone all three. Burr found he could stand with a crook in his neck, bend at the knees—which he could not keep up for long—or lean forward and stand with his hands on his thighs. Or, he supposed, he could sit on the ledge and let his feet dangle in the water. But over time he might regret letting himself get wet and cold. The ledge was too narrow—less than the span of his boot—to sit on it with his heels pulled up beneath him. For the moment he stood uncomfortably with his head bent to one side. Barely audibly, the priest murmured a *Salve Regina.*

Despite his discomfort Burr smiled briefly as he thought how the three of them would look to anyone who could see them standing there: on one end the long old servant with cocked head, on the other the short, bandy-legged craftsman with muscled arms crossed, and between them the fat, spindle-legged priest with muttering lips.

As the noise and clamor above their heads increased, the three risked a few quiet words. At first most of the talk was of why Jack had twice begun his descent, twice abandoned it, and then replaced the jakes. None of them had a good answer. Even so, Garnet seemed unworried. It was Owen who asked, "Can we trust him? Father, you heard his confession. Was there aught in it that would—"

The priest cut him off. "You know I cannot tell you that."

Burr said, "Well, there is this. If he had betrayed us I think we would be in the hands of the pursuivants already."

Owen grumbled his reluctant agreement. Then he said, "Or. . . . Well, I know not."

"Keep faith," the priest said. "Whatever befalls us, God is with us."

For a long time—long enough for the light that crept through the cracks in the mortar to fail altogether—they heard little or no noise overhead. So the three remained silent, standing in utter blackness. Burr wondered how they could get back up the garderobe. Once the pursuivants had gone and the jakes was slid away from its place again, he and Owen could probably climb up the way they had come. But Garnet. . . . Burr thought glumly that if the search lasted long, the priest might lose enough of his fat to make the climb.

At length boots again clattered and floorboards creaked overhead. Burr asked, "How long will they search?"

Owen said, "There is no reckoning. Once some other of us were down here five days. Sometimes they sit quiet and wait for us to come out. But we wait longer. Sometimes they break apart the house and leave. When the jakes is pulled back from the wall, then it will end; we are delivered or caught."

"If we are freed, how do we get back up?"

"The way we came," Owen said.

The priest said wryly, "I wonder."

"Or," Owen continued, "we go through the foundation wall."

Burr asked, "Is it not solid stone?"

"All but in two places. The foundation has two openings well beneath the water's crest, one at each end of the house. So the water can move. A yard below the surface at our feet I have attached a chain that extends underwater to one of the portals in the wall. All we have to do is hold our breath and pull ourselves along the chain. When we pass through the portal, we come up in the moat and swim across to the shore. Do you swim, Master Burr?"

"I do."

"Good. We must wait here as long as we can, though. No doubt the infidels have men watching all sides of the house. Only if they discover that the jakes can slide or if they pry up these floorboards over our heads will we make the attempt. Or if hunger drives us. After a week, perhaps."

"A week!" Burr said in a harsh whisper.

"If it comes to that. Let us pray it does not. But it is good you can swim. Father here swims like a fish."

Garnet said, "I hope I am a fish and not fish-bait for these scabrous pursuivants."

Fish and bait. The priest's image reminded Burr of a poem Jack had written for Lady Bedford just after he had lost her bracelet: lost it or, as was more like, sold it. Something about Lady Lucy's being her own bait, catching the love-besotted fish called Jack Donne. Plainly she had been pleased by the verses, or she never would have shown them to her manservant.

Burr knew Lady Bedford better than she thought. She would say, maybe even half-believe, that such verses as these were merely an artful example of poetic fashion. She would say a clever woman of her standing should support clever poets. Burr would not be taken in, though. He had seen the way she looked at this Jack Donne. Lady Bedford was no strumpet, but a poem like "The Bait" could open a way straight to her bed. As far as Burr knew, Jack had not made his way there yet. But the least provocation might land him there.

Burr painfully shifted his weight. Uncounted times he had chafed at Lady Bedford's imperious ways, but always he had kept his grudgings to himself. And what was his reward for all those years of faithful service? She had ordered him to travel with this Jack Donne. It was all Lady Bedford's doing that her faithful old servant had just descended a sewage shaft and now stood in distress. Already the pain stabbed in his neck, his knees ached, and his hams were beginning to cramp. Crafty and fiery as Lady Bedford could be, he would give all the money he had hoarded in all those years if he could be back at Bedford House now.

For a few minutes more he bore the pain, and then, as the pursuivants talked loudly while they walked overhead, he slipped into the water. Ignoring the fierce whispers of protest from Owen and the priest, Burr took a deep breath, dropped beneath the surface, and found the chain.

Four days later Owen and Garnet still stood on the narrow ledge. During that time they had sometimes leaned against each other to relieve the burden in their legs and had occasionally sat on the ledge with their feet in the water. But the air and water under the house were cold, so they stood as much as they could, bobbing up and down on the balls of their feet to keep warm. For the whole four days they had eaten nothing. To quench their thirst they had dipped up handfuls of the murky water at their feet. No footsteps had sounded above them for the last two days, then light ones—Eleanor Vaux's, or young Ned Tidwell's, they hoped. But the pursuivants had their tricks, and they were patient. If they found a Jesuit priest—especially Garnet, the leader of the English Jesuits—they would receive a rich bounty. If they learned Owen was a lay brother in the Jesuit order, even he would bring a good price.

At last the two heard the jakes above the shaft slide from its place against the wall of the upstairs room. Owen waited until he heard three sharp taps against the stone at the top of the shaft. He held still for a few heartbeats, then heard two more taps. The pattern repeated. "That's the sign," he said.

"Thanks be to God," the priest replied.

Owen pulled open the concealed, half-submerged stone door, then stepped down into the knee-deep water inside the shaft. "Clear," he heard from above. It was Eleanor's voice. Had pursuivants discovered the hidden shaft, they might have forced her to say such a thing. But she would not have revealed the coded signal of the taps against the stone.

"We'll soon be up," Owen replied to Eleanor. Turning to the priest he said, "You first, Father."

"No," Garnet replied.

"I'll go first, then, and pull you from the top."

"No, I say. Not again. My scrapes are sore, and have but begun to crust over. I am loath to tear them open again. I'll take the chain to the moat; the pursuivants are gone."

"We don't know that," Owen persisted. "They're out of the house, but it may hap they watch from the wood. And your flesh has fallen away somewhat in these hungry days. The shaft is safer."

"Even so, I have no love for tight places. I will try the moat."

"Think, Father, of what they will do to you if they catch you."

"I have thought, Nick, and I have prayed. I say I will try the moat."

Owen paused for a time, then said, "If you can wait another hour, I will go up the shaft and venture outside."

"I like not to use you as bait, Nick."

"Better if I am caught than both of us. And you are known to them; I might talk myself free."

"True," the priest said. He exhaled heavily. "Well, I will allow it."

Together the men murmured a Paternoster and an Ave Maria. Then Owen said, "I'll pull up the rope after me and ask Eleanor to lower you some food."

"I would relish it," the priest replied. "Take some food yourself before you venture outside; I can wait."

Owen nimbly climbed the rope, and when the garderobe became too narrow for him to bend his knees and use his feet, pulled himself up with his arms alone. Eleanor was waiting at the top with roast mutton, bread, and clear water from the well. Owen told her the plan.

"And what of the old servant?" she asked. "Burr. Isn't he coming up?"

"Burr went out by the moat four days ago."

"Why?"

"I don't know. Had he been caught, we had all been betrayed."

As they talked she tied some of the food and a corked bottle of the water into a cloth, pulled up the rope, secured the bundle to the end, and lowered it to the bottom of the shaft. Meanwhile Owen ate hastily, took a long draft of the water, and asked, "What happened to Donne? Why didn't he come down after us?"

Eleanor said, "I wish I knew. To help us below, I think. Perchance to delay the search. But he is captured. They bound his hands and took him into the wood."

"Hm. I like not the sound of that."

Owen stepped into the hallway. The house looked as if a storm had raged through it. Boards had been pried out of some of the walls in search of hidden closets. Owen shook his head. The pursuivants could have simply used a string to measure the rooms, and they would have seen that no closets lay behind the walls; there was no need for such destruction. Beds had been overturned and the thicker mattresses slit open. Bones and scraps of food lay strewn everywhere. Coals had scorched the floors where the pursuivants raked out the fireplaces to look up the chimneys. What was left of the heavy door to the bridge hung racked and splintered, its iron hinges twisted out of shape. Owen looked up at the portcullis, wondering how the pursuivants had raised it without a winch; the thing was heavy as a brace of oxen.

Before venturing outside he whistled the call of a chaffinch. An answering song, a good imitation of a short-eared owl, came from the woods. That would be Ned Tidwell: the boy had been watching the grounds, and the owl was the all-clear signal.

Owen stepped onto the bridge. What a blessing simply to stand in the sunlight and breathe in the clean air of day. He crossed the moat and walked to the barn. To his surprise he found all the horses still stabled; he had expected the pursuivants to steal some of the animals. But they looked well fed and watered, no doubt by Ned. Owen patted Jack's big bay mare on the neck and went to check the tool shed. A mattock and spade were missing. Not a good sign if Donne had been led into the forest.

Owen found traces of boot-prints where the men had entered the wood. He followed the signs of their passing. At every turn he expected to come upon a fresh grave. But he found none. The woods were thick, crossed with animals' trails and indecipherable marks on the ground. At least Owen could not make sense of them; he was not an expert tracker. Soon he lost the trail altogether.

He walked back to the grounds of Baddesley Clinton. He would signal Father Garnet that it was safe to escape into the moat. After that he would tell Ned it was safe to go back to his fishing. Then he would resume his search for Jack.

The scrape of the wooden trencher sliding into the chamber sounded against the stone walls, waking Jack from his fitful sleep. He shivered, stood, paced, and smacked his open hands against his thighs to start the blood flowing. The walls reluctantly gave up their dull echoes. He cupped his fingers and blew into them, his breath swirling in ragged wisps and fading in the dim air. As always, the smell of stone that had mouldered through the centuries, stained with every fluid these frail sacs of human skin contained, lingered dankly in the nose. Barring the Second Coming of Our Lord, the stones would remain for millennia more with their ever-thickening accretions of human misery.

Warwick Castle. Months ago, it must be by now: upon painfully coming to his senses on the floor of this dimly lit chamber—there must be a high window somewhere out of sight from the cell—he had guessed he lay in the dungeon of Warwick Castle. His wounds were still fresh when he awoke, so he could hardly have travelled far from Baddesley Clinton. And apart from Warwick Castle, what structure near Eleanor Vaux's house could hold among its foundations such thick-ribbed walls as these?

He had been cast into this darksome place in June but had since lost track of the days. Weeks had passed, surely, even since the chill in the air had betokened the turn from summer into fall. It was October, he guessed, or thereabouts. For perhaps the thousandth time he thought of Anne and the children. What would they be doing now? Would they be outdoors in the crisp fall air? Would their breath be fogging too?

In all his months in the dungeon no other human being had spoken even a single word to him. In the early weeks he had tried every day to talk to his gaoler, plying the dusty-haired old man with questions, or attempting idle chatter, or demanding an audience with someone in authority. But the old man was deaf and mute, or only half-sentient, or under some strict command to utter no word. All Jack heard from him was the sound, once a day, of the shuffling feet as the old man descended the long stone stairway. If Jack stood near the bars, the approaching gaoler would stop, set down the trencher of food, the vessel of water, and the empty jordan, move the fingers of one hand as if to scratch an invisible itch that hung in the air, and wait until his prisoner had moved to the far wall. The old man would deliver the food and drink, then replace with the empty jordan the full one Jack had left by the bars. No matter what Jack said, the keeper would turn and climb stiff-jointed up the stairs. Weeks had passed since Jack gave up trying to talk with the man.

During the months of his confinement the only human voices he heard came echoing from a great distance away. His shouts when he heard them always went unanswered. He must be the only prisoner in the castle—or at least in this part of it. Once again he wondered: why would local pursuivants led by a mere constable accord Jack Donne such singular treatment? Why had they not killed him in the forest and left him in the shallow grave? After all, he had done his best to kill them. This must be Cecil's doing somehow. For whatever reason, *Robertus Diabolus* wanted Jack alive but out of the way.

He thought about his last hours at Baddesley Clinton, his last memories before waking up in this dungeon. The pursuivants had bound him to a post in Eleanor's house, then for the rest of that day and most of the next, ransacked the place in search of priest-hides. Eleanor had been right to warn Father Garnet and the others away from the hidden closet Owen had fashioned in the attic. From where he sat bound to his post Jack could hear the pursuivants shouting to one another about the discovery. Then he heard their anger at finding the closet empty. During the rest of the search Jack neither saw nor heard Eleanor, Ned Tidwell, nor the boy's sick mother upstairs. Probably they had been taken away somewhere. He trusted they were safe. Even pursuivants would not dare to injure or kill a woman with a family as prominent as Eleanor's, Catholic or not. And she would see to it that no harm came to the boy or his mother.

When the pillaging finally stopped on the third day, Jack asked once again for a drink of water. Once again he was refused. The constable said, "Tell us what you know of these scurf-ridden Catholics, and you will get a drink."

The constable left the room for a while to talk with the others. Jack could hear them but could not make out what they said. When they were finished they released him from the post, retied his hands—in front of him this time—and prodded him before them through the shattered door, over the bridge, and across the lawn. They sent Ridgely to fetch a mattock and a spade from the tool shed. The vacant-faced man they left to watch the house. Jack heard him whistle once. Two whistles answered from different points in the fringe of the woods. The constable and the red-bearded man stopped with their prisoner at the well and filled three wineskins. Had there been spit enough in his parched mouth to do it, Jack would have salivated at the sight, the sound, the very smell of the fresh water. Ridgely joined them, the tools from the shed propped on his shoulders. They entered the forest and walked for perhaps half an hour. Jack's thirst made him weak in the knees, but he struggled on.

The constable stopped them at a small clearing shaded by ancient oaks and poplars. He turned his rough-hewn face to Jack. "Who lies hid in that house?"

Jack said hoarsely, "I swear by Almighty God, on peril of my salvation, not a soul lies hid in that house." He did not utter such oaths lightly. What he said was true: the three fugitives hid under the house, not in it, and they did not lie but stood. The constable eyed his prisoner for a long while before nodding to the red-bearded man, who gave Jack a backhanded blow across the face.

"Not too much too quick, Sam," the constable said. "While he lives, we want him where he can talk." The red-bearded man grinned and shrugged his innocence. The constable turned to Jack. "Dig," he said.

With his hands still tied before him, Jack took the spade from Ridgely and started in. The men stood back to let him work. Jack thought darkly that they did well to back away. The constable did well to draw his sword, and the red-bearded man did well to take the mattock from Ridgely. If they did not keep their distance, Jack would use the shovel to lay waste the lot of them. But they watched him carefully. Twice Jack had to trade the spade for the mattock to chop through roots too thick for the shovel.

After the hole was some two feet deep, the constable held out a skin of water and asked, "Do ye want a drink?" Jack glared at him and nodded. "Then tell us where to look," the constable said. Jack recommenced his digging. At the sound of water pouring onto the ground, Jack looked up. "Just tell me when to stop," the constable said stonily as he held the slackening skin at arm's length. Jack spaded up another scoop and tossed the soil onto the wet ground at the constable's feet. The man stopped pouring. "Go ahead, Sam," he said.

This time the red-bearded man handed the mattock back to Ridgely, then strode over to Jack and used not the back of his hand but his fist. Jack staggered in the hole he had dug but kept his feet. Blood welled in his mouth. He spat out a piece of a molar and went back to his digging. "That's your own grave you're standing in," the constable said. "You know that, don't you?" Jack dug some more. "Damn his eyes, Sam, give him another."

Jack scooped up another shovelful as the red-bearded man approached. In one motion he flung the soil into the constable's face and continued his swing, meeting his assailant with the edge of the blade. The red-bearded man stood wide-eyed with his cheek laid open. Jack leapt from the hole and jabbed him in the midsection with the butt-end of the spade. With the red-bearded man doubled over, Jack darted toward the cursing constable to take his blade.

It was Ridgely he hadn't reckoned on, Ridgely with the mattock. Jack had the constable's right hand in his grasp and had already heard the man's wrist snap when he glimpsed something coming at him from the right. A white-hot jolt fired through his head, and then he woke up stiff and bloody in this rocky cell.

Now, months later in the dim light and boggy air of the dungeon, once again Jack saw or heard—his senses had begun to blend over the days and weeks—a rat scuttling toward his trencher of food. He was there before the animal, unaware of crossing the space in the cell, but ready to snatch the creature and dash it against the rocks. First, though, he would look closely at the beast struggling in his grip. If it was not Nellie, he would kill it. When he did so he always reached between the bars and threw the carcass as far as he could. He did not like to kill the creatures, but it would not do to let them overrun the cell. Besides, he worried one of them might hurt Nellie or one of her little ones.

In the first days of his imprisonment Jack had feared he might soon have to eat the animals raw rather than fling them away, but so far he had avoided that: as the weeks wore on, the keeper unaccountably began giving him increasing amounts of food. Perhaps the old man had, in the dim chambers of his mind, taken some sort of liking for his prisoner. If so, the quantity of food he brought was the only sign of it. But Jack was grateful. By now he had daily offerings of more than enough moldy bread and barley-meal stew, usually with greens and sometimes with bits of some sort of meat, not only to keep him alive but to keep up his weight.

Still, of all the rats only Nellie and her little brood could he afford to feed. After perhaps three months of soul-numbing loneliness he had lured her to him with a few crumbs of bread. Now he fed her and her three young ones from his daily portion. The mother rat and her children had lost all fear of him. They would frisk about his cell at their play, and Nellie would let him pick up her little ones and hold them in his hands. He learned to interpret the family's chirps and squeaks: learned when they were hungry, when they wanted to play, when they smelled another of their kind, when they were frightened by some sound inaudible to him. They did not respond when he tried to imitate their little noises, so he spoke to them in human words: sometimes English, sometimes Latin, French, Italian, or Greek. They did not seem to care which.

Especially when Nellie and her children were away on some business, Jack kept up his strength by whatever exercises he could fashion. He had room, at least, to move freely: the cell must once have held a dozen prisoners, maybe more. Sometimes he darted from corner to corner, hundreds of times, until he stood panting with his palms on his knees. Sometimes he contorted his body in one direction or another, then pushed against the bars or the stone walls as hard and steadily as he could, counting his pulse-beats until he could bear no more. Then he turned a different way and began again. He remembered the counts for every position and each day tried to increase the numbers. Sometimes he scaled the walls as far as he could, gripping with his fingers and toes the cracks between the massive stones. After a few weeks he could almost hang pendant from the beams overhead.

When his strength finally gave out and he sat chastened and quiet, he would try to pray, try to listen for any faint echo of encouragement. But God remained silent, inscrutable. Still, Jack kept at the meditations, hoping for the light. At such times he could not escape the plaguing sense that he had brought all his dark loneliness and misery on himself, that he was a damned soul, rightly forsaken by God and man. Then he told himself it was only the voice of the fiend trying to lure him to despair. But the whispering would not relent. It troubled not only his waking hours but crept into his dreams. So he prayed. He prayed long and tearfully. Two or three times he thought he caught a glimmer of the becalmed radiance of the Blessed Virgin, but such moments were painfully rare. All the rest of the time his prayers brought him no consolation at all.

When the silence grew too heavy to bear, he talked to himself. In the absence of pen and paper he composed aloud his poems, devotions, and letters. He spoke the words, mentally recast them, and began again. The poems he committed to memory. Some were darker than any he had written before, but they did more than his prayers to still the beating in his soul. He used the verses to confess his fears, used them to pray. Today he paced as he recited the words:

As due by many titles I resign
Myself to thee, O God; first I was made
By thee, and for thee, and when I was decayed
Thy blood bought that, the which before was thine;
I am thy son, made with thy self to shine,
Thy servant, whose pains thou hast still repaid,
Thy sheep, thine Image, and, till I betrayed
My self, a temple of thy Spirit divine;
Why doth the Devil then usurp on me?
Why doth he steal, nay, ravish that's thy right?
Except thou rise and for thine own work fight,
Oh I shall soon despair, when I do see
That thou lov'st mankind well, yet wilt' not choose me,
And Satan hates me, yet is loath to lose me.

After praying the lines aloud he continued pacing in silence for a time, then felt led to compose a letter to Anne—one she would never receive, for the words died like a vapor in the air no sooner than he gave them voice. But maybe somehow she would know. . . . Each time he composed one of these evanescent letters he asked Anne about their third child. If the infant had lived, the little one must be three or four months old by now.

And if Anne had survived the birth: he did not even know that.

During the early days of his travels, part of him had found that the search for Guido somehow freed him to look about him at the wide world, to let his mind range, to laugh broadly among men in a way he had not done since his time at Lincoln's Inn and then in the wars. But as the distance from Anne and the little ones increased, so did the pain of separation. On chilly, wet nights he had longed for the fireside, for Anne's warmth, for the fresh intelligence of her conversation. He wished he could hold the little ones in his lap. The months in the dungeon had turned the longing sometimes into an ache and sometimes into an emptiness, a hole in the soul. The search for Guido now seemed utter folly. If only he could be granted it, any sight, any sound of his family—even the children's crying—would gladden him for days; he was sure of it. A single word from Anne would allow him to sleep in peace through a month of cold nights. It now seemed unforgivable he had not written more letters to her while he could. Time and again during his travels he had told himself it was not safe to send her messages in the absence of a courier he trusted, but could he not have written of inconsequential things? It would have been enough simply to describe the color of the plants, the shifting of the clouds, the shape of the lands he crossed. She would have been grateful for whatever he wrote, would have understood why he could not confide more.

As it was, it grieved him that as the months of living among these desolate stones passed, he found it harder and harder to recall Anne's face, or Constance's, or Little Jack's. He could describe their features: the color of hair and eyes, the shape of the nose, the line of the jaw. But these descriptions did not coalesce into any familiar likeness. Sometimes the images of his loved ones seemed on the verge of coming into focus, but then they receded before him, watery and insubstantial, like the fading scenes upon first waking from a dream. The mind cast after them, but the net returned empty. It was maddening: these were the faces he loved, and he could not recall them.

Yet Cecil's face remained clearly etched in his memory. Lady Bedford's too.

Chapter 14

Elbows on the table, Anne propped her head in her hands, trying once more to make sense of the matter. Maybe the Queen had told Cecil of Anne's illegal visit. Why else would the man have summoned her? Yet it had been months since the Queen's message to her that Guido was in Warwickshire. If the Queen had lately warned Cecil that the royal household was in danger, why had she not done it sooner? Well, even if Cecil was bent on punishing Anne for her effrontery, she was ready to suffer the consequences. What worried her far more was the prospect—a likely one, much as she hated to think it—that the Queen had said nothing to Cecil, but the twisted little man had news about Jack. If so, the news were not like to be good. No word from her husband had come through the whole summer and into the fall, not since he sent the poem about the bracelet of her hair. In the letter with the poem Jack had assured her he had received her news about Guido. Her husband should long since have been back in England, in Warwickshire, not even three days' ride away. Why had he sent her no word, no hint he was safe and well? Twice she had sent one of Wolley's servants to inquire about Jack in various towns throughout Warwickshire, but each time the servant had come back without news. She prayed that the image of the circlet of her hair embracing bare bone did not prophesy Jack's early end.

The paper's folded edge protruded just above the pocket in her dress. She pulled out the page and read the poem yet again, searching for any meaning she had not yet discovered, maybe even the clue to some code. But she found none. The poem was exactly like Jack: witty, earthy, religious, wonderfully enamored of Anne herself. It was a poem to be treasured, but she would gladly cast it into the flames if it meant she could see the man himself, if for only an hour.

Her husband did not even know that five months ago she had been delivered of their third child.

It was the sound of men that woke Jack. Men talking! One spoke, the other answered, and they were coming down the stairs. He scrambled to his feet and stood waiting at the bars. At the foot of the stairs the two took shape by the light of a lantern. They were moving directly toward him. The one carrying the lantern was the familiar gaoler with his shuffling step. Well, then, he was not a mute; he had been talking with the stranger. The new man dwarfed the keeper. Broad-shouldered and well over two yards tall, he carried with him a bracing scent of the outdoors. Dressed in a leather jerkin and breeches—a country gentleman just home, perhaps, from a hunt—he gazed into the cell and said, "Aye, that's the man. Let me in."

The gaoler handed the gentleman the lantern, fumbled for his keys, and put a large one into the lock. He could not get the key to turn. The big man growled something, reached for the key, and gave it what looked like an easy twist. The lock fell open. The door squealed on its hinges as it swung into the cell. Jack backed away to let the stranger enter. "Chairs," the big man said to the keeper. "You have chairs hereabout, do you not?"

"Aye, sir. I'll bring you a brace of joint-stools."

"Not stools," the stranger snarled. "I said chairs. Two of them: real ones. This man needs to remember what it was like to sit in comfort."

"Well, now, sir, that would be a matter for—"

"Are there chairs in Warwick Castle, or no?"

"Well, now, as I was saying, sir, there are. But—"

"Fetch them." The stranger's tone said he would brook no more hesitation. The gaoler reached to retrieve the lantern, but the big man said, "We'll keep it here: this man needs light. And by God's bloody bodikins, he needs food. Bring him a good supper instead of whatever you've been feeding him. Something with meat in it, and good, fresh bread. And bring some wine."

"Well, sir, that all would take some time."

The big man swung his leather satchel from his shoulder and tossed it into the middle of the cell. "And what have you in this Stygian hole apart from time? Take what time you need, but mind you make it a good meal. First bring the chairs."

The old man stood looking bewildered. "But sir, you must needs understand—"

The stranger glared at the dusty-haired gaoler, who turned, shook his head, and muttered to himself as he stiffly climbed the stairs.

The tall man looked familiar to Jack, but he could not make out where he might have seen him. Then again, Jack had tried for months to remember what his own wife and children looked like, and he could not. The man standing before him could be his best friend, and Jack might not recognize him. "Pardon my failing wits," he said. "I know you, but I misremember."

The stranger held up the lantern, pulled back his hair, and turned his head. The top part of his left ear was missing.

"Robin Catesby," Jack said.

"Aye. Tell me how you came here. Did a judge sentence you?"

"I don't know how I got here, and I remember no judge; I'd taken a knock to the sconce with a mattock."

"Ah, that were enough to tamper with the memory. Can you recollect who was there before the mattock?"

"There was a stout red-bearded man. I think I laid his face open with a shovel. And a constable."

"A constable."

"Yes. But how did you know I was here?"

"Word travels."

"Well," Jack said, "it took its time in traveling."

The big man shrugged. "Some arse-licking pursuivants led you into the woods, and that's all we knew. We thought you were dead."

The old gaoler was descending the stairs backwards, dragging two chairs after him. They thudded on each step as he came.

"Sirrah!" Catesby said. The gaoler stopped. "Who sentenced this man?"

"I have my orders."

"But who was the justice?"

"Orders, sir."

"Whose orders, then?"

The old man would not reply, but began again to drag the chairs down the steps. When he had pulled them to the cell, he made his way back up the stairs.

Catesby looked as though he might follow the man and give him a clout, but then he mumbled something, turned back to Jack, and set the chairs a few feet apart. He gestured toward one.

Jack hesitated. It seemed unnatural, somehow extravagant, to sit in a chair: especially one like this, with a padded, upholstered seat and back. Bare-chested, his buckram shirt having given out entirely a week or two since, he felt ill at ease. The shirt's noisome, tattered remains lay in the corner of the cell for a makeshift pillow. Come nesting season, he would perhaps parcel out buckram strips to Nellie for her new brood.

Jack looked again at the chair. Instinctively he brushed the remaining rags of his breeches with his hands, as if there were any hope of removing the grime. Catesby stood patiently, the light from the lantern reflecting a gruff compassion in his eyes.

Jack put his palms on the arms of the chair and eased himself into the seat. Why such a simple act moved him he could not say, but it did. There was quiet wonder in his voice as he said, "We used to sit in these. We thought nothing of it."

Now Catesby sat. "If I have aught to do with it, you will have chairs again, and not ferried down the stairs to a dungeon by that old fool of a Charon. But in a real house. And a bed. Think of it: a bed. The service you have done Father Garnet, Nick Owen, and Eleanor Vaux will not be forgotten. And Eliza Vaux prays for you daily at Harrowden."

Elbows propped on the arms of the chair, Jack covered his eyes with his hands. All this was moving too quickly. Something inside him pressed against his ribs. Breathing was an effort.

Catesby said, "This constable, now. What did he look like?"

"Face made of stone."

Catesby nodded. "And the sculptor left off before his carving was half done?"

"The very man."

"Swetnam. I know him. He is easily managed."

Jack raised his eyebrows. "That were news to me."

"Ach, never fear him." Catesby looked around. "So how do you pass the time?"

"I weary my muscles with climbing the walls."

"Aye, the sinews in you stand out like stones, with no fat earth to cushion them. So you climb. What else do you do?"

"I pray. I write poems."

"Poems?"

"Yes."

"But how do you write them? Does that withered husk of a keeper bring you pen and ink?"

"No. I don't write them. I . . . compose them. In my mind."

"And then you con them?"

"Yes."

"I were never overfond of conning poetry; it would never stay in my mind. Even in school when I could start with the words laid out before me."

"One grows accustomed to it, I suppose."

"Aye, like anything else. But I could never see why anyone would write, still less con, this prancing poetry. Men don't speak in rhymes."

"True. But the rhymes, the rhythms, the strange conceits, all of it sharpens the language, like good steel hammered and honed to an arrow-head."

"Ha. Now, I'd never thought of it like that." Catesby paused, then added, "Say one of them for me."

"A poem?"

"Aye."

"Of what sort?"

"I don't know, a hunt maybe. Have you anything about a hunt?"

Jack turned over some possibilities, then said, "Have you ever been boar-hunting, and you heard the beast charging at you through the brush, snorting and squealing, and you stood firm, for you knew you were a man and he was but a beast, and though others might turn and run, you would not?"

"Aye, now you're frisking sharp." Catesby stood, moved to within a foot of Jack, unlaced his breeches, and let them drop to the floor. He picked up the lantern. Jack pulled his head back as he found himself at eye level with Catesby's swaying ball-sac and what might have served for a bull's pizzle. But Catesby was pointing to the inside of his left thigh, which bore a cruel, crescent-shaped scar. "I've been *that* close to a charging boar," he said. "He had a tusk in me." Catesby set down the lantern, pulled up his breeches, and sat again in his chair. "Say on."

"Well. Yes. That kind of hunt. The boar thought he had you. But you were a true man and you were determined to have him for dinner despite all his bristle and his snarl and the ripping of his tusks."

"Aye, that's the touch of it! By God's wounds, you've hunted these boar yourself."

"I have. And the beast's godless, bloodshot eyes say he's torn you already and he'll soon have you, but your eyes lock on his, and that makes him furious all the more."

"E'en so, e'en so!"

"And then he's spitted on your boar-staff, with a look of surprise on his hairy face, as if to say, *I never knew.*"

"Aye, *there's* a poem for you. Tell me that one."

"Well, this one is like the hunt, but the boar is named Death."

"Say on."

Jack recited the lines:

Death, be not proud, though some have called thee
Mighty and dreadful, for thou art not so.
For, those whom thou think'st thou dost overthrow
Die not, poor death, nor yet canst thou kill me.
From rest and sleep, which but thy pictures be,
Much pleasure: then from thee much more must flow.
And soonest our best men with thee do go,
Rest of their bones, and soul's delivery.
Thou art slave to fate, chance, kings, and desperate
men,
And dost with poison, war, and sickness dwell,
And poppy or charms can make us sleep as well
And better than thy stroke; why swell'st thou then?
One short sleep past, we wake eternally,
And death shall be no more; death, thou shalt die.

Catesby paused, as if he were expecting more. Then he said, "So Death himself is going to die, no matter all his boasting."

"That's it. Like the boar."

"But. . . ." Catesby paused to think, then said, "But Death is going to die later, on the Last Day, not like the boar in the hunt."

Jack hesitated. "Yes, but—"

"And we're going to live forever."

"Just so."

"And that's your poem."

"It is. The words are like the boar-staff. There is no real boar in this cell, but that poem kept the beast at bay through more than one long night."

Catesby rubbed his beard. "So you're the poet, but you're like the hunter."

"Yes. Both at once."

"But if that's what you mean, why not just say it plain?"

"The plain words have their use, but they can be like a blunt staff instead of a spear-head."

Catesby considered the matter, scratched the back of his head, and said, "I like a good tale of a boar hunt, none of your mincing poetry."

"Ah. Well." Jack looked up the stairs where the gaoler had disappeared, then turned back to Catesby. "Robin, are you here to set me free?"

"Of course I am. What did you think?"

"Why don't we do it, then?"

"Why don't we. . . ."

"Leave. Why don't we leave?"

"Ah. Because I'm hungry. Left without breakfast when I got the news, then rode all day."

"But . . . we could get something to eat on the way. What if the keeper betrays us, and comes back with more of the guard?"

"If there's more of them, then we'll see some fun. I've a dirk for you, and two blades of my own." Catesby paused, then looked mildly disappointed as he said, "But no fear of it, he'll come with the food. I've paid him enough for his trouble, and besides I've put the true fear of the Catesby clan in him. We'll eat and then be on our way."

"Well. You know best, I suppose." Catesby nodded as Jack continued: "You said you came as soon as you heard the news. You mean the news I was mewed up in this dungeon?"

"Aye, that, and the tidings from Father Garnet."

"What tidings?"

Catesby reached for his satchel and pulled out a well-sealed letter. "Here. He sends you greetings."

By the lantern's light Jack looked at the letter's cover-sheet in his hands, addressed with only the initials *J D.* The cover was folded from coarse vegetable parchment flecked with bits of still-green plants. He ran his stone-callused fingertips over the waxen seal. The touch of the letter brought back a vast world of reading and writing all but ebbed away: the faint crackle of a long-neglected book opened at last, the smell of ink, the sound of a goosefeather quill's liquefied scratch, thc stuttering heat of a candle, the purr of molten wax dripped for a seal, the signet's cushioned imprint that bulged the edges of the cooling wax.

"Well," Catesby said, "aren't you going to open it?"

"Yes." Jack called himself back from his distraction. "Yes. Of course." He carefully lifted the paper's edge, tearing slowly though the seal, as if it would be sacrilege to do more damage than needful. He let the cover-sheet fall away and unfolded the paper inside. The first words were *Caveat: for your eyes alone.*

"So what does Garnet say?" Catesby asked. "Let me see."

Jack held up a finger to signal he was still reading. Garnet's penmanship was not the best, and the lantern was not in the right place. Jack leaned forward to lift the lantern. At the same time, Catesby reached toward him and said, "Let me do it for you. I can read the Father's scratchings well enough. Your eyes are dim from all these months in the dark."

Jack took the lantern and pulled back. "Give me a minute. Ah: the light suits better here. So far Garnet only sends his greetings. Let's see: then he thanks me for my good service at Baddesley Clinton, and he says what you already told me: he thought I was dead. But now that he knows I live, he is sorry it was my cross to bear to lie in prison so long, and he hastened to send you as soon as he learned I was in Warwick Castle. He prays for us both. That is all."

It was a lie. The letter said, *Remember Coombe Abbey. It will happen ere long. Make your way there, and do my former bidding. Pause only to burn this paper.* So the attempt to kidnap the Princess had not yet been made. And Father Garnet had hinted that Catesby had a part in the conspiracy to seize her.

The big man eyed Jack and said, "Let me have a look at it. Sometimes with Garnet there are words behind the words, so to speak, and I know the man's ways."

"No need," Jack said. "It's but an ordinary letter."

"Then why did he charge me to ride here with such haste?"

"I suppose he wanted me free. As I told you, he is grateful for my service."

Catesby looked unconvinced.

Jack had no shirt, no pocket, and tatters for breeches. He tucked the letter under him on the chair, watching Catesby's eyes follow him as he did. It was best to distract the man. Jack said, "Robin, now I bethink me, I've come to see you're in the right: the story about the boar is better than my poem."

Catesby's face lost its suspicious edge and once again turned open and frank. "Oh, but it was a good poem, as these things go, and I don't say it wasn't. You should keep writing such."

"Maybe I will. But tell me the rest of the tale of that hunt, and what happened after he gored you, and you ran the boar-spear through the beast. You must have lost enough blood to fill a wine-cask."

"Oh, that I did. . . ."

Jack kept Catesby busy telling stories of hunts and whores and drunken brawls until the old gaoler limped down the stairs, straining under the burden of their supper. Catesby glanced the old man's way once, then finished telling about how his nose was broken in a fight with four Scotsmen. The dinner arrived: roast mutton, beef stew, and a plugged goatskin bulging with wine. No sooner had the old man set down the food than he turned and muttered his way up the stairs.

Catesby laid out the food on trenchers and in bowls the keeper had brought. It pained Jack to adulterate such a feast, but as Catesby dug into his food, telling stories between mouthfuls of meat and long pulls from the wineskin, Jack quietly tore Garnet's letter into shreds and dropped the pieces into his bowl of stew. He took his time with the meal: had he not, such fat-laden fare would have come back up in any case. In the end Jack thought it a fine meal despite the parchment, and the two finished all the gaoler brought them, with Catesby eating and drinking perhaps thrice again Jack's share.

Looking glassy-eyed and sated, Catesby sat back in his chair and belched. "So: where are you off to now? Home to your wife in London, or a nunnery first? I know some good ones."

"My wife, of course." The full weight of Garnet's message did not sink in until Jack had said the words. He would not be going directly home to his wife and children, but to Coombe Abbey first. There he would warn Sir John Harrington of the plot to kidnap the Princess. Well, his stay at Coombe Abbey would be short—time enough only to convince Harrington of the danger.

But if the Princess was there, so was her tutor: Lucy Harrington Russell, Countess of Bedford.

Catesby shrugged. "Ah, well, whatever suits." He wiped his beard with his sleeve. "I'm going the other way. But Garnet sent a purse for you. Your wife will want to see you arrive with some clean clothes on your back." He reached for his satchel, pulled out a small, coin-filled purse, and tossed it to Jack. "I never counted it, but I trust it will serve."

"I'm sure it will. Thank Father Garnet when you see him."

Catesby sat back in his chair and was soon breathing heavily, on the verge of sleep. Jack thought about leaving without him, but he didn't want to arouse Catesby's suspicions.

After a few minutes the keeper halted his way down the stairs. He shuffled to the cell and held before him a large blacksmith's rasp. "Strike me," the old man said.

Catesby stirred from his torpor. "Eh? What's that?"

Jack looked at the piece of ribbed steel in the keeper's hand. "Strike you?"

"Strike me, one of you. Not hard enough to crack my pate, but hard enough to part the skin."

"But why?" Jack asked.

"If anyone questions me, you knocked me down and escaped."

Jack shrugged and said, "Hold steady." He weighed the rasp in his hand, trying to decide just how much force to use. Only a little, surely.

By now Catesby was standing. He took the rasp from Jack's hand and tossed it onto the stones at the foot of the stairs. Then he said to the gaoler, "I need no iron rod to open your head."

The old man flinched a little, and Catesby gave him a backhanded swipe to the forehead. Catesby belched again. It looked to Jack as if the big man had merely waved away a fly, but the gaoler staggered and fell. Blood flowed freely from his forehead. Catesby strode over and retrieved the rasp, held it to the old man's head until the steel was covered in blood, and tossed it back onto the floor. "There," he said. "You'll mend. Tell your tale as you will, but don't go saying it was Robin Catesby who had to take a piece of metal to you. Say it was the poet here."

Lady Bedford looked up from her book to smile as the Princess Royal primly said, "Checkmate." The girl moved her knight to capture her opponent's rook. Incredulous, the squat-bodied Earl of Bedford fingered his beard as he studied the board. Studying the board, like so much else pertaining to the intellect, took the Earl a long time. He scratched behind his ear, then wiped his broad, lumpy nose with his sleeve. "Luck," he said. "Luck of the bairn." The young Princess looked at him with her wide eyes in a good imitation of guilelessness. "Agh," Lord Bedford said as he placed his hands on his thighs, "I'd best be on." Turning to one of two gentlemen in waiting, he said, "Tell Throckman to saddle my roan."

As her husband rose, Lady Bedford asked, "Does my father hunt with you?"

"Aye, that's the plan." He thumped out of the room.

Lady Bedford put her book in her lap and looked at the Princess. The child reminded her of herself at that age. "Nicely played," she said. "Checkmating my husband does well. But you must never defeat your father."

"Why mustn't I?"

"Because, Your Highness, no nine-year-old girl—" Lady Bedford checked herself—"Because *no one* should best the King at chess. Even the Lord Cecil lets your father win."

The Princess wrinkled her nose. "*Does* he? I have wondered. Lord Cecil can defeat me with ease, and yet he never defeats my father." The girl pursed her lips. "So I am never to best my father."

"Never, Your Highness."

"Then answer me this. My father is a king. Is not the purpose of the game to defeat the king?"

Lady Bedford laughed. "*That* game, yes. But when he lets your father win at chess, Lord Cecil is playing a different sort of game."

The Princess remained pensive for a time, then said, "I think I understand."

Lady Bedford tipped her head toward the girl. "I think you do."

The man who had left the room to arrange for the Earl's horse returned with another gentleman, this one green-stockinged and cross-gartered. The man bowed to a point midway between the Princess and Lady Bedford as he said, "Begging Your Royal Highness's pardon, but, Lady Bedford, a man waits without who craves an audience. He would give no name but insisted you would want to admit him. The man would not be put off."

"Why would I admit a man without a name? What manner of man is he?"

"Dressed to please and fair of speech, but haggard of form: tall, pale, with a distracted eye, his beard and hair long and wild. Altogether he looks a very woodwose."

"Well!" Lady Bedford said. "What did you tell him?"

"That you were like not to admit him, my lady," the gentleman said. "Yet he importuned me in courtly terms that so misfit his form, I thought it best to inform you of his entreaties."

"I thank you for your information. But a nameless man so crazed can have little to tell me, pretty of speech or no. Send him away."

"Yes, my lady." The green-stockinged gentleman bowed to the Princess and said, "Your Highness," then straightened himself to leave the room.

As he reached the door the Princess said, "I should like to

meet such a man."

Lady Bedford said, "Oh, Your Highness, that were ill-advised. The man sounds far beneath your station, and he might be dangerous."

At the word *dangerous* the Princess's eyes grew larger. "He sounds like an eremite from the tales: a wise hermit with a prophecy we must heed. Or if he be a woodwose I should like to see him even more. Take me to him."

The green-stockinged gentleman shook his head and said, "Be ruled, Your Highness; the man is not for you."

The Princess narrowed her eyes and gave the gentleman such a look that he took a step back. The girl said, "I will not be ruled. It is your function to advise, mine to rule. I will see this man."

The gentleman turned to Lady Bedford, who returned him an exasperated look as if to say, *When this child turns peevish we have no choice.* She asked the gentleman, "Has my father left for the hunt?"

"This morning, my lady, with Lord Hay. The Earl is to meet them. Perhaps he has yet to depart. Shall I send for him?"

Lady Bedford waved away the idea.

Turning to one of the men who stood waiting, the green-stockinged official said, "Post me some three or four of the guard in the chamber, and then admit Her Royal Highness." To the other he said, "Alert the guard without the house. They are to watch for any mischance."

When all the men had left the room, Lady Bedford turned to the Princess. "Did not His Majesty make it clear that while you remain here at Coombe Abbey under my father's protection, you are to heed the counsel of your protectors?"

"He said I am to heed your father the Lord Harrington's counsel. But your father left this morning with the hunt."

"So he did. Well, we shall see this eremite."

CHAPTER 15

All knelt as the Princess entered the chamber. The child gazed happily upon the haggard stranger while Lady Bedford watched him closely. Never had she beheld a man whose grooming so mismatched the rest of his appearance. His clothes did credit to his thin but well-muscled form, and he bore himself as a man who could easily make his way among courtiers. But his dark eyes bore a look haunted, guarded, and wild. His tangled hair reached the middle of his back, and his beard bristled thick and untrimmed.

The Princess said, "Rise, woodwose. What do you crave?"

"Audience, Your Highness. Audience with the Lady Bedford."

The voice sounded familiar, and there was something about those eyes. . . . Lady Bedford took a step closer. "Donne!" she exclaimed. "Jack Donne!"

Jack nodded.

"But why did you not give my man your name? I almost turned you away."

"I was afraid, my lady, you would not . . . recognize me. I have . . . fallen off somewhat, of late."

"But how did this come about?"

"Prison," he said. "A dungeon. Sickness of heart from living in a stone cage."

"And my servant Timothy Burr? He was to remain with you, and I have had no word from him since midsummer. Was he in prison too?"

"No. Or not that I saw. We parted ways just before my arrest."

The young Princess said, "Woodwose, you speak beside the point. What of this message? What have you to say to Lady Bedford that you would not say to me?"

"Your Highness," Jack said, "I have sworn a vow to deliver some news to her and none other."

The Princess's tone changed from imperious to curious as she asked, "Did you break your chains and lay waste the dungeon? Did you kill all the guard?"

"No, Your Highness. I meant the guard no hurt."

The child seemed disappointed. Then her eyes brightened as she asked, "This message: is it a prophecy?"

Jack paused. He appeared to be studying his reply. "It is," he said. "And heavy will rain the ruin that falls upon us all if I utter it in the presence of any but the Lady Bedford. So it has been decreed."

The child nodded; she seemed to know this story. "And good is to come of it if you speak with her?"

"Much good, yes."

"And a happy marriage in the end?"

"Yes, most happy."

"Is a dragon to be slain first?"

"No, Your Highness, no dragon. But a creature still more dire, one that beggars all description."

Her eyes ardent, the Princess put her hand to her lips, then said, "More dire than a *dragon*. . . . Let us all leave the woodwose and Lady Bedford to their conference."

Two or three gentlemen began at once to speak their objections. Lady Bedford interrupted them. "I know this man. He has no more harm in him than I have in myself. Do as Her Highness says."

The green-stockinged gentleman opened his mouth to protest

again, but Lady Bedford cut him off with a glare. After a sweeping gesture that ended with an upward flourish, he said, "Away."

Alone with Jack, Lady Bedford pulled one chair to face another and said, "Sit. Please." When they had sat she took his hands in hers. Sensing his discomfort, she asked, "Did others share your prison cell, or did you remain alone?"

"Alone. Purely and utterly."

"How long since you have . . . touched another?"

"I know not. Month upon month."

She gave his hands a little reassuring squeeze before saying, "I want to hear everything that has befallen you. It pains me to think what you must have endured. But first you had better tell me: who has sent this message for my ears alone?"

Lady Bedford felt a tinge of disappointment as he said, "In fact the message was for your father." She tried to dispel her petty thoughts as Donne continued, "But the porter told me Lord Harrington had ridden out some three or four hours since. Your husband too was preparing to ride when I arrived, but I thought it best to say nothing to him and speak with you alone."

Ah, there was that at least. "You did well to let my husband ride. Coombe Abbey is no more his house than mine. We stay but a time as guests of my father, at the Queen's request, while the Princess resides here."

"And why does she reside here?"

"Protection. The royal family must not all remain in one place, lest the Spanish or some other force attack."

Donne nodded, then looked directly at her. To see in his eyes such intelligence conjoined with such suffering moved her more than she would have thought. He said, "The message concerns the safety of the Princess. One in a position to know—one whose name I cannot reveal—warns of an attempt to attack this house and capture her."

"Capture her! *Who* means to attack? The Spanish?"

"I think not. English rebels, more like, perhaps in league with the Spanish."

"To what end?"

"That I know not. Ransom, I should think."

"But you must suspect something more. Is it gold they want?"

Jack shook his head. "Mayhap, but I would hazard they mean to use the child to bargain for some other gain. Maybe a favorable marriage to someone of the old faith. Or some such religious advantage."

Lady Bedford gave him a mildly exasperated look and said, "All of which is to say we know nothing but that they are Catholic. How large a force?"

"My lady, I wish I knew. All I can say is that the plan is afoot, and we would do well to heed the warning."

"How soon do they come?"

"Nor do I know that. A matter of days, I think. The sender of this message says the Princess should be spirited away to some safer place."

"But this house is well guarded. Few estates are better fortified. Were she not better off here? We could send for more troops."

"Kenilworth Castle is hard by and might serve better."

She had to agree. With its broad moat and thick walls, Kenilworth was all but unassailable. Something in her misgave, though. She did not know this Jack Donne well; he could be laying a trap. Watching closely for any hint of betrayal in his response, she said, "Perhaps these attackers mean to waylay her along the road, or perhaps conspirators already lie within the hold at Kenilworth."

Donne shook his head. "The assailants know nothing of the message I received, or it would never have been sent. They think the Princess will remain here."

"The message comes from some spy, then."

"Not a spy, no. But . . . one, as I say, in a position to know. One who does not wish any harm to the royal family. I cannot say more."

"So the sender of this message is a Catholic in a position to know of a conspiracy against the Crown. He is some conspirator whose conscience betrays him. Or a priest! He is a priest who has heard of this plan in a confession."

"Lady Lucy, I have said too much."

"A Jesuit?"

"I cannot tell you that."

"Ah, so he *is* a Jesuit." Lady Bedford had detected no sign of lying in his eyes—only discomfort at her guesses—and she was good at reading the heart's expressions in the face. Even so, she had best try again to find any sign of dissimulation. If Donne were a member of some rebellious confederacy, or in league with the Spanish, he might try to lure the Princess into peril. "Kenilworth would serve," she said, "but what of Warwick Castle?"

She was surprised at the suddenness of his response. His hands twitched in hers as a momentary shudder ran along his limbs. Such a reaction seemed triggered by something more than a mere desire to lie to her. "What is it?" she asked.

"It is in Warwick Castle that I have lain these last long months. In the dungeon."

"The dungeon of Warwick Castle? I didn't know it was still in use."

"I think I was the sole prisoner. Cecil must have wanted me alive but buried under stone." He watched her closely, and she returned his gaze. His was not the face of a liar; anything but. She slowly lifted one of his hands and kissed the back of it. He let out a small, inarticulate sound, like a dying man's last breath. His eyes brimmed.

They sat this way for a time. Then he pulled his hands from

hers and said, "I hurried here, taking time only to buy these weeds I wear and try to bathe in a stream along the way. I fear I must look—and smell—the very woodwose the Princess believes me to be."

Lady Bedford smiled, then put her face to the side of his neck and inhaled deeply. "I don't care," she said. Then, all business, she spoke briskly: "Yet you would no doubt enjoy a real bath. I will order water to be heated. In the meantime I will decide what to do about the Princess. Regardless, the first thing is to order greater numbers to defend the house." She smiled at him again, then rose and left the room.

Jack had been given food: a whole roast capon, fresh bread, rich red wine, and a sweet-cake covered with berries and cream. He had eaten slowly, very slowly, while men bustled about the house to bolster the guard. Now a drowsy numbness settled along his limbs, and he rested his head on a cushion. Perhaps he dozed.

He was roused by a servant who came to lead him down a series of hallways, then let him into a large chamber with a great featherbed beneath a shuttered, east-facing window. Nearer the door stood the huge basin, presumably the one Lord Harrington used for bathing. It was the biggest brass vessel Jack had ever seen; he guessed it must be two and a half yards long. Lit only by candles on low stands around it, the polished brass danced with flickering light like something from a dream.

Soon three servants began to come and go with bucket after bucket of hot water. They must have a dozen fires blazing, Jack thought, to heat so much of it. When the tub was over halfway full, one of the servants entered with a fresh stoup of wine, set it beside the basin, and felt the water for temperature. "There: that is the way Lord Harrington likes it. I trust it will serve."

"Of course," Jack said. The servant left the room and closed the heavy door. Jack pulled off his clothes and eased into the bath. The water was very hot but bearable. He stretched to his full length, closed his eyes, and floated on his back. If this was a dream, he hoped he never woke.

After a minute or two he heard the door open. He sat upright and watched as Lady Bedford entered, carrying a pewter urn with a wooden handle protruding from the top: a lye-cask and brush, Jack guessed. She also carried a small, stoppered glass vial of some rose-colored liquid. Without speaking she set the cask and vial beside the tub, turned, latched the door, and began to unlace her dress. With a wry smile, she slowly let the dress fall to the floor. She stood before him naked. Lady Bedford was small-boned but as shapely as Jack had ever imagined her.

Still without a word she stepped into the tub, facing him as she eased into the water. Then she leaned forward, laid her breast against his, and kissed him. She picked up the wine, drank some, and tipped the flagon for Jack to drink.

At length she drew the brush from the lye-cask and laid the soft bristles against his cheek. The lye-wash had been mixed with spikenard. He moved about—now on his knees, now with his back to her, now standing—until she had cleaned every inch of him. By then the water had cooled. Hand in hand, they stepped from the tub. They dried each other with soft, thick towels, then let them fall to the floor.

She picked up the little vial, pulled the stopper, and poured some of the rose-colored oil onto her hand. She rubbed the perfume into his skin and hair. He did the same for her. The aroma was intoxicating. Lady Bedford said, "Lavender to heal the roughened skin, jasmine to ease the beating mind."

She led him to the fireplace. He turned to look back at the basin. The candles still glowed around the polished brass, reflecting waves of shifting light interfused with the red glow of embers in the fireplace. She pulled him close, and they stood watching the dying fire. From time to time a yellow flame licked around a half-spent log.

She stood on her toes and pulled his head toward hers to whisper, "The servants are well away from here. Even so, we must make little noise." He murmured some half-hearted protest that faded into the heavily spiced air.

Jack was wakened by a shaft of light that flared between the shutters. He draped his forearm across his eyes. As in so many fitful dreams of late, he lay next to Anne at last but somehow could not see her. His mind cleared, and he knew: he was not home, and next to him lay not Anne but Lady Bedford. He groaned.

"What is it?" she asked.

"Nothing," he said. "My head. Too much wine. And this light." He recited the lines he had fashioned months before:

Busy old fool, unruly sun,
Why dost thou thus,
Through windows and through curtains, call on us?

Lady Bedford interlaced her fingers with his. "That sounds like the start of a poem."

"It is," he said. Still shading his eyes, he turned his head toward her. "Have you forgotten? I sent it to you from an inn near Harrowden Hall last winter." With a sinking in his gut he remembered he had sent a copy to Anne, too: an act of duplicity befitting an adulterer.

"I never received it," Lady Bedford said. "I would have remembered such verses. In fact I meant to chide you when the time sorted. I charged you to send me poems, and through all those months I never received any."

He rose on one elbow. "None?"

"Not a single one."

"But I sent you four or five, some from the north country and some from the Netherlands."

"To Bedford House?"

"To Bedford House."

"But I never received them. And letters received at Bedford House are brought here once a week."

Jack collapsed onto his back again. She sounded sincere, but he had never been sure he could tell truth from craft when she spoke. Especially not now. After all, last night she had committed adultery, apparently without the least qualm.

A queasy sense of the enormity of what he had just done washed over him. He had committed adultery too—lured into it, perhaps, but in full command of his wits. He had betrayed his loving wife on the very point of his long-awaited return. He had sinned against his wife and against God. And with whom had he done this thing? With a powerful woman whose motives might extend beyond mere lust, a woman influential enough to destroy whatever future was left to him.

And now she claimed she had never received his poems, sent one at a time over a period of several weeks. The posts were uncertain enough that one might have been lost, conceivably even two. But four or five? No, either Lady Bedford was lying or someone—most likely some agent of Cecil—had intercepted them.

Lady Bedford had requested that he write the poems as to his mistress. She liked to be flattered, he had thought, and so he had flattered her. She liked to be cast in the literary role of the unapproachable object of male desire, like Sidney's Stella or Petrarch's Laura or Dante's Beatrice. So each of Jack's mailings had begun with an effusive salutation: hardly unusual for a poet addressing a patron. But Jack had chosen titillating terms of address, suggestive of not only his desire but also the possibility of its fulfillment.

Well, his desire had been fulfilled last night. As had hers, and with a vengeance. He looked at his left hand, bandaged and faintly throbbing. Despite her warning last night to make little noise, she had made more and more of it as she approached her climax. To muffle her cries he had reached an open hand around her head and worked the web of flesh between his thumb and forefinger into her mouth. After a spasm she had bitten down hard, then turned and kissed him fiercely, his blood still on her lips. Only then had she torn the edge of the sheet into strips and wrapped his hand.

Now as daylight made its way into the room, she lay placidly beside him, lightly trailing her fingertips along his cheek. She kissed him gently, and he did not resist. Then she said, "Stay with me here, if only for a few days, at least until my father returns."

"No, I need to get home."

"But you mustn't. An attempt on the Princess's life is at hand, and we need wise counsel to defend the house. You have served in the wars, and with my father gone, you are the man most fit to be obeyed." She slowly sat upright, looking like a naiad rising from a stream. Her delicate nakedness deferred to his strength. "You owe it to the kingdom to stay."

Jack could see the game she was playing, and playing it well. This woman who was perfectly capable of giving orders to the household guard, and who enjoyed doing it, was telling him—with her words and with her body—that she needed him. Yet the beseeching, almost helpless look in her eyes seemed convincing. Maybe she was telling the truth, admitting that she needed help in an unaccustomed matter. After all, the household guard would soon be supplemented by troops from London, and how much could Lucy Harrington know about managing preparations for battle? Or maybe she merely wanted him to stay only because she didn't like the idea of letting him go home to Anne.

Jack knew his place was beside his wife and children, and he ached to see them. He should leave this house, find some forsaken spot along the road, get on his knees, and beg the Lord's forgiveness for the thing he had done. And Protestant or not, he should seek out a wise priest of the old faith and confess, then ask whether it would be more loving to keep Anne ignorant of her husband's infidelity or to tell her all, begging her forgiveness along with the Lord's.

All this he should do. Yet Lady Bedford might have a better idea than she knew. If Jack could command a successful defense of the Princess's life, would not that one act acquit him of all debt to Cecil, even advance him in the eyes of the King? Jack owed it to the kingdom to stay, she had said. Whatever her motive, maybe she was right. If some group of overzealous Catholics succeeded in capturing the Princess, full-scale war could ensue. He had waited all these months to see Anne and the little ones. If he remained at Coombe Abbey for a few more days, maybe he could go home to them afterward for good. During his time at Coombe Abbey maybe he could even keep clear of Lady Lucy's bed.

Yet there she was, leaning toward him, her skin creamy and her dark eyes wide with anticipation. "A few days only," he said, then pulled her to him.

She should have arrived at the chapel by now; what could be keeping her? Cobham taking his time, no doubt, subtly preparing her for what was to come. Cecil shifted his weight a little. The stone floor hurt his knees, and his back would soon go into spasms if he kept kneeling here. Once again he tried to weep, straining to make the tears come. His face needed to be red and wet for this encounter. He thought of his long-suffering wife and her early, painful death; he remembered his humiliation upon learning he had delivered his sonnet to Anne on the very day Sir George discovered her elopement with Donne; he rubbed his eyes with the heels of his hands; he strained some more. Still no tears. His back ached, both at the sidewise crook in the base and the hump behind his shoulders.

He cursed himself for not simply having had Donne killed months ago. But he had reasoned that if Anne found out her husband was dead—for despite all precautions, word of such things did travel—in her eyes he would always be a martyr, Cecil his executioner for forcing him into such dangerous work. If her husband remained missing, she would blame Cecil for his absence and always hold out hope for his return. No, she must be made to think her husband remained alive but had betrayed his wife and his country. She must think he had abandoned his family to take up with another woman, all the while plotting a Spanish takeover of England.

Some of the elements of this deception were already in place. Beside him lay the rolled-up document he had hastily penned not half an hour before: a royal writ of annulment of the Donnes' marriage. Twice before, King James had refused to sign such a document despite Sir George More's requests, saying he did not like to overturn chancery-court decisions unless the good of the realm depended on it. So Cecil had written the document and signed the King's name, something he had learned to do well enough. In place of the King's signet seal he had used one of his own, twisting it as he pulled it away from the wax to leave a blurred image. Certainly it should be enough to convince Anne. A week ago the rumor of Jack Donne's defection to the Spanish cause had been whispered into a few ears, and now everyone at the royal court had heard it.

But then Donne had somehow escaped the dungeon at Warwick Castle, setting all the preparations at risk. It was a stroke of good fortune that the man had not gone directly home but had turned up at Coombe Abbey. Well, Cecil would not make the same mistake twice. Now that Donne had emerged, the man would soon cease to trouble the world. And his death would seem a traitor's. Cecil had not had time to work out the details, but Donne's death would make the forged writ of annulment moot, and in her confused and bitter grief, maybe too in the exhausted clarity afterward, Anne would come to see that Cecil, and only Cecil, had loved her all along.

Finally he heard the distant click of Cobham's boots on the flagstone. Having summoned no tears, Cecil quickly took the little stoppered vial of water from his pocket, tilted his head back, winced once at the stabbing pain between his shoulder blades, and poured several drops into each eye. His hands trembling, he replaced the stopper and dropped the vial into his pocket. At last: a polite knock. The latch slid softly, and a faint creak sounded in the little chapel as the door swung open. He made a mental note to have the hinges oiled. Cobham said quietly, "Lord Cecil, pardon my intrusion, but your guest has arrived."

For a few seconds Cecil kept his head bowed on his folded hands. He appeared holy, as he imagined, but not too brightly revealed; he had chosen with care the number of candles around the altar. His lips moved in apparent prayer. Then he rose as smoothly as he could. He did his best to stand erect. As he turned he said, "No matter, Cobham; my prayers were almost finished. In an hour or two I will return to them. Ah! Mistress More—excuse me, Mistress *Donne*—too much time has passed since last I saw you. And your beauty exceeds even what it was! The Lord has smiled on you; the difficulties of your marriage have done nothing to diminish your loveliness."

Anne gave a shallow curtsey as she said, "It is kind of you to say so." Cecil looked and listened for any hint of insincerity, but he could discern none.

As he walked toward her he limped a little despite his effort to move smoothly. With a white handkerchief he wiped his cheeks, taking care not to remove all the moisture around his eyes. "I am afraid you have caught me at my worst," he said. "My prayers have moved me out of all countenance."

"For what do you pray, Lord Cecil?"

With a delicate wave of a hand—his hands, at least, were well formed and graceful—he said, "Oh, always I pray for the good of the realm, for an end to the wars, for the relief of those who suffer, for the peaceful conversion of all papists to the true, Protestant faith." He looked her steadily in the eye as he said, "But what has moved me in especial this last hour has been the plight of your poor husband."

She blanched, pale as the face of the moon. "My husband! Oh, I feared it in my soul. Is he in danger? Is he . . . is he alive?" She reached toward him, then withdrew her hand and held her fingers to her lips. Delicate fingers and full, supple lips. He longed to put his own fingers to those lips, to stroke her long, lovely neck, to remove her dress slowly, listen to it rustle to her knees, and kiss her beautiful breasts.

"Oh, he is alive," Cecil said. "I would not for the world have it otherwise. In all I have done, I have taken great care to preserve him. Yet. . . ."

"Yet what?" Her green eyes dazzled. "Is he hurt?"

How did she summon the tears so easily? Could her commoner of a husband really mean so much after all he had done to her, after disgracing her with a bad marriage and doing her out of her fortune? Well, regardless, it was best to proceed as if it were true, as if she really loved the man despite all his selfish recklessness. If Cecil underestimated her desire for this son of an ironmonger, the next hour or two could go very badly. He must remain on his guard, must proceed slowly, must not let his own desire supplant his reason.

"No, no, I do not think he is hurt." He looked at her closely, tried to share her worry, her sorrow. To his surprise the tears began to well in his own eyes. "Would it were only bodily hurt," he said. "But come, sit. I am sorry to have to bring you these news."

"Oh, what is it? Tell me."

"Please, sit." Her mind could hardly have been on her appearance, but the simple act of lowering herself onto the backed bench looked graceful, effortless. Cecil wanted to respond to this, to tell her she moved with liquid ease, but now was not the time. She sat lightly, anxiously looking up at him, unconsciously sliding along the bench to let him sit beside her. And he needed to sit; to have so close to him all her attentiveness, all her beauty, all her grace, left him light-headed where he stood. As he tried to move with equal grace to join her on the bench, he knew he failed—but knew also that she paid his awkwardness no mind at all. Such things did not matter to her.

She took his hand! He let a little involuntary gasp escape, then placed his other hand on hers, enfolding the delicate fingers as tenderly as one would hold a frightened bird.

He spoke softly: "You cannot know my sorrow for having to say this to you. But I am duty-bound to tell you that your husband has betrayed you. He has betrayed me, betrayed us all."

"How . . . no! How do you mean?"

Cecil sighed deeply before saying, "He has joined the papists. Now he is one of their confederacy. And. . . ." He held her hand closer to him. "Your husband has taken another woman, one I know to have been happily married before she met him."

"No. No!" She pulled back her hand. "You are misinformed. He but feigns all this, or someone has misreported him. Or. . . . No. Not Jack. Not. . . ." She sounded like a lost child half-afraid to speak as she asked, "Who is this woman?"

"None but Lucy Harrington Russell, Countess of Bedford."

She sat stunned for a minute before saying, "How. . . . Who has told you this?"

"He himself has told me." Cecil pulled from his pocket a sheaf of five poems addressed to Lady Bedford. He quietly admired his own gesture as he gave her the papers; the very shape of his hand expressed sorrow.

She glanced quickly through the pages. "These are but poems. She is his patroness. They are . . . fictions."

"Read them. I am sorry. The verses but shadow forth the substance of what he has done to you."

She looked at the topmost poem, *The Sun Rising.* She had seen it before. *Busy old fool, unruly sun.* . . . Jack would say he had merely copied it out for Lady Bedford after writing it for Anne. Still, she did not like to think of Lady Bedford reading the poem and picturing herself in bed with Jack as the morning sun interrupted their night of love.

Anne turned to the next paper: *The Relic,* surely written for her alone. It was the last bit of correspondence she had received from him. She was the one who had given Jack a bracelet of hair to keep about his wrist, the bracelet his poem said would last until Judgment Day. Her eyes moved swimmingly over the verses as she searched for the place that mentioned her by name, that spoke of the marriage that eternally bound their double flesh in one. In its place she found words that drained her spirits:

If thou and I at last might couple,
Bodies willing, lithe and supple,
Saint Lucy's glist'ning radiance
Would slide all darksome shadows thence.
Thy husband and my wife
Might soon forgive a love like thine and mine,
Their jealousies consign
To dull Oblivion's unrememb'ring life.

Forgive such a love? The thought was bitter. Forget it? Never. The last of her breath left her as she read the final three lines:

If I could kindle thy bright spark to fire,
And lightened, prick the strings of thy quaint lyre,
We'd sing the world a miracle entire.

Anne trembled to the next poem. It was one she had never seen, titled *To His Mistress Going to Bed:*

Off with that girdle like heaven's zones glistering,
But a far fairer world encompassing.
Unpin that spangled breastplate, which you wear
That th'eyes of busy fools may be stopp'd there.
Unlace yourself. . . .

Enough. She turned the whole sheaf of pages face-down on the bench.

Cecil said, "It is your husband's hand, is it not?"

Her response was barely audible: "It is." She slowly shook her head. "The words here: they are hurtful to read, to think. . . . Yet I say again: they are but poems. They do not mean he has committed the acts."

In the halting speech of one reluctant to part with his words, Cecil said, "I am afraid . . . it is all true. Your husband has . . . dwelt . . . nearby of late. He might have come home to you, but instead he has remained at Coombe Abbey, where Lady Bedford stays with the Princess. While her husband was away hunting, your husband spent his nights alone with the Countess in her bedchamber. Two nights ago Lord Bedford returned to Coombe Abbey unexpectedly and discovered the two lovers . . . in . . . *flagrante delicto.*" The part about Lord Bedford was not true, but one of the household servants—a man in Cecil's employ—had reported the noises of lovemaking.

"No," she said in a hoarse, sobbing whisper. "It cannot be."

"The good Lord Bedford has come to me asking my help in procuring a divorce from Lady Lucy."

Anne buried her head in her hands. Cecil continued, "And in the meantime Lady Bedford has somehow convinced the King to grant the thing he has denied your father Sir George all these years. It is . . . you cannot know how it pains me to tell you this . . . a writ of annulment of your marriage to John Donne."

Anne slowly turned to face Cecil. Her eyes took on the look of a cornered beast's. In a voice both frightened and fierce she said, "An annulment! Oh, tell me of no annulments. Jack and I are married; there is no undoing that. We are married in the eyes of God, the kingdom, the Church of England, and the chancery-court. This lawful marriage has produced three children. Are they to be made bastards at the sweep of a pen? How can such a marriage be unmade?"

Cecil let his eyes express his sadness. He said quietly, "I have the writ here, signed and sealed by the King. It is your husband, I fear, who has urged Lady Bedford to use her influence with the King to attain it."

"Not Jack. Not the Jack Donne I know. Has this witch Lucy Harrington cast him under some spell?"

"That's as may be; I know not. But I cannot say I have ever trusted her."

Anne lifted her hands vaguely, as if she had no more words.

Cecil continued. "And . . . you had as well hear it all at once. From another trusted source—I cannot tell you who it is—I have learned it is most certain that . . . your husband has joined the Catholics in earnest, and is in league with the Spanish. He means to work with them to overthrow the realm."

She sat staring straight ahead. "That were as hard to believe as anything other you have said."

"Do you have cause to know otherwise? Have you heard

aught from him in these last few months?"

She shook her head, apparently unable to speak.

Cecil took her hand again, and she allowed it. "I feared as much," he said, then asked tenderly, "Have you not wondered why?"

She let forth a moaning cry and sat awhile convulsed in her grief. He slowly reached his arm around her, softly placed a hand on her copper-gold hair, and coaxed her head onto his shoulder. None of this did she resist. For four years he had dreamed of such a moment. He trembled, but perhaps she did not notice beneath her own racking sobs.

When at length she had quieted he said, "It is not good for you to go back to Pyrford Place, or at least not yet. The memories there will be too bitter. For a little while come to live at this house. There are diversions here aplenty: people come and go, there is music, there are gardens. You may play with your children, or let our maidservants tend them. And if you want a quiet place to read, there is my library."

She looked tired, perhaps on the point of accepting the offer. "Thank you Lord Cecil, but—"

He lightly put his hand to his chest. "Please. If only for a little. It would do you good, and it would set my own heart at ease."

She took a deep breath, let it out, and whispered, "Very well."

"Ah. That is something, at least. A coach stands ready to go to Pyrford Place. A trusted maid will ride in it, gather your children, and bring them back here. She will pack your clothes and whatever else you desire to bring."

"All right. Thank you." She sounded as if she had no more resistance in her.

"Again, nothing would please me more."

Cecil told Cobham to bring the maidservant, then sat with Anne in silence for a while. In time she would see the rightness of coming to live with him here. With her marriage to John Donne dissolved, or so she thought, she would begin to consider what it would be like to wed a man above her station, not below. Soon she would see that while the man who loved her truly was not imposing of stature, he could impose his power anywhere in the realm, giving scope to her own powers. She would come to savor the wine of ambition but would not grow giddy with it. And how she would grace his arm at affairs of state!

Before proposing any of this, Cecil would take her from room to room and let her remember what it was like to live in a wealthy household—and a household better suited even than Loseley to a woman of her sensibilities.

The library he would save for last, having been told by Sir George More of her great love of books. It was with Anne in mind that Cecil had spent four years buying books and whole libraries. He would give her time to read, time to listen to the woven voices of madrigal singers, time to watch her gamesome children play. For a few days only, he would tell her, he would ask her to stay: only until she could begin to bear the sorrow her husband had brought upon her. Those days would become a week, then a fortnight, and all the while he would attend to her every wish. In the ripeness of time he would proclaim his love for her, would propose the marriage that would bring them both joy. As the well-born wife of the King's chief minister, she would exercise powers rare for a woman: powers far greater than even Lady Bedford's. Lady Anne More Cecil would take charge of all the charitable endeavors of the Crown. She would see to it that the hungry enjoyed food in plenty, that the old and the infirm found loving care. All in the ripeness of time. He had waited four years and more; he could wait another few weeks before declaring his love.

Nor was he merely employing craft. Her happiness would be

real, and so would his. Little wonder he trembled in sympathy as she wept on his shoulder.

CHAPTER 16

The shadows lengthened as Jack made his way along the road. No attempt had been made to capture the Princess. After a week-long search, news of the threat had at last reached the hunting party. Lord Harrington, with Lord Bedford in tow, had arrived at Coombe Abbey three days later. Jack had reviewed with Harrington all the battle preparations. Lord Bedford had eyed the tall, fierce-looking stranger narrowly, his puffy face red and his nether lip abob, but Jack had paid him no mind.

Ten days ago he had arrived at Coombe Abbey looking like a pallid vagabond. Now with good food in his belly and money in his purse, he strode toward home. With his hair and beard still long—combed but untrimmed, as Lady Bedford had decided she liked it—and with eyes she had said looked haunted still, perhaps Anne would not recognize him at first. But like faithful Penelope upon seeing the truth and welcoming her Ulysses home, she would fly weeping to his side, hang upon his neck, and rain down kisses upon him. He smiled at the thought. Then, as in a dream, she was not Anne but the light, firm-bodied Countess of Bedford wrapped about him and kissing him savagely. Just hours ago as he took his leave from her, she had said, "We cannot live together as man and wife." Then she had stood on her toes and taken the lobe of his ear between her lips. She had given it a little tug, then whispered, "Not yet."

He shook the image free. No doubt, he assured himself, the memory of Lady Lucy would fade over time, and he would think of none but Anne. Pyrford Place lay a four-days' walk from Coombe Abbey, but with the few miles he would cover before nightfall, he could perhaps make it home in three more, two if he rose with the first light and moved quickly. As he walked he began to compose a poem for Lady Bedford. She had asked him to send her his verses often. He told himself that even if their time together was a mistake—two hungry souls sating themselves and then parting, never to indulge their lust again—there was no reason she could not remain his patron. Did not his family need the money?

He wanted something light, something to amuse the wits rather than stir the passions. He pictured a comic version of what might have been if Lady Lucy's husband had arrived on that first night.

In another half an hour he had a few lines:

Once, and but once, found in thy company,
Thy husband's irksome wrath now falls on me.
All unawares you rubbed into my skin
That which betrayed us in our sweetest sin:
A strong perfume, which at his entrance cried
E'en at thy husband's nose; so were we spied
When, like a tyrant king, that in his bed
Smelt gunpowder, the fat wretch shivered.
Had it been some foul smell, he would have thought
That his own feet, or breath, that stench had
wrought.
This perfume vial I freely give t'embalm
Thy husband's corpse, its fate within my palm.

Well. It was a start, at least.

As night approached, a sole horseman came thundering toward Jack at a gallop. The horse and rider passed, then pulled up short, turned, and trotted back toward him. Jack put his hand to the sword Lady Bedford had given him when he left. The blade was one of her husband's. Jack had to smile at the woman's boldness.

The rider reined the horse to a halt in front of him. Even in the dim light Jack recognized the animal: it was his big bay mare. The horse snorted and nuzzled Jack's shoulder. "Donne?" the rider asked.

Jack knew the voice.

"Owen! Where do you ride in such a rush? And why on my horse?"

"As for your horse, you are welcome to it. I ride it because until today I thought you were dead. Father Garnet is in London. I've been finishing a new priest-hide near Northampton. Some two hours ago I got word from him that you are alive but your success is uncertain. He wrote that I am to warn Harrington at Coombe Abbey of Princess Elizabeth's danger, lest your attempt meet some mischance. Are you come from there?"

"I am. The house is well fortified, and the guard increases daily."

Owen swung himself from the saddle. "Good. Then I need not hazard being recognized in a houseful of Protestants. And we can give this fine beast a rest." He patted the horse's flank. "Where do you walk?"

"Home. London and Pyrford Place. Home."

"I'll turn and walk with you, and when your bay has breathed we'll ride together."

"That sorts well. But the light fails. I'm tired, and so is this mare. Is there an inn hard by?"

"Not half a mile back—or ahead, as we go now."

When the two had stabled the horse at the small barn attached to the inn, they went inside and ordered tankards of ale. They were the only customers in the house, so the mistress told them which bedroom to use upstairs, brought them their ale, and told them to keep track of how much more they dipped from the cask. Then she went to bed. The men sat at a corner table to talk. Although they were alone in the room, they leaned toward each other over the table and spoke in low tones; there was no need to risk being overheard.

Jack said, "Let me be sure I understand this. The Princess is a Protestant under the Protestant Harrington's protection. A Catholic plot is afoot to abduct her. And you, a Catholic, are sent by a Catholic priest to risk discovery and capture in an attempt to foil this Catholic plot."

"All true."

"And the reason, I take it, is that the attempt is not backed by the new Spanish Armada but by hot-headed English Catholics, too few in number to be sure of victory."

"True again. Or so Father and I think. We've heard no rumor of Spain's hand in this business."

Jack took a deep draught of the ale and held his tankard poised in the air as he considered the matter. Then he said, "And so if the rebels fail, the Scotsman and Cecil will use the attempt to spread fear of all Catholics. Cecil will seem justified in killing us all."

"Or driving us from the land, aye."

"Owen: could Cecil lie behind this rumor of an attack on the Princess?"

Owen furrowed his brow, then rubbed his beard. "That were a new thought to me. Cecil would do it if he could; I doubt not that. Yet I think it is not so. Father Garnet would not tell me, but here is my guess: one of the rebels feared for his soul and confessed his part in the attempt." Owen took a drink.

"But Nick, this man with the troubled soul: he could be a Protestant, one of Cecil's spies. His confession could have been feigned."

Owen considered the matter, then said, "I doubt it. If a man lied about such a thing, Father Garnet would know."

"I'm not so sure," Jack said darkly.

"Well. Whatsoever this informant be—true man or liar—I'll hazard London holds a nest of Catholic souls giddy with bloodlust. We must go there and find out what we can."

"No. I'm going home. I'll pass through London on the way and take you wherever you want to go there. After that I'm riding home to Pyrford Place. I have done with these affairs."

Owen spread his hands in protest. "But the fate of all English Catholics might lie with the two of us."

"No, it lies with the one of you. I tell you I'm going home."

Owen drained his tankard. On his way to refill it he said, "Give the matter some prayer."

"Fair enough. But the Lord did not answer my prayers while I lay in Warwick dungeon."

Owen returned to the table. "No answer?"

"None."

"But at times you felt the Virgin loved you despite your sins."

Jack looked at him carefully. "How did you know that?"

Owen took another sip of ale. "I didn't have to know it. I know the Virgin."

Jack nodded. "Still," he said without conviction, as if in a weak attempt to convince himself, "most of the time God was silent. Absent. He did not answer my prayers."

Owen considered the matter, then said, "You're here, aren't you? Free."

"Free." Jack looked at the tankard before him. "What I want to be is home."

The stone of Pyrford Place, with its variegated reds and golds, shone much as it always had. Well, little wonder. Although it seemed a lifetime ago, only three seasons had passed since Jack left the house. He did not take time to stable the bay mare but tethered her to a chestnut tree in the yard, the saddle still on her back. He wanted to see Anne. She would be sitting by the fire, three children playing on the floor around her.

The door was unlatched, so he walked into the room. No one was there. The air felt colder inside than out, as if no fire had warmed the room for a long time. A sense of foreboding grew in him as he climbed the stairs. His knees went slack when he saw that Anne's clothes were gone, and so were the children's.

Jack braced himself, took two deep breaths, then hurried downstairs and back outside, strode across the lawn to the other end of the house, and stood before Francis Wolley's door. He knocked loudly. After half a minute a beef-faced servant Jack recognized opened the door. "Is Francis here?" Jack asked as he stepped inside.

The servant held up a hand to stay him. "And who might you be?" he asked.

"Jack Donne. You know me."

"I know Master Donne, but you. . . ." The servant peered at him. "Why, so you are. Pardon my . . . misremembering."

"Of course. Is Francis home?"

The servant led him to a room Francis had redecorated since Jack last saw it. Three walls were pale yellow with an ornately painted lavender border, and on the fourth hung a richly woven arras depicting a young woman with a unicorn resting its head in her lap while one shepherd boy led another in a merry chase. Meanwhile, a short-horned Pan with sly eyes sat by a stream in one corner, playing his pipes. All this Jack took in at a glance.

Francis stood. "Jack! Good God, what happened to you? We thought you were dead. And really, you'd look better as a ghost."

"Thank you, Francis. You're looking fine yourself."

"Well, I try." He gestured toward the arras. "But you haven't told me what you think."

"Very fine work, Francis. Where is Anne?"

Wolley's face darkened instantly. "Oh. Anne. You don't know?"

It was just as Jack feared: Anne had died, perhaps in childbirth—had died longing for her husband, maybe, and he had not been there to comfort her. His breath failed him, and he could barely get out the words: "When? When did this happen?"

"Not long ago. A week, maybe. Oh, I'm beyond sorry to be the one. . . . Jack, this must be terrible for you. Truly, we thought you were dead."

His mind nearly numb, Jack asked, "But did she say anything? Did she want me there?"

"Well, she hardly. . . . But where *were* you? We didn't know."

"Of course you didn't. That was Cecil's plan. He had me secretly imprisoned."

"Cecil. So then he *knew:* knew you were alive. Yet he. . . ."

"What? Yet he what?" Jack put his hands on Francis's shoulders and gave him a little shake. "Did *Cecil* have something to do with Anne's death?"

Francis pulled back. "Death? Is Anne dead?"

Jack threw up his hands. "You just *said* she was."

"Did I? No, I never. . . ."

"Wait." Jack thought back. "You said there were some news I didn't know: something that would be terrible to hear. What are these news?"

Wolley shook his head. "Jack, I don't want to be the one to tell you. Maybe you'd prefer to think she had died."

Jack took a step toward Francis, who took two steps back. "*Tell* me."

"All right. All right." Wolley took a deep breath, then said, "Anne has married Cecil."

Jack stood stunned. "Married. But she's married to *me.* How could she . . . ?"

"I tell you we thought you were dead. And in case you weren't, Cecil got a writ from the King dissolving your marriage."

"But. . . . No! I will go to the law. I will take this thing to the courts. Sir George already challenged the marriage, and I won the case."

Francis said softly, "Jack." He put a hand on his friend's shoulder and eased him into a chair. Jack did not resist. Wolley continued, "Sir George is not the King. No court will deny the King's will."

"But. . . ." Jack sounded like a frightened child as he asked, "But did she consent to this?"

Francis took one of Jack's hands and held it in both of his. He spoke tenderly. "She did. I am sorry."

"But *Cecil.* That twisted little. . . . And Anne: how could she . . . ?"

"Anne was thinking of the children. You had died, she thought, or no longer cared about her if you lived. Cecil was a good match for her: an excellent match. She has wealth again, and he has given her scope to use her powers. She is to work on behalf of the kingdom to help the poor. Oh, Jack, I am sorry."

"But none of this sounds like Anne. How could she love such a man?"

"You should see him with the children. He dotes on them."

"Children! Did the third one live?"

"Oh, yes. George: his name is George, after her father. This new marriage has reconciled her to him."

Jack rose, moved uncertainly toward the door, and muttered, "I will kill Cecil. They will put me to death, but first I will kill him."

"Jack, don't talk that way."

"Thank you, Francis. I must go."

Francis moved quickly, blocking Jack's way to the door. "You cannot do this. Tell me you will not kill Cecil."

"Oh, Francis," he said with menace in his voice, "I will tell you no such thing." He started to shoulder Wolley aside.

"Wait. *Think,* Jack. Think what this would do to Anne. She loved you, I am sure. But now she is happy. The children are happy. Let their new father live. And live yourself. You can stay with me in this house as long as you will."

With a firm sweep of his hand Jack shoved Francis out of the way. He strode ahead, out of the house, making no reply as Wolley called to him. The crisp air braced his lungs. His horse snorted and smoked, eagerly shook her mane, and pawed the ground at his approach. He swung himself into the saddle and rode at a canter toward London.

After a few minutes he reined the mare to a trot. She had already travelled far that day, most of the way with two riders on her back. Not long after he had begun to clop along, hoofbeats came thundering behind him. He pulled his mare to the side of the road to let the horseman pass.

The wait was not long. Horse and rider galloped by in a flash of violet and white, a rush of flying mane, fiery eyes, and snapping velvet. Jack turned his head away as clods of turf rained about him, then turned back to see the horseman disappearing ahead. He recognized the animal: it was Wolley's Andalusian stallion, all churning hocks and flashing hoofs. Wolley's lush, purple cloak flapped behind him. Despite Jack's troubles he sat still for a moment on his whinnying mare to admire the sight.

Well, there was no going to Cecil's house now. Willing and strong as she seemed, his bay could never overtake Wolley's Andalusian. Francis would soon be warning Cecil of Jack's murderous intent. And why shouldn't he? Anne, Wolley's favorite cousin, was happy for the first time in years, and the marriage would prove advantageous to Francis. Wolley was fond of Jack, too; Francis would have no desire to see his friend hanged for murder. So, Francis would think, Cecil must be warned.

Despite this setback, Jack kept the mare on the road to London. Somehow he knew his alternative course; he would go to Nick Owen. The man would not likely support a murder plot, but he bore no love for Robert Cecil. Part of Jack knew he could not trust his own bloody intent, and so he needed counsel from a cooler, wiser head. Owen was just the man for that. And Jack knew the house where Owen stayed, having dropped him off there earlier that day.

Anne sat in an apricot-colored dress, nursing little George in Cecil's library. A handwritten volume bound in calfskin lay open on her lap. The book was a gift from Cecil: a volume of Petrarch's love sonnets written in the poet's own hand nearly two centuries before. The book must have cost Cecil more money than Anne and Jack had seen in their marriage. Her mind, though, was not on the book itself or its price but on the poet's lovely Italian cadences. Restrained in form but heartbreaking in feeling, the verses reflected perfectly Petrarch's unrequited desire for Laura. "You are my Laura," Cecil had told her the night he gave her the gift, "but our story has a happier end."

"After he first met with you," she had replied, "Jack told me of a sonnet you wrote for me. He called it a *cri de coeur,* a poem worthy of Petrarch. I have longed to read this poem. Do you have it still?"

"No. When I learned of your marriage I burned the poem."

She let out a little cry of dismay. "It is lost, then?"

"No. I remember the words. How could I forget them?"

She took his hand. "Might I hear it?"

He nodded, then closed his eyes, breathed deeply, and began:

If but thy lightsome footfall might but pause,
While, halting, limping, I made up the pace
To take thy side; if thou wouldst turn thy face
To mine and not recoil despite just cause,
And were thy touch a balm to mend my flaws,
Or would thy beauty's gentle force new-trace
Some faintest shadow of thy soul's sweet grace
Upon this visage bent from nature's laws,
Then, then, dear Anne, my upright noble form
Which never in this life was blessed before
Could smile on tempests and could laugh at storms.
Thy whispered prayer, enriching one most poor
In spirit, breathing godly strength, ensures
Though trembling still, I dare to ask for More.

Tears had gathered in her eyes as she kissed his hands and said, "Will you write those words for me? I desire nothing so much as that."

"Of course," he said. "How could I deny you anything?"

Now Anne had the poem, penned on fine parchment by Cecil in his own hand, rolled into a green-ribboned scroll in her pocket. Constance and Little Jack played with brightly colored wooden blocks on the floor nearby: red, yellow, and blue cubes of finely sanded and painted wood. Walnut, the craftsman who made them had told her. Some of the cubes had one color on one face, another on another.

A patient, smiling, quiet-voiced servant girl named Judith sat with them. Cecil had offered a wet-nurse as well, but Anne had declined. She smiled as Little Jack held up a shining blue block for her to see. When the child turned back to his playing, Anne read another of Petrarch's poems, switched baby George to the other breast, and turned a page.

★ ★ ★ ★ ★

The sound of the Andalusian's hoof-beats had hardly faded when the wind picked up, swirling fallen leaves before it along the road. A jagged flash of lightning. Jack's mare turned back her ears in anticipation, and a thunderclap split the air. She leapt into a gallop. Jack reined her in, slowed her to a walk, and patted her neck. He leaned forward and told her not to worry, speaking soothing words to calm her frightened eyes. Then the storm arrived in driving sheets of cold rain, drowning out his voice. His wide-brimmed hat held out the rain for a while, but before long it was soaked and sagging. Gradually the rain faded to a steady drizzle.

Jack plodded along on the mare. The water collected along the road in muddy channels clogged with twigs and the soggy remnants of brown-veined leaves. In the last hour he had arrived with ardent heart at Pyrford Place, discovered his wife had left him, and gathered his resolve to kill his rival. Even this last, desperate hope now felt threadbare, tattered.

And what hope lay with Owen? What counsel could he offer, when Wisdom herself had fled the world, leaving in her place the mere thrusts and counter-thrusts of Power? It now seemed he had set his course on Owen simply because he had nowhere else to go. The dismal day perfectly reflected the soddenness within him. The world's whole sap had sunk, and he was at one with the God-forsaken earth. The mare's hoofs sucked the mud with every step.

The thought returned: all his troubles were God's perfectly just punishments for Jack Donne's own doings. God had given him chance after chance, and he had rejected them all. His youthful fire to serve the Church, a fire fanned by his Jesuit uncles, he had suddenly doused upon his brother Henry's death. Reluctantly, with reasons in plenty but with lukewarm faith and feeble embrace, he had turned to the Church of England. There he had proved an unproductive servant. Meanwhile, the loving family of his youth shunned him as an apostate. Only by lying had he now regained his mother's faith.

The pattern went back ten years and more. He had joined the Inns of Court but left without a law degree. His service in the wars had gone unrequited, and afterward he had spent his time seducing young women rather than fighting for his rightful place with Essex or Raleigh. Then at last the Lord Keeper had seen his talents. But Jack had stolen the man's niece from under his nose, and in the theft had ruined his young wife's fortunes along with his own. And Lady Bedford. Despite all his lust for her, Jack had not seduced her; she had seduced him. What Machiavellian purposes she harbored, he could scarcely guess. No doubt she would soon make them known. Finally and most terribly, the love of his life—the dear wife he had neglected even before being cast into prison, even before committing adultery—had thrown in her lot with Lord Cecil. Anne was gone, and so were the children, including a son Jack had never seen. Even Constance and Little Jack would forget altogether the man who had begotten them, always thinking of the twisted little schemer as their father. A few months ago Jack had been sure he could outwit *Robertus Diabolus.* But Cecil had utterly defeated him. All Jack's boldness had proved foolishness, all his confidence the Devil's own snare, all his prayers empty wind.

He stopped his horse, dismounted, and fell to his knees in the mud. At first he did not pray but simply waited. Horsemen, oxcarts, and foot-soldiers passed him by, some of them laughing or muttering, but he paid no mind at all to what they said. None of it mattered. He simply knelt in the mud and waited. At length words began to form within him. It was not as though he heard a separate voice. But he sensed that he was not alone, and the words arose without much effort on his part:

Batter my heart, three person'd God; for you
As yet but knock, breathe, shine, and seek to mend.

That I may rise, and stand, o'erthrow me, and bend
Your force, to break, blow, burn, and make me new.
I, like an usurpt town, to another due,
Labor to admit you, but Oh, to no end,
Reason your viceroy in me, me should defend,
But is captiv'd, and proves weak or untrue.
Yet dearly I love you, and would be loved fain,
But am betroth'd unto your enemy:
Divorce me, untie, or break that knot again,
Take me to you; imprison me, for I
Except you enthrall me, never shall be free,
Nor ever chaste, except you ravish me.

He staggered to his feet, aware for the first time of his stiff joints and cold limbs. Whether God had decided to break him down and make him new was not clear, but he felt chastened if not chaste, unfettered if not free. He pulled himself onto the mare. She was cold too, and no doubt hungry. Well, London was not far away, and she would soon be warm, dry, and fed.

Half an hour later the rain had let up. Jack crossed London Bridge and doubled back along the Thames toward the house where Owen stayed in a rented room above a chandler's shop. He found a stable for the mare nearby. The shop stood just across the palace yard from Westminster Abbey. The towers of the abbey loomed overhead on one side of the yard and the old palace on the other, its grounds sprawling with shops, houses, and inns. Bills advertising this or that performance besprinkled the posts, lean-ribbed dogs sniffed the ground for scraps of food, and dirty children chased one another in their shrill-voiced games. The blind, the half-witted, and the crippled sat here and there against the palace walls, their clack-dishes for alms before them in the dirt. Most of the dishes were empty. Tinkers, bawds, and ballad-mongers hawked their wares.

Before he stepped onto the curb to climb the set of stairs beside the shop, Jack heard someone call his name. He looked around but could not find the source. It was a voice he knew from somewhere, an old woman's voice. She called again, and this time he looked up. It was Mrs. Aylesbury, his old landlady from his time at the Inns of Court. She leaned out an open window and waved an arthritic hand. "Master Jack! Come up, come up."

Chapter 17

The same set of stairs served for Mrs. Aylesbury's room and Owen's. An odd coincidence, unless. . . . Well, Jack would find out soon enough. The two doors at the top of the stairs stood directly across from one another on either side of the narrow landing. Jack had lifted his hand to knock on the door to the left when he heard the thumping of canes and the shuffling of feet on the floor within. He waited. The sound stopped, and the latch slid. The door creaked open. Mrs. Aylesbury stood hooped over two canes supporting her burled hands. A red, tightly woven mantle hung around her shoulders. She tilted her head and looked up at him, a merry smile on her sparse-toothed, wizened face. He embraced her gently, unsure of how much pressure her fragile bones could take.

"Oh, Master Donne," she said, "it's wondrous good to see you. I'd know your walk anywhere, as I've said often enough before. But how strange you look! Come sit, come sit. I've two chairs by the window. One for you and one for me. But you're wet and cold. And the insides of your belly must be knocking together for want of a supper. But there's plenty in the larder. The Earl has seen to that, bless him forevermore. He's seen to it something wonderful. But look at you! It's a blessing to my old eyes to see you here. I've heard all about your time in that prison, you know. The good father told me, and told me all you did to help him escape them pursy-wants. And the Earl! The Wizard Earl *himself* sought me out at the Savoy and brought me here. His very self. Back a year ago, it must be. Paid for the room, paid for the food, and his man still brings me money, more than enough to live on, as the good Lord knows. Often enough have I tried to send some of the money back, but the Earl won't have it, says his man. So when I go down to the yard two times a week as I try to do, I give what's left to the lorn and the lame there. But Master Donne: it's all 'long of you I live in plenty! The Earl *himself* told me so, told me it's all 'long of you. Told me you asked him to look after me, back last winter it was, as I said before. No, this is your chair here, on this side. I'm to sit by the magic glass, as the Earl asked me to do. It's easy enough to sit here, I'll warrant you that, and it gives me somewhat to do. And the glass is wondrous magic. It brings people close, all in the instant, as if they stood before you in the air. But how fare you?"

She paused long enough for Jack to say, "Well enough. It's good to see you."

He waited for her to sit. She propped one cane against a table, put her hand on the low windowsill, and slowly lowered herself into the chair. On the table, which Jack saw had been nailed to the floor, stood one of the Earl's optic glasses. Its base had been fixed to the table with screws, and the brass tube with lenses inside had been mounted in such a way that it could swivel, slide along a rail across the table, and move up or down a vertical rod. Jack smiled at the Earl's ingenuity.

"This glass, now," Mrs. Aylesbury said. "There's magic in it, but Father. . . . Oh, Master Donne, Father told me you came back! Back from your heretic ways. Back to the Old Faith. It's God's own doing, it is, as I told Father when he said it to me. It's Father has told me of your coming back from your heretic ways, same as it's Father has told me of your time in that prison. And damn the eyes of the pursy-wants that sent you there, and

I don't care a jot who hears me say it, in heaven or hell or earth."

"Thank you, Mrs. Aylesbury. But—"

"We prayed for you, every morning and every night, you know."

"I much appreciate that, Mrs.—"

"And the Lord has answered our prayers, and here you sit before me: looking strange and hollow, somehow, though your body seems hale and strong. I misremembered to ask the Lord to send you as your old self. But no matter. I trust the Lord knows what's best, as I said before."

"I thank—"

"The prayers of the three of us: Father's prayers, and mine, and yours, all mingling together, like. Streams joining to make a river. And it's our prayers as freed you."

"I thank you for your prayers. You prayed when I could not."

The old woman looked puzzled. "But why could you not? Did the pursy-wants have your mouth bound?"

"No. These lips could speak, whether in sorrow or attempted prayer. I tried, Mrs. Aylesbury, but at times the words would not come. Or not from the heart, such was my misery and confusion."

She scoffed and waved a gnarled hand at him dismissively. "You were ever over-precise, Master Donne, like a Puritan o' Sunday. Why, there's no trouble to praying. You just . . . pray. You say the words. Or even if you're struck mute, you *think* the words, for the Lord can read thoughts. Though I'm of the mind that words is best, for there's such a deal of thinking in the world nowadays, it must be a great trouble to the Lord to sort it all out. So I'll warrant words is best. Though I have to say there's a deal of words about, too. And there's some folk as do more talking than what they do thinking!" She cackled at her joke.

"You are right, Mrs. Aylesbury. As usual." Before she could

reply he said, "But I have two questions."

"Well, what's to stop you asking them?"

"The first is this: you said some of the prayers were Father's. Do you mean Father Garnet?"

"I do."

"And so he stays nearby?"

"Just across the hall is how near. Now as you're back in the fold, there's no harm in saying it."

"So he stays with Owen."

"He does. Though Owen comes and goes."

"The second question is about this optic . . . this magic glass the Earl has set up for you."

"Father says it's not magic at all, but I know better, now, don't I. 'If it's no magic, then you're not looking through it proper,' I says to him. So he gives me one of his looks—you know his looks, Master Donne—and he says, 'Then you may be assured it is good magic, acceptable to the Lord.' 'Well, if it's good magic,' I say to him, 'why did you not tell me so at the first?' And he gives me his look again. Well, bless him for a Jesuit entirely, head to toe."

"I see. You said the Earl wants you to look through the glass. To what end?"

"Why, to the small end. The large one faces out to the yard."

"Yes. But *why* does he want you to look through the glass?"

"To spy out those we suspect. Did I not say so before, clear as day?"

"Ah. Then tell me again, Mrs. Aylesbury: whom do you and the Earl suspect, and of what do you suspect them?"

"Why, mischief, of course. The Earl's cousin Thomas Percy for one. There's a man I could see was up to no good the first time ever I saw him. Guido for another, Catesby—"

"Guido? You've found Guido?"

"Found him? I didn't know he was lost. And don't I see him

every day through the glass?"

Jack stared at her, then rose, took her head in his hands, and kissed her wrinkled brow.

"Well," she replied, "I'm glad to see you too, same as I said before."

With some difficulty Jack extracted from her that Guido, Catesby, the Wizard Earl's cousin Thomas Percy, and a few others must be planning some mischief, for the Earl had asked her to spy out the men's doings. She watched them through the glass and from time to time made the labored descent to the palace yard to inquire about them. She told Jack that Guido posed as Percy's servant, styling himself John Johnson. There was not much to recommend the name, she said; if one were going to the trouble to counterfeit a name, it should fadge better than *John Johnson.* But, she said, that was not to the point. The point was that this Guido or this Johnson had loaded a deal of firewood and coal into an undercroft Percy had rented in the cellars of the old palace, a huge deal of firewood, as if they meant to sell it. But they never removed any. There were doings around the undercroft at night, too, but she could not make them out. "Catesby I would trust not a whit," she said, "and Tom Percy even less. As for that fox, I'll warrant he's up to some unholy trick."

"Guido, do you mean?"

"Aye, Guido: same as I said."

Jack asked her to point out this undercroft. She used the optic glass to show him.

"Do you think they mean to start a fire in the palace?" he asked.

"Lord only knows."

"I'm going to have a look in that undercroft."

"Oh, do be careful, Master Donne. After the good Lord took the pains to set you free because we prayed for you, I were loath to put him to the trouble again."

"I'll be careful. Have you a lantern hereabout?"

"Why, Master Donne, are you addled? It's broad day."

"But it will not be broad day in the undercroft, will it?"

"Well, there is that. But the chamber will be locked. They always use a key to enter it, and lock it again when they go. But yes, the Earl's man left me a lantern in the larder there. And help yourself to some salted ham before you go. Eggs, too; the Earl's man brings me eggs."

"When I return. Use the magic glass, Mrs. Aylesbury, to watch for Guido and the rest. If you see any of them, hang your mantle from the window." She looked about the room as if to find her mantle. Jack said, "The one you're wearing: it's red, so I can see it from a distance. If you see Guido, Catesby, or any of the others, hang it from the window." She fingered the mantle's woven wool. Jack asked, "Have you another to wrap about you if you put this one out the window?"

"Have I another. . . . Aye, but it's not red."

"That's all right, Mrs. Aylesbury. Only hang the red one out if you see the men, and use the other, whatever its color, to keep you warm."

"Oh, I see. Why didn't you say so?"

Jack smiled. "I must have been confused."

"Well, no wonder to that, what with the deal of trouble you've seen. But never fear it, I'll take care of you now."

Jack thanked her, put the lantern in his leather satchel, descended the stairs, and crossed the palace yard. No one appeared to be watching the door to the undercroft, which had been fitted with a new-looking lock, a sturdy work of brass and steel. He looked around. People milled about the yard, none of them paying him any mind. No mantle hung from Mrs. Aylesbury's window.

A blacksmith's hammer sounded from somewhere nearby.

Jack followed the sound around a corner and down a side street to a shop where an apprentice worked the bellows of a forge while the smith hammered a red-hot horseshoe he held with a pair of tongs. Jack picked up a stick from the streetside gutter and laid its end in the glowing coals. He took the lantern from his satchel, raised the sheet of translucent horn on the face, and used the burning stick to light the wick. The smith glanced at him and nodded, apparently uninterested in a stranger's lighting a lantern while the day was yet full. The hammer's rhythm held steady.

Jack looked around the shop. On a workbench he found several thin strips of hammered steel: trimmings, perhaps, chiseled hot from some larger implement, shards to be re-melted for another use. After picking out three, he waited until the smith stopped hammering to temper the horseshoe in a vat of water. As the iron hissed and the steam rose, Jack asked, "Might I buy these?"

The smith glanced at them and shrugged. "Half a groat."

"Good. And might I use your tools to bend them?"

"That were hard steel," the blacksmith said, "and too brittle to hold the bending cold. Ye'll want to fire it."

The smith went back to work, and Jack laid the ends of the strips in the hot coals. It did not take long for them to glow red. He drew one from the forge with a small pair of pliers, fixed the cooler end in a vise, and used the pliers to bend the tip at a right angle to the shaft. He tempered the rod in the water, then pulled the second from the fire and bent it at a different angle. And so with the third. He left a full groat on the bench, thanked the smith, and walked back around the corner to the undercroft door. He looked down the street to Mrs. Aylesbury's window above the chandler's shop. No mantle. Trying not to attract attention, he set to work with his new tools. If anyone glanced his way, Jack might seem to be merely plying a stubborn lock with a key. The lock did not seem to be as simply made, though, as the ones he had opened before.

There had not been many; what he knew came mainly from his early childhood. When he was very young his father had sometimes brought home broken or keyless locks from his iron-mongery. From time to time, both before his father's death and after, Jack had amused himself by taking the locks apart. And once, years later, when a girl's jealous father had locked the front door to her house, Jack picked the lock by moonlight and spent half the night with the girl not a dozen paces from the old man's room.

But for what seemed a long time the lock to the undercroft door did not yield to his makeshift tools. He was at the task, he guessed, over a minute before he heard the tumbler click into place. The door swung into the room on well-oiled hinges. He glanced back at Mrs. Aylesbury's window again. Still no mantle. Jack picked up the lantern, stepped inside, and closed the door behind him.

The room looked unremarkable except for its high ceiling and the size of thc pile of wood against the back wall. Fireplace-length staves of quartered hardwood had been heaped from floor to rafters, the bottom of the pile reaching halfway across the floor. Pieces of coal lay intermixed with the wood: an odd thing. Why would anyone who unloaded the carts of firewood and the carts of coal not have kept the two separate? Jack set down the lantern, scrambled a few feet up the pile until his head nearly brushed the cobwebs descending from the ceiling, and began to pull away pieces of wood. It was not long before he uncovered the smooth, rounded face of a large barrel. He moved more firewood. Beneath the barrel was another, and beneath that still another. He picked up the lantern and held it close enough to see that there were yet more barrels behind these, stacked three deep against the back wall. They stood three high and four abreast. He quickly made the calculation: thirty-six. Thirty-six large barrels had been hidden under all this firewood.

He pulled the stopper out of the cask nearest him. Black powder spilled onto his hand. He sniffed it, then realized that from his other hand hung a flame just a few inches from a barrel of gunpowder. Thirty-six barrels of powder would easily reduce Westminster Palace to rubble, would probably kill hundreds of people nearby. Thousands, maybe.

Jack stumbled back down the woodpile and looked up. What room, he wondered, stood atop this one? Then he remembered from his brief time in Parliament; he now stood directly beneath the House of Lords. Commons Chamber lay nearby. Jack grew queasy at the thought. Every soul in Parliament would be blown to the heavens in a single blast the moment anyone touched off all this gunpowder. And the new session was to begin in a few days. Also the King: the King would be there to inaugurate the term. Probably both princes, too. Jack picked up the lantern and began to back away. Bloody war would follow, with nobody left to put it down. Then Spain would invade: that must be the conspirators' aim. England would be Catholic again, at a cost of thousands of lives. Tens of thousands, most like. Spain would have little trouble after an initial slaughter of the remaining Protestant nobility.

Jack half-registered a change of light in the room. Before he had a chance to think what this might mean, a faint noise sounded behind him. He spun around. For an instant he saw Timothy Burr's face. The old man was swinging something at him. Before Jack could react, the brick slammed against the side of his head.

As Jack began to come to his senses he could not see clearly. Something was moving beneath him, and he felt a tugging at his arms. Gradually his eyes found their focus. He was looking down at the toes of his boots as they carved shallow, uncertain trenches in the dust. Half dragging and half carrying him, two strong men, one a little taller than the other, had draped his arms around their shoulders. One of them was saying something in a deep, resonant voice, but Jack could not make out the words for the ringing in his head. He tried to gather his thoughts, to remember where he had been and what had happened. At one point his head lolled to the side, and he found himself looking at a distant red mantle hanging from a windowsill. People milled about. A hard-faced woman and two dirty children stared at him. All went dark again.

He woke on a straw-filled mattress against a wall of bare planks. His head felt about to split. Perhaps it had split already. He lifted his left hand to feel whether his brains lay exposed. The hand rose heavily. A chain. A shackle about the wrist. His right hand, he thought vaguely, remained unfettered. But it felt like someone else's hand, a fleshy weight at his side. The fingers moved thickly, without sensation. He shifted his weight a little. The prickling burn of renewed feeling began to radiate along his right arm and into his fingers.

After a while he heard a door open. Footsteps. A bolt of fire shot along his neck as someone lifted the back of his head and put a bowl to his lips. Ah, water: he hadn't realized his thirst until he began to drink. He finished the bowl and said, "More."

"Wait a little, Master Jack. You'll want to be sure you can keep that much down."

Jack knew the voice. "Burr," he croaked out.

"Rest a little."

"You betrayed me." His voice was hoarse, a rasp along the throat.

"No, you betrayed us. Or you would have if we'd left you to your will."

"I don't under—" Then it came to him. "Gunpowder. Gunpowder under the wood. Parliament. You're going to blow Parliament to the heavens."

"No, Master Jack. To hell. We're going to blow these bloodsucking Protestants back where they were spawned. You would have stopped us. I'm sorry about your head, but it was the best I could do. Guido wanted to kill you. So did Catesby."

Jack groaned. "I'd feel better if they had."

Burr chuckled. "That's my old Master Jack. You'll mend. It was but a tap with a brick."

Jack coughed, and the action made him wince. "By God's bodikins, if that was a tap I'd hate to see a clout."

"Well, I'm the one has kept you alive, with your thanks or without them. If Catesby and the rest had their way, your head would stand so tickle on your shoulders a milkmaid could sigh it off. And it's the same head that broke in twain a good English brick."

"Hm. Sorry about your brick, Tim. I trust you'll find another if you fetch a fancy to batter my skull again." He took a labored breath. "But you said Catesby wanted me dead. Robin Catesby is my friend."

Burr's eyebrows peaked. "Friend? If that man is your friend, then might I suggest you never make an enemy?"

The pain flared behind Jack's left eye, then settled into a throb. He tried to ignore it. "Burr, already twice this half-year past I've had my headpiece cracked. First it was an addle-brained Protestant pursuivant; then it was you, a bloody-minded Catholic, as it would seem. I tell you I want no more of this spying, for knaves on every side desire to break my pate."

Burr smiled. "You're right that a brick does little credit to a studious mind. Here, take some more water."

Jack drank. "Well, Tim, you may be sure of this: your hatred of Robert Cecil can be no more rooted than my own. I am resolved to kill him, come what may. So if you'll but unlock these chains, I'll set about the task."

"Ah. Much as it pains me to deny you that pleasure, we will see to it for you: Cecil will be blasted into particles with the King and the rest of the nobility. And think, Master Jack, how edifying you'll find it to be rained upon by such exalted personages."

Jack closed his eyes and tried to breathe deeply, evenly. Burr's deceitful performance, he had to admit, had in a way been admirable. For months Jack had travelled with the old scoundrel without once suspecting him to be a bloodthirsty Catholic.

"So, you have bested even *Robertus Diabolus.*"

"I suppose so," the old man said. "The arrangement had a certain beauty to it. Cecil hired me to pose as a Catholic, never suspecting I had been one all my life."

Burr gave Jack another drink of water, then set the bowl on the floor. Jack rested his head. A wave of dizziness washed over him, then retreated. After two long, slow breaths he asked, "What of Lady Bedford? Is she part of your confederacy?"

Burr raised his heavy brows again, multiplying the folds on his forehead. "The Lady Bedford? Never think it. No, no, a lifelong Protestant, she, insofar as she is anything."

"In league with Cecil?"

"Despises him. And yet she wants something from him, has wanted it for years. A divorce from Lord Bedford, I think, or an annulment. I know not the whole tale. Still, I would hazard a good piece of gold on this much: she traded me as part of some bargain, handed me over to Cecil to use as he would, in exchange for his support in procuring this divorce. She wants not to be Lady Bedford but some other. I cannot say I blame her. But the King opposes it, and so her hope lies with Cecil. Yet all this I have pieced together guessingly."

Jack narrowed his eyes. A divorce. So when she said not *yet* could she and Jack live as man and wife. . . . No. She must have been toying with him. Lady Lucy Harrington Russell, Countess of Bedford, could hardly aspire to become Lucy Donne. What woman on God's earth would divorce an earl to marry a commoner? Yet the Countess of Bedford was unlike any other woman Jack had known. . . .

The pain behind his eye sharpened to a white-hot point. In the very instant he let out an inarticulate little cry, he knew the flash of pain was not only suffering but also an admonition, a reminder that whatever the Countess wanted, it was not what Jack Donne wanted, or wanted when the Devil wasn't riding him. Jack Donne wanted Anne Donne. He had just asked himself who would give up the life of a noblewoman to marry a commoner, and his own wife had already done so. Why was he even thinking about Lady Bedford?

The door opened again. More men entered—two of them, Jack guessed from the sound of their boots on the floor. He tried to turn toward them, but moving his head even an inch to the left sent a searing jolt of pain through his eyes.

One of the men pulled a three-legged stool to the low mattress, sat, and leaned forward so that his face hovered directly over Jack's. Broad-shouldered and with a face to make women swoon, he wore a tall hat and a neatly trimmed beard. His almost-black eyes seemed to pierce to the marrow. The man said nothing. Jack's vision blurred again, but he knew the other man by his voice soon enough. From somewhere in the room it was Robin Catesby who said, "You're right, Burr. Garnet says we're to let him live."

"Catholic," Jack lied. "I'm a true Catholic."

There was silence for a few pulse-beats until the man hovering above Jack said in a deep, velvety voice, "Well, there's Catholics and then there's Catholics. And you're not the sort we can trust." It was the voice of a leopard at the moment a purr begins to slide into an echoing snarl.

"Trust," Jack said. "You mean I cannot be trusted to blow a hole in England."

"That's just what I mean," the dark man said. "And a big enough hole and a big enough blast to hoist the tyrant back to Scotland. I'm the munitions man, so I should know. On the field of battle I can plant a petard that will land a Protestant's parts wheresoever I wish to watch them fall."

"Protestants at war, yes," Jack said. "But those barrels of powder are not under a battlefield. It's a new Parliament. Both princes will sit with the King at the opening. They're only boys. And what of the Catholics? Will you blow up the Catholic nobles with the King? Think of the Wizard Earl. Monteagle. Northampton. Worcester. Stourton. The list goes on. And in the Commons: both houses have Catholics in them. Do they all know about the powder?"

The stranger scoffed. "Of course they don't. D'ye think we could risk that? None of 'em know. They'll be martyrs to the cause, is what they'll be. If they knew what they died for, they'd embrace it like a bride."

"But Father Garnet won't let you do this."

"Well, now. There's a hard one; I'll give you that. He won't and he will. His words say no, but his eyes say blast away. And I side with his eyes. There'll be time enough to repent hereafter."

Catesby said, "Fawkes, we need to get to the undercroft. This meddler here pulled half the billets and coal away from the barrels."

Fawkes rubbed his beard. "Aye. We should have made him stack the wood again, and then we should have tied him to a rock and dropped him in the Thames." Fawkes stood. "Well, he might yet find time for a swim to the bottom. Burr, if he gives you any trouble, just say the word and we'll tell Father we dropped him in the deep by mistake."

Catesby laughed. "Well, Guido, you were ever loose-fingered. But let's go cover that powder. It's just as well we let him live awhile. If he tells us how he knew to find something by picking a lock and digging through a wood-pile, it may hap he'll 'scape a drowning."

"Catesby!" Jack said with as much authority as he could muster. "You freed me from a dungeon, and now you sty me with a shackle?"

Catesby strode into view. Looking down at Jack, he said, "I had my doubts about you from the start. I told you plain enough at Harrowden when first we met: for intelligencers and spies, I said, things will go hard. Well, they're going hard. And they're like to go harder."

Jack did not reply, but looked at Catesby as steadily as he could. Sometimes there seemed to be two of him, sometimes three ghostly Catesbys swimming, weaving, combining back into one before his eyes. Jack's vision played these tricks but, he thought, his mind and speech were clear.

Catesby continued, "Yet I did as I was bid. Father Garnet told me to carry a sealed message to you in the dungeon at Warwick Castle, so I carried it. But he never told me I couldn't follow you. And where do you go? Straight to Coombe Abbey, where the Princess lies. And what do they do? They let you in. And what comes next? Messengers scatter along the roads, the house bristles with guards, soldiers pound the way to Coombe Abbey."

"What were you going to do, capture the Princess? Carry her to Spain? Kill her?"

Catesby said, "Never mind what we were going to do. Here's the question: what did Garnet tell *you* to do? For it seems you betrayed him in going to Coombe Abbey. Or he betrayed us all in telling you to go there. One of the two. So you were best out with it. What was in that note?"

"Have you asked Father Garnet, Robin?"

"Oh, I will, be sure of it. But first I mean to learn all I can from you. Give some thought to what you'd like to say, and it had best match the tale Garnet tells. It'll be the truth from you, or you'll find yourself lying here still when Guido here touches off the fuse. If you lie to us, then in a twinkling you'll lie in a thousand places at once." With the look of a man accustomed to speaking but not attending to his own words, Catesby appeared to register an epiphany. "Ha! If you lie to us, then you lie here in chains, and then you lie everywhere! That were nimbly spoken, eh, Guido? Look, Jack, I'm a poet too."

Fawkes smiled, but in a way that made him look at once canny, smug, and cruel. He stood. As they walked out together, Catesby clapped him on the shoulder. "What cheer, Guido? The day of liberty is at hand." Fawkes did not react, but looked straight before him and strode through the door ahead of Catesby.

CHAPTER 18

When the men had left, Jack said to Burr, "So that's Guido."

"That's Guido."

"Well, Cecil and I agree on one thing: we've no great love for the man. Guido Fawkes, is it?"

"Aye, Guy Fawkes. He travelled to Spain to tell the king there of our intent, and since then the man has styled himself a Spanish Guido and not an English Guy."

"But Tim, do you really wish to serve a Spanish king?"

"Better an honest Spaniard than a Janus-faced Scot."

"An *honest* Spaniard? I think a feather will tip the balance between them. Tim, thousands will die in the blast and the bloodshed to follow. Thousands. You know that, don't you?"

"Believe me, Master Jack, I have thought the thing through and have settled my mind that this is the nearest way. Spain will invade, whatever we do. If the English nobles live to fight, then you will see war indeed. No, my conscience is clear. As Guido says, the nature of the disease requires a sharpish remedy." Burr put a hand on Jack's shoulder. "Just think, Master Jack: Robert Cecil's bulging head will soon explode. You need not turn a finger to kill him yourself, and you may live still thereafter."

"Tim, none of this sounds like you. When did you fall in with this faction?"

"Oh, long ago, when you were but a pup. It was Lord Burleigh, this same Cecil's father in the bastard-queen's reign, that dispatched my own father to his grave. I have but bided my time."

Jack managed to turn his head without much pain as the door opened again, and someone entered with a large armful of firewood. The man said, "Burr, Father Garnet says we're to keep this wretch warm. I'll watch him; Father wants to see you."

"Then watch him close," Burr replied. "This miscreant knows how to pick a lock." Burr rose, and a few seconds later the door closed again. Jack heard the new man loading the wood into the fireplace, then walking to the bedside. The man sat on the stool Fawkes had put there. Jack looked up into a face with a thin-whiskered chin and a watery, furtive look. Jack had seen him somewhere before, but he could not call to mind the time or place. Nor could he remember the man's name. Even before the sparse-bearded man had said a word to him, Jack could see he lacked the hearty resolve of Catesby or Fawkes. Here was a man with doubts. "So," Jack said, "you've conspired with these desperate men. I thought you were smarter than the rest."

The man eyed Jack suspiciously. "And when would you have done any thinking of any sort about me? I don't know you."

"Jack Donne, if you've forgotten. Or if you like, John Donne. Did Father Garnet not commend me to you?"

"Father Garnet said nothing of you but that I'm to watch you close and keep you warm. If the good father is such a friend to you, why do you lie here chained to a machine, with a lump the size of a chamber-pot on the side of your head?"

"Why, there's little enough to that. I but ran afoul of Catesby and Fawkes for trying to talk sense to them."

The man barked out a scornful laugh. "Ye'd as well try to talk sense to a brace of oxen next time, and then go home and hit yourself on the head. I warrant you'd give yourself a lesser knot."

Jack risked a guess: "You fought at Cadiz under Essex, did you not?"

"Ah. Would that I had. But this same Robin Catesby and I were cast in the Tower in '96. The bitch-queen Elizabeth had taken sick, and Cecil gathered up some of us Catholics. Said we'd poisoned her."

"Did you?"

"Didn't have the chance, or we'd have jumped to it. But no, it was all one of Cecil's tales. I did rise with Essex in '01, but you know what happened there."

"So that's where I remember you."

"You were of the Essex party?"

"Do you not remember?" In fact Jack had been of the opposite party. In 1601 he had not yet married Anne, had still worked with the Lord Keeper. Maybe he remembered the watery-eyed conspirator from one of the Essex rebels' trials. "I've forgotten your name."

"Tresham."

Now the name came back: "Francis Tresham?"

"The same."

Jack tried to think what he knew of the Treshams. "You're a cousin to Lord Monteagle, are you not?"

"Brother-in-law."

"Ah. A good man, Monteagle, and a good Catholic. A shame he has to go up in flames with the rest." Jack slowly shook his head despite the pain it caused him. "Think how he'll cry out for help, and none will arrive."

Tresham pulled the stool an inch or two closer, leaned forward, and spoke in a low voice: "There you have it. There's no cause for him to die. None."

"Maybe he doesn't have to. You could warn him."

"Ah, Catesby won't hear of it, and if Guido found out he would gut me like a fish."

"Does Catesby have to know? Does Fawkes?"

Tresham narrowed his eyes in thought. After a time he said, "Monteagle's house is in Hoxton. I can't risk being away to warn him; Catesby and Fawkes would suspect me. And there's this: I love Monteagle, but I owe him money. He waxes wroth in my presence. What if he holds me at Hoxton until I name others of our number? No, I cannot risk warning him. Yet I love him well, if only for my sister's sake."

"Pen a message, then, and send a courier. Do not sign your name." Tresham eyed Jack warily but did not immediately dismiss the idea. Jack pressed his advantage. "Get pen and paper," he said. "I'll help you with the words. You must say enough to warn him away from Parliament but not so much as to cast suspicion on yourself or any of our friends."

Tresham hesitated. "But how can you—"

Jack tried not to give him time to think. "Father Garnet wouldn't want to see Monteagle die."

"That much is true."

"Is there pen and ink hereabout?"

"Aye." Tresham disappeared from the room and soon came back with quill-pen, knife, ink, and paper. He said, "I promise nothing. Only to write the letter. Then I'll let Father decide."

Jack said, "Of course. Now: no names on the paper. Disguise your hand, and we'll keep the style strange. No man among us must appear suspect." He dictated:

> *My lord, out of the love I bear to some of your friends I have a care of your preservation. Therefore I would advise you, as you tender your life, to devise some excuse to shift of your attendance at this Parliament. For God and man hath concurred to punish the wickedness of this time. And think not slightly of this advertisement, but retire yourself into your country where you may expect the event in safety. For though there be no appearance of any stir, yet I say they shall receive a terrible blow*

this Parliament and yet they shall not see who hurts them. This counsel is not to be contemned, because it may do you good and can do you no harm. For the danger is past as soon as you have burnt the letter. And I hope God will give you the grace to make good use of it, to whose holy protection I commend you.

When he had finished writing, Tresham asked, "That will keep him away? I would not for the wide world see my sister lose her husband."

Jack said, "It will keep him away. And we could warn other good Catholics: the Wizard Earl, Northampton, Stourton. . . ."

Tresham pressed the heels of his hands to his eyes and let out an agonized groan. He said, "Do you not think I would spare all of them if I could? But some one or other of them would betray us to Cecil, and then all our enterprise were lost. The tyrant would rule still. No, we must hold with the plan. Monteagle only. He will keep his peace. And Guido *must not know* of this letter. Nor Catesby."

Jack said, "Of course they won't know. Ah, Monteagle: a good man and a good Catholic. That's one be spared, at least. And think of it: there's a godly deed you'll carry with you all your days, and may they be long and full of plenty. But we have a little time before Parliament begins. Until then, do one thing more: pray to discern God's will in sparing the others. That's all I ask: only pray."

Tresham nodded his agreement. Jack said, "Leave the paper here, and let me talk with Father."

Looking stunned, relieved, and frightened all at once, Tresham laid the letter on the joint-stool. Then he left the room.

Perhaps fifteen or twenty minutes passed before Father Garnet entered. During the interim Jack forced himself to stretch his neck and try to massage the stiffness away. The side of his head was too sore to touch, so he tried to ignore the pain there. His left eye was swollen almost shut. Garnet looked taken aback when he entered the room, as if a grotesque stranger lay where the priest had expected a friend. He crossed himself and said, "I am sorry to see you like this. Your chains are needful but for a time."

"Father, you know I am a godly man. These chains are not needful at all."

"I know. I know. But others don't."

"Who? Guido? Catesby?"

"Aye."

"And when did you start letting them rule a priest of the Holy Church, and a Jesuit at that?"

Garnet looked about him as if someone would make his answer for him. Then he said, "You speak true. I will take them to task, but for a little time I must proceed with care. You of all men know how hot-blooded they can be."

"In other words, you fear for your own safety."

Garnet looked at him through pale eyes cold with accusation. "You seem to forget the depth of my steadfastness. It was I who was ripped through the bowels of that garderobe at Baddesley Clinton."

"And are you forgetting that an ill wind blew my way too?"

Garnet's glare softened a bit. "No."

"Well. I thank you for my release from Warwick dungeon."

Garnet nodded his acknowledgment, then said, "I will not deny that my safety, if not my life, hangs in the balance of late with Catesby and Fawkes. Yet that life I will turn over as frankly as a pin if the Lord so directs me. The question is not what I am willing to sacrifice but how best to manage these men. There I but exercise prudence."

Jack could not disagree. These Jesuits were ever artful in sifting together the mysteries of the faith and the demands of the moment.

As if he wanted to change the subject, the priest said, "Eleanor Vaux was here last month. She brought us a powerful blessing, and she told me of all your good service when the pursuivants came. She thought you were dead, as did we all. For weeks after the pursuivants' attack she sent parties into the wood and beyond to search for you. All they found was a shallow grave, unoccupied, but stained with much blood. We thought the worst until I learned, some fortnight past, where you lay. Within the hour I sent Catesby to work your release. Jack, you thanked me for setting you free. I thank you most humbly for all you have done."

"One might desire better thanks, Father, than to be knocked about the sconce and chained to a . . . what is this? A printing press?"

"Aye. If we are to print answers to the Protestants' published lies, if the people are to know the truth, we must have our presses. And we must move them from house to house before they are discovered."

"This thing must weigh as much as three or four men. And you move it?"

"In pieces."

"Well. The truth, you say. Why have you seen fit to chain me to the truth?"

"Catesby is right when he says these are parlous times. He thinks we must detain you for a little while. I will do what I can to mollify him and the rest, but I cannot promise much. They will be guided by me in some things but no longer, it would seem, in all."

Jack decided there was little to be gained in chastising the priest. "That Fawkes looks like a hard man."

"None harder. Yet so far he has done all as Catesby has directed. He will not listen to the orders, though, or even the counsel, of any other."

"Well, it is Catesby who enfetters me here. Did you know

that he followed me to Coombe Abbey where the Princess lay?"

The priest closed his eyes and let out a little groan. "So that is why he was late in returning. But why does he suspect you and not me in aiding the Princess?"

"He suspects us both."

"Ah. Since his return he has stood aloof from me. Now I understand why."

"Well," Jack said, "to the point. Tresham means this paper on the stool to go to Lord Monteagle, and I think it should."

Garnet picked up the letter and read it. "Tresham wrote this?"

"The manner of composition is altered so no man among us will be suspected, should the letter miscarry. I am to deliver it."

"Tresham speaks here of a terrible blow, come Parliament. What does he mean?"

Jack stared at the priest. "Are you telling me you do not know?"

"I know there are foul doings afoot. I know Catesby and the rest mean some hurt to Cecil and some few of his men, but they will not confess to me how it will come. Pistols, I would guess. They have purchased several of late, and you are enchained here because he does not want you spoiling the plan."

"Pistols? Father, they mean to blow Parliament halfway to the moon: king, princes, nobles, commons, all. I counted thirty-six barrels of gunpowder in the undercroft."

The priest's eyes widened, and he crossed himself tentatively, as if he had forgotten how to do it. He said in a whisper, "No."

"I tell you it is so. I discovered the powder, and so Catesby and Fawkes have chained me to this machine. Set me free and I will deliver the letter to Monteagle."

The priest did not appear to be listening. He mumbled, "I must dissuade them." Turning to Jack, Garnet said with more conviction, "I will not allow it. The Holy Father will not allow it. I will . . . I will write to him."

"There is no time. The Holy Father is in Rome, and the new Parliament is upon us."

"Then I—"

"Will Catesby listen to you? Will Fawkes? They'll chain *you* to a printing press first."

"I fear you're right. Perhaps I should turn myself over to Cecil and tell him all. Another could tell Catesby and the rest to take to their heels."

"Madness, Father. You are a Jesuit. Cecil would hand you over to Topcliffe, who would slowly flay you alive and feed your flesh to his dog while you watched. No, you cannot go to Cecil. And you need not."

The priest was beginning to sweat. "What is your counsel?" he asked.

"Seal this letter well, and let me deliver it to Monteagle. If Monteagle stays in Hoxton, that's one Catholic spared, at least."

The priest nodded. "But you are hurt. Can you make it even as far as Hoxton?"

Jack had wondered the same. But what he said was, "Of course I can. I know my strength."

"Well. I'll work what I can. The good Lord knows this land is ruled by evil men, but Catesby is no such. I will confess to you that when I suspected he might do harm to Cecil, I did too little to dissuade him. But so much gunpowder. . . . We cannot allow this thing."

"Believe me, Father, this letter is the nearest way to stop it. Do you know this man Monteagle?"

"Not well, no."

"I do. In better times I worked with the Lord Keeper, and I often corresponded with Monteagle in matters of state. If ever a politician knew how to butter his bread on both sides, it is Monteagle. I'll wager he will take this paper straight to Cecil."

"And if he does not?"

"Then we're no worse off than now, and he is spared. Only set me free, and I will go to Hoxton. I will give the letter to Monteagle. Then I'll watch from a distance. If Monteagle goes to Cecil, I will come directly back to you. Or if that's not safe, I'll post on the undercroft door a warning to Catesby and the rest, telling them they are discovered, and their only hope is to flee. In the meantime you need to clear as many people from this part of London as you can."

"This part of London. . . . Do you mean this gunpowder has that much force?"

"Father, I have been in the wars. I have seen what ordnance compounded can do. That much gunpowder will leave a smoking hole where the heart of London used to be. Thousands will go up in the blast and the burning thereafter, and then thousands more in the bloodshed to follow. Just free me from these fetters, and I'll set about the task."

The priest looked dismayed. "I cannot set you free. Guido brought a smith here who heated an open link and then closed it as the last ring on your chain. There is no lock."

A wave of nausea passed over Jack. He closed his eyes, took a deep breath, and said, "Father, do you not understand? Fawkes and Catesby do not mean to free me. When that powder is touched off, I will be blown into so many shivers the Lord himself will take half an hour to find them on the Last Day."

The priest paled, wiped his brow, and said, "What should I do?"

"If I cannot be freed, the first thing is to find a courier you can trust. Send him to Monteagle in Hoxton with Tresham's letter."

"I will. What else?"

"Say little or nothing to Fawkes or Catesby about this. In fact, say nothing to Fawkes at all; I think he is beyond all cure.

Your hope lies with Catesby, though he suspects you. Father, you may be sure that in the dungeon I said nothing of what you wrote in your letter to me, but told him only that you sent greetings and prayers. So: get Catesby alone and try his faith. Learn whether he will be ruled. If you cannot move him at the start, leave him to God. Your only hope then is to save as many souls as you can by moving them out of the way. Begin, I pray you, with old Mrs. Aylesbury."

Half-distractedly, the priest said, "Yes, I know her." He crossed himself, as did Jack with his free hand. Garnet was reading Tresham's letter again as he left the room.

Jack did his best to ignore the pain on the side of his head and along his neck as he sat up. He carefully turned to see just how he was fettered to the press. The chain was securely linked around the metal framework; there was no freeing himself that way.

Then, without hint or warning, he heard a voice—or did not hear it, exactly, but the words somehow imprinted themselves directly in his mind as clearly as any sentence he had ever heard: *The fire of adversity leads to freedom.*

As he was wondering what such a strange message could mean, something compelled him to turn farther around and look at the fireplace. His breath left him. There was Thomas More, or what was left of him, on the mantelpiece. The message had come from him: Jack was sure of it. He crossed himself. So the skull was the powerful blessing Eleanor Vaux had brought from Baddesley Clinton. More's eyes, or the sockets where they had been, were staring directly at him. No longer did the bones look lifeless or vacant; it was as though More, in some form, had returned to speak to his descendant.

"What do you mean?" Jack asked aloud. The skull stared at him sternly but made no reply. Jack turned over the words in his mind: *The fire of adversity leads to freedom.* Perhaps More, the one who had died so well, was simply preparing Jack for his own death. The adversity he had been suffering for months, the smoldering loneliness, searing betrayal, and soon perhaps infernal gunpowder, would result in his eternal freedom in the Kingdom of God. "Is that it?" Jack asked. Again, no answer.

Below the skull the flames in the fireplace had already begun to warm the room. The wood, burning now in earnest, must have been touched off by live coals from an earlier fire, or it would not have sent out waves of heat so quickly. *The fire of adversity leads to freedom.* Then Jack had it. The message was no metaphor. He needed to work some part of the chain into the fire. But the room was large and the chain only four or five feet long; he could not get within three yards of the fireplace. With difficulty he stood. He had to pause and brace himself against the printing press to keep from fainting back to the floor. Soon, though, the blood returned to his head, and the pain it brought kept him alert.

He slowly bent down and tried to lift the press. The strain made him feel as if someone had stabbed him behind the left eye. But still he bent all his strength to the task. The press moved, if only an inch or so. He waited to catch his breath, then lifted and pulled the press again. Three or four inches this time; he was already learning how best to use his leverage.

In this way, over perhaps a quarter of an hour, he moved the press to within two feet of the fire. Through it all Thomas More looked down on him with something like satisfaction. At one point Jack asked, "Why don't you help, then?" But he didn't like the way he felt afterward. He needed to show reverence, not wit. And perhaps his kinsman *had* helped him.

A large iron pot hung from a hinged steel arm angled away from the fireplace: someone had been heating a stew earlier, with the pot swung in over the fire. Jack looked into the vessel. Some of the cold stew remained. He tore off a large piece of his shirt, dipped it into the stew, and wrapped the wet cloth around his left hand and the first few links of the chain shackled to his wrist. He flicked the heavy chain whip-wise, three times, until a loop lay in the hottest part of the fire. Even with the wet cloth to shield his hand from the heat of the fire and the chain, he soon grimaced. *The fire of adversity.* The cloth was steaming, and no doubt drying fast. Without disturbing the loop of chain in the coals, he unwrapped the smoking cloth as quickly as he could, dipped it into the stew, and wrapped his left hand again.

After doing the same three more times, he lifted the pot from its arm, set it on the floor, and tore off another piece of his shirt. The heat on his left hand and wrist was fierce. He dipped the cloth into the last of the stew, wound the fabric around his right hand as best he could, and gripped the end of the hinged arm. He lifted, then pulled the steel toward the floor. Again and again he did this, trying his best to ignore the pain of the burns his left wrist and hand were suffering as he worked.

At last he had pried the metal arm free of its mooring in the stone, so that he held a piece of stout steel with a hook at the end. He pulled the chain from the coals. Several links glowed bright red, one almost white-hot. He stood, worked the hooked end of the steel into that hottest link, moved back from the fire until the chain stretched taut, and leaned away from the press. He pulled hard on the hinged end of the steel rod and felt the softened link of chain give way. He kept pulling to be sure he had opened the link as far as he could, then slackened the chain and inspected the result. He had opened the link more than enough to set himself free. All that remained was to wait for the chain to cool enough to slip off the opened link.

His plan was to go to Cecil's house and watch for a chance to kill the twisted little schemer, perhaps strangle him with what was left of the chain. He was nearly out the door when he heard the voice again—or apprehended whatever spirit it was that came to him more clearly than sound: *Child, don't be a fool.* He stopped in mid-stride and turned to look at More. This time the skull watched him with tenderness, perhaps even a hint of amusement. Here was the other Sir Thomas More: not the formidable chancellor who refused to do the bidding of even the eighth Henry, but the More of wit, of learning worn lightly, of good cheer.

But what could he mean? Jack approached him, knelt, and crossed himself. He said an Ave Maria and a Salve Regina. He stood and placed the palm of his right hand on top of his kinsman's head. Thomas More would make his way back into Jack's family, Eleanor Vaux had said: she was utterly certain of it. Now he trusted she was right. "I will welcome you," Jack told him.

Child, don't be a fool. Well, Jack was, after all, More's child—or great-great grand-nephew, at least. *Fool.* In his days on earth, More himself had punned on the nearness of his name to the Greek *moros,* fool. So Sir Thomas could be saying *Jack, my son, don't be like me.* But how could that sort? Jack could hardly do better than his famous kinsman.

Just before Sir Thomas sent or spoke the message, Jack had been bent on killing Cecil. As soon as the thought of strangling the little man with the chain had entered his mind, Jack's veins had surged with murderous desire. Then a man dead these seventy years had directly told him not to be a fool. Sir Thomas More must be sending a message not to kill Cecil, not to send himself to certain death at the gallows. More's death at the block had been a glorious martyrdom, an embodiment of steadfast faith that made the whole world take notice. Jack's execution would be a mere waste.

Of course. Of course More was right. Jack's place was with Anne and their three little children. Surely Anne's new marriage to the bunchbacked toad would not stand. Jack had not been through so much for so long to be kept now from rejoining his family. How could he have seriously intended to kill Cecil with his own hands? There must be another way.

He looked at More again, then unstoppered the bottle of ink, took a piece of paper, and wrote a simple message: *Listen to Monteagle.—Your erstwhile servant.* He folded the paper and wrote on the outside *URGENT: CONFIDENTIAL TO SIR ROBERT CECIL.*

So if Monteagle received Tresham's letter and took it to Cecil, the little hunchback would know to take the warning seriously. Jack could then warn Catesby and the rest to flee. After the conspirators had abandoned their plot, the gunpowder would be discovered and the disaster averted. If Monteagle took the letter seriously and made some excuse to stay away from Parliament, Cecil would not know of Monteagle's absence until the new session of Parliament began. Until then he would have thought Jack's note meant Monteagle had something important to say in Parliament, perhaps in a speech. Now Cecil would know something strange was afoot. He would investigate all the possibilities, including Monteagle's absence. Either way, Jack would have done what he could to make sure Fawkes never lit the fuse.

On a different piece of paper Jack wrote, *YOU ARE BETRAY'D. CECIL IS COMING. FLEE!*

His black, broad-brimmed hat lay under the writing-table next to his satchel, his black leather jerkin neatly folded beneath the hat. He put on the jerkin he had purchased just after his escape from the dungeon and tucked the letters into one of the three hidden pockets he had asked the tailor to stitch into the jerkin's lining. The hat he fitted tenderly onto his head. Despite the swelling around his left temple, the hat was not too small; Jack even fancied the pressure on his temple relieved the pain there somewhat. He retrieved the satchel.

When he left Mrs. Aylesbury's room to search the undercroft, the satchel had contained only her lantern and the generous supply of money Lady Bedford had given him when he departed Coombe Abbey. The lantern was gone, but remarkably, the purse filled with gold coins still rested in the satchel.

So these militant Catholics were, in their odd way, honest men. They would enfetter one who meant them only good, would blow him to bits in a Satanic blast. But they would not steal his money. These terror-merchants aimed to bring England to her knees and subject the whole land to foreign rule. Yet they would not take a man's money even when it would go up with him in an explosion such as the world had never seen. Once again, he had to admire the conspirators. But he also had to stop them.

Jack walked out into the night air. His breath fogged in the cold, then slowly faded; not a hint of a breeze pulled it one way or another. Nothing stirred in the cathedral yard. He looked at the stars through a gap between the shops: two or three in the morning. Probably the city would be awake and bustling by the time he accomplished his tasks.

He needed to set about his work, but he stood motionless. Something was amiss. For a moment he thought it was a sound, but when he strained to listen, he heard nothing but the ringing in his left ear. Something or someone, though, was singling him out, as if by an internal summons. He turned. Without knowing why, he walked back to the room he had just left.

He eased open the door and peered inside, half expecting Catesby or Fawkes to spring from the shadows and attack him. But everything in the room stood just as he had left it.

It was then that he caught Sir Thomas More's eye. Or More caught his. In any case the meaning of the strange silence in the wintery air now became clear. It was More who had called him back, More who had further business with him. With a sickening pang Jack realized what he had almost done; he would have left his venerable kinsman to be shattered in the blast. Or Cecil and his agents would find the skull when they ransacked the houses surrounding Westminster. Jack felt as if he had left his mother or wife or child behind. He crossed himself and said aloud, "I am sorry."

Sir Thomas did not reply, but Jack was sure his kinsman had already forgiven him.

He looked around the room. The straw-filled mattress would have to do. He ripped open the fabric and shook the straw onto the floor. Then he tore the cloth into two pieces, one larger than the other. He carefully lifted Sir Thomas's skull from the mantel and used the large piece of cloth to wrap it. He wrapped the jaw in the smaller piece.

Jack distributed the coins from Lady Bedford among the jerkin's three hidden pockets, took a little straw from the pile on the floor, and lined the bottom of his satchel. He laid both pieces of Sir Thomas on the straw, packed in a little more around the wrapped bones, and fastened the satchel's clasp. Jack shouldered the bag and left for the second time.

He crossed the yard to the locked undercroft door, took from a pocket one of the shards of steel he had bent to pick the lock, pierced the paper warning Catesby and the rest to flee, and wedged the shard between two of the door's boards. Anyone approaching the door would immediately see the message and know to get as far away from the undercroft as possible.

Then Jack hurried to the blacksmith's shop where he had spent a groat on the steel for those same lock-picks. He looked about him. No constables, not even a drunken vagrant asleep on the street in the bleak chill of the night.

Jack set down the satchel and backed away two paces from the locked double doors of the smithy, then lunged against the boards. He heard one of them splinter a little into the shop. He rubbed his shoulder, then made another lunge. After half a dozen more, his head blazing with pain, he had broken two boards enough to kick them into the smithy. He picked up his satchel and climbed through the splintered opening. In the near-total dark he felt for the blacksmith's tools until he found a cold chisel and a weighty hammer. He remembered where the smith had mounted his heaviest vise.

He clamped into the vise the bottom half of the chain's nearest link, the one that looped into the holes in the hinged shackle on his wrist. He tore off what remained of his shirt, folded the cloth, and put it into his mouth to cushion his teeth.

It was awkward work, but he bent down with his head sideways and held the chisel in his mouth, its bladed end against the link of chain whose top rose above the vise. He tried a few carefully aimed taps with the hammer. Then he began to strike the end of the chisel with more and more force. Only once did the hammer glance off the chisel's head. Luckily it bounced away from Jack's face; otherwise he would have shattered his nose. But the force of knocking the chisel off center drove its shaft sidewise between his upper and lower teeth, hitting hard against the back of his mouth.

Renewed pain in his head, already swollen and painful from Burr's assault with the brick, drove him to his knees. He tasted blood, let the cloth fall from his mouth onto the vise, and worked his jaw. Nothing seemed to be broken. With his left wrist still chained close to the vise, he dangled there for a few seconds before a surge of nausea rushed through him. He had time only to turn himself as far away from the vise as his left arm would reach, and vomited until he hung where he knelt, weak, clammy, and spent. He turned and sat, his left arm raised above him, as if he had made some abortive, half-hearted attempt to test himself in Topcliffe's manacles. *Breathe,* he told himself. *Breathe.*

Somewhere in the night an owl called to his mate. The answer came from such a distance that at first Jack thought it might be an echo. But too much time had elapsed for that.

The call of an owl on a still, cold night always made Jack feel desolate, but on this night the hollow, plaintive sound made him shudder. He thought of such owls calling to each other some week or two or so hence, when much of the city would lie in blackened ruins. The owls and other birds of prey would feast themselves on unidentifiable bits of humanity. If Jack could not prevent the blast, or at least find a way to remove his wife and children from Cecil's house in Ivy Lane to Pyrford Place or somewhere else safely distant, some of the charred morsels that fed the birds would be theirs.

It was unthinkable. Faithless to him or not, Anne deserved nothing but God's blessings. Jack chafed against the thought, but he knew she had been a better wife than he was a husband, a better woman than he was a man. And those little innocents of theirs who had probably forgotten their real father: how could they possibly die in an infernal conflagration? How could any deity worth the name allow this unholy terror to go forward? Yet Jack knew that God the Father had allowed thousands of his adoptive children—millions of them—to suffer worse fates than to be alive and well one minute, dead the next. Even the Father's only child not adopted but begotten had drawn his last, tortured breath in the horrific realization that his father had abandoned him.

Well: maybe God's secret plan allowed such terrors, but Jack Donne would not, if he could find another way. His head pounded as if he had hit it directly with the heavy hammer, and his burned hand and wrist sent searing bolts of pain up his arm and into his neck. Yet he must not let these things distract him from the business at hand. Soon the owls would give up the treetops to the harmless songbirds of dawn, and by the light of day someone would find him in the smithy. Jack picked up the bloody cloth from the floor beside him. He took one more deep breath and stood, put the cloth in his mouth, and started in again with the hammer. After a few more blows he finally broke through the link.

Jack repeated the process with the chisel's blade an inch or so away from the link's open spot until he had broken through again. He slipped off the link, and since it was no longer holding the hinged shackle closed he was quickly free altogether. He dropped everything—tools, chain, shackle, and bloody cloth—onto the floor and felt his way to the barrel of cold water the smith had used to temper his hot steel. The room was utterly dark, but still he closed his eyes and gritted his teeth, then plunged his badly burned left hand into the water. The pain ripped through him with such force that his knees buckled again, and he slumped beside the barrel. Perhaps he lost consciousness. But when he rose stiffly to his feet, his hand was still in the chilly water, the pain numbed, if only for a time. He pulled his hand from the water, picked up his satchel, and climbed back out through the broken door.

The blacksmith who owned the forge might have been the same one Catesby and Fawkes had brought in to close the link that fettered him to the printing press when Jack was knocked senseless. Or the smith who had left him in chains might have been some other, and the honest craftsman whose shop Jack had smashed would come to find that someone had senselessly wronged him. The good man had already allowed Jack to make his lock-picking tools in the forge, had charged him only a pittance for the steel.

Either way, Jack hoped he lived to come back and pay the smith. If he was the honest man Jack took him for, the blacksmith would receive money in plenty for the damage to his shop. But if he was the one who had closed a link in a chain without a lock, a chain that left a man slender hope of escape, then Jack would pay him a different way. First he would ask Sir Thomas More's advice, and then, if his kinsman permitted it, Jack Donne would match strength for strength with a blacksmith. He would do a better thing than the smith had done to him: Jack would not leave the man to die, but he would make him think again before he consented to enfetter another.

Now, though, more pressing matters lay at hand. Jack tried to put the blacksmith—along with the pain in his head and his hand—out of his thoughts as he shouldered his satchel and made his way toward Ivy Lane.

Chapter 19

Robert Cecil sat at his writing-desk, where he had spent three hours hastily signing some documents and hurriedly composing others. The new session of Parliament was about to begin, and a fair amount of preparatory work remained. On the fifth of November, King James and both his sons would preside over the new session's opening ceremonies. The morning would be taken up with processions, speeches, posturing, applause . . . all the trappings of statecraft Cecil found distasteful. But it all had to be efficiently arranged, and Cecil was the man to do it.

After the morning festivities the King and both princes would depart, and the real work of the new Parliament would begin—but not until the members of both houses had been sated with food and drink. Cecil preferred his lawmakers dull-witted and pliable in the afternoons. Some would doze through their enemies' arguments. Or if they stayed awake and the wine they had drunk made them angry, Cecil could assert control by chastising them in public. In the end the bills Cecil wanted to pass would pass, and the men in both houses would take their entertainment in the city or go home for the evening. But he doubted anyone would look forward to going home as much as he.

These days Cecil spent altogether too much time dealing with matters of state: far less time, though, than even a week or two ago. Then the work had proved a welcome distraction from his troubles; now he chafed against his duties, always yearning with half his mind to return to Anne and the children. Their presence in the house filled him with a sense of purpose, with eagerness to finish his mundane tasks and spend his leisure with them. Never had Cecil liked young children, but Constance, Little Jack, and the infant George, despite their occasional bouts of tetchiness, delighted his eyes. He loved to hold George in his arms, to rock him to sleep while the other two frisked about at their games. Never mind that doting on children did not suit a man of his station—did not in fact suit a man at all. If the servants whispered, let them whisper; he cared not a jot.

And Anne: more than ever, Anne shone with an effortless grace. Even in the simplest dress she looked radiant next to the ambassadors' wives, the painted ladies-in-waiting, the gilded butterflies that flitted about the Court. She could converse wittily about nearly any topic on God's green earth.

Queen Anna liked her, a fact that could only redound to Cecil's good. His dealings with the Queen had been strained from the start, probably because he continued to urge the King to dissuade her from keeping her Catholic Masses. The King ignored his chief minister's wisdom, but Cecil knew it could not be good to have it bruited about that while ordinary Catholics were heavily fined for going to their Masses, and while papist priests were tortured and killed whenever they were caught, the Queen of the realm held Masses at whatever palace she kept. But this king had his crotchets.

The Queen, though, had already asked Anne to tutor the Princess in Greek. Lucy Harrington Russell, Countess of Bedford, had been looking after most of the girl's education. But Lady Bedford's Greek was not strong, so the Queen had turned to Anne.

What a blessing: already in her brief time living at his house—a matter of days—Anne seemed to intuit the ins and outs of statecraft. Without scheming or posturing, she won over heart after heart, mind after mind. The woman was a wonder.

And to think that she loved him! It hardly seemed possible, but all her motions told him it was true. She had not yet shared his bed, but Cecil understood that. Donne had destroyed her faith in a marriage she had at one time thought unassailable. It would take time for her to accept a new lover. Not much more time, though. Cecil was confident his joy would soon be complete.

He was near to setting the last of the agenda. Perhaps only an hour's work remained before he could return to Anne. He had barely started in again when men's voices sounded in the hall. One was Cobham's, telling the other he would have to wait: Cobham would see what he could do, but he could promise nothing. A tap on the door. Cecil said irritably, "Come in, come in."

Cobham slipped into the room and closed the door behind him. He braced his foot against it, as if he expected the man to force his way inside. "The Lord Monteagle waits without," the servant said. "He says he will not be put off."

"Monteagle? What can he have to say to me? Dismiss him."

"Yes, my lord. And there is this, delivered by the strangest courier—or courtier—that ever I saw. He waits with Lord Monteagle without. The man spoke in such fair terms and in such firm knowledge of the affairs of these times that I knew him for a man of statecraft. Yet he would not give me his name, but only this missive for you."

Cecil took the paper. The cover-sheet said the letter was urgent. Cecil found such histrionics from a stranger who would not reveal his name distasteful. But he tore through the seal. The message was but three words long: *Listen to Monteagle.* It was signed only *Your erstwhile servant.* He looked at the back of the paper. Nothing.

Cecil asked Cobham, "Why, apart from his withholding his

name, is this fair-spoken courier-courtier so strange?"

"For one, he is wild-looking, as if his eyes had seen too much. For another, his beard is long, and wavelets of hair flow all down his back—hair to make many a maiden sigh, and a form to match—but he put me in mind of some eremite away from his hermitage for the first time in his life, an eremite with some urgent business in the city."

Cecil said, "Wavelets. Sighs. You read too many poems, Cobham, hear too many plays. First your man is a statesman, then an eremite. I desire no traffic with any such, fair of form or not."

Cobham raised his chin a bit. His tone was crisp. "There is one more thing. He appears to have been tortured."

Cecil looked at Cobham closely. "Tortured, you say. Topcliffe?"

"I think not," Cobham said. "These methods would not have been Topcliffe's. They are not . . . precise enough. No, the eremite has been beaten about the face, and his left hand has been held to the fire; it is badly burned. He appears to take no note of either injury."

Cecil looked once at the papers on his desk, papers that would have to be dealt with before he could return to Anne. He hoped this business with Monteagle and the stranger would not take long. "Well," he said, "let both in at once."

Cobham replied, "Lord Monteagle, begging your Lordship's pardon, is easily managed. But I will say again the tortured one looks like a man on a mission, a man not to be trifled with. Pray let me post some guard before admitting him."

"Very well," Cecil said, waving Cobham away as if he were sweeping drying-sand off a sheet of paper.

Cobham exited through a door opposite the one he had entered, and a minute or two later reappeared with three soldiers. He directed one to stand by each door. The third he stationed a few feet behind Cecil. Then Cobham slipped out the door and into the hallway where Monteagle and the fair-spoken stranger waited. "Three minutes only," Cobham said. "Lord Cecil has an appointment for which he must on no account be late."

Remaining seated at his desk, Cecil watched Monteagle bustle into the room, winded as if after a long ride, followed by a tall, well-muscled, black-clad man with a broad-brimmed hat. Cecil wondered at this second man's temerity in baring his chest—he wore no shirt beneath his open jerkin—and in failing to remove his hat during an audience with the Secretary of State and chief Privy Counsellor. The strange man's eyes were not clearly visible in the shadow of the brim, but Cecil could see that the side of his face was badly bruised and grotesquely swollen. Could Monteagle have been the torturer? Something about the black-clad man's bearing told Cecil it must not be so; the stranger did not look the sort who would willingly let an assailant live.

Monteagle was waving a paper in the air. "Treason, my Lord Cecil," he said. "Treason! I hold treason in my hand."

"Then by all means take the treason out of your hand and place it upon my desk." Monteagle did as he was told. Cecil read Tresham's letter hastily. "Who wrote this?"

"I know not, my lord. A common courier delivered it to me in the night."

"So you don't know who wrote it."

"No, your lordship. But—"

"Come, Monteagle, you must suspect someone. Why was it delivered to you and none other?"

"I swear to you, my lord, I cannot think who sent it. There is no signature, I do not recognize the hand, and I do not know why—or whether—I alone received it. Mayhap there are others."

"No such that I know," Cecil said. "You are the only one, or perhaps only the first, to come to me. Well. The author must be some hot-headed Catholic, if what he says is no mere ruse. The writer is a papist in league with other papists. If the man be not mad, or attempting to trick us, some conspiracy is afoot, some dread stratagem. He who wrote it must be a friend of yours, or a kinsman. A fellow-Catholic."

"No, my lord, I am a good—"

"Oh, spare me your protestations, Monteagle. I know well enough you're a Catholic."

"But my lord, I have brought this thing to light. I am a faithful—"

"Yes, yes, if the warning here proves true, you shall have your reward." Without taking his eyes off Monteagle, Cecil said, "Cobham, Francis Wolley remains in the house, does he not?"

"Yes, my lord, in the gaming room when last I saw him."

"Find him and bring him here. Then tell McCrae to saddle Wolley's Andalusian."

Cobham made a slight bow to Cecil and left the room.

Cecil muttered, half to himself and half to Monteagle, *"They shall receive a terrible blow this Parliament and yet they shall not see who hurts them."* What could this mean? Poison? A barrage of cannon from ships in the Thames? Fires set in the halls of Westminster? Or under the chambers, perhaps. How long since the houses and shops around the palace yard had been searched? Well, they would be searched now.

Cobham entered without knocking, followed by Francis Wolley, who looked fine in an oxblood doublet of crushed velvet and umber hose. "Wolley," Cecil said, "Is the King hunting still?"

"Yes, my lord, in Cambridgeshire. His Majesty means to make his way to London leisurely, arriving on the eve of the new Parliament. Shall I deliver him some message?"

"I think so, but hold a moment." Cecil closed his eyes in thought, finger and thumb on the bridge of his nose.

When Monteagle said, "My lord," Cecil raised a hand to silence him; he needed to consider the steps he must take. The first would be to augment the naval force at the mouth of the Thames, the second to search the rooms around, above, and beneath the Lords' and Commons' chambers. Until he knew more, he wanted to keep the search quiet; only a few trusted men should be involved.

Then he would have to deal with this nervous, suspicious king, whose own father had been blown to bits, the king known to dive beneath his bed at the sound of fireworks. Once James Stuart knew he was safe, he would suspect everyone, even Cecil himself—no, *especially* Cecil himself—of inventing the plot to curry favor by pretending to discover it. No, the King should not be informed yet. If the search turned up evidence, Cecil would send for the King and subtly lead him to search out this same evidence; the King must think he himself had discovered the plot. All would stand amazed at His Majesty's instinctive powers, at the divinely appointed sovereign's providential knack for sniffing out treason with the Royal Nose.

Cecil turned to Wolley. "No message to the King. Not yet. But remain about the house. It may hap I will send you to him or to another on a moment's notice." Cecil said to Monteagle, "Come with me; I've a task for you." He gestured toward some of the household guard. "You three: gather the rest of the soldiers, within the house and without. All of you are to meet me here in one hour's time." From their separate places in the room, the three soldiers knelt in unison. Cecil admired their precision. Well, after all, he had himself chosen them as part of his household guard. He turned to his manservant. "Cobham, fetch me Suffolk, and John Whynniard."

"Yes, my lord," Cobham said as Cecil limped out of the room, followed by Monteagle. Cobham nodded to Wolley, then walked out and closed the door after him.

Wolley strolled casually about the room, inspecting books and paintings, idly looking over the papers on Cecil's desk. Jack shifted his weight, and Wolley glanced at him and then winced as if coming upon an ugly piece of furniture in Cecil's otherwise well-appointed house. He said, "Now *that,* my good man, is a nasty bruise. I don't know when I've seen so many colors on a single face. And ugh! You'll need some balm on that hand." His gaze lingered along Jack's bare torso for a few heartbeats. Then, with a practiced flourish of his cloak as he turned, Wolley walked out of the room, looking like a sprightly soldier on leave from the wars.

Jack wondered how his own appearance could be so altered that even his old friend, the man in whose house he had lived for four years, the man he had visited only days before, did not recognize him. Maybe it was the broad-brimmed hat that kept his face in shadow. Or, more likely, Wolley was simply acting like himself; the man could be very observant, but only when the thing he was looking at interested him. A battered stranger was not much to his taste.

Alone in the room now, Jack sat in Cecil's chair at the desk where the agenda for the new session lay atop other papers. The chair was uncomfortably high; the little man must want to seem above his visitors in physical as well as political stature. Jack found blank paper and pen. He composed a message warning Garnet and the others that Monteagle had betrayed the conspirators. The search would soon begin. All of them—Garnet, Owen, Burr, Tresham, Catesby, Fawkes, and the rest—needed to flee. When he had finished writing he folded the paper, waxed the seal, and put Owen's name on the cover-sheet; naming the priest posed too great a risk.

Jack left the house through a back door. He made sure to slide out the heavy bolt even though the door was open. He eased the door back into place; the bolt held against the doorjamb. If no one discovered the unlatched door, Jack could re-enter the same way. He strode off to seek out a messenger.

Three streets away he found a livery stable and overpaid the puff-eyed, grizzle-pated owner. By the light of a candle the old man examined the gold coins in his hand: more than the weather-bitten stabler earned, Jack supposed, in a good month. Wide-eyed, the man looked up at Jack and promised to go himself, immediately, and deliver the message. Jack leveled his gaze and said, "Fail me not, as you value your skin. And forget this face; you have never seen it."

The man bobbed his head. "Already it is forgotten."

Jack finished giving instructions, then turned and walked back toward Ivy Lane.

He re-entered Cecil's house through the same door he had exited not a quarter of an hour before. He stepped into the hallway. Where to find Anne? Cecil's library, maybe. If not, he'd keep looking. He checked several rooms on his way to the library, then rounded a corner. There she stood in the hallway, a book in her hand. She glanced up at him, dropped the book, and had begun running toward him almost before it hit the floor. She fairly leaped the last few feet, threw her arms around him, and held him tight, convulsed with sobs as she pressed her face against his neck.

Jack did not know what to think, and it did not seem to matter: he could hardly think at all. Dimly he was aware that his intent had been to chastise her. At the moment, though, he desired nothing but to embrace her. All that mattered was that he keep holding her close to him, keep kissing her hair as she wept.

At length she pulled her head away and looked at him with

love and pity. "Oh, Jack, what happened to your face?" She reached up to touch his cheek but drew her hand back before making contact.

"It doesn't matter," he said. "A brick."

"And your hand: it's been burned."

"It has, but do not think of it."

"And your eyes. . . ."

"A few months in a dungeon, nothing more. But none of that matters; I'm here now." In an attempt to show her his wounds were not serious, he gently caressed her hair with his burned hand. His palm was burned much less than the back of his hand or his wrist, but the pain of even his light touch on her hair was surprisingly sharp. He did not let on. "Only tell me: are you happy here?"

"*Now* I am, yes. Now that you're here. I've never been so happy." She took up his unburned hand and kissed it. Then with tender sorrow in her voice she said, "A dungeon. Was it Cecil put you there?"

"Yes, but that doesn't matter. I will deal with him. What I want now is to know: how could you . . . ? Why did you ever consent to marry that twisted little Machiavel?"

She took a step back. "*Marry?* Why do you ask such a thing? I didn't marry Cecil. How could I? I'm married to you."

"You didn't . . . ?"

"No! It's true I feared you were dead; we all did. But even if you were, I'd never. . . . No. No! I moved to this house but to learn something that would help you, if you still lived. That's all: I wanted to do whatever I could. And here you stand! But what made you think I had married the man who had wronged you so?"

"Your cousin made me think it. Wolley told me so."

"He *what*?"

"He told me you had married Cecil."

"Jack," she said softly, "are you thinking aright? Such a blow with a brick. . . ."

"It's not the brick; it's Francis Wolley. He's here in the house. Ask him yourself."

"Oh," she said, "rest assured I *will.* But not now. I have something to show you." She led him down the hall. They walked past a spacious room with tables set up for various games. A girl of some twelve or thirteen years sat on a cushion, singing a sad, lovely song as she played a lute. Sprawled on a couch a few feet away lay Francis Wolley.

Jack said to Anne, "Wait. There he is."

Anne said, "But I want you to see. . . . Oh, very well: Francis first."

Wolley glanced up, looked at Anne and the dark-clad man she led by the hand. Then horror spread across his face along with the recognition that had eluded him before. "Jack! You're. . . . That was you!"

"I made no attempt to conceal the fact."

Wolley stood and backed away. The girl stopped her music. "Leave us, Emilia," Anne said without looking at her. After propping her lute in a corner, the girl got up and skipped lightly away through the door opposite the one Anne and Jack had entered.

Wolley held his hands before him as if to fend off an attack. He opened his mouth, but it took some time for sound to emerge. "I . . . I . . . he made me do it, Jack. I had to do it. He made me."

"*Who* made you do it?" Anne asked.

"Cecil. He made me. Oh, I'm sorry. I'm terribly sorry. But I had no choice."

Anne's tone was businesslike as she said, "Francis, you had better tell us plainly what happened."

Wolley took another step back, then slowly let his hands fall.

"It was a lover," he said. "A week ago at Whitehall. I . . . I took some pleasure with Sir Thomas Kerr's son Robbie—no mere boy by now, mind you, but fully grown—and Cecil caught us in the very act. Well, how was I to know the King himself fancied this same Robbie Kerr? So Cecil sent me back to Pyrford Place, and told me if ever Jack Donne came to find Anne there, I was to tell Jack—oh, I'm such a fool—that she had remarried. Then I was to ride post-haste to this house and tell Cecil where to find you. When I arrived here I told him you had ridden toward London from Pyrford Place despite my attempts to keep you there, but I knew not where you lay. I had to lie to you, Jack. I had no choice. You know how Cecil. . . . Anne, I'm sorry. Truly. I love you both, but if Cecil were to tell the King. . . ."

Anne took a menacing step toward Wolley. "Oh, Francis," she said as he retreated still more until he had backed against a wall. "Oh, Francis. When I have done with you—"

They heard men's voices in the hallway. "No, eighty," Cecil was saying to Monteagle as he walked past the open door, glancing into the room on his way. "Eighty foot-soldiers, but sixty of the other." He had passed the doorway.

Anne stood with panic in her eyes for a moment, then collected herself. She hissed at Wolley, "Mouth shut, whatever we say." Apparently ready to do anything to avoid more trouble, Wolley nodded eagerly. The men's voices in the hallway continued for a few seconds, then ceased. Anne turned to Jack, stood on tiptoe, and hastily whispered into his right ear, "Forged annulment, I think. Check the seal. Cecil's desk. Steal it."

She gave Jack a little push toward the doorway opposite the one Cecil had just passed. He slipped out of sight.

Anne turned to face Wolley and assumed a posture that suggested she had been talking with him for some time. An instant later Cecil reappeared in the doorway. He seemed puzzled. "Wasn't there . . . ? There was another man in here. I thought I recog—. That man in black, where did he go?"

Anne turned to him, smiled, and put on a quizzical look. "What mean you, my lord? What man in black?"

"The one here in the house. I saw him in this room. He looked like. . . ."

Anne said, "Whom did he look like, Your Grace? Francis and I have been alone in this room."

"No, he was here. In this room. Even now, as I passed. He looked like. . . ."

"He looked like whom, my lord? You speak in riddles."

Cecil turned to Wolley. "Where is he?"

Wolley raised his palms. "Whom means Your Grace?"

"Him! Donne! You know very—Monteagle, you saw him, did you not?"

"Of course, my lord," Monteagle replied. "I saw. . . . Whom did I see, my lord?"

"Donne! Or a man very like him. In this room. The man in black. With the hat and a jerkin but no shirt. Don't tell me you have forgotten. I think the man is Jack Donne."

Anne put her hands to her lips: "Donne? You say you saw Jack? But where? Perhaps you saw some spirit betokening trouble that has befallen him. Maybe it seeks our help."

Cecil narrowed his eyes. "Spirit? *That* is the best you can do? Please. The man I saw was no spirit. Come, where is he? The two of you dissemble, or one of you does. You cannot both have missed him: he was here but now." Cecil turned to Monteagle. "You saw him, did you not? Jack Donne."

Monteagle said, "My lord, I am afraid. . . ." Cecil glared at him. Then Monteagle said, "Yes! Yes, of course I saw him! Standing in this very room. Dressed all in black. I did not know his name until this moment, but of course I saw him."

Cecil looked at him murderously. "So you did not see him."

"My lord, I must protest: I was *listening* to you."

Cecil pointed at the doorway Jack had exited. "Go and find him! No. First alert the guard, within the house and without. Tell them my orders are now that they *not* meet me as planned, but to have some of them guard the doors and others find the man. Then bring him to me here."

"Yes, my lord." Monteagle began an elaborate bow.

Cecil said, barely audibly, "As you value your skin, go."

Monteagle stopped in mid-bow, righted himself, and hurried out the door.

His brow contracted with suspicion, Cecil looked at Anne.

The stabler plodded toward Westminster on his dependable old gelding, the frightening, black-clad fellow's letter in his pocket. The message was of the highest import, the man had said. But who could trust such a fierce-eyed, battered stranger? Well, no matter: the pay was more than generous, and all the stabler had to do was deliver the letter to a gray-headed fellow, a short, bandy-legged man called Owen. The stabler had but to knock on the door of a room above a chandler's shop across the yard from Westminster Palace. If Owen answered, or if any man answered who knew Owen, the messenger had only to hand over the letter. Or if no one was in, the stabler would find across the stair-landing a stooped old woman called Aylesbury. She could receive the letter, but only if she could be made to repeat three times that she was to give it to Owen. Failing that, the stabler was to wait until one of the men arrived.

The old man's mouth watered as he thought of the Blue Boar, two or three doors down from the chandler's shop if his memory served, where a bit of the battered stranger's gold would buy the best ale in the house.

Leaves began to swirl in little eddies along the paving-stones as the gelding made his way toward the chandler's shop. The stabler guided the horse to the side of the street as he approached a hooded man, plump and thin-legged, and a stooped, arthritic-looking old woman who hobbled beside him. She wore a red, tightly woven mantle draped around her shoulders. The hooded man seemed to be trying to hurry her along, but she hung bent between two canes and moved haltingly, as if she were trying to step carefully on every cobblestone.

The stabler turned a corner and pulled the collar of his coat about him; the wind was rising, funneling along the street. He glanced at the sky and frowned. Banks of clouds were moving toward each other, some churning in off the Atlantic to the east and some sweeping down from the north. He hoped to make the delivery and sit warm and safe in the alehouse before the storm hit. From the windows here and there, arms reached out to pull shutters closed. Street-vendors hurried to cover their stalls. He clucked the gelding to a trot.

The first of the large drops had begun to smack against the pavement by the time he pulled up before the chandler's shop. As he dismounted, the stabler had to hold his hat on his head to keep the rising wind from carrying it away. After looking longingly toward the Blue Boar, he pulled the stranger's letter from his pocket and turned to climb the stairs.

Cecil had been pacing for perhaps ten minutes. Anne and Wolley sat, as they had been told to sit, side by side on the couch. Anne had tried a number of times to tell Cecil that he must have been mistaken; she had seen no man in black, least of all Jack Donne, standing in that very room. Wolley had said the same. Clearly, though, Cecil was not convinced. Two or three times he had pointed out that Anne and Francis had been facing one another, so that at least one of them must have seen a tall man standing not four paces away. But both insisted that if such a man had in fact stood so near them, neither had seen him.

At the sound of men's voices all three turned to face the doorway Monteagle had exited. A guardsman holding one of Jack's arms pulled him into the room. Another held Jack's other arm, and Monteagle gave the prisoner a little shove from behind. Half a dozen other guardsmen followed into the room. Jack's hands had been tied securely behind him, but some of the guard had drawn their swords and now held them pointed at him. Jack looked at Anne and gave her the slightest of nods.

She sprang from the couch as if she had only that instant recognized him, took a quick step toward him, and said through gritted teeth, "You! Who let you into this house?"

Cecil said, "Leave him to me, my love. I will make him speak truth."

Anne turned to Cecil and held up a hand. Sounding as if she had never been so certain of anything, she said, "No! Leave him to *me;* there's time enough to shackle him hereafter. For now, my lord, I shall make him answer to *me* for his misdeeds." She turned to face Jack again, then strode up to him and with both hands shoved him in the chest, hard. Had Monteagle not been standing directly behind him, Jack would have been knocked into the hallway. As it was, Jack stayed on his feet after colliding with Monteagle, who stumbled to the floor.

Anne reached up, grasped the collar of Jack's jerkin, and pulled his face to within an inch of hers. Anger flashed across her eyes. She said, "You dare to come to this house. You who are a traitor to the Crown and a traitor to your own family." She shoved him again, and this time he tripped over Monteagle, so that both lay sprawled on the floor. "Get him up," she said to no one in particular. Two of the guardsmen helped Jack to his feet. Monteagle picked himself up and moved off to the side. This time Anne grasped Jack by the beard and pulled him to her. With slow menace in her voice she said, "Do you think I do not know of your betrayal?" A third shove, and this time he kept his feet, but his back slammed against the doorjamb. Then Anne venomously spat out the words: "We thought you were dead and I wish to God you were. I know of your treason and I know of your doings with that seamy hobbyhorse Lucy the Whore of Bedford."

Anne made a fist of her left hand. With a broad sweep of her arm she smashed her fist against the right side of Jack's face: the uninjured side, but still the blow jarred him. For an instant both sides of his head sent such jolts of pain through him that it took a moment to clear his mind. Never would he have imagined Anne could strike with such force: rather more force, he thought, than the circumstances merited.

Still, he knew how to play his part in this strange drama. He raised his own voice. "Whore of Bedford? And what of *you*? It is you and not I who married four years ago, only take another husband while the first yet lives. What does the God who just heard you request my death think of *that*?"

She worked her face into a cruel smile and said, "What you call my marriage to you is dissolved." With a little two-handed gesture suggesting dissipation into mere air, she repeated the word: "Dissolved."

Anne turned to Cecil and said, "Oh, my lord, I pray you let me curse this man into particles. Then you may have your way with him."

Cecil stood, apparently struck speechless, and looked at her as if he had never seen anyone so beautiful.

Chapter 20

Still talking to Cecil, Anne said, "No. Now I bethink me, I will not waste my curses upon this spotted Jack, this knave of spades. I will but hold up a glass to him, that he may see himself for the thing he is." Cecil extended his hand in invitation as if to say, *Far be it from me. . . .*

Anne turned to Jack and said, "From the start you deceived me, pretending you loved me when all you wanted was a name for yourself. Favor with the Lord Keeper. And my father's money. From the start you cared about me not one whit. Then with my father's money and the Lord Keeper's power, you could secretly abet these traitorous Catholics. Well, I thank Providence, my father knew better. As did my uncle the Lord Keeper. And now at last *I* know better. Lord Cecil has taught me to read the charactery inscribed on your paper-thin soul. *He* has given me a home. *He* cares for these children you abandoned at your first opportunity. Whether he fathered them or no, Lord Cecil knows how to love them. And he has given me love. Real love. For all your talk of it in your pretty, witty verses, I doubt you have ever known what love is. But it doesn't matter. Our marriage—would that it deserved the name!—built as it was on your greed and your ambition, and defiled by your lechery with the Lady Bedford and who knows what other alehouse-queans, is dissolved. With these eyes I have seen the writ of annulment."

Jack said to Cecil, "This cannot be. Four years ago her father filed a challenge, and the ecclesiastical court upheld the marriage. It is legal. From the start it was legal. What court has overturned its legality?"

Cecil smiled, but he said nothing.

Jack said, "Where is this writ of annulment? Produce it."

Cecil luxuriated in a period of cold silence before saying, "I do not answer to your demands, Master Donne, and in any case there is no need. You need know only that your marriage is dissolved. *My* marriage—mine and Anne's—will soon take place."

Anne turned to Cecil. "But why hide our glad tidings? Why not bring out the writ and show it proudly to all gathered in this room?"

Cecil stepped to her and put his hand on her shoulder. He said softly, "My love, there is no cause. Why need we display our good fortune, baring it to all these uncomprehending souls?"

Jack knew well enough why Cecil did not want to bring out the document. The little schemer must have composed it in the King's name only in order to persuade Anne that nothing stood in the way of her remarriage; he had never meant it to be examined carefully. But after Anne had told Jack to steal the document and hurried him out of the gaming room, he had returned to Cecil's study and found the writ of annulment on the desk. The handwriting was Cecil's, but that alone did not damn him; the King could hardly be expected to pen his own edicts. It was the signature. The signature as well as the seal should have been the royal one. The signature was a fair approximation of the King's but still bore traces of Cecil's strangely crabbed penmanship. In his days with the Lord Keeper, Jack had seen Cecil's scribblings often enough. And the blurred image in the sealing wax was not the King's; Jack was sure of it. Probably the seal had been stamped with some signet of Cecil's, then smeared: intentionally, no doubt, to fool Anne. But she had seen through the ruse.

Jack's whole examination of the document had taken perhaps

a dozen heartbeats. Then there were noises in the hall. Jack had folded the writ and slipped it into an inner pocket of his jerkin just before three soldiers from the household guard entered the room and bound his hands behind him.

Now Anne was asking Cecil to produce the writ. Jack hoped she knew what she was doing; now that Jack Donne had reappeared, surely Cecil's plan would be to have his rival searched, then quietly killed as soon as possible. After that, there would be no need for any annulment; Cecil's marriage to Anne would be unimpeded.

Unless Jack was misreading Anne's actions, she must have seen the truth: Jack would soon be dead if she did not find a way to prevent it. At least, Jack prayed it was so. And probably she knew that Cecil's next step would be to destroy the false writ.

Anne turned to Cecil's servant. "Mr. Cobham: I pray you, fetch the writ of annulment. I think I saw it yesterday on my lord's desk."

Cobham looked at Cecil, who said to Anne, "Again, my love, there is no need."

Anne backed away. "My lord, will you deny me this one small pleasure? I but wish this Catholic Jack, this puppet of the Pope, to see that in the eyes of the law his marriage to me has never been." She turned to the servant. "Mr. Cobham, if you please."

The servant glanced again at Cecil, who gave him a knowing nod. Cobham stepped into the hall.

Anne gaily clasped her hands together and held them to her breast. "My lord, let us have a great spectacle of a wedding, with all the lords and ladies in London attending."

Cecil eyed her a little suspiciously. "My dearest, I thought we had agreed. A small wedding were best: a private affair with some few well-chosen guests."

She gave him a coquettish look, then said, "Well, we shall

see. Only for now, announce our plans to all assembled here. Perhaps the ceremony will not be large, but today I would have the tidings of our joy proclaimed to the world."

Cecil looked at her as if surprised to hear her saying these things. "My love," he said, "this is not the world, but two nobles—Wolley and Monteagle—along with one traitorous prisoner and a few common soldiers."

"Even so, I would like everyone, especially this traitor, to hear the words. Call it a bride's whimsy."

Cecil exhaled audibly, then said, "Very well." He raised his voice to the stentorian level he used before Parliament and other assemblies: "Let it be known to all here assembled that Sir Robert Cecil, Earl of Essendon, and Anne More of Loseley, erstwhile supposed wife to one John Donne, whose illegal marriage is now dissolved by express order of King James the sixth of that name of Scotland and the first of that name of England, will marry at the earliest opportunity, expecting to enjoy, by the grace of God, perpetual felicity thereafter." He turned to Anne. "Will that suffice?"

"Yes, my love. It is just what I longed to hear."

Cecil's face contorted into what Jack took to be a smile.

Cobham entered and said, "My Lord Cecil, may I speak aside with you?"

"My good man, tell me what you have to say; we have no secrets from these good people."

Cobham looked uncertain, then said, "Very well. My lord, the writ of annulment is not on your writing-desk."

Cecil made a sweeping gesture to include everyone in the room. "Ah, well, we shall present it hereafter, once it is found. Probably I misremember where I laid it."

Cobham looked uneasy. He said, "My lord, I don't think you understand. The writ is *not* on your writing-desk."

Still looking at others around the room—the good-natured,

caring gaze of a born politician—Cecil said to Cobham, "Yes, I heard you well enough the first time. I must have placed it somewhere else."

"My lord, I will say it again: *the writ is not on your writing-desk.*"

Cecil now looked at Cobham directly. "Not. . . ." Cecil turned to Anne, then Jack. His expression said he had suddenly seen the truth. The little man's eyes widened. He hissed at Jack, "Where is it?"

"In a safe place, rest assured."

"How could—? When?"

"When you had perused Monteagle's letter, and had gone off with him to make preparations. You will recall you left me in your study."

Cecil narrowed his eyes. "You! *You* wrote the letter Monteagle carried."

"I assure you I did not."

"But you stole the writ of annulment."

"I did."

"Where is it?"

"With one I can trust to follow my instructions. If you ask Wolley here, he'll confirm that I sat at your desk as he left me soon after you had departed the room with Monteagle. When he had gone I took the writ—it is forged, you know—and had time to exit the house through a back door and give it to a third party."

Cecil asked suspiciously, "Which door?"

"It is painted a dark blue, with a steel bolt and a trigger-latch. I left the bolt out so I could get back inside, if need be. And if you but inspect your desk, I think you will find I have helped myself to some of your paper and ink as well as the writ. By this time the document and its accompanying message will have been delivered by the courier I hired. I thank you for your generous gift of writing materials."

Cecil looked at Anne again, then at Cobham, then at Jack. "And what might be these instructions?"

"That should any ill fortune befall my good wife here, or me, or any of our children—*any* ill fortune or accident—then the keeper of the writ, with its forged royal signature and its false seal, will turn the document over to the King. And I assure you, this person is well placed to crave admission to the royal chambers."

With a deadly look in his eye, Cecil turned to Anne. "And you knew of this."

She returned his gaze. "Knew it? I designed the stratagem. And I saw to it that you announced before all these witnesses your plan to marry a woman you knew to be married already. With that pronouncement you confessed your treasonous lie that His Majesty King James of England had annulled my marriage." She turned and looked each soldier in the eye, then Wolley, then Monteagle, and last, Cobham, as she said, "Each of you is a witness. I pray to each of you: in the name of all you know to be good, do not perjure yourself in a court of law."

With a note of desperation in his voice, Cecil said, "You told me you loved me."

A cold fire burned in Anne's eyes as she said, "And you told me lie upon lie about my husband. You told me he was well when you had cast him into a dungeon and left him to die. You told me he had committed all manner of wrong and infidelity: that he had turned Catholic. That he was an agent of Spain. That he plotted terror against his native land. That he loved another woman."

"But all these things are true!"

Anne narrowed her eyes. "If I were a better Christian I would pity you and your shrunken little soul."

Jack said, "Tell me this, Cecil: Why did you not have me

killed at the start?"

Cecil looked at him stonily, then said, "Because I told you I would not. Because no matter the precautions, word of such a death *will* spread. Because I would not have your wife think you a martyr. Because I thought you might do the realm good service. Choose what reason you will. But I *should* have killed you, and with my own hand." Then with a despairing look at Anne, he said in an almost infantile tone, "I trusted you."

She glared at him. "And I knew better than to trust you."

Cecil closed his eyes, took a deep breath, and said, "Well. I shall take my leave." He turned to go.

"Not yet," Anne said. "There is more."

The stabler sat on the topmost stair, the letter still in his hand. He had knocked on both doors, knocked his knuckles sore. No one was within: no Owen, no Mrs. Aylesbury. Probably the stabler had been waiting only an hour or so, but it seemed more. His throat threatened to wilt within him for want of drink. When he thought of the Blue Boar, he felt he would soon die of thirst.

Finally, he stood. He would have one stoup of ale, maybe two, then return to knock again. Surely the bare-chested stranger did not mean him to sit waiting until he had pined away altogether. He descended the stairs and pushed open the door.

The cold rain was now driving so hard that the street had become almost a river. The stabler saw that his gelding stood looking miserable, fetlock-deep in water, where the man had tethered the poor beast to a post outside the chandler's shop. As he stepped onto the street, the water swirling about his boots, the stabler held together the collar of his faded buckram coat in a vain attempt to keep himself dry. In a few seconds he knew it was no use; already, in only half a minute, he was soaked to the bone. He gave up trying to fend off the rain, and stopped to pat the gelding's neck. "Just a drink or two," he said. "Then I'll be back. If this Owen is still not home, I'll stable you for the night. I'll buy you oats." The horse looked at him as if he understood but did not believe what he heard. "Ach, never fear it," the stabler said. "Just a stoup or two."

Cecil turned slowly and looked at Anne. "There is more?" His expression said he had never been addressed in such a way, had never fathomed the depth of depravity to which a woman could descend. He slowly shook his head.

"You wrote me a sonnet," Anne said. "Wrote it, burnt it, and then recited it to me from memory. Feigning admiration, I asked you to pen me a copy." She patted her pocket, which contained a rolled parchment tied with a green ribbon.

Cecil's shoulders hunched even more than usual, and his eyes took on a haunted look. No sound came as his lips moved, forming the word *feigning*. Then he spoke: "You said you treasured that poem."

"I do treasure it, and for this reason: should anything go amiss with the revelation of the writ of annulment, I have made arrangements that your love poem be read aloud at the royal court, to the amusement of all present. All will be encouraged to inspect the parchment, composed, as it is, in your own inimitable hand."

"So it is not enough that you would ensnare me in the sticky web of your deceit. You would ridicule me as well. Is there anything else, you she-spider, you brach?"

Jack lunged toward *Robertus Diabolus*. Hands tied behind him or not, he meant to throttle the twisted little man, come what may. But two of the soldiers moved with such speed to restrain him it was clear they had been watching for him to attack their master. Three more of the guard quickly moved to help the first two. Jack allowed them to hold him back, then said to Cecil with deadly menace in his voice, "Hold. Your. Tongue."

Cecil's response was barely audible. "Very well. I am sorry; I repent me. I am not. . . . I am not myself." He seemed unable to look Anne in the eye. He glanced toward Jack. The hunchback sounded as if he were trying to control his tone, but what he said came out as a hiss: "What else?" Jack looked at him. Cecil's face was behaving oddly, twitching and slowly contorting. Then he gradually regained his composure.

Anne had been watching as if the little man were some strange beast. Cecil looked to her pocket. He jerked toward her, moving like a grotesque insect, and snatched the scroll. Anne did not resist. Cecil slid the ribbon off the scroll and unrolled the parchment. He seemed confused as he looked at it. "What is this?" he asked.

Anne said, "Read it aloud."

Spittle formed at the corners of Cecil's mouth. He stared at Anne, who nodded calmly and said, "Proceed."

Cecil read through clenched teeth: "I, Robert Cecil, Earl of Essendon, do hereby order and direct the following three items: First—"

Anne's voice was firm: "Louder."

Cecil stared at her for a time as if he could wither her with a mere look.

Unruffled, she returned his gaze, and it was he who turned his eyes away first. He took a deep breath and raised his voice to a defiant shout. "First: should John Donne or any member of his family meet any mischance, I, Robert Cecil, hereby direct that the sonnet beginning *If but thy lightsome footfall might but pause* become the centerpiece of a comic court masque to play before the King and Queen, said masque to be fully funded by me. *Nota bene:* Anna Stuart, Queen of England, Scotland, Ireland, and Denmark, has consented to oversee the production of said masque. Second: I hereby direct that this same John Donne's mother, Elizabeth Heywood Donne Syminges Rainsford, now residing in Antwerp, be granted, at my expense, free and open passage to England. Further, should said Elizabeth ever be molested in England for worshipping where and as she chooses, I, Sir Robert Cecil, pledge to do all in my power to have any charges or punishment imposed upon her be declared void, and her public record utterly expunged of any record of wrongdoing. Failing the success of my efforts to spare punishment to Elizabeth Heywood Donne Syminges Rainsford, the masque aforementioned is to be performed. Third: I hereby direct that for so long as Elizabeth Heywood Donne Syminges Rainsford desires to remain in this country, she be granted at my expense a pension, for so long as she lives, of three hundred pounds *per annum.*"

Cecil stared coldly at Anne. "And have I assurance that you and your family will maintain public and private silence about this agreement?"

She said, "You do. And to be clear to you and all others present: my family includes Sir Francis Wolley here; he is my cousin. No harm is to befall him."

There was something like death in Cecil's eyes as he said again, "Is that all?"

Anne said calmly, "That is all, except that the document you hold requires your signature and seal."

Cecil looked almost numb. Cobham quietly slipped from the room. Cecil limped to a little chest of drawers against one wall, took pen and ink from one of the drawers, and signed the document. Such silence hung in the air that the only sound was the scratching of the pen. Cobham returned with a lit oil sconce and a stick of chestnut-colored wax. He bowed slowly, according Cecil as much dignity as ever, before handing the sealing-wax to his master and holding the lamp over the parchment. He tipped the flaming spout slightly to give the molten wax a clear path through the air. Cecil held the stick to the flame and let the wax drip onto the parchment. He waited only a moment for the little pool to begin to congeal, then pressed his signet ring into the center. The thickened edges, which must have been hot still, swelled to touch the flesh of his ring-finger, but if Cecil felt the burn, he did not let on.

Jack watched this self-inflicted punishment attentively—it would have been easy enough for the little man to remove his ring—as his own hand throbbed at his side. Perhaps Cecil was offering some gesture of minor atonement for causing the burn. In any case, this time the little man did not twist the signet but waited for the wax to set around the embossed image before lifting the ring. He handed the parchment to Cobham, who silently blew the ink dry, then rolled the document and gave it to Anne. She retrieved the green ribbon from the floor and slid it onto the scroll.

Cecil straightened his doublet and attempted to stand erect. He looked at Francis and said, "Wolley, what have you witnessed here today?"

Francis did not hesitate: "Exactly what you fear I witnessed, Lord Cecil. But should you grant the items my fair cousin requested, and should no harm befall her family, then I too pledge to maintain public and private silence."

Cecil nodded stiffly and turned to Monteagle. "What of you, then?"

Monteagle bowed deeply. "My lord Cecil, I swear that I comprehend nothing whatsoever of what has transpired here today. Nothing whatsoever. No man, woman, or child shall ever hear from me any breath of the day's doings, for I understand none of them. *None* of them."

Cecil turned to his chief servant. "Cobham, I pray you speak with the soldiers. Make them understand what is required of them."

"Of course, your lordship."

No one seemed to have heard him coming, but a clear-eyed military officer—in fact his clothing proclaimed him the commander of a regiment—stood in the doorway. "Lord Cecil," he said, "I must speak with you."

"Well, speak."

"Without door, my lord. Upon the instant, so please you."

Cecil lifted his hands, as if it didn't much matter who gave him his next orders. He stepped into the hallway with the officer. Once outside, the commander closed the door to the room.

It seemed only a few seconds later that Cecil reappeared, looking like a changed man. The canniness, the sense of shrewd command, had returned to his eyes. "Guard: to your posts!" he said. "You two: a coach approaches, carrying a young boy. Admit him and the lady who accompanies him to the house, then bolt the door. Open it for no man without my order. Bring the boy and the woman to this room."

Cecil then turned to Wolley. "Now: if I have the leave of everyone in this household, down to the greasiest scullery-wench—" here he looked at Anne—"and the sootiest turnspit—" he looked at Jack—"I have a kingdom to protect." With that he was gone. Monteagle hesitated, then followed him.

The Blue Boar was not where the stabler remembered it. As he stood where the alehouse should have been, he looked up and down the street. But the rain hardly allowed him to see a dozen feet in front of him. He made his way past several more shops, all of them shuttered against the storm, then doubled back. He patted the drooping neck of his rain-soaked gelding again as he passed, and kept walking. At last he found the alehouse.

The room was not crowded, but the drinkers were noisy with

merriment. Their clothes appeared to be dry; the stabler must have been the only one to arrive after the storm. He stood dripping and cold. But seasoned wood blazed in a big fireplace, and one chair near the fire stood unoccupied. The stabler ordered a tankard of ale from the tapster, then took the open chair. His clothes stuck to his skin. Soon they would be steaming. He rose to take off his coat, then sat again and spread it out on the floor before him. No doubt it would still be wet when he went to knock again at Owen's door, but perhaps the fire would dry it somewhat.

Anne turned to Jack. "Come: I was on my way to show you something when we stopped here." She took her husband's right hand and led him down the hall, then opened the door to a room fragrant with blue and yellow flowers as well as potted herbs. They stepped inside. Constance, a head taller than Jack remembered her, looked at him as if some glimmer of recognition troubled her eyes. She darted to her mother's side and clung to her skirt.

Little Jack smiled at him and went back to pounding one wooden block against another. Anne reached into a cradle and lifted out the sleeping baby. "This is George," she whispered.

For the first time Jack looked upon his infant son.

The stabler glanced down at his soggy buckram coat steaming in the warmth of the fire. By the shifting light he could see the corner of the stranger's letter protruding from a pocket. He pulled it out, intending to make sure it, at least, had dried by the time he left.

To his horror he saw that the ink on the cover-sheet had not held fast; only faint, smudged traces of it remained. Since the soaked cover-sheet had torn free of the seal, the stabler pulled out the note inside to make sure it could still be read.

But it was no better than the cover. No words remained; only black smears on the paper. To be certain of it, he stood and held the letter near the fire, closely examining the paper by its light. No, the message was entirely gone. The stabler was unlettered, but he could easily see that the learnedest in the kingdom could not discern a single word on the page.

Anne laid the sleeping child in Jack's cradled arms, then turned to the maid-servant and said, softly enough not to wake the baby, "Judith, there is much bustle in the house, and I would have the children away from it and back at Pyrford Place. Pray you come with us."

"Yes, my lady, if Lord Cecil—"

"You need not ask Lord Cecil; affairs of state have his whole mind, and in any case I give you my leave to join us."

"Very well, my lady."

"See whether you can arrange to have a coach carry us there. Meet us in half an hour's time in the gaming room."

"Yes, my lady." The servant curtsied and left the room.

Jack's eyes glistened. "This child is beautiful. George. I am glad for your father's sake you chose that name."

"Well, my father has softened toward you. I have said nothing to him about it, but I think he guesses you have undertaken some dangerous task on behalf of the Crown."

Jack looked at the sleeping child's beatific face: perfectly formed lips, delicate ears, a nimbus of copper-gold hair. "A beautiful bairn. George."

"Well: thanks be to God, the boy will have a father."

"Yes, thanks be to God. But it is 'long of you that Cecil dare not now have me killed."

" 'Long of us both." Anne picked up Little Jack, who let fall a bright blue wooden block and reached after it but did not make a stir when Anne turned him away. She led Constance, who still clung to her mother's skirt, back to the gaming room. She meant to see whether Francis wanted to return with them to Pyrford Place or remain at Cecil's house. The latter, she guessed: probably Francis would want to stay and try to mend his tattered bond with Cecil.

They had not been back in the gaming room for half a minute before a commotion arose down the hallway. There were footsteps—a good many of them—and men's voices, along with a child's. The regimental commander and two other soldiers entered the room, followed by a boy with a rust-colored cap and a woman in a dress of dazzling yellow silk. After them came three more soldiers. A fourth remained outside. He closed the door.

Jack did not want to betray any attraction to the striking woman who stood only a few feet before him; he made an effort to keep his eyes on the boy, a child of some nine or ten years.

Jack thought he had seen the lad somewhere. The child looked like a smaller version of Prince Henry, older son of King James and Queen Anna, but this boy's features were softer, his expression cannier. Nor could the child be Prince Charles, younger son of the King and Queen; Charles was only four or five years old. A cousin, perhaps.

Jack exhaled heavily. Both princes—Henry, who must be twelve years old by now, and little Charles—would attend the new Parliament's opening session. They were but children. Yet Catesby, Fawkes, and the rest aimed to blow them up along with everyone else. Well, not if Jack Donne could prevent it. He had shepherded Tresham's letter to Monteagle into Cecil's hands, and he had done what he could to spare the conspirators along with everyone else. But he would do more, if need be, before allowing the carnage Catesby and Fawkes intended.

The boy returned Jack's gaze, then brightened and said, "Woodwose!"

Jack looked closely at the child. "Princess?"

The girl removed her cap, letting fall her long, dark hair. Wolley was looking at her as she did so. He hastily knelt, bowed his head, and said, "Your Highness." Then others, including Jack and Anne, knelt. Lady Bedford made a perfunctory curtsey.

The Princess gazed around the room, nodded, and said, "Rise, one and all, and take your ease." She turned to Jack and asked, "What happened to your face, Woodwose? Did a wicked sorcerer put some horrid spell on you?"

Lady Bedford asked, "Yes, Jack-a-napes, what did happen to your face?"

Jack turned to Lady Bedford. Her eyes were bright, and a half-smile teased along her lips. Sure his expression betrayed nothing, he said, "It was no sorcerer, but your old servant Timothy Burr. With a brick."

"Burr? And with a brick? Why would he do such a thing?"

"We had a difference of opinion."

Lady Bedford smiled. "Did he convince you?"

"That, like a brick, were a hard matter."

"Well. You can both be hard-headed. I have not heard from that miscreant Burr in these several months. If you see him again, take your own brick to that thick pate of his, and it may hap the knock will put him in mind of his duties."

Lady Bedford turned to Anne. "Ah, there you are; you're the one I wanted to speak withal."

"Oh?" It was only a syllable, but Jack registered a tautness in Anne's tone.

Lady Bedford said, "I would speak with you alone."

Anne hesitated before replying. Jack watched her, waited for her to speak. At last she said, "Jack will join us."

"*Will* he?"

Jack sensed that Lady Bedford had turned back to him, so he met her gaze. Her face was now entirely unreadable, at least to him. Somehow he knew, though, that Anne was looking from rival to husband, no doubt divining what each must be thinking. Jack tried to keep his expression neutral. He thought it best not to look away.

"Very well, then," Lady Bedford continued. "Perhaps there is no harm in it. I merely wanted to congratulate you both on your reunion after all this time. You must be delighted to find yourselves together again after so many trials and . . . such tumult!"

Anne hesitated, then said, "I thank you."

"As do I," Jack added. He could tell by Anne's tone that she suspected some other motive beneath Lady Bedford's words. Jack thought the same.

"And I especially want to thank you, Anne," the Countess continued, "for letting me borrow your husband for some week or two."

"You are kind to thank me, I suppose," Anne said, "although I do not remember granting any permission that would deserve your thanks. Nor did I even know, while you kept him, that my husband lived."

"Owing to an impending attack, it was unwise to dispatch messages from Coombe Abbey, or I would have sent word to you immediately. But I needed a man to command the troops in my father's absence, and your husband performed the task admirably. In fact, in *all* he did he was . . . masterful."

Anne took a moment to gather herself as if recovering from a blow. Then she said, "Well. I am glad your father has returned and that all is well. And I understand your *husband* returned with him?"

"Yes. But in his absence *your* husband did all that mine might have done—and more. Really, his performance was breathtaking."

Anne closed her eyes, then opened them, inhaled deeply, and

said, "But he is here, now, as you say, and here to stay."

"Well, it may hap I will borrow him again. I *do* like his poems, and I am sure he would very much enjoy my continued patronage."

"It may hap," Anne said briskly. "That's for time to tell. As for now, though, I think Jack and I will return to Pyrford Place."

"I see," Lady Bedford said. "The Princess and I will remain here for a time; my father deems it unsafe to remain at Coombe Abbey. One of Lord Cecil's spies has told us an attack there is imminent. In the meantime, I think I can speak for Lord Cecil when I say that you would be most welcome, Anne, to return to this house at any time. And the woodwose, here: I am certain *he* will be made welcome."

Anne said, "We shall see."

Jack quickly calculated his best course. Yes, his first duty was to get his wife and children to Pyrford Place, out of harm's way. Once there, he would return to London to lead Cecil, if he had not already found it, to the undercroft. If the gunpowder had been discovered, Jack could hardly go to make sure the conspirators had fled; Cecil's spies would be watching the buildings surrounding Parliament, and they would suspect his hand in the plot. Well, he had twice warned the plotters already: once with the message on the undercroft door and once with the note the stabler carried to Owen.

Lest Anne worry that Jack was returning to London for some tryst with Lady Bedford, he would tell her all—or all but the particulars of his time with Lady Bedford. Anne would worry about him but would insist that he do what he must to spare all those lives.

The fire had been fed and now blazed hotter than before. The stabler's coat had all but stopped steaming: at last it was near to drying. The man belched his pleasure. He could hardly know that not a quarter of a mile away a second soaked note of warning, a note written by the same black-clad stranger, sagged from the shard of steel that fastened it to an undercroft door. The door was partly sheltered from the weather, but such was the force of the swirling wind that the wood was wet almost to the lintel.

At the instant the stabler tipped his fourth tankard of ale, the rain-soaked paper pulled free of its pin on the undercroft door and dropped into the flooded street, where the current hurried it toward the Thames.

The coach carrying Judith and the two older children to Pyrford House creaked slowly ahead. Although the storm had passed only half an hour before, the road was well drained and walkable, so Jack and Anne followed along behind. With his bandaged left hand Jack held the sleeping baby against his shoulder. The fingers of his right were interlaced with Anne's as they walked side by side.

For a while they did not speak. At length Jack said to her quietly, "George. You named him after your father."

"I did. Much as I misliked his treatment of us, I never left off loving my father." Jack nodded, and Anne continued: "And he was most pleased with the name I chose. He attended the christening."

"*Did* he. Praise be for that."

"Praise be."

They walked on in silence as the infant George slept against Jack's shoulder. Still Jack held Anne's left hand with his right. After half a mile or so he said, "I take it that were no mere ruse, then. Is it Queen Anna who keeps Cecil's poem in her care?"

"Be assured she does. I took it to her at Whitehall yesterday. The Queen is a good woman, and she bears little love for Robert Cecil."

His eyes beamed as he looked into hers. "Anne, you are a wonder."

She smiled. "I will not deny it."

Jack lifted her hand and kissed it. Their fingers remained interlocked. She asked, "To whom did you send the writ of annulment for safekeeping?"

"I had no time to send it." Jack released Anne's hand, reached into an inner pocket of his jerkin, and pulled out the writ.

Anne smiled. "Well. You almost make me sorry I hit you."

"I do not doubt you are almost sorry. Anne, my head has suffered repeated battering these last long months. I fear the next man—or woman—who strikes me shall knock my pate clean from my shoulders. If that happens, I pray you retrieve my headpiece and keep it in a box under our bed."

She put on a purse-lipped, concentrated look as she appeared to think carefully about the request, then said, "I suppose such a box could be found."

"I thank you. Oh! And speaking of a head in a box, I have something—many things, in fact—to discuss with you about my doings of late."

She looked up at him, and her eyebrows rose. "A head in a box, you say. Not your putative head under the bed, but a different one." He nodded, and she continued, "Now, *that* is the sort of tale that should warm us on a winter's night. Or chill us on a warm one." They walked a few more paces. Then she added, "After all these long months of trouble there will be time for tales of that sort, God willing."

"God willing," Jack said.

Anne took his hand again, and they walked for perhaps half a mile in complete—and Jack thought contented—silence.

Then Anne pulled Jack from a reverie as she asked, "Is any of it true?" He thought he detected a hint of hesitant fear in her voice, as if she had found it difficult to ask the question.

"Any of what?"

"The things Cecil said about you: that you had turned Catholic. That you worked for a violent Spanish overthrow of England. That you . . . that Lady Bedford was more to you than a mere patron."

He did not answer for a while, then said tenderly, "My love, I will tell you all. But now is not the time."

Anne said nothing but released his hand and reached for the baby. She lifted the still-sleeping child and held him against her right shoulder, leaving free her left hand, the one that had been holding Jack's right. They walked on as the coach rolled ahead. After a while she asked, "Have you turned Catholic?"

"No."

"Do you work for Spain?"

"No."

She nodded, and when Jack stole a closer glance he could see that her brow had contracted and her eyes had reddened. He felt something tug hard at his gut, but he did not let on.

They walked, and the carriage creaked.

After a time he reached his hand to take hers again. She glanced at his hand but did not take it.

She did not take his hand, but she walked close to him.

AUTHOR'S NOTE

What we know about the past is but a sliver of light in the broad beam of human experience. While *Love's Alchemy* aims to do justice to that bit of bright light, it remains a novel, not a history. In the penumbra of history's light I have freely invented some of the characters and great swaths of the plot. Time and again I have responded to the demands of storytelling first, history second. My hope is that the reader will approach *Love's Alchemy* as a well-informed tale, not a chronicle or biography: a tale that yields a rich sense of the real-life brilliance of John Donne and the torments within him, of the beauty and the tumult of his times.

Post-Elizabethan England gave rise to a peculiar blend of politics, theology, and language that merged the old world with the new. John Donne was a microcosm of that world. We admire Donne above all else for his witty, sexy, stunning poetry, and it is right that we do. Yet his poems were never static; the man was an inveterate reviser. Some of the poems embedded in *Love's Alchemy* are presented just as we now know them, and some, or parts of some, are fictive trial runs, putative early versions of poems Donne would later polish into the gems that dazzle us today.

ABOUT THE AUTHOR

An English professor at Loyola University Maryland, **Bryan Crockett,** PhD, teaches and writes about the interplay between literature and religion in the works of Shakespeare and his contemporaries, including Marlowe, Jonson, and Donne. He has published a good many scholarly works. *Love's Alchemy,* though, departs from the author's usual academic writing. As literary fiction rather than literary scholarship, *Love's Alchemy* aims simply to tell a good story: a tale of spying and intrigue, of faith and love.

When he is not spending time with his family, teaching, or writing, Crockett enjoys reading (of course), poker, playing in the surf, and working with his hands. In writing this novel and in a great deal else he has been aided immeasurably by his wife, Pamela Crockett, a teacher and artist. Pamela and Bryan live just outside of Baltimore. They have three quick-witted children, all of them with an artistic bent: Joe, Becky, and Rosie.

The author can be reached through his website at www.crockettbryan.com.